Moving to the Country

Moving to the Country

Anna Cheska

THOMAS DUNNE BOOKS
St. Martin's Press New York

THOMAS DUNNE BOOKS.
An imprint of St. Martin's Press.

www.stmartins.com

ISBN 0-312-28132-3

First published in Great Britain by
Judy Piatkus (Publishers) Ltd.

First Edition: December 2001

10 9 8 7 6 5 4 3 2 1

For June

I should like to give special thanks to my agent Teresa Chris for her enthusiasm, advice and support.

Thanks also to Sue and Kate Monnery, Heidi Percival and those lovely, supportive friends who know who they are. Thanks to Keith for inadvertently making me fall in love with Italian opera. And to the rest of my family, to whom the words THE END will always have a special meaning.

For frequent tears have run
The colours from my life

Elizabeth Barrett Browning
(*Sonnets from the Portuguese* 1850)

Chapter 1

'Here we are, then.'

Felix's voice nudged Jess awake. She roused herself blearily from her somewhat slumped position in the passenger seat beside him. 'What? Where?' The countryside was lush, green and unfamiliar.

'Brocklemouth – where d'you think?' From his tone, they might have been driving to the supermarket on a Saturday morning, instead of executing – with the help of a firm dubiously entitled Removals Intact – a complete shift of worldly goods from East Sussex to West Dorset.

Jess smiled. In their case, removal included even the kitchen sink, which was enamel and perfect for the watercress bed she had planned for the garden of their new house.

Felix might sound calm. But she knew how much this meant to him. *A new start for us, Jess. For us, and for the company too.* Wasn't that what she loved the most about her husband? His blissful, childlike optimism?

She eased herself upright and assumed a look of intelligent observation of the countryside they were passing through. 'Already?' And sure enough they were slowing and turning left along the lane that led down to the bay; she remembered it vividly from their one visit three months ago.

1

It couldn't decide on a direction – a bit like Jess herself, come to think of it – and it was too narrow for any traffic to even contemplate coming the other way. And ... *there'll probably be a bloody caravan site at the end of the road*, Felix had grumbled in a voice that told her he didn't care, not really, because he'd already decided he loved the place.

'Already,' he said now with a smile that warmed her.

'Do you think we've beaten the removal men?' Jess screwed up her face at a blast of unexpected afternoon sunshine and began scrabbling in her bag for her sunglasses. She found a purse positively bulging with loose change – why was it that clearing out a room produced more pennies than your average wishing well? – the inevitable sketchbook and pastels she carried with her everywhere; wet wipes – although those days should surely be over now that their daughter Sophie was not only eighteen but also at university; keys – new ones – that made her shiver with anticipation, and at last her slightly battered shades.

This made Felix laugh. She liked the way he laughed; there were never any half measures, he threw back his rumpled dark head and roared. 'I should bloody well hope so in that thing they were driving.' Smoothly, he swung the Alfa Romeo into a right-hand turn that seemed to demonstrate its utter contrast with the vehicle to which they had entrusted their possessions.

'We did stop for coffee. Twenty minutes.' In a motorway service station, Felix drinking his scalding hot, he was so keen to be away.

'And they'll stop for forty. At least.'

'Mmm.' Jess quite wanted the dirty white removal van to be there when they arrived; for some of their things to have taken up residence, to be waiting for them. It was daunting to think that the van she'd last seen chugging down Sompting Lane held nineteen years of accumulated memories in its fat belly. Memories that were now squashed into cartons with saucepans, crockery, and the glass cake tray that the Slatterslys had given her as a leaving present (and no, of course she'd never use it). Nineteen years of *stuff* accumulated in parallel with Sophie's childhood, Sophie's teenage years, Sophie's leaving . . .

For a moment her eyes glazed over the Dorset landscape; the trees and the high grassy banks lining the lane they were whizzing along to get to their new home. Her gaze moved into the distance, to the farm buildings and criss-cross fields of yellow and green apparently sprinkled over the slopes of the hills by some generous god with a pepper pot. Patchwork Dorset. She let the landscape go from her mind, until it was replaced by a female figure and a rucksack. A bit too tall, a bit too thin, Sophie would call herself, with a mass of brown hair that was as frizzy as Jess's own, and dark blue eyes that dominated her face. A perfect duplicate of her father's eyes . . . Jess sneaked a glance at him in the driving seat beside her.

She thought of Sophie as she had seen her last, standing outside Bishop Bell at the Chichester Institute, the hostel that was to be her new home, grinning madly and waving as Jess and Felix drove away. Yes, Sophie had looked happy – relieved almost. And if anything she had encouraged this move to Dorset. *I'm grown up now, Mums. I'm independent. I've got my own life to live.* All true. So why did Jess feel as though she had deserted her? Why did she feel the precarious closeness, maintained against the odds in the teenage years, stretching as if it might break without her even noticing?

Jess squirmed uncomfortably in her seat. And why did this image of Sophie remind her so vividly of the younger sister she had as good as lost? Of Louisa, who had also taken a rucksack with her when she left, but who, in sixteen years, had never come back?

Almost there. Jess stretched out her legs, aware once

more of Felix's contained excitement close beside her. The closeness had been precarious with Louisa too. Perhaps that was it. Or maybe it was the fact that her wild-haired gangly daughter reminded her so much of Louisa to look at. It would have been nice for Sophie to have grown up with an aunt close by. Jess could imagine the kind of aunt Louisa would be – someone more like a friend, someone a girl could talk to in a way she couldn't always talk to her own mother ... She gave herself a mental shake. It hadn't happened, and there was no point brooding about it. Only ... where was Louisa now? She didn't even know.

'Jupps Lane.' Felix took a left and placed a hand on her knee.

Jess curled her fingers over his knuckles. 'Jupps Lane.' It sounded OK and it had looked pretty good too, on the change of address cards she'd scribbled two weeks ago. *Cliff Cottage, Jupps Lane, Brocklemouth, Dorset.* It was the kind of address she'd always wanted. It was simple, and kind of said it all.

'And very upmarket, darling,' her friend Patti had commented, reading the card. 'Not to need a number.'

Now, Felix drew up outside the cottage and for a moment Jess took stock of her new home: of the broken paving stones on the flag path, the number of dark patches where burnt orange tiles were missing from the roof, the beautiful – but worn – slabs of yellow Dorset stone cloaked with honeysuckle and Virginia creeper, and she smiled with satisfaction. Not upmarket in the least.

'It needs loads doing to it,' she had told Patti.

And Patti, who knew her well from their weekly lunchtime meetings in the Café Continental on the shopping precinct where they both worked, had said, 'Now you're talking,' and tapped the sketchbook that always seemed to be bulging provocatively out of Jess's bag. 'Then it's even more up your street than I realised.' And she was right. Jess couldn't wait to get her hands on the place.

'Come on, then.' Felix ejected the tape of the Italian tenor who had been serenading them through rural Dorset and jumped out of the car.

Jess didn't need telling. She got out, pulled herself upright and stretched properly at last, her eyes not straying from the cottage, taking in every detail of flaking paintwork on wooden window frames, the neglected geraniums in pots outside the front porch. The paintwork outside would need a face-lift before winter set in, if only to halt the rotting process that had clearly begun already. She would plant campanulas between the flagstones, and in the summer they'd have big pots of poppies and cornflowers outside the cottage.

'No time for dreaming.' Felix grabbed her hand and pulled her towards the front door.

'I thought you said we'd have loads of time before they got here,' she protested, half-laughing.

Felix dangled his keys in the air and adopted a mysterious expression. 'Time for exploring, my sweet.' He opened the porch door, inserted his key in the second lock, and stepped back out again.

'What . . .?'

'A grand entrance, I think.' He bent slightly and before she could guess his intentions, he had scooped her up, lifted her in his arms fireman-style and was staggering into the porch groaning loudly.

'This isn't how you're supposed to do it.' She held on to her bag with some difficulty while depositing a sharp slap across his back at the same time. 'There's no fire. And whatever happened to romance?'

But she loved it, loved this moment, the way he had of making her feel like a girl again. At times like these she could almost sweep her worries right out of her mind, instead of only out of sight in the small mental cupboard she used for the purpose. Jess was good at that. She tucked them in the cupboard – to be added to until the door almost wouldn't shut (what then? Would they all fall out on top of her?) to be glanced over occasionally . . . but mostly to be denied.

Felix heaved her across the threshold and dumped her unceremoniously in the dark hallway. 'Romance is getting older. Some of us are getting weaker. And some . . .' He narrowed his eyes and looked her up and down, 'Could even be getting heavier.'

'Damned cheek.' But Jess was distracted, already running her forefinger along the dark blue paintwork and pock-marked wood panelling of the hall. Where was the source of light? She looked up the staircase and spotted a small square of window. From there, and from the mottled glass in the front door that looked like a fifties replacement for something decent. And that was about it.

'Let's open some windows.' She flung open the sitting room door and pulled the nets away from the window bay. They were ghastly grey cobwebby things. But the cottage stood close to the roadside so they'd have to use something if they weren't going to open their sitting room up to public viewing every night.

Felix was standing grinning in the doorway. 'Just imagine what Immaculate Interiors would make of this place,' he said.

Jess thought of her old boss, Sandra Slattersly, with her teased orange hair and veins and lipstick to match. Would Sandra have liked such an empty canvas to paint her ideas on? No, she would have been scared stiff. She could match a pair of velvet curtains with scatter cushions and a throw, but that was about her limit. Not that she'd let anyone know it . . .

'Charming, my dear,' Jess breathed, in Sandra's husky voice, sticking out her bosom – which unfortunately lacked the generous curves of Sandra's – and looking vaguely over Felix's head. Sandra always held conversations with the air above people, so that you spent the entire time she was talking feeling nervous that some unidentified flying object was fast approaching and about to let rip on your best linen jacket. 'But we must take it one careful step at a time, you know. Mr Hasty always has to clear up his own mess.'

Felix laughed. 'Well this Mr Hasty would get rid of these shit-brown walls for starters.'

'Absolutely.' Jess pulled her sketchbook out of her bag and made rapid notes. She'd thought it before. Whoever last decorated this cottage wanted to live in a mausoleum. Of course she had mentally redecorated the entire cottage already, several times and with a good deal of variety, but memory played tricks. On their previous visit she'd made so many drawings that Felix had retaliated with his own pencilled caricature in her book of a mad artist with equally crazy hair and with something very rude written in the speech bubble. And yet she had still got some things wrong.

Felix went over to the fireplace and craned his neck to look up the chimney. 'This is going to need a good sweeping.'

'And this . . .' Gingerly, Jess poked the scrambled egg and firework carpet with her toe, 'can go on a long journey to the nearest tip.' But it was a nice big room. Under the carpet there might be some decent floorboards that could be bleached and varnished, and with a roaring log fire the narrow window seat under the bay would be perfect for sketching or reading.

But what was she doing in here when she hadn't even gone through to the kitchen yet? And there was one thing Jess was waiting for as she opened the door that led on from the hall: the glimpse through the window straight ahead, the window with the view that had sold the cottage to her when they first visited it. She was conscious of the silly smile pasted on her face as she walked across the room to the sink. Bliss . . .

7

This, at least, was exactly as she had remembered it. It was a wonderful view of an overgrown back garden, small and sloping with a trickle of a stream running into a tiny pond; of a wooden gate that led out to the cliff, and in the distance the enticing shimmer of sea.

Jess reached forward and pulled at the sash window. It was stiff with disuse but she managed to yank it up. She breathed in deeply. It was all there in her nostrils – the grass, the cliff, the sea.

'You'll have something to look at,' Felix had said, three months ago, coming up behind her and putting his hands round her waist. 'While you're washing up.' And she had pushed him away, laughing, aware of the estate agent's curious glance.

Felix did the same thing now. Only this time he didn't say anything about the washing up. He just held her and they looked at the view together. She was aware of the solidity of him, the tightness of muscle as his arms wrapped her close. Her heart skipped.

'Oh, Jess,' he said after a while.

In that moment she loved him – perhaps almost as she had loved him nineteen years ago – with the same intensity, only with some wisdom from the passing of time too. And then she remembered what she had told Patti. About their silences, their drifting. *I'm not sure of what I want any more.* But what she had not told Patti was even worse. Her secret worry – that it was happening again, as it had happened before. That Felix was . . .

'No.' She spoke aloud. It was impossible.

'No?' Gently, Felix turned her round.

She surveyed the walls surrounding them, not wanting to meet his eyes. 'No to magnolia,' she said.

'Oh, you.' His face softened. 'Let's go take a look at the pond.'

They passed through the long narrow workshop. 'Plenty

of room for all your tins of paint,' Felix teased. 'All your rollers, brushes, bottles of white spirit, what have you.' His voice slipped into the Australian twang that he had never quite managed to eradicate, although she knew he had certainly tried. Felix's family, Felix's background were far away in Australia, but *he* had moved on.

Jess brushed some dust from the old pharmacy cupboard that the previous owners had left, thank goodness. She had practically begged them to. Lots of cupboard space. And so many nooks and crannies for glues and glazes, stencils and sponges.

Outside in the garden they stepped slowly through the long wet grass towards the pond, peered into murky depths. 'Too much surface exposed to the light,' Felix said knowledgeably. 'Algae.'

'See any fish?' she asked him, bending closer. 'We must have fish in our pond.' And a rockery would be good. Not a neat, landscaped one, but something a little wild and craggy – the garden, Jess felt, was meant to be a little wild. And there were lots of bog plants and marginals that would love it here. Not to mention the watercress. She would have to fix up the sink so that it got the benefit of some running water from the stream.

'Ah, you want so much, woman.' Felix grabbed her hand. 'You're never satisfied. Come upstairs.'

'But Felix . . .' She didn't want to be guided; she wanted to wander as the fancy took her in these precious minutes before Removals Intact brought their furniture and men demanding cups of tea. Before they were invaded by reality and the need to start unpacking. 'I want to walk to the cliff.'

She could see from his slight frown that he was reluctant. Like a child Felix always wanted to play things his way, but today he was being good and loving and so he walked with her to the gate, one arm slung over her shoulder.

Jess lifted the catch. The cliff path pulled her irresistibly.

She waded through the nettles and stood on the muddy stone path, arms hugging her chest to protect herself from the chilly sea breeze. She stared out into the distance.

God, it was beautiful here. They had come to Dorset a few times for family camping holidays when Sophie was small, and she'd loved it then. The grass always seemed greener than it did in Sussex, the flowers brighter. 'Must be all that rain,' she had said once, when their camp site was washed out *again*.

And so she had to admit that the thought of a move to Dorset had been appealing when Felix had first mentioned it. She had been surprised because the jewellery business of Beck and Newman had seemed to be thriving in Sussex; but apparently she was mistaken. 'Peter's looking for pastures new,' Felix had told her. 'He says we're in a slump. He wants to expand.'

That didn't sound like Peter. Jess knew Felix's partner – who ran the design side of the business – pretty well, and ambition had always seemed rather more Felix's department than Peter's. But as the senior partner and the money side of the partnership, Peter Beck had the biggest say, much to Felix's perpetual frustration. 'But . . . Dorset?' The location had seemed even more unlikely.

Felix told her that Marilyn Beck's mother lived in Axminster, that she was suffering from angina and that Marilyn wanted to be living near her just in case. That explained it. Marilyn wore the trousers in that relationship; if she wanted to move, then her husband and the business would be forced to follow.

Still, Dorset had certainly been appealing, Jess thought again now, as she breathed in the sea scent and the late autumn edge of decaying leaves, mud, stone, gorse or whatever it was that seemed to be creeping into all her senses. Why shouldn't they move? What ties did she have to Sussex? She had friends, of course, like Patti and her neigh-

10

bour Ruth. But all her family were gone.

She was reluctant to be so far away from Sophie, but she could hardly use this as an objection since Sophie would be at university and more to the point seemed actively to want them to go. And she *could* have regretted leaving her own job at Immaculate Interiors where she was at least working with design ideas, colours, fabrics and refurnishing – even if only on the retail side. But she couldn't pretend to Felix that she suddenly loved both the place and the woman she'd been slagging off for five years.

In truth, this was just the kick up the backside she probably needed. It was about time she thought about doing something that she really wanted to do, instead of just playing at it. This was her chance. A new location, a new start. For her, for Felix, for them.

Jess turned to her left, assessing the coastline, already half-planning her first walk. The path snaked on along the coast: beside it the rust-coloured cliff dropped down to a ribbon of sand and fine shingle, the waves curling around the edges and then stretching out into the endless blue, grey and green of a merging horizon.

At last she turned back to Felix who was watching her, his eyes thoughtful. 'Mmm. I love it.'

'Let's go back in,' he said. 'It's cold.' And then, 'Let's go and have a look at the upstairs.'

'All right.' She recognised both the gleam in his eye and her own slight shiver.

He went into the north bedroom. 'Which one shall we have?' They had already debated this. Felix wanted the larger room, the one they were standing in, because it had a fireplace and a bay window identical to the one downstairs. Jess wanted it to be the small south room because of the view.

Felix spread out his arms. 'In here we could have a huge bed.'

11

'We've already got a huge bed. And there's space for it in the other room.'

'I could find a bigger bed.' One dark eyebrow rose suggestively.

'I bet you bloody well could.' Jess laughed.

'You could use the other room to work in. You could have a desk under the window . . .'

God, he knew all the right things to say to tempt her. But there were only two bedrooms. 'What about Sophie?'

He shrugged. 'She's a visitor now, Jess, you know that. Most of the time she won't even be here. And there'll be plenty of room for a sofa bed in there.'

'What about the holidays?' She tried to stop herself going on. But she did not want Sophie relegated to a sofa bed. She might be at university but this was still her home.

'All right.' Felix's mouth barely tightened. 'Let's look at the other room.'

They retraced their steps along the landing.

Something about this room had appealed to Jess from the moment she'd first seen it. It wasn't just the view – which was beautiful, more complete than downstairs of course, encompassing the cliff, a wooded area to the west, and the mouth of the river Brockle to the east, curving into a bay that was fractionally and intriguingly out of sight. It was also the shape of the room with the sloping eaves on either side of the window and the little alcove to the right. She could see her dressing table sitting right there in a space practically designed for it. The carpet was a loud purple. The walls were painted delicate primrose. The room was small but secure. Small but warm.

'You want this room?' Felix took a step towards her.

Inside Jess something flickered into life. 'Oh, yes. I want this room.' It was one of his games. But they weren't playing at partnerships, playing at marriage. It was always something she had really wanted to work.

12

Felix was very close to her now. He only had to bend slightly and his lips were half touching hers, that delicious tickling not-quite-but-any-second feeling that was like Felix's whisper in her ear, his whisper on her lips. 'Then I guess we'll have to christen it.' He put his hands on her waist and brought her closer.

'What about the removal men?' she whispered.

'Bugger the removal men.'

She giggled. Felix had given them the spare key. It would be a terrible shock if they were to struggle upstairs with the walnut double wardrobe, only to find the new owners of the house indulging in gleeful new house celebrations of a physical nature on the carpet.

'Take off your jacket.' His voice caught.

Jess felt a stab of desire as he eased it from her shoulders. She shrugged it off and it fell to the floor.

Slowly, painfully slowly, one by one, Felix undid the buttons of her blouse. He bent to kiss her breasts, swept back the unbridled frizz of her thick brown hair from her face and nuzzled into her neck.

'Shouldn't we be cleaning the house or something?' She pulled him closer, loving the warmth of him, the wet mouth moving across her skin, the fingers playing one of their familiar tunes, caressing her breast; not needing to look, knowing exactly what he was doing. 'Getting it ready . . .'

'You want to go clean the house? I'd rather go on doing this.' His voice was muffled. 'And I'm ready as I'll ever be.'

She felt herself folding inside. 'Felix . . .' She tangled her fingers through his dark hair and clung to him.

In one smooth movement his head bent lower, and he took her breast in his mouth, sucking greedily, his hands on the curve of her buttocks, moving her closer still.

Despite herself, Jess wondered about the neighbours. Were they the type to bring round welcoming flapjacks?

13

Were they in their gardens listening out for removal-type noises and hearing only the odd grunt of lust? But then Felix's hands went to work on the business of unclasping her bra, which he had got down to a fine art over the years, and the thoughts spun away. All thoughts – apart from the fact that she wanted him.

Her hands were on his shoulders and together they sank to the floor, half-laughing, catching at what clothes remained on one another's bodies.

'Do you think we'll be happy here, Jess?' Felix's eyes – his beautiful, sleepy, come-to-bed (or the nearest floor will do) dark blue eyes – were insistent. He knelt and tugged at the belt of his jeans.

She helped him. 'I want us to be.'

'We *have* to be.' He sounded like a child. He began to pull her jeans away from under her and she wriggled to make it easier for him. She'd been in much the same position when she'd squeezed herself into them this morning.

'Mmm . . . ouch!' The coarseness of rough carpet on bare skin brought back memories of teenage passion and thinly carpeted floors. With Felix. All of her sexual memories belonged to Felix. There had only ever been Felix. And she might not be as slim as she'd been twenty years ago, but at least Felix still wanted to get her down on the carpet occasionally.

She kissed his fingers, lightly, taking the middle one in her mouth, sucking, waiting, knowing his body so well, each tight muscle. Felix played squash, did weight training and kept himself in shape; he was only five ten inches tall, but perfectly formed. She smiled.

He eased himself on top of her, not all of his weight but just enough so she had the pressure of him and so that his hands were free.

'Felix . . .'

In what seemed like seconds – when she was aware only

14

of his fingers, his hands, his mouth on her breast, his skin only a breath away, the warmth of him – she shuddered into orgasm. 'Mmm, Felix.' Saying his name was still a pleasure to her. Still . . .

Gently, he transferred more of his weight. He slipped inside her, making love slowly, gently, and in so precisely the way she liked it, that it was almost frightening. Was there such a thing as a perfect coupling?

His rhythm changed at the right second when she was almost there again; they didn't have to wait for one another. He seemed to grow harder still, there was an isolated moment when she lost the sensation that it was all for her pleasure. It was a moment that was his, when he lost control; a moment that she found precious. And then he came inside her.

They lay there for a few minutes. Jess became aware of a musty smell. 'This carpet stinks.' Another one for the tip. And never in a million years did purple go with primrose yellow.

'That's what I love about you.' Felix propped himself up on one elbow. 'Your timing and your finer feelings. You always say the right things. You never make a man feel cheap.'

Jess laughed and he reached out to touch her lips. 'You know we belong here, you and I,' he said.

And feeling as she did right now, with the warmth of him still so close, it was easy to believe that he was right.

An hour later Jess stood in the middle of furniture from the old house that didn't quite fit into its new surroundings, and found herself once again thinking of Sophie. Was the phone connected yet? She picked it up and the dialling tone confirmed that it was. She located her bag squashed between cartons labelled 'kitchen' and found the college details in her address book. Bishop Otter College, in Chichester, but a part of Southampton University. Bishop Bell hostel was a house with six rooms on the ground floor, six – including Sophie's – on the first. It was a small and pleasant campus; Jess had no real worries.

Moments later, she heard the phone ringing. Come on, Sofe . . .

'Sophie?'

'I'll get her.' Of course, if there were twelve of them, it was unlikely that Sophie would answer.

Jess sat on a carton to wait.

'Hi!' Sophie sounded excited and apprehensive at the same time.

'Darling . . .'

There was a slight pause. 'Oh. Hi, Mums. I wasn't expecting you to call. What are you doing? Where are you? Is everything OK? Aren't you meant to be moving today?' The questions tumbled out.

Her Sophie. Jess laughed. 'Yes, we are, and everything's fine. We're in Cliff Cottage and right now I'm surrounded by boxes. It's utter chaos.' She was relieved, she found, to hear her daughter's voice. What had she been worrying about? 'How's it going so far, darling?' she asked. 'Have you settled in?'

'Oh, it's OK. The others seem cool.' This was about all Jess had expected. It was a mixed hostel both in terms of gender and subjects being studied. Details of her daughter's new life would no doubt take their time to emerge gradually.

'They're not working you too hard?' In the background she heard the removal men arguing about where to put an unlabelled carton.

'Oh, well, you know, Mums. Not bad. So far, at any rate.'

'Mrs Newman? Where d'you want this one, love?' one of the men yelled.

Jess got to her feet. 'Hang on,' she said into the phone.

16

'Sitting room,' she yelled back, without even looking.

'Sure?'

'Positive.' Jess took a deep breath. There was something she wanted to tell her daughter. 'It's not so very far, Sofe,' she said. 'If you want to come home for the weekend or anything. Any weekend. I'll be around.' *I'm still here for you*, was what she wanted to say.

But she realised that Sophie understood. 'I know, Mums.' Her voice softened.

'And you will come soon – to see the cottage?'

'Try and stop me.'

'Good.'

'All done now, then.' Both men entered the kitchen, waiting expectantly. 'That's the lot.'

Jess waved her arms at them. Hang on, she mouthed again, indicating the phone. Was she supposed to tip them as well as pay them? Should she check that all the boxes were where they were supposed to be? And where had Felix sloped off to?

'I've got this essay to write,' Sophie was saying. 'So I gotta run. And it sounds pretty crazy there. Can you phone next week?'

Next week? Jess had been thinking of tomorrow. 'Of course I can, darling.' She tried to think herself into casual and liberated parent mode. Words like *own life, independent,* and *mothers who are unable to let go*, spun through her mind. She'd get there – eventually.

''Bye, then.' Already, Sophie had gone.

''Bye, darling.' Jess put down the phone.

Sophie Newman ran back upstairs to her room and the overnight bag she'd been packing when Karin had called her to the phone. Thank God she hadn't missed her mother's call; her absence might have taken some explaining.

She picked up the nightie with the teddies on that Jess had

17

bought her and tucked it back inside the covers of the bed. She wouldn't be needing that where she was going.

It made it easier, she thought, zipping up the bag, that her parents were safely ensconced in Dorset. There wouldn't be any surprise, *oh, we thought we'd just go out for the day,* sort of visits, or unexpected meetings in Brighton town centre. When she was supposed to be in Chichester.

She repressed a twinge of guilt. She loved her mother – of course she did. Dad was OK, but Mums was great. Great, but not always cool about things. She couldn't always see that Sophie had her own stuff going on now. She wasn't some kid who had to run back to Mummy for help every five minutes. She was a woman. Sophie stood upright and heaved the rucksack over her shoulder. And she was going off to meet up with one very attractive man.

The removal men had removed themselves, Felix had gone off to see Peter Beck about something that apparently just couldn't wait until Monday, and Jess drifted out into the garden with her cup of tea to get some fresh air, pausing only to pull on the old waxed jacket and gumboots that miraculously turned out to be in the black bin bag labelled 'workshop'. From there it was only a few steps to the gate, and a clump of nettles to the cliff path. I'll just go a little way, she told herself, putting her mug down in the long grass by the gate. Then I'll turn back.

It was already growing dark and cold, the sky was charcoal grey and gusty, and the ground underfoot had a damp and mossy give under Jess's boots as she walked east along the path, heading towards the mouth of the Brockle.

She passed another wooden gate. Neighbours . . . She peered curiously into the garden. Thankfully it was as scruffy as their own, so flapjacks and keeping up with the Joneses seemed equally unlikely. And Jess would swear she could hear the faintest sound of a violin playing. A CD or tape perhaps? An orchestral maestro? She chuckled and walked on. Ahead was a gap in the undergrowth of gorse and nettles. Should she go any further? Shouldn't she be turning back?

But she had to find out where it led. She eased herself through. A small patch of green with no trees. A viewpoint, complete with wooden bench. She sat down. But how many walkers would find this? Not many, hopefully.

Jess looked out towards the dark sea. A faint-hearted band of moonlight filtered on to the crust and spittle of trundling waves. If it were warmer, she might have climbed down there, flung herself into the water, swum the removal dust from her skin. But not in this weather. Already, she could hardly feel her fingers and toes.

'So this is where you've got to.'

She jumped, looked up to where Felix stood beside her. Everything about today seemed weird and dislocated, and yet perfectly natural at the same time. Perhaps it was always like that when you moved house. 'All those boxes,' she wailed.

'And I deserted you. I know.' He held out his hand. In his eyes was a glimmer of a laugh, half-hidden, a twitch of his lips. 'I'm despicable.'

'Yes.' She took his hand and he pulled her to her feet.

'Do you forgive me?' He smelt of expensive aftershave, from one of the many jars that would soon be sitting on a new bathroom shelf. A new bathroom shelf, a new bathroom. The scent, vaguely heady, slightly musky, made a bizarre contrast to the autumn sharpness of mud and leaf, the sea salt, and fragrance of change in the air. A woman's perfume?

Jess shook the thought far away. *That* part of their marriage was over. Everyone was allowed one mistake. 'If you come back and help me with all those blasted boxes I might see my way clear.'

They walked back slowly, arm in arm. 'It'll work, you

know, Jess. I mean it. I know things haven't been great. I . . .'

'Yes.' She didn't want him to say more. There was no need.

They passed the neighbouring cottage. There was an acrid flavour to the air now. 'Bonfire,' she said.

'Good idea.' Felix's mind had clearly latched back on to emptied cartons. Jess smiled. Everyone needed a change of direction from time to time.

A new start. She nodded. That was what it would be. Life was too short to brood about past mistakes, to worry over daughters leaving home, to wonder if she would ever see Louisa again. Life was for living and she would live it to the full.

Silently Jess braced herself for all those boxes. 'Come on, then.' She was ready to move into their new cottage. Ready to meet head on whatever her new life in Dorset might decide to throw at her.

Chapter 2

'You're telling me I have to leave?' Louisa Parris said this in English because she was cross, and because she knew Monsieur Dumas spoke it fluently. Didn't he boast about it often enough?

'Ah, Louisa. *Je regrette . . .*' Off he went again. Why couldn't he say it in plain English, or at least plain French? And why the big pretence that he was devastated to lose her? Louisa was a realist. She could see precisely what her boss – this little Frenchman with his fluffy dark hair and brazil-brown face – could see, that Café Noir wasn't full enough to justify paying two people to work behind the bar and wait at tables. The tourists had all left Trégastel and gone home. The proprietor had a choice. He could sack Louisa or Claude, or he could keep both of them on for the winter and watch his profits go down the nearest French sewer.

'When I promised you could stay the whole winter . . .' he was saying in French. Not slowly, for the French never spoke slowly, but Louisa had been living in Brittany on and off for long enough for her to understand every word and most of the implications. She could have stayed, but in return for what, exactly?

21

'So that I'd still be here when the tourists come flocking back for the spring?' That had been the reason given. So that she might be available for his bed, more like. It was odd, having a conversation in two separate languages, each determined to hold his own, so to speak. And each with a very different agenda.

'*Oui, oui.* I will need more staff then, of course.' He patted her hand in a conciliatory manner that she had always previously considered repulsive.

'Yeah?' Yes, he fancied her. But as she hadn't taken him up on any of his offers so far, would he still want her working in Café Noir next spring? There would always be other women – women who might view the situation differently, with an eye for the main chance perhaps. And Louisa would always be the sort of too-tall Englishwoman whose parrot-bright clothes and make-up were altogether too garish for the carefully understated French taste.

'*Oui, certainement. Mais maintenant—*'

'Oh, stuff it.' Louisa walked away. If she stayed she'd tell him exactly where to put his *certainements*. And it was a good time to move on. Any time, she told herself firmly, was a good time to move on. Especially now she was temporarily manless. Jean-Pierre had gone back to his wife last week, and good riddance to him.

She would pack her things in her rucksack. Louisa took care not to accumulate more than she could carry in one bag: a few clothes, minimum make-up, her Walkman, one good book and Scarlet, her battered blue teddy bear. And she would hit the road, just as she always had before.

Since leaving Sussex behind at the age of eighteen, Louisa had preferred to stay on the move. What had there been to keep her in the place of her childhood? Their parents had died two years before, Jess had Felix, and living with Aunt Pam had been an experience she didn't care to prolong. And if you kept moving, there was less chance of feeling too safe, less chance of building a love, a home, only to have it snatched away.

Louisa smoothed back her short dark hair and strode away from Monsieur pain-in-the-bum Dumas. It wasn't as if she never contacted Jess; she usually sent a postcard to let her sister know where she was. But often she would have moved on before Jess had the chance to reply. No forwarding address provided.

It was better that way, though not always of her own choosing. Often, she didn't know exactly where she would end up. A girl had to take work where she could find it, and since work was in the tourist bars, cafés and clubs, this meant saving up a bit of a stash. For the hard times, the winter times, when sane people like Jess were tucked up in their secure little houses with their nine to five jobs, their attentive husbands and a glass of wine at six o'clock before dinner.

Another world. For those on the move, November meant finding a place to eke out the winter with a few like minds. Decent inside work in bars or restaurants was still available, but competition was fierce. And the place to choose would be a city, not a village like this one.

But she liked it here. Louisa glanced behind her. Apart from bloody Monsieur Dumas . . . This part of Brittany had always been close to her heart; memories of childhood holidays here with Jess and her parents had drawn her back, bonded her to the place, making her return time and time again. But there you go. Louisa pulled on her apron. There was no point in being sentimental. Perros Guirec down the coast had a lot more buzz to it in the winter months than Trégastel. She was more likely to find work there.

'Will you give me a written reference?' she called over her shoulder to Monsieur.

'*Naturellement*. Of course, of course.' He gave a Gallic shrug. 'I don't want to lose you, Louisa. I told you . . .' There he went again.

23

She joined Claude behind the bar. For all his pretty verbals, her boss was a hard man, and not a particularly fair one either. Oh, he had said she must leave because she had been with them for the shortest time. But if she had shown him the slightest encouragement, let alone slept with him, it would be Claude – not Louisa Parris – walking the streets tomorrow.

And she wouldn't wish that on him. Claude was a darling.

'Trouble, *chérie*?' Claude, dressed in his usual uniform of tight black trousers, white shirt and red cravat, eyed her sympathetically.

'You bet. Last in, first out,' she said.

''E took you the chop, *non*?' Claude was eager to learn English – so many of the French were; rather surprising since the English rarely reciprocated. So Claude spoke it whenever possible, to the string of British tourists who had passed through Trégastel this summer, many of whom – of the male variety anyway – had ended up in Claude's bed. Thus giving a new dimension to the term pillow talk, Louisa thought, having watched this performance over the past months with grudging admiration. The result was that Claude had acquired a mixed vocabulary of idiosyncratic English phrases and swear words, not to mention a smattering of Irish, Scottish and Welsh. His difficulty concerned the appropriate use of them.

'*Non*, I mean, yes.' She picked up a pastis glass and began drying it slowly and deliberately with the tea towel. 'He gave me the chop, all right.'

'And will you 'ang off?' Claude asked.

'Huh?'

'I mean, er, will you be bumming off some place?'

Despite herself, Louisa laughed. 'You hang around, bum around and take off, Claude. And yes, I'll be leaving.' She paused, looking around the café in which she had spent the

24

entire summer – a heck of a long time for Louisa – at the traditional gingham tablecloths and wooden chairs, the sketches of the stunning Granite Rose coastline pinned to the walls. She loved the Côte de Granite Rose. 'But I've got nothing to stay for, have I?'

'Not Jean-Pierre?' Claude knew most of the lurid details of Louisa's summer romance from the late-night, wine-drinking gossip sessions they'd shared after closing times this summer. And he probably had him down as the reason Louisa had stayed here so long. In a way he was right. But even without a Jean-Pierre, these days she often had to search for the restlessness that had always driven her on before. It no longer came easily. To her chagrin, it was becoming all too tempting to stay.

'Jean-Pierre – like I told you before . . .' Louisa picked up another glass. 'Is now back with his wife playing happy families.' She had been only a temporary diversion and quite a profitable one for Jean-Pierre as it happened, since she was sure the bugger had nicked her camera, practically her only possession of value in the entire world.

'Happy families . . .' Louisa could see Claude storing that up for the future. He would probably use it to proposition his next young man. *You want to play happy families with me,* non?' The reaction might be an interesting one.

'And you will work in another bloody place? Another bar?' Claude asked.

'Probably.' It might be unfashionable to admit it, but Louisa enjoyed bar work and waitressing. It was a social way of life, a casual way of life. Working was necessary for food and shelter, but playtime was another thing entirely. There should be lots of it, in Louisa's opinion.

She put down the wine glass, leaned on the counter and stared outside. It was beginning to drizzle with rain. The dusty pink granite paving outside was spotting – changing colour like the rocks in the bay, washed by an incoming

25

tide; ashtrays on tables were filling with water, the crimson umbrellas were starting to sag. It kind of summed up her feelings. Just how sad was she getting to be?

In the charcuterie opposite old Philippe was just closing, looking up at the sky and shaking his grizzled head. And beyond the shops, she could see the slow rise of the dunes that signalled the beginning of Coz Porz beach where she and Jean-Pierre had spent her time off on all those lazy summer afternoons. Louisa sighed. Glorious days climbing rocks and dipping their bodies into the clear blue sea when the sun got too hot to handle. But what a bastard. She hadn't even bothered to call Jean-Pierre, to ask him about the camera. Not because she was afraid his wife would answer – he had admitted one day that they had what he called *an arrangement* – but because she knew there was no point.

'An arrangement?' She had traced a fingertip coated with oil across the dark brown skin of his back, along the knobbly ridge of his spine. It all sounded terribly civilised.

'*Mais oui.* She has a lover.' He turned over, shielding his eyes from the sun, probably not even seeing the utter consternation on Lousia's face as she let her oily fingers drop to the sand.

'I see,' she said. But of course, she didn't.

How naïve I still am, she thought now, as she leaned on the counter and remembered that day. How naïve, despite having travelled alone halfway round the world, to be shocked at what was probably a typically French arrangement. It was, she thought, so very English of her. And her lip curled because she didn't want to be very English, no way. So on that day with Jean-Pierre she had laughed a little too brightly and asked him what would happen when his wife's lover left. Would it be at the end of the summer?

'Why should we worry, *chérie*?' came the reply, as Jean-Pierre slipped his fingers inside the top of her bikini. 'When we are having such fun?'

It wasn't what Louisa had wanted to hear.

She wiped the counter with a damp cloth. He probably still was having fun. Still having fun with his wife and Louisa's bloody camera.

'Do you want me to 'ave a word?' Claude was watching her, his brown eyes filled with concern.

'With whom?' Her mind was still with Jean-Pierre.

Claude made a very French gesture, half-shrug, half-wave, towards Monsieur Dumas's back room. 'With 'im inside.'

She shook her head. 'I know when it's time to leave.'

'Still searching, *non*?' Claude brushed her cheek lightly with his fingers. 'Still searching ... or still running, *chérie*?'

Louisa turned away from him. She loved Claude; he was one of the best friends she'd ever had. But what did he know? And what else could you do but run, when there was nowhere to call home?

In Cliff Cottage, Dorset, the lights went out.

'Shit.' Jess stared into the darkness. She was using silver spray on the frame of a mirror she'd picked up in the local salvage yard this afternoon. And she was only half done. It wasn't a good time, but when would be? Was it a general power failure? Their power failure? A blown fuse?

She fumbled at her feet, put down the spray can, began to edge cautiously out of the breakfast alcove. Easy does it. Keeping close to the kitchen wall, she felt her way along it with the palms of her hands, knocking over her jam jar full of nails and treading on her hammer in the process. She swore softly. First thing – find a torch to minimise personal damage. Second thing – check out the rest of the street. There was no point in searching for the fuse box if the other houses were also in darkness.

On her way to the door, she banged a shin on one of the

27

chairs. 'Ouch. Bloody hell.' She rubbed her leg. It took time to learn the contours of a new house; you weren't expecting to be plunged into darkness before you had grown accustomed to its shape. And where was Felix? Still working – never around when she needed him.

She reached the understairs cupboard. Logically, this was the place to keep a torch. But who was logical round here? She groped among the hooks, her fingers encountering something clammy . . . a plastic carrier bag; something distinctly animal . . . Felix's old leather jacket, and various vacuum cleaner attachments that weren't attached to anything. 'Shit,' she said again. No torch.

The hall was obstacle-free and she marched to the front door and yanked it open, peering into the different kind of darkness outside. There wasn't much of a moon, but she could see quite clearly so her eyes must be getting accustomed. There were lights in the house opposite, chinks of brightness peeping through curtains up and down the street. 'Our power failure,' she muttered. Blast it. That meant tackling the fuse box – and the understairs cupboard again. But first, candles.

Jess shut the door and leaned against the wall. Now where might a candle be lurking? She shivered. It was very quiet. Spraying her mirror under the bright lights of the kitchen, earlier, she hadn't noticed any particular silence. But now it was here, part of the cottage, as if her ears could only work efficiently when her eyes couldn't see. A strangely oppressive silence. A slow creak. Wind. The cottage was creaking in the wind, as if it were tired of standing on the cliff all its life. Felix had told her they were too far back from the edge to worry about erosion, but what about in a hundred years or more? Maybe Cliff Cottage knew its days were numbered.

'Poor old cottage.' And as for her, not only was she talking to herself, but she'd have to start the mirror all over again, and she couldn't even go out for candles, since the second-hand car she'd bought last week had needed an overhaul from the local garage in Lyme. Which was where it was sitting right now.

She'd have to phone Felix. He could pick up some candles, maybe even fuse wire, on the way home. It would probably mean talking to the awful Hilary Buchanan . . . but needs must.

Jess made for the kitchen. This would teach her to be less concerned with basics like the state of the wiring than the cosmetics of the silver-grey bathroom.

Be sure of your basics, Sandra Slattersly had been in the habit of saying to any customers of Immaculate Interiors who would listen. *If your basics are right, the rest will follow*. Jess sighed. It was beginning to look as if the basics of Cliff Cottage were ropey to say the least.

But, 'Hyacinth,' she said, glancing at the black phone-shape in front of her. It was digital – how was she supposed to remember which button was which? You looked, didn't you, when you punch-dialled; you didn't do it from memory.

'Hyacinth.' This was the lingering scent of the soap favoured by Sandra; the soap forever squatting in the wash-basin of the staff loo. And perhaps coincidentally it was also the fragrance of the candle in a blue porcelain holder that Sandra had given Jess last Christmas. She had never lit it. But if she could only remember where she'd put the damn thing . . .

Ten minutes later she found it in the sitting room on a very high shelf. Matches turned out to be in the junk drawer (bottom) of the dresser; Jess began to feel quite pleased with herself.

She phoned Felix who was – according to horrid Hilary – *unavailable at present*, and located the fuse box in the understairs cupboard. But she didn't fancy fiddling around

29

with God knew how many volts with only a hyacinth-scented candle to light her way. Maybe she should have bought herself one of those maintenance books for idiots that male friends gave single women, so they wouldn't be called upon to change plugs and unblock drains every five minutes. But why should she? She had never even been single. Felix had always been there. Apart from the one time, that was.

She pushed this thought aside and wandered back into the kitchen. It was odd, seeing the cottage from this new perspective. Was she getting to know the real Cliff Cottage for the first time? Because that was how it was, wasn't it? The dark sometimes helped you see things.

The power cuts when she and Louisa were young had done that too. It was the three-day week, she supposed. Probably very inconvenient for adults, but for kids it had been both exciting and an excuse for not getting homework in on time. Jess smiled as she remembered her mother cooking dinner on a primus stove, herself reading *Bunty* by candlelight, endless games of cards – whist, sevens, Newmarket. The charades. And most of all, she could see their father's face. It was as clear now as then. Even by candlelight, especially by candle-light, she could see the love in his eyes as he watched her. As he watched Louisa. *My darling child*, he would say to her. But only to her. Jess had never known that before.

She stared into the fluttering flame of her hyacinth candle and wondered again as she did so often. Where was Louisa? What was she doing? Did she think of Jess as often as Jess thought of her?

The door knocker punctured the silence and she jumped. Either Felix had forgotten his key or she was about to receive her first visitor at Cliff Cottage – in the middle of a power cut, wearing a baggy blue boiler suit daubed with silver paint, and armed only with a hyacinth-scented candle.

*

Felix Newman was looking at Hilary Buchanan's legs.

Peter Beck had just left the office and now Felix's PA was standing in the doorway in her dark stockings and high heels, narrow hips encased in the clinging jersey of her black skirt. But then Hilary could look sexy in anything, and Felix was in the mood for a diversion. The weekly meeting with Peter had been a bore as it always was; but how else would they get to discuss company progress?

Felix tapped his fingernails on the desk. OK, so he didn't have a lot of time for his partner. Peter was a talented designer, he couldn't deny that. He'd helped establish a good client base in Sussex; no doubt he'd do the same here in Dorset. Thanks to Peter's abilities in the field of jewellery design (not to mention Peter's money that had put them on the road to start with) Beck and Newman was now a relatively successful company. But as for Peter Beck himself . . . well, he wasn't much of a man, was he?

'Letters to sign,' Hilary said in her clipped voice. 'I want to get them in the last post.'

'Pass them over then.' He watched her as she approached his desk, as she stooped slightly to put the letters in front of him. Whereas Hilary Buchanan, thought Felix, opening his pen with a flourish, was all woman indeed.

'Did the meeting go well? Are we still solvent?' Hilary perched on his desk. She had been with them so long, she knew as much about the company as he did. They had expected her to leave when Beck and Newman moved to Dorset. In a way Felix had wanted her to leave; in his mind that had been part of the deal.

'You know the answer to that one,' Felix growled. Not that he would have relished taking on a new PA – Hilary was the best; she was efficient, she protected him from clients when he needed to be protected, she ran his engagements diary like clockwork; she was on his side against Peter whenever he needed her to be, and she shielded him

31

from any stress that threatened to spoil his day. But she was also a complication.

'I think we need to do some more advertising,' Hilary said, smoothing her skirt.

'For Peter's stuff?'

She shook her blonde head. 'For the antique pieces. And insurance, of course. We should build up that side of things again.'

Felix smiled. *His* side of things. While Peter had worked to gain himself a reputation as a jewellery designer, it was Felix who had seen the need to diversify, who had expanded their first small workshop to incorporate a retail outlet dealing with insurance queries, valuation and private sales – not to mention the antique jewellery that Beck and Newman bought, restored and sold. It was Felix too who had developed the contacts for selling their jewellery in other retail outlets, so that the name of Peter Beck was at least known in the right circles even while it remained exclusive. Oh yes, he had played a large part in the evolution of Beck and Newman, and at least Hilary appreciated that. Jess admired Peter's jewellery more than he would like – that Deco stuff was right up her street. But Hilary recognised the immensity of Felix's achievements. She knew that Peter Beck would be nothing without Felix Newman. 'Perhaps you're right,' he said. 'Mustn't get complacent, must we?'

'Absolutely not.' The vague smile that he had never been able to pin down flitted across her face. 'Oh, yes . . .' She seemed to connect this with something else in her mind. 'Your wife phoned ten minutes ago.' Although they had met at office social occasions, as infrequently as possible if Felix had anything to do with it, Hilary never referred to Jess by name.

'And?'

'Something about the lights going out.' Hilary dismissed this with a cool shrug of her shoulders.

32

'In the cottage?' Felix eyed her breasts under the cream silk blouse. He knew better than anyone that at thirty-nine, Hilary's sexuality had risen to its peak. He knew, because for eighteen years he had been indulging in an on/off affair with her. On more than off – until six months ago.

Hilary nodded. 'I should imagine so. Perhaps you should buy her some candles on your way home.'

'Mmm.' Felix began to clear his desk, which was not easy, since Hilary was still sitting on it. The affair had begun when Jess was pregnant, and he had no excuses for that. Except Hilary had always been an alluring woman. Bloody stupid it might have been, but if they were honest, what man would turn her down?

After the first time he'd tried to cool it, but it was bloody difficult to say no to Hilary Buchanan. She was every man's dream. The only demands that she made were sexual and occasional, she accepted that he was married, she even saw other men (he didn't like that so much, but was hardly in a position to say so) and she provided some of the best sex Felix had ever had in his life.

Had Jess ever had any idea? It made him grow cold to think of it. She'd never said anything. Although that first time . . . she had seemed different, but that could be his guilty conscience, or the fact that she had a newborn baby to contend with. She couldn't know. And what had been happening between him and Jess – the gaps in their togetherness, the times when they weren't on the same wavelength, when they barely communicated, when it seemed as though they wanted different things – all that had nothing to do with Hilary Buchanan. How could it, when Jess didn't *know*?

'Bas is coming round to the flat in an hour,' Hilary said. She was watching him. But had he ever known what she was really thinking?'

'Final wedding preparations?' When Hilary had told him six months ago that she was marrying the wealthy businessman Bas Nicholson, and when Peter had suggested they move the company to Dorset, everything had begun to fall into place for Felix. This was the new start he needed for himself and Jess. No more Hilary – she was bound to stay in Sussex and besides, she would never jeopardise her relationship with Bas. It was what he had been waiting for. No more temptation, no more guilt. The answer had been handed to Felix on a plate.

Hilary slipped neatly from the desk. 'Not really. There's nothing more to be done.'

Of course. There wouldn't be. If Hilary was frighteningly efficient at work, what on earth would she be like organising her own wedding? Felix felt a germ of sympathy for Bas.

'Nothing will change.' She was standing by the door.

Felix blinked. What was she talking about? 'No babies, then? No leaving work and leading a life of luxury?'

'Life of luxury?' Hilary's lip curled. 'Luxury is a limited kind of fun, Felix, you must know that.'

'Hmm.' He didn't agree. He certainly wouldn't say no to a taste of it himself.

'And talking of fun . . .'

He didn't twig, even when she reached out to turn the key in the lock of his office door. 'Hilary?'

'Nothing will change,' she said again, advancing towards him.

Self-discipline had never been one of Felix's qualities, and the last vestiges were soon drowned and forgotten in the headiness of Hilary's perfume as she approached his chair, as she bent close to loosen his tie, to undo the buttons of his shirt. Hilary had always been the one to do the touching and taking, and he had never stopped her. He was a man, and she was the sexiest woman he'd ever known. He didn't ask her if everyone else in the office had gone home. As always, he simply let Hilary take care of everything.

Chapter 3

The man standing on Jess's doorstep was a complete stranger to her. He was dressed entirely in black and was holding a bottle of wine, casually, the neck of it supported between three fingers as if he were about to use it in a game of tenpin bowling.

'Hi,' he said.

'Er . . . hi.' Perhaps he was looking for a party? At any rate he showed no surprise that Cliff Cottage was in darkness, nor did he seem to find the sight of Jess, standing on the threshold in an outsize paint-stained boiler suit, with wild hair and candle in hand, at all unusual. 'Can I help you?'

'I thought someone was in. I saw the light moving around.' He thrust the bottle towards her.

'Um – thanks.' Automatically, she took it. It was homemade – definitely suspect.

'Dandelion wine,' he said. 'Welcome to your new abode and all that.'

'Ah.' She was beginning to see. 'You live . . .?'

'Next door.' Sure enough he waved in the direction of the cottage of scruffy garden, evening bonfire and violins.

She looked him up and down. Tall, dark and interesting.

Cropped hair and hungry eyes. A variation on Nigel Kennedy; but he didn't look dangerous. 'Come in.'

'Thanks.' He held out his hand. 'Rupert Sumner.'

She would never have christened this man Rupert. He wasn't a bit cuddly, from what she could see of him in her dark hallway. But he had nice hands and a strong grip. 'Jess Newman,' she responded. 'The lights have gone out.'

'I guessed as much.' He spoke solemnly.

Jess giggled. 'And this is the only candle, I'm afraid.' In the light of it she saw his beak of a nose wrinkle. 'Stinks, doesn't it?' she commented cheerfully. 'Hyacinth.'

'I might have some of the white and unscented variety next door, if you get really desperate.' He made his way into the kitchen as if entirely used to being in the dark. And he seemed perfectly at home. 'Shall I open the wine?' He grinned. 'Or do you want to save it for later?'

She didn't hesitate. 'If it's in the least restorative, I think I need it now.' Luckily, Jess knew exactly where the corkscrew was, and the glasses too. She was getting better at this already. Progressing in leaps and bounds.

'Want me to take a look at the fuses?' he asked. Jess had placed the candle in the centre of the pine kitchen table, and the light flickered across his prominent features, emphasising the hollowness of his eyes.

Did she? It was rather a cheek. But on the other hand, how much burning time did this disgusting-smelling candle have left? She was hardly in a position to refuse neighbourly assistance.

'After a drink,' she said firmly. 'Cheers.'

For a moment they drank in silence. This was so weird; Jess shifted uneasily in her chair. It would be a great story for Patti the next time she phoned. But the wine was surprisingly good – a much better proposition than flapjacks, at least.

'What brought you to Dorset?' Rupert gazed across at

her. He had a direct way of talking that she found rather refreshing.

'My husband's company has moved here.' Although this wasn't entirely accurate. 'We wanted a change.'

'From?'

'From Sussex.'

She cradled her glass with her hands, leaning back into the shadows. 'It's meant to be a new start.' Jess had no idea why she said this. But sitting here in semi-darkness opposite a stranger, drinking his dandelion wine, had removed all the usual rules of social conventions. And she sensed that this was a man to whom social conventions were not a high priority.

He nodded as if he understood. Then removed a small pouch of tobacco and a packet of cigarette papers from his back pocket. 'Do you mind?'

Jess shook her head.

He rolled the cigarette deftly in the dim light. Probably, she thought, he could do it with his eyes closed. 'I did the same,' he said.

'Oh?'

'I dropped out of university. Moved away from my family. That was my new start.'

'When was that?' She tried to fathom his age, but it wasn't easy in this light, and the way he was dressed provided no clues.

'Back in the days when dropping out was what people did.' He laughed.

Probably about her own age then. And able to poke fun at himself, which was a plus. She began to warm to him. 'And did it work – this new start of yours?' Jess got to her feet and managed with some difficulty to locate the blue ceramic ashtray she always kept on the dresser. A throwback, she supposed, to visits from Patti back in Sussex; she smoked like a chimney.

37

His eyes met hers. They seemed to have grown darker and there was a strange expression in them that she couldn't read. 'It would have,' he said.

Would have? That seemed an odd thing to say. Would have worked if what?

'It's OK,' he amended, his expression lightening once more. 'I choose how I live. I don't have to do what others expect of me.'

He reminded her of Louisa. She too had defied society's conventions; done exactly as she chose. 'Are the choices always black and white?' Jess murmured, sipping her wine. She envied those who made it seem so easy.

He shook his head. 'No. But I lead a simple life.'

'No wife? No children?'

'None.' His eyes seemed to darken once again. But in this light, who could tell? It might be a trace of some former sadness, a memory of what might have been; it might be Jess's overactive imagination.

'My sister's like you,' she blurted. 'Although it's easier, isn't it, to make choices just for yourself when you don't have a family to think of?'

'Perhaps.' But he smiled, as if to deny her words. 'And family is important to you.' He poured more wine. 'Isn't it?'

'Well, yes.' Perhaps too important. 'Though I'd still like to be more like Louisa.' Not to care so much for family ties ... But the bond of family had always been strong for Jess. That was why she missed her parents, why she would have preferred to have Sophie living nearby, why – despite all the differences between herself and Louisa over the years, despite the miles that separated them – she couldn't accept the thought that she would never see her again.

'Do you ever see your parents?' she asked this strange man sitting opposite her in the near-darkness. 'Are they still ...?'

'Alive?' The light from the candle flame played momentarily across his face as he moved in his chair. 'Oh, yeah. They send birthday cards, invitations for Christmas, that sort of thing.' He sounded bitter.

'But you never talk?'

'No.'

'And so you don't know how they feel?'

He shot her a searching look. 'Don't I?'

With her forefinger, Jess pressed the soft outer edge of the blue candle in towards the centre, being careful not to burn her fingertip. She would give almost anything to find out what her parents had felt. What her mother – so passive in her everyday life, so deferent, so . . . bloody dutiful – had really felt. And as for her father . . . She would like to ask him why he had loved Louisa so much more. Ask him what the hell *she'd* ever done to be passed over. Why it was, that the best memory she had of him was evoked by a piece of stupid pink granite she'd found on the Ile de Bréhat in Brittany. Jess tugged at her hair. For God's sake. They had admired it together, polished it together, and now it sat on her dressing table – a precious thing. She had felt close to him that day. She grabbed her wine glass and took a huge gulp. Pathetic . . . 'You should find that out,' she told Rupert. 'Before it's too late.'

'Before they die, you mean?'

'OK.' She could be equally direct, if that was what he wanted. 'Before they die.'

He was watching her thoughtfully. 'Is that what happened to you? Did you leave it too late?'

Jess blinked in surprise. But she was drawn to him; she even sensed he could be a friend. She looked away, over his shoulder, into the black mass that was the cooker and the shelves of pans, skillets and woks above. 'My parents died in a car crash,' she said. 'A drunk driver went over some traffic lights that were on red.' Easier to state it baldly; almost the only way. They had never had a chance. And

Jess had never had the chance to make them love her.

'How old were you?' He was still watching her. Did he think she was about to cry? Had he bargained for this when he decided to take a bottle of dandelion wine over to his new neighbours?

'Seventeen,' she told him. 'I had Felix.'

'Your husband?'

She nodded. They had only been seeing one another for a few months. But after the crash he had gathered her up, cared for her, persuaded her to move into his flat. Not that she'd needed much persuasion. Felix was charming, and, at twenty-four, very much the sophisticate to a girl of seventeen. He had taught Jess how to have fun again, he had replaced the void in her life that was her father and her father's lack of love; he valued her. 'We were married a year later.' If it weren't for Felix . . .

Rupert poured more wine for them both.

Jess realised with a shock that they'd almost finished the bottle. The candle flickered on the table. The wick was low; soon she'd be in the dark again. And instead of doing anything remotely constructive about it, here she was telling practically her complete life story to a total stranger. The wine had not been restorative so much as opening the floodgates. Perhaps she was missing Patti and their weekly lunches in the Café Continental more than she'd realised. And Ruth, her neighbour back in Sussex, who had provided a lot more than the odd onion or cup of sugar.

Female support, Jess mused drunkenly. They had made her laugh too, and one or other of them had always been around if she needed someone to moan to about Felix or Sophie or Sandra Slattersly, if she were concerned about Sophie, or even if she wanted someone with whom to visit an art gallery. Patti, who ran her own boutique, changed men in the casual way that some women changed hairdressers, but she had a heart of gold. And Ruth, who had just got her degree at the age of forty, and who lived with her mother and five cats, was a million miles away from this man sitting opposite her. Very disparate neighbours . . .

But then again . . .

'I think I should take a look at that fuse box now,' Rupert said.

Ruth would never have said that. Jess smiled. So there were compensations. 'If it's not too much trouble.' She squinted at her watch. 'Felix is awfully late.'

He got to his feet, seeming taller than ever. In a few strides he was in the hall.

Jess grabbed the candle and followed him.

'In here?' He pulled open the understairs cupboard door.

'Yes.' Jess repressed a twinge of guilt that the independent nineties woman she was supposed to be wasn't au fait with fuses. 'It's very nice of you—'

'I can hardly leave you here on your own in the dark. Damsel in distress and all that.' He shot her what she was beginning to think of as one of his looks, stooped, and filled the cupboard. All elbows and legs.

'If I can't fix it you'll have to come next door until your husband gets home.'

'All right.' She was humble. Maybe all women liked being dominated once in a while. For a knight in shining armour he didn't quite look the part, but who cared? In Dorset, neighbours clearly helped as well as confided in one another.

She squatted and held the remains of the hyacinth candle, while he flicked off the mains switch, opened the fuse box and peered inside. He seemed to know what he was doing. She realised that despite their rather outlandish heart to heart, she hadn't even found out what he did for a living.

'It's a pretty antique system,' he said.

'It would be.' Felix had been very confident about the survey. But had it included the wiring? It seemed unlikely.

41

'But if I can see which fuse has blown . . .'

Jess inched closer, allowing the candle to illuminate the row of fuses.

Rupert emitted a low whoop of triumph. 'This is the bugger. Look how black it is.'

Jess looked. 'Can you fix it?' she enquired hopefully. She needed the bathroom, but now was not the time.

'There's a card.' He picked it up, inspected the wires wound round it like embroidery thread. 'I can put some new wire in. There's some here that's the right amperage.' He produced a penknife from the back pocket of his jeans with the air of a conjuror.

'Wonderful,' Jess breathed from her position on the floor.

'I'll just loosen the retaining screw.'

Knowledgeable too. 'Whoops.' Jess lost her balance. She had leaned forward so far that she almost fell into him. It must be the wine. But half a bottle of homemade dandelion didn't seem to have affected *his* hand and eye co-ordination.

'Shine the light up a bit.'

She watched him remove the old bit of wire and secure in the new. 'You've done this before.' A thought struck her. That would be ironic. 'You're not . . .?'

'An electrician?' He laughed. 'Nope. I deal in furniture. Antiques and restoration.'

Restoration is a dying art, Jess remembered Sandra Slattersly saying on one occasion, tossing back her orange hair. But then, she probably wanted it to die – Immaculate Interiors would sell more furniture that way.

Rupert replaced the board. 'All done.'

'Fixed?' Jess couldn't believe it was that easy. Maybe she'd buy herself that manual after all.

'Should be.' He paused, his hand on the mains switch. 'But it might blow again. It depends.'

'On what?'

'On what caused the short circuit in the first place.'

42

'And that could be?'

He shrugged. 'With an old wiring system like this it could be almost anything. I mean, the insulation might have rotted, it could have been chewed by mice.'

Jess pulled a face. She began to feel he was rubbing the old system stuff in a bit. What did you expect when you bought a cottage in the country?

'Or your roof might be leaking. That's pretty likely come to think of it.' He scratched his chin. 'What with all that rain we've had today. If it's gone through to the ceiling—'

'We had a survey done. The roof's OK.' She ignored his look of surprise. 'So, shall we go for it?'

'Why not?' He shrugged, turned back and flicked the switch.

The bright light from the hallway flushed into the cupboard, illuminating them and their rather unorthodox positions. Rupert was bent almost double, his arms cradling the fuse box. Jess was squatting at his feet in her paint-stained, oversized boiler suit surrounded by dust and vacuum cleaner attachments, not to mention the body parts of the man next door. It was a touch embarrassing, to say the least.

She eased herself half-upright, but was hampered by the floor mop and the ironing board. This cupboard wasn't big enough for the both of them.

'After you.'

She giggled, backing out, still clutching the remains of the candle in the bowl. In the hallway it was worse; it seemed as if all the lights in the cottage had come on at once, and they were twice as bright as usual.

He came out after her, with dark and dusty hair, looking less hungry and less unusual under the bright lights, more like your average male (violinist? – with those hands anything was possible) who built bonfires in the dark and

43

lived in the cottage next door. He flicked a cobweb from his shoulder.

'Thanks, so much.' She wasn't sure what to say to him now. Should she offer him another drink – coffee was safer this time perhaps? – lead him to the front door, or what?

'That's OK.' He didn't look at her. Already, their conversation, which had flowed easily into the beginnings of friendship in a candlelit kitchen under the influence of dandelion wine, had become stilted. So that Jess was almost relieved to hear at last Felix's key in the lock.

'Sweetheart . . .' In his arms he carried a spray of white lilies and a box of purple candles. Hilary bloody Buchanan must have told him about the power cut. His dark suit was hardly crumpled at all. And—

Not lilies . . . There had been lilies once before.

'This is Rupert,' she said quickly. 'He lives next door. He fixed the lights.'

'Bloody good of you.' They shook hands, but Jess saw Felix's glance of faint distaste. They wouldn't like each other. And Felix wouldn't twig that the dust in Rupert's cropped hair was *their* dust.

Rupert shrugged once more. 'Just lucky I was here.'

'You must come again.' Felix, clearly not suffering from the kind of indecision Jess was prone to, led the way to the front door.

'Come to dinner.' Jess smiled.

'Yes, come to dinner.' Felix frowned, moved back towards the kitchen. 'Bring your wife.'

'Don't have one, I'm afraid.' Once more, Rupert raised his beetle brows.

Sorry, Jess mouthed. Felix could be so damned dismissive at times. As if the whole world owed him a favour.

'Girlfriend then, whatever.'

'Shut up, Felix.' Jess put a hand on Rupert's arm. 'Come round again soon, won't you?'

'Sure.' He smiled, and the friendship that had begun so easily in Jess's dark kitchen seemed to resurface between them. 'But you ought to get that wiring fixed.'

'I will. We will.'

Jess watched the tall dark figure disappear down the lane before returning slowly to the kitchen.

Felix picked up the empty bottle of dandelion wine and deposited it gingerly in the bin. 'We'll never be able to get rid of the guy if you encourage him,' he said.

He'd never said that about Ruth. 'We need to get the wiring looked at,' Jess said.

'Not by him.'

'I didn't say by him. By anyone. The lights could go out again any time.' The anger bubbled inside her. Felix could be so irresponsible too.

'I'll phone someone in the morning.' He opened the oven door as if expecting dinner to materialise from within.

But when he turned round again to face her, he was smiling. 'Fancy a takeaway?'

'S'pose so.' She might be a sucker for that boyish grin, but she was still feeling cross. Cross and a bit drunk too. Felix was like a child and right now she didn't want that.

'Anyway, I don't know what you're so peeved about. Look on the bright side. At least you made a start on the kitchen walls.'

What was he talking about? She followed his gaze. Silver handprints from where she'd felt her way along the wall shone from the magnolia, beginning from where she'd been standing spraying her mirror, with a gradual fade-out towards the door.

Jess trudged upstairs into their primrose bedroom and peeled off the boiler suit. She peered into the dressing-table mirror. Frizzy hair streaked with silver was not about to become a fashion item. She liked the man, but what had their new neighbour thought of her, for heaven's sake?

And in the background, behind this silver-haired woman was . . . primrose. What did primrose really say about a person? Jess whirled round. Absolutely nothing, that's what. Primrose merely implied, and what it implied was that you lacked the imagination to think of an alternative to primrose. It was girlie, bland and safe. But she didn't want to be safe; she wanted to be . . . what? A laid-back colonial? With muslin draped at the window, lots of ivory, terracotta and a linen throw on the bed? Or hot and spicy, with cumin walls and chilli on the ceiling? (Not literally, of course.)

At any rate she wanted to be something. And she'd rip up this awful purple carpet for starters. It was perfectly tasteless and it smelt of mould and decay so badly that she couldn't believe she and Felix had actually made love on it. She would have bare floorboards with matt honey varnish. And a rug – something exotic and warm to the toes on a cold winter's morning. What she wanted, was change. Wasn't that what moving was all about?

From downstairs, Jess heard the firm tenor of Placido Domingo getting into the unmistakable rhythm of 'La donna e mobile' from Verdi's *Rigoletto*. She could fathom Felix's mood from the Italian arias he chose. This one said he was pleased with himself. But what did that mean?

Tomorrow she would buy more paint; visit the salvage yard again. And do something about the lighting. One spot-light over the mirror to illuminate each new line as it appeared on her face (but worrying about it would only create more); a reading light beside the bed; an up-lighter for a romantic glow. The single bulb above her would be redundant, that was for sure. As she looked up at it she noticed a slight blackening, a stain around the ceiling rose. Water. Earlier today it had rained nonstop as Rupert had said, although it was drying out now. What had Rupert told her about the possible reasons for a short circuit? The bloody roof *was* leaking. So much for Felix's survey.

46

She sat down on the bed, stared up at the ceiling and listened as the rain began once more. The decorating would have to wait. Apparently Sandra Slattersly had been right after all and this amateur designer had to follow her advice. The woman was still haunting her. It was all a question of going back to the basics, and that was something that Felix had never learned. If the basics were right, the rest would follow.

Jess tried to phone Sophie the following evening. Once more, she got the girl called Karin. *The best of the bunch*, Sophie had called her.

'She's not here, I'm afraid.'

'Will she be long, do you know?' Jess was hoping to persuade Sophie to come to Dorset the following weekend. They were going to Hilary Buchanan's wedding – a forth-coming event that left Jess with very mixed feelings – and she was hoping for some moral support. She also had a childish desire to show her daughter their new cottage. Sophie had half-promised . . . And Jess missed her, she really did.

'Probably.' The girl seemed to hesitate. 'At least, I'm not sure.'

Why the reluctance to give out any information? Jess was curious. 'Gone to a disco, has she?' She seemed to remember the College held them regularly. 'The student union bar? Or does she have a new boyfriend in tow?' Sophie was eighteen. And besides, Jess trusted her daughter. She had gone through the usual teenage rebellions. She had learned at a party at the age of fifteen how sick alcohol could make you, and she had calmly accepted the condoms her mother offered her a year later when she had her first 'serious' boyfriend. But she had never stopped studying and – as far as Jess knew – she had never been involved in anything dangerous. As Patti and Ruth often used to remind her, Sophie had always been sensible.

'Um . . . perhaps if you ring tomorrow?' Karin hedged.

47

'Fine. I'll do that.' Girls that age always stuck together. It was probably nothing to worry about. But Jess was thoughtful as she replaced the receiver. There had been something in the girl's tone. And why had Sophie been so keen for her parents to move to Dorset?

Sophie Newman let herself into the flat that was 'on loan', though she didn't know who from. Not that it mattered. She could use it whenever she wanted to be in Brighton (which was quite a lot of the time, actually) so long as she rang the doorbell first, and always replaced the key under the broken flowerpot when she left.

She dumped her rucksack on the kitchen floor and examined the contents of her Sainsbury's carrier bag. Fresh chicken breasts (boned and skinned; Sophie had been a vegetarian not so long ago), olive oil (extra virgin, her mother always said, was well worth the money), an onion, garlic (OK if they were both eating it) fresh tarragon; tinned tomatoes, pimentos, and a packet of Italian rice. For pudding, she'd chosen Häagen-Dazs ice cream, mainly because the adverts oozed erotica. Nick, presumably, could be trusted to bring the wine; in Sophie's admittedly fairly limited experience, men could always manage that.

Sophie began making the tomato sauce according to her mother's recipe. Jess made the same basic sauce for lots of meals – she simply threw in different meats, fish, vegetables or pasta to ring the changes. But Sophie would become more of a discerning cook, she had decided. If she didn't have time to create properly, then she would simply go out to eat or get a curry. What was the point of settling for *second* best? She wanted the best that was available.

Like Nick. Dreamily, she stirred the garlic and onion into the sizzling green olive oil. Nobody could ever accuse him of being second best – even her mother; although certainly her mother wouldn't understand.

Sophie laughed. Her mother might say: *You kids, you're so young. You think you know it all. But what can you know about men, about love?* She'd heard them going on about it, Jess, Patti and Ruth, or the three witches, as her father had once called them when Jess had forgotten to meet him for lunch because the three of them were gassing away in the Café Continental. Well, her mother was way out of touch, absolutely stuck in the dark ages, because she knew nothing about the men of today. Whereas Sophie . . .

She flung the tomatoes in the pan and stirred them about a bit. She had met Nick at Amy's eighteenth. He was a friend of a friend, tall, blond and pure hunk. Horny, Amy had called him. And he was straight with her. Right from the start she felt the attraction . . . she cut into a tomato . . . shooting from one to the other of them. He felt it too, she was sure. Neither could help it. You couldn't, could you, when it hit you for the first time? You just went kind of wobbly and goggle-eyed and threw yourself into it. Well, Sophie did anyhow. But he was straight with her because he told her even before their first kiss.

I'm married, he said. But in his eyes he wanted her; she saw it. And Sophie felt the same. Too right. There was no deceit. It had been Sophie's decision, right from the start.

And she didn't regret it. Nick was nothing like the guys she'd hung out with before, guys whose idea of a good time was a late-night movie and a few cans of beer. God, they were so crass, so young. Nick was different. He was ten years older than Sophie. He made her feel cared for and loved. He asked her what *she* wanted to do, he made her laugh, he bought her presents, he knew so much about the world – not just about a poxy little student community, but about the real world. He was sophisticated and he was good company. He made the rest of them look a bit pathetic really.

She had already applied to Southampton, and there was

no question of not going, although Nick filled all waking thoughts and dreams. Nick and how to get to see him more often, Nick and where they were going to make love – in the summer it was on the South Downs or in his car, but both were unsatisfactory for Sophie – Nick, Nick, Nick. The rest was a haze.

While the tomato sauce was simmering she found another pan, heated more oil and browned the chicken. She could have found a flat in Chichester, which would have made things easier, though she wished to God she was even closer – perhaps at Sussex University instead. But her mother had wanted her in residence. *Just for the first year, darling.* And a year was a lifetime.

There had been a B&B in Brighton, and some sleazy motel. But this place was by far the best arrangement. And Brighton was only an hour away from Chichester by train. Sophie put the chicken and pimentos in to simmer with sauce and began to run the bath water. It was by far the best arrangement. For now . . .

Chapter 4

Once Louisa had made the decision to go, she was restless, unable to choose where she should go *to*. 'What do you think, Claude?'

'Do you want the heat, or do you want the snow?' He shivered melodramatically, wrapping his red cravat closer round his neck.

Louisa pulled a face. 'Heat, I suppose.' But she always headed south in winter. Sometimes she longed for the grey drizzle of a November day in England, for the rush of a north-easterly wind scoring into her skin – if only to wake her up. And then there was the depressing thought of Christmas. What a downer. Her least favourite time of year.

'Sitges.' He named a place in southern Spain. 'I have a friend there, *chérie*. He will look after you.'

'Darling, you have a friend everywhere.' Louisa laughed. But from her position on the other side of the bar she saw Claude's expression freeze as the ring of the door chimes and the blast of a cool breeze on her back told her the door of the café was opening. Nothing unusual about that, even in November. 'What?' She frowned, about to turn.

'I am perfectly well,' Claude said politely. But he was staring straight in front of him and Louisa recognised the look in his eye. Lust. She'd seen it often enough this past summer.

She turned to follow his gaze. Walking towards the counter was one of the most gorgeous men she'd ever seen in her life. He wasn't tall – although since Louisa was five ten in trainers most men lost out in her height assessments – and he was a little on the heavy side. But that was appealing after the lean dimensions of Jean-Pierre. His hair was dark and slicked back with a few sexy strands flopping untidily over his forehead, and as he drew closer his eyes proved to be a delicious drown-in-me-hazel. But it wasn't any of that. It was instant impact.

'I see what you mean,' she murmured. Either Louisa or Claude would be very disappointed. But surely this man was about as hetero as they came?

The mystery man – he definitely hadn't been here before, she would have remembered – was accompanied by two others; one thin and spotty, the other with a beer belly hanging over his jeans and at least four days' ginger growth on his chin. A happy foursome with Claude seemed increasingly unlikely.

Louisa turned her attention back to number one and treated him to her most dazzling smile. This kind of thing didn't happen too often, and when it did, well, a girl had to go with it. '*Oui?*'

'Hi. Any chance of getting something to eat?' This was spoken in English. So they shared a nationality and spoke the same language. Louisa smiled to herself. But would it be any more than that?

'Sure. What do you fancy?' Or who? She and Claude needed to get a few things straightened out, so to speak.

'You're English.' He seemed surprised.

'Guilty.'

'And you live here?' His eyes flicked over her.

'I was here for the summer. But I won't be around for

much longer.' She kept her voice casual. Didn't she always? Even when she fell for a man hook, line and nasty habits, she worked hard never to let them know. As a rule, men couldn't be trusted. It was the give-'em-an-inch syndrome. As soon as they thought they had you they took advantage, didn't they? But not if you took advantage first.

'What about the food?' One of the other guys looked bored – and hungry.

'There you go.' She pointed to the menu scribbled on the blackboard. She'd gladly translate for them if necessary – she knew from experience how useless the English were abroad.

They drifted over to take a look.

'Do you think he'll be having *des huitres*?' Claude whispered in her ear. 'The gorgeous thing.'

'The oysters are off, darling, remember?' She knew what Claude was getting at, though personally she considered aphrodisiac food to be largely dependent on who you were sitting with at the time. 'He'll have to make do with *moules et frites*.'

The gorgeous thing in question shrugged off his leather jacket to reveal a sleeveless vest in acid green, a tanned skin, a fair bit of muscle and the tasteful tattoo of a blue rose on his right forearm.

Claude sighed. 'He is a lot of all right, *non*?'

'Bit of. Mmm.' And exactly her type. So much so that she wondered if she should leave Trégastel after all. A man like that was worth changing your plans for, and she didn't have a train to catch, did she? 'So what do you think, Claude?' She got down to the nitty gritty. 'Straight or gay?'

The million-dollar question. But if she couldn't have him, then she was happy for Claude to do the honours. Claude was the nearest thing to a best friend she'd ever had. Brittany was one of the places she couldn't seem to stay away from, and Claude had been around for most of that

53

time. That was the trouble with moving from town to town, country to country – friends became few and very far between.

He put his head on one side. 'Search me. He could, how do you say it, go each way?'

'Either way.' Louisa smiled and took out her notebook. And there was also only one way to find out for certain . . .

'This looks . . . er, wonderful.' Nick had swept in, wrapped her in a long and passionate embrace, and was only now surveying the feast she had prepared, hot and still sizzling in its serving dish, on the dining-room table. It felt like he was coming home, but Sophie noted his hesitation.

'You did want dinner?'

'Of course.' He squeezed her hand. 'But where did you get all the stuff?' He glanced towards the kitchen, probably worried that she had both raided and demolished it.

Sophie laughed at him. 'Where d'you think? From Sainsbury's like everyone else.' She nudged him forwards. 'Come on, come on, we can't let it get cold.' This was fun – she couldn't think why women complained about cooking for the men they loved. It hadn't taken her very long, she'd had a gorgeous soak in the bath before getting ready for him, and it had all left her with such a good feeling. Warm and kind of contented. This was what life was supposed to be like. Not poring for hours over an essay about something that might or might not have happened hundreds of years ago.

Nick sat down. 'I never knew you could cook.' But he entered into the spirit of the thing, unfolding his paper napkin with a flick and a flourish, and producing a gold cigarette lighter with which to light the candle.

Sophie ladled Italian rice and then chicken and pimentos on to the plates. 'Oh, I'm full of surprises,' she said.

He rolled his eyes. 'I don't doubt it.'

The dinner was good. The tarragon gave the dish a unique and scented flavour, and the chilli sauce she'd added provided the necessary zing. The rice was perfect, and so was the company.

Nick had her wide-eyed at the story of the female estate agent in his office who had been propositioned in a client's bedroom that day. *Why don't you measure my proportions at the same time*, had been the line. *I don't think you'll be too disappointed.* 'But she was,' Nick said, face deadpan. He followed this up with the one about the client who had been frightened to death by a huge spider in the bathroom of an empty house. *We couldn't possibly buy it now* . . . Nick mimicked the woman's horrified and snooty accent to perfection.

Sophie pushed the food around her plate. He made his job sound such a laugh. She began to wish she worked there too. At least then she'd have a chance to see more of him, and maybe they could find a few empty houses of their own.

But her appetite was never dormant for long. She finished her chicken as they (or rather he) went on to politics – particularly Tony Blair and whether New Labour was a cop-out. According to Nick, it was, and he told her quite a few reasons why. She didn't agree with anything he said, but relationships were about two different people getting together, weren't they? It would be boring indeed if those people agreed with one another all the time.

Still, it was great – it was like, real life. It made all those student-type debates in the union bar about surrealism and philosophy seem silly. What did any of that matter when she could sit here with Nick, having dinner, discussing the realities of the world they lived in. Almost as if they were married.

But he spoiled it by asking her about college. 'Did you get that essay done?' He promptly began to devour his

Häagen-Dazs with a hunger that wasn't quite the kind of hunger she had intended.

This was it. The moment when she was supposed to drape herself elegantly on top of him, preferably on the sofa, although the dining-room table might do, while they spoon-fed one another with the crème de la crème. Until the warm sensuality mingled with cold Häagen-Dazs became too much and red-blooded passion took over from ice cream. But asking her about an essay? That was more her mother's area of concern.

'What essay?' she asked grumpily, grinding the ice cream into a pulp with the back of her spoon.

He pushed his chair back. That was better. Movement led to action. They were one and the same. 'The essay you said you had to give in tomorrow.'

'Oh. That one.' She had complained about the workload at uni, not dreaming he would bring the subject up again. In fact, she hadn't expected him to be remotely interested in her assignments.

'Well?' His smile was disconcertingly like that of a tolerant parent.

She took a spoonful of ice cream, playing for time. The truth was that the course was proving more difficult than she'd expected. She'd coasted her A levels and imagined a degree would be much the same, only you'd have more time to yourself. It wasn't like that at all, and no, she hadn't done the bloody essay. She'd come here instead.

'Of course I did,' she said. 'Only, sometimes . . .'

'What?'

'I wonder what I'm doing it for, that's all.' Who wanted to learn history? It was only about dead people when all was said and done. And half of it – the early stuff – could just as easily have been made up by someone for a laugh; no one knew for sure. As for all that studying, what was it actually achieving? It wasn't changing anything or adding anything to the world. So what was it for? Everyone at school had been expected to go the further training route if they did well in their A's: poly, university, college, whatever. It was as simple as that. But why?

Sophie had looked at the possibilities, discussed them, *endlessly*, with her mother. And still been no wiser when they'd done. Eventually she had chosen history, not because she particularly enjoyed it, or because it would be good for her future career (truth was, she didn't have one in mind) but because it seemed to be what she was best at, and so she fondly imagined she'd be able to breeze it more easily. Nobody had questioned her decision.

Sophie was about to say some of this to Nick; she had never told anyone, although she knew Karin had a good idea. But his next words stopped her in her tracks.

'Don't give it up, Sophie.' There was real entreaty in his eyes.

'Why not?' If she did, they'd be able to spend more time together. She could get a job and a flat of her own for them to spend time in, make love in. She would be an independent working woman and she would be able to do what the hell she liked.

He stood behind her, his hands on her shoulders. 'Angel, if you finish your degree you'll have a qualification that really means something.'

Huh. Means something to whom?

'You're clever. It would be a waste not to use all those lovely brains.'

Brains? Lovely? Was she missing something here? 'You sound like my mother.'

Jess was always moaning about having missed out in the education department. But she could go and do it now, couldn't she, if it meant so much to her, like her friend Ruth had done? Ruth was pretty much old fogey material – she was at least forty; education wasn't just for the young. And when her mother was a girl *she* hadn't had anyone breathing down her neck. She had chosen Sophie's father. Freely chosen. But would she let Sophie do the same? No way. Sophie was being pressurised from all sides, even from Nick, the man she loved.

'I'm only thinking of you, angel.'

That was more like it. Because now, his fingers were exploring under the neckline of her crop-top, thumbs firm on her collar bone. 'Mmm.' The last thing she needed was a lecture. This was so much nicer.

'I want you to go back and work hard, so I can be proud of you.' He bent to kiss her neck.

'You'd be proud of me anyway.' She leaned her head back, felt his fingers smoothing her hair from her temple, from her neck and shoulders.

He picked up her bowl of ice cream. 'And you haven't finished your pudding.' With his other hand he pulled her to her feet, and led her into the bedroom. 'Let's take it in here.'

Sophie forgot about the essay. This was what it was all about. She knew it. Just like in the adverts . . .

Afterwards they lay naked on the rumpled sheets, and he lit a cigarette.

She watched him, his smooth estate agent's look all gone now. His fair hair, layered and usually brushed back neatly from his face, was dishevelled. She reached out her hand to touch him; his skin felt warm with the faint glow of damp sweat and exertion that she found so sexy. And his blue eyes had the dreamy expression she loved. 'Nick?'

'Mmm?'

'You are staying the night?' It was almost midnight and he seemed in no hurry to leave. Just this once, Sophie allowed herself to hope . . .

But Nick seemed to change, his eyes grew alert once

58

more, he shifted uncomfortably on the bed. 'Angel, you know I can't.'

Any second he would sit up, swing his legs over the side, get up, shower, drink coffee, kiss her, leave her. And that would be it until the next time. She knew the pattern.

'Hey ...' She trailed her fingertips slowly across his chest. The hair was scanty – she didn't go for the gorilla type. Lots of guys these days shaved their body hair, but Nick didn't need to.

'Sorry, angel.'

'It's OK. No sweat, honestly.' She would die rather than be one of those whining women who always wanted more. She had as much of Nick as he could give, as much as he was willing to give. That was as it should be. It was all she wanted: what was freely given.

He relaxed instantly. 'Maybe I'll be able to fix up a weekend away sometime. Would you like that?'

Paris would be heaven. 'Forget it. Everything's cool.' She pictured a hotel. With a balcony. Croissants and brioches with coffee for breakfast in bed.

'And I'd stay tonight – you know that. If I could only think of something to tell Barbara ...'

Sophie shrugged. She didn't want to think about Barbara. Didn't want to think of them sharing a bed, sharing a life. He wouldn't stay with Barbara for ever of course, Sophie knew that. Someone like the anonymous Barbara could never hold a man like Nick. They didn't have children, so she wasn't breaking up a family, and these days marriage wasn't for ever. But she would never pressurise him into leaving his wife. Nick must make that decision for himself.

'We both have other commitments,' she said. 'We've always known that. We'll just be together when we can.' Had she read that in a novel somewhere? Sophie yawned. Maybe she should suggest he came to Bishop Bell? You were *supposed* to sign in guests – for fire regs and so their car didn't get clamped or whatever, but most people didn't bother. But the hostel was so *studenty*. She couldn't imagine Nick there somehow.

'You know I would stay if I could. I really, really want to.'

'I don't blame you.' Sophie stretched luxuriously. 'This is a gorgeous bed.'

He bent towards her. 'And you are a gorgeous girl. A very unusual and gorgeous girl.' He kissed her mouth, slowly, very slowly, then deeper, exploring with his tongue. His hand cradled one breast, his fingers playing with her, drawing tiny circles with his fingertip. Tiny circles getting wider . . .

Sophie arched, offering herself to him again with a small moan. She pulled the firm shoulders closer, ran her hands along the fine hair of his arms, up and along his shoulder blades, as he eased himself on top of her once more. 'Mmm, Nick.'

With a deep pleasure she saw his eyes glaze as he moved inside her, and she shifted her hips as she had learned to do, gripping him with her knees, rocking to his rhythm, their rhythm, wanting it to go on for ever, for his warmth to seep right into her, until he was part of her, until they were together.

'When can I see you?' he whispered in her ear much later when she was almost asleep. 'Next weekend?'

She smiled. It was so late. What would he tell Barbara now? 'I can't make next weekend. I have to see my parents' new cottage.' And then there was this stupid wedding that her mother seemed to be so hung up about. She'd like to get out of it, but Mums obviously needed her to be there. Anyway, she mustn't make it too easy for Nick.

'The weekend after?'

God, not two weeks without him. She couldn't face that. 'I could come down on Thursday,' she murmured. 'If you think you can fit me in.'

He chuckled. 'So soon?'

'I've got some free time.' Who cared about not making it easy? And one thing was for sure – she wouldn't be telling him about her assignments any more.

'Thursday then.' He kissed her ear and swung himself out of bed.

The bed felt empty without him. 'I'll miss you,' she said to the space beside her. And with a smile on her face, she fell asleep.

*

'What d'you mean he won't talk to me?' Felix was in his office at Abbotsbury pacing up and down the room as far as the flex would allow, the phone in one hand and a silver bangle in the other.

'It's not you.' He heard Marilyn's sigh. 'He won't talk to anyone.'

'Have you told him how important this is?' Felix knew he was hassling her, and of course it wasn't Marilyn's fault. But she was his wife. Surely she knew how to get through to Peter?

'I tried to.' There was a pause.

In the past, Felix had considered his partner's wife a bit of a pain with her constant demands. But lately he was beginning to have more sympathy for her. Peter was such a bloody dreamer. 'And?'

'And he said he'd get back to you. You know what he's like. It's the big *do not disturb a creative artist at work* thing, isn't it?' He heard the derogatory tone in her voice and sensed her support.

'Yeah, but let me explain it to you, Marilyn.'

'If you think that'll help.'

'It might.' Felix took a deep breath. 'The position is that I have a whole chain of jewellers waiting for Beck and Newman bangles . . .'

'Which Peter is supposed to make?'

61

'Which Peter is supposed to have made,' he corrected. Three weeks ago, to be precise, and their non-appearance had forced Felix to postpone the order. 'We were supposed to deliver last week. We didn't.'

'I see.'

Felix wondered if she did see. Marilyn had expensive tastes. Customers wouldn't keep reordering from an unreliable firm, no matter how good the merchandise. Their reputation was at stake, and with it their profit margin. 'Peter promised to get them to me this morning,' he said patiently. 'Last chance. And now he's gone on walkabout. He hasn't come to the office and he hasn't even called in and told me why.' He twirled the bangle between his fingers and waited for her response.

'I do see.'

'And don't you think he owes me an explanation?' Felix was getting bored with this. He was wasting time.

'*I* do. But . . . Hold on, will you Felix? I'll give it another try.'

This time he thought he could hear her in the background. But was she getting anywhere? It was all very well having your head in the clouds, but business was business. Letting people down was not on. Next time they wouldn't even want any bloody Beck and Newman bangles. And Peter probably wouldn't give a damn.

She came back. 'Peter still says he'll call you later, Felix. He says he can't stop what he's doing right now. I'm sorry, but—'

'Right, that's it.' Felix slammed down the phone. He grabbed his jacket and left the office.

Hilary looked up in surprise. 'Where are you—?'

'I'll be back in an hour.'

He reversed his car out of the reserved parking space and pressed a button on the CD. Giordano's 'Come un bel di maggio' from *Andrea Chenier* burst forth – heavy, dramatic,

62

confrontational – perfect for his current mood. Felix swung out of the car park and headed for Litton Cheney. It was time Peter Beck was taught a lesson.

Chapter 5

Felix barged past Marilyn as she opened the front door. 'Where is he?' he demanded.

She laughed. 'Where do you think?'

What was so funny? He hesitated. Then he remembered the tone in Jeremy Browne's voice when Felix had told him, *again*, that the bangles wouldn't be arriving – the tone of voice that as good as announced Beck and Newman to be some cowboy outfit, unable to keep the smallest of promises. Felix charged on down the hallway.

'Peter!' he bellowed. He'd be in the studio on the other side of the kitchen, of course. That had been one of the selling points of this overpriced bungalow for Peter. More fool him. Some sort of artist's sanctuary. Not so much a workshop as a retreat from the bloody world.

'What's all the racket?' Sure enough, Peter emerged from the studio, blinking, his hair messed up as it usually was, the round red mark of an eyeglass livid on his face, his big hands dusty. 'What's going on?' He wiped his hands on jeans that were filthy already and stared at Felix. 'What are you doing here?'

Felix stopped in his tracks. How could he even ask? The funny thing was that Peter in all honesty probably *didn't* know. When he was immersed in a job he forgot everyone and everything. Marilyn's words had no doubt gone in one ear and out the other without making any lasting contact with his brain. 'The bangles?' he managed to say at last. Christ Almighty, the man must be hell to live with.

'Bangles?' Peter scratched his head. 'Bangles? Oh . . .' Felix saw the light dawn. 'Bangles, oh yeah, sorry about that.'

'You said I'd have them this morning.'

'Bloody hell, so I did.' Peter hit his forehead with the heel of his hand. 'This morning. What an idiot.' He turned to his wife. 'Could we have some coffee, Marilyn? Would you mind, darling?'

Marilyn's expression told Felix that this darling did mind. She had been standing, arms folded, watching them, with a look almost of pleasure on her face. Now, she scowled.

'I don't want any coffee,' Felix said. 'I want the bloody bangles.'

'Tomorrow – first thing. I only need to spend another hour here, and then I'll come in to work and get it sorted. It won't take long. They're almost finished.'

'Are they indeed?' That made it even worse. If they were almost finished now, then wouldn't they have been almost finished last night? And if so, then why the hell hadn't they got sent off this morning? 'Why do you need to spend another hour here?' Felix kept his voice calm, but he could feel himself getting more than a little hot under the collar. Peter was so damned frustrating.

'Ah!' His business partner clapped his hands together, and a light of pure animation, that Felix both recognised and loathed, appeared in his grey-blue eyes. 'It's this brooch for Evie Vaughan.' His body language spoke of passion for his work. Oh yes, Peter had plenty of *that*.

'Evie Vaughan?' He might have guessed – another of Peter's *special* clients. Another old trout with more money

65

than sense. If Peter had his way there would only be special clients. His prioritising this morning had made that clear enough. The scatty artist routine had been pretty damn good, but there must have been a time when Peter had put the bangles aside and picked up Evie Vaughan's bloody brooch instead.

Felix raked his hands through his dark hair. And sure, the exclusive and handmade stuff that Peter designed brought in good dosh. But it was the bread and butter part of the market that kept the company going when Peter was going through a quiet patch. The valuations, the insurance deals, the antiques, the jewellery they sold on to other retail outlets. It was a part of the business they had to protect. Felix's part. Like the bloody silver bangles . . .

'It's going to be good, come and see, both of you.' Taking their interest for granted, and apparently oblivious of Felix's feelings on the matter, Peter led the way into the studio. Felix looked at Marilyn; she shrugged, and they both followed.

Peter was working amid characteristic chaos. Every available surface was covered in clutter: saws, drills and blades, files, pliers and hammers, and the selection of flour-grade sandpapers and emeries that he used for polishing. There were sheets of metal, trays of semi-precious stones, jewellers' scales and shears, a blowtorch, pencils, what have you. It would be hell for Felix to work in such disorder, and he saw Marilyn's delicate nose wrinkle with distaste, but his partner seemed to thrive on it.

'I've used jade with coral and gold leaf.' Proudly he showed them the brooch – a perfect piece of Art Deco symmetry, like most of Peter's work. 'I only need to polish it up now.'

'Still setting in platinum,' Felix commented, knowing perfectly well that the polishing could take almost as long as the original creation. Setting the semi-precious stones in the

66

malleable metal of platinum had been considered very daring back in the nineteen thirties. But that was *then* . . .

Peter was obsessed by the period of Art Deco, of course. But it simply cheapened the piece in Felix's eyes. It was a waste of the precious, to be frank, it looked too much like silver to the untutored eye. And most eyes were. Sometimes – in his more modern pieces – Peter even combined precious metal with base, less a design statement than a blasphemy, as far as Felix was concerned. What was the point? It was self-indulgent crap, nothing more.

'But do you like it?' Peter held the brooch up to the light he'd had fitted over his workbench, so that no shadow could fall across the piece he was working on.

Aesthetically it was appealing, but Felix wouldn't give him the satisfaction. 'I'm sure Evie will love it,' he said, conscious of his own sneer. 'But aren't we missing the point here?'

Peter's expression changed. 'Perhaps you'll enlighten us, then?'

Felix leaned closer. It was tempting to grab him by the collar but Felix wasn't a violent man, and anyway Peter Beck was much bigger than he. 'We might have lost the order on those bangles,' he hissed. 'For good.'

Peter shrugged. 'Peanuts.'

'Look after the peanuts . . .' Marilyn contributed from the doorway.

'I'll make more from this one brooch than I would a hundred bangles.' Peter selected a fine grade of sandpaper and continued to polish it lovingly, using his buff stick to remove the surface marks from the metal.

And that was the point, wasn't it? Felix watched him in exasperation. He was in love with his bloody designs. He didn't give a fuck for silver bangles. 'And would you like to explain that to Jeremy Browne and all the rest of them?' Felix loosened his tie and undid the collar button of his shirt. Jesus, but it was claustrophobic in here. 'Would you like to tell them exactly why we make promises that we don't keep?'

What made it worse was that in a way, Peter was right. His designs *were* exclusive, he could charge high prices for them, and he had established a healthy clientele base of those, like Evie Vaughan, who didn't mind paying. And, despite their move to Dorset, the quiet patches when Peter's work was not in demand were becoming fewer and fewer.

'Evie wanted it for tonight.' Peter seemed unaffected by Felix's outburst. Lightly, he blew the particles of dust from the brooch. 'There was no other way. I couldn't tell her no.'

Felix snorted with derision. Some chance.

'And last week I thought I'd get it finished in time. I've been working all hours, Felix.'

Marilyn nodded to confirm this.

'Fine.' Felix turned on his heels. 'I'll just carry on running the business without the least idea when anything will be ready, and you go off and do your own thing completely ignoring me whenever I try to discuss what's going on. Fucking perfect. How every business should be run, I guess.'

'Don't be like that.' Peter's tone was conciliatory as he followed Felix out of the studio and into the kitchen. 'I said I was sorry.'

'Yeah . . .'

'And I also keep telling you that I can't keep up with the demands for this kind of stuff you're asking me to churn out.' He brushed the dust from hands on to jeans, grabbed an apple from the fruit bowl and bit into it noisily. 'You'll have to tell them we can't supply so often. Or at all. I've got my own work to think of, don't forget.'

'Not likely to, am I?' Felix conveniently overlooked the fact that this had been the original agreement between them. Peter's work would come first, the other demands of the company second.

'Well, I don't know about this bangle thing . . .'

'What don't you bloody know?' Felix was furious. He had negotiated the contracts for the 'bangle thing'. He had considered it a triumph.

'If we should keep it going—'

'Stuff that,' Felix snapped. 'That is not good enough - no way.'

Peter seemed to get taller by about two inches. 'If you don't like it, Felix . . .'

'Yeah?' Felix almost didn't care any more. He'd had just about enough of this man.

'Then you know what you can do.' Peter stomped back into the studio and slammed the door.

Typical. All the things Felix would like to say to him . . . (but he couldn't, because basically Peter had control of the company). He hit the wall with his fist and looked round. Marilyn was watching him, laughing.

He glared at her, then found himself laughing too. 'We're as bad as a couple of kids. Isn't that what you think?'

She beckoned him closer. 'What I think is that you could do with a stiff drink.' She poured him a scotch from the expensive brand Peter favoured and handed it to him.

Felix swallowed it in one. It burned his throat, made him thirstier than ever.

'Another?' She was watching him, like a cat. She picked up a pack of cigarettes from the counter and lit one, slowly, bending her face towards the flame.

Reluctantly, he shook his head. 'I'm driving.' For the first time today he observed her with some attention. She looked sexy - done up a bit more than usual with her sleek dark hair pinned away from her face, some dark eye make-up, a smart rust-coloured jacket and a short skirt to match. She would never be beautiful, but Marilyn knew how to make the best of herself. 'You're looking pretty good these days, Marilyn.'

'Well, thank you.' She smiled.

'Going out to lunch?'

She flicked ash into the ashtray. 'Felix, I don't know a soul in Dorset apart from Mother – who for the time being is bedridden – and I don't imagine Peter's about to whisk me off somewhere, do you?'

He smiled, but the business with Peter still rankled. As a matter of fact it rankled like hell. 'I'll take you to lunch, then. How about that?' Why had he said such a thing? Was he crazy? How many times had he and Jess discussed what a manipulative bitch Marilyn Beck could be, how she was only interested in money, how neither would give her the time of day if it weren't for Peter . . . But then again, it was only lunch.

Marilyn narrowed her eyes. 'You're on.' She picked up her bag and keys, ground her cigarette out in the ashtray, and led the way out of the kitchen.

'Not going to leave him a note, then?' But Felix was pleased. He approved of people who were able to make a quick decision; of women who didn't need a flight check before they could leave their houses.

'Let him stew.' Marilyn opened the front door. 'And don't imagine I don't know why you're doing this.'

They walked down the path and he opened the door of the car for her. 'Lunch with a beautiful woman. Do I need a reason?'

Her laughter was husky and touched some chord within him. 'Stop trying to flatter me, Felix. I know you want to annoy Peter, and as it happens, so do I.'

'Really?' Now, why would she want to do that? Felix started the engine and put the car in gear. He knew the perfect place to take her, a small pub just outside Dorchester where atmosphere and intimacy were equal to the food. He didn't just want to annoy Peter – that was the trouble – he wanted to teach him a lesson he would never forget; teach him some bloody respect. It drove him crazy that when it came down to anything important, Peter had the final say. How could Felix ever get to run the company his way? When would come the time that he no longer had to defer to a guy whose head was stuck in jewellery design bloody wonderland?

'And it's so much more fun,' Marilyn let her scarlet-taloned hand rest on his for just a moment, 'to do it together.'

Well, well, well. Perhaps they had more in common than he had ever realised.

'How about some lunch?'

Louisa looked into his delicious drown-in-me hazel eyes. It was probably the best offer she'd had in years. She had been acting casual – maybe too casual? – since his arrival in Trégastel and the only intimacy she'd achieved so far was knowledge of his name – Stevie Black – and the fact that he played in a band. Considering that he'd come into the café several times, this wasn't a lot. But he seemed to be hetero-sexual since Claude had found out even less. and now, from the look of invitation in his gorgeous eyes, Louisa was beginning to suspect she'd played it right.

She shrugged. 'OK. Lunch sounds good.' Actually lunch sounded fantastic.

'Do we have to rush?' His voice caressed her.

No, no . . . Perhaps he sang in the band? Deep and husky, words running into each other, coating your eardrums with honey. 'Um . . .'

'I mean, are you free for the afternoon?'

Louisa looked at the rose tattoo inked on to brown skin. Perhaps he played the guitar. She could imagine that – quite graphically. 'As a matter of fact . . .' It was Friday, her last day, and yes, she was *supposed* to be working this after-noon. 'I'm free, from this moment on.'

71

He grinned. Melting material. 'You just left?'

'I just left.' It was a good feeling. It was always a good feeling to walk out of the door, though she'd miss Claude, of course.

They left the café and strolled towards the dunes of Trégastel and Coz Porz beach. And this time Louisa didn't think of Jean-Pierre. Not even for a millisecond.

Together they scanned the seafood restaurants. Some had closed down for the winter, others had moved their tables inside. But it was an exceptionally mild day and the green and yellow umbrellas of Le Tas de Crêpes were still in evidence. They settled themselves on the yellow metal chairs and the waiter, with whom Louisa had been on grinning terms all summer, brought them a menu.

'You said you'd be leaving Brittany soon. That day ... when we first came into the café.'

Was it her imagination or did he seem sad about that? Had he been casting long, lingering and lustful looks in her direction in the Café Noir, without her knowing about it? 'Mmm. So I am.' Still playing it cool – and why not, when it had worked this far?

Louisa loved this restaurant. The seafood was so fresh – you could guarantee it; it almost still tasted of salt and ocean. And perhaps that was why she preferred to eat it outside in the fresh air. The langoustines here were melt-in-the-mouth perfection. She ordered some and he did the same, along with a bottle of crisp Muscadet.

'And since you sound so pleased about it,' (had she been too convincing?) 'I guess you're a lady who likes travelling?'

'I love it.' Louisa smiled at the waiter as he brought the wine, and wondered if this were still true. Of course she had loved it in the beginning; but that had been a long time ago. 'I've been doing it for sixteen years,' she told Stevie.

He whistled through his teeth. 'That's a long time to be on the road. Where have you been?'

'Mostly Europe.' She took a sip of her wine, feeling quite proud of herself. Other women married and had babies or stressed themselves out in some career or other. Louisa experienced the world first-hand. Not to move on was to stay still, to become stuck in the material world, slave to convention. Like Jess. 'I've lived in France and Spain a lot of the time. But I was also in Portugal for a year or so, Italy for two summers, Germany . . .' She ticked them off on her fingers. 'Malta, Israel.'

'You make me feel dead suburban.' He stretched out legs of blue denim. He didn't look at all suburban. He looked sun-bleached from a hot summer and gorgeous and as if he'd feel at home anywhere. He reminded Louisa of what she missed about the English – a kind of amused cynicism, so you weren't sure if you were being laughed at or not.

The waiter brought some salad of red oak-leaved lettuce, frisée, rocket, watercress and slices of huge plum tomatoes dressed with vinaigrette and cubes of goat's cheese.

'How did it start?' he asked her. 'Did you just take off one day and never go back?'

'Kind of.' She had always known she wouldn't stay in Sussex with Aunt Pam. And Jess had made it clear that Louisa wasn't going to be asked to share her life with Felix and her new baby. Jess had become a stranger; mumsy and distant. The father who had loved her was dead. In truth Louisa hadn't known where to go, or what to do. She had been lost, and all she could think was – just go, and see where it leads. And keep moving. When you stay too long in one place, you only get too dependent. It all begins again: love, trust . . . You forget that in the end you can only depend on yourself.

She met a gang of people her own age on the ferry going over from Newhaven to Dieppe – people who were drifting, who had no timetables, to whom life was a slow-moving affair. These people didn't judge, they didn't hassle, and they had a knowledge of life that astounded her. One of them, Jimmy, made love to her that first night and gave Louisa her first taste of grass, her first lesson in sex, her first scent of freedom. It was mind-blowing. She agreed to go with them to pick grapes in Provence, and by the time Jimmy moved on six weeks later, she found she didn't much care. She had adopted their lifestyle. She was free.

'So when will you be moving on?'

She wouldn't admit it to anyone but herself, but this might depend on him. 'Tomorrow, maybe,' she said, In hitchhiking terms Saturday could be a safe day for travelling, but any other Saturday would do.

'And where will you be heading?'

He was asking a heck of a lot of questions. Was that a good or a bad sign? 'I might take the train to Rennes,' she said. 'Then head south.'

How she got there would depend on the price of fares, More and more often these days she took the bus or train, though it ate into her precious stash. It was dangerous to hitch, she knew that, but she was careful, and over the years had written her own rules. She never took a lift from anyone who looked dodgy or who'd obviously been drinking. And she kept a spray in her pocket that was illegal; but if it saved you from rape, who cared? Add to that the course in self-defence that was the best thing Aunt Pam had done for her. Mostly, she could take care of herself.

'Or I might go across to Spain.' Only . . . she was feeling strangely tired. Maybe she was getting too old for all this stuff. Maybe she should be more like her sister, whose biggest worry was probably getting Felix's shirts ironed on time. 'How about you?' she asked.

'We've been doing some gigs round the country,' Stevie told her. 'All summer. It's been a ball.'

'I bet.' Louisa smiled. She could imagine. 'What kind of stuff do you play? Rock?' She could see ginger-jaws on drums; the least good-looking ones always played drums.

74

He flicked back his hair in a manner wonderfully reminiscent of Bryan Ferry. 'Jazz and blues. Some of our own stuff, some that's more well known. We're good – though it's not up to me to say it, I guess.'

'Someone's got to.' Her image of him changed. This time he became a saxophonist playing a sexy solo that crawled up and down your spine – melting guaranteed. 'I would have liked to hear you play.' Only, Trégastel wasn't the kind of place that had venues for musicians. It was strictly seaside and seafood. For anything resembling culture (with the dubious exception of the aquarium) you had to venture further afield.

'It's not too late.' His gaze held hers.

'It's not?' The langoustines arrived, but she waited, fingers poised, for his reply.

'We're playing tomorrow night, in St Malo. It's our last gig. We'll be leaving here first thing in the morning.'

'Ah.' Louisa selected the smallest langoustine – she liked leaving the best to last – and divested it neatly of its shell. 'St Malo.' She felt a stab of disappointment. That was the opposite direction to where she was heading. St Malo was to the north, only a Channel crossing away from England. 'Shame . . .'

'But you could still come.' He selected the largest langoustine on his plate, peeled it and dipped it in garlic butter.

Louisa felt her mouth watering. 'Not really.'

'Here.' He held it out for her.

It was very tempting. She opened her mouth and bit into the soft flesh. 'Mmm.'

'I mean, like you said, you're free, aren't you? No plans, no ties . . .'

She could feel herself about to agree, so she looked away from those eyes and concentrated on her lunch. 'Ye-es.' But what exactly was he proposing?

75

'We've got a van.'

'I'm sure you have.' Louisa wiped her mouth with her napkin.

'So, obviously, getting there wouldn't be a problem.' He picked up her hand, playing idly with her fingers.

The melting continued at an alarming rate. In desperation, Louisa grabbed a slice of buttered baguette and took a bite. Maybe something as mundane as buttered baguette might keep her sensible. If she was too old for hitch-hiking then she was getting much too ancient for one night stands. 'If I'm travelling south, it's out of my way,' she pointed out.

'Not by far. We're on a peninsula here, don't forget. You said you'd be heading for Rennes. That's due south from St Malo. Keep going and you get to Nantes, Bordeaux. You're practically in northern Spain.'

Men. She hadn't asked for a geography lesson.

'But then there's other places you could get to from St Malo.'

'Like?' Louisa was conscious of a sliver of fear; or it might have been anticipation – she wasn't sure.

'Paris, Le Mans . . .' He let go of her fingers and took a sip of his wine.

Louisa wished he would pick up her hand again. She wished he would touch her. She wished she were the wine that he was savouring, rolling around his tongue as if it were the finest champagne. She wished she were going to St Malo. 'And what will I be missing – if I don't come?'

'An experience.' He smiled and she was done for. 'So what have you got to lose?'

Chapter 6

Jess took a break from distempering the bedroom walls. She needed a cup of tea. And a chance to study the leaflets she'd picked up from the library this morning. Again.

She couldn't help reading them over and over; just looking at the glossy promises sent her all-of-a-shudder with excitement. And this time she had promised herself she would do it. This time she wouldn't let work or family or this lack of self-confidence (it started with pregnancy and increased year by year until the menopause finished you off) prevent her. Moving to Dorset had kick-started her into action. Her time had come.

A knock on the front door broke into her thoughts.

Rupert. 'Hi, there.' She let him in. Since their sojourn in the understairs cupboard their friendship had progressed rapidly. He often dropped round on his way back from work, and although he wasn't Patti or Ruth, Jess enjoyed his company. But it could never be as uncomplicated as friendship between women, could it? Felix wouldn't like it, for starters.

She waved the brochures at him. 'I got them. All the college courses available.' She pointed. 'This looks favourite. It leads to a City and Guilds 7819 qualification.' She read aloud from the brochure. 'Studying colour, presentation drawing, all aspects of room design, decorative techniques ... blah blah. And a design project.' The words tumbled out; she'd been itching to tell someone all day. This was her new beginning.

'Great. When would you start?' Rupert grabbed the brochure from her, and lounged against the dresser to read it for himself. As always he seemed rather too tall for Cliff Cottage.

'January. And you're encouraged to take on outside projects.'

'This place? You've only just moved in and you've redecorated half of it already.'

'Hardly.' She laughed. Maybe she was taking on a lot, but it was all part of making the cottage hers. Theirs, she corrected herself. 'It has to be someone else's house, anyway. Otherwise you could say you were thrilled with the results when you weren't. And I'm not too old. It says—'

'Mature students are positively encouraged to apply.' He finished for her, reading from the leaflet. 'Sounds perfect for you then, Jess.'

'Ha ha, very funny.' She aimed a playful swipe at him but he dodged out of the way. 'I'd make you some coffee but I've got to finish distempering the bedroom walls, so you'll have to make your own.'

He did so and a few minutes later brought it upstairs on a tray.

'Cheers.'

Rupert wrinkled his nose at the smell. 'Distemper? Isn't that something to do with dogs?'

'Ignorant heathen. Distemper allows a wall to breathe.' She had to admit it looked pretty awful at the moment, all wet, uneven and blotchy, but she knew from experience that the paint would eventually fade to a creamy opaque texture that would be perfect for the stencils she had prepared while munching a cheese sandwich at lunchtime.

Rupert did not look impressed. 'What are you aiming for in the looks department?'

'Swedish. Larsson-esque.' Bright, whitewashed rooms, painted furniture, simplicity, light. That was the look she had eventually decided on.

'Come again?'

She clicked her tongue. 'Ikea?'

'Now I get you.'

Jess continued to wash the walls with long sweeping strokes. It was good to get painting. She enjoyed the entire decorating process; especially the satisfaction of the final design touches – like the muslin she would drape in the window area, the Larsson 'Red' (decidedly orange) mixed from cadmium orange and deep red with which she planned to paint the bedroom chair, the red-oxide-tinted tulip stencils for the walls. But it was the painting that she found the most liberating. And God, did she feel liberated. Last weekend the roof had been given a patch-up job and some urgent retiling; yesterday the wiring had received the all clear.

She planned to finish this room and then start on the garden. There were a few jobs that needed doing before winter frosts set in; she'd prune the wisteria and the philadelphus, fix up her sink for the watercress she intended to plant in the spring, and cut down some of the long grass and nettles. Since the move she'd felt her energy really flowing, as if there were no limit to what she could achieve. And it took her mind off other things . . .

'What will Felix say?' Rupert asked, breaking the silence between them. Not that she minded his silences – she had quickly grown used to them. Silence gave her space for her own thoughts, and she had plenty of those.

'What about?' All this painting must be building up her muscles. Jess paused for a moment and thought of Felix. He had been distracted lately. Still pleased with himself too, but that didn't necessarily mean a thing. They hadn't made love for a long while either, but there was so much to do; when evening came they were both pretty exhausted. Or was she making excuses for him, for them?

Rupert was watching her closely; this was a habit of his that Jess found harder to get used to. 'The college course. The interior design thing.'

'Oh, he'll be pleased,' Jess said airily. He was always saying she should take it up professionally. And the only reason she hadn't mentioned it lately was because, well . . . because Felix could be funny about art. Perhaps he got cross because he couldn't impose any order on it; it was out of his control because he didn't really understand it. She smiled to herself. Maybe that's why he got so fed up with Peter Beck. He admired what artists achieved but he hadn't a hope of pinning it down.

Rupert began to wander around the room. He picked up the postcard that Jess had stuck on the windowsill. 'From your sister?'

'Yes.' Jess had told him something of Louisa. That she was restless, that she'd practically travelled the world with a rucksack, that it didn't seem as if she would ever come home.

Now, she didn't stop painting; her brush-strokes barely faltered. 'It took forever to get to England and then it had to be forwarded from Sussex.' There was no address on the card. Had Louisa done that on purpose, or simply forgotten? It was a picture of the rocks at Trégastel – the tortoise, the hare and all the rest of them. Almost against her will, Jess's gaze drifted to her dressing table. Under that white dustsheet was a perfect piece of the darkest pink granite; one perfect memory.

'You miss her?' Rupert had never asked her why Louisa had not gone to live with Jess and Felix after their parents' death, though they had often talked about that time. Louisa was only fourteen when it happened.

It had been so long since she'd seen her. But, 'Yes, I do.'
Jess could still picture her small face bruised with pain. *Let me come and live with you, Jess.* 'I always felt responsible for her. But—'

'You were only seventeen.' Rupert took a couple of steps towards her, she swallowed hard, and felt his arm round her shoulders.

Yes, she was only seventeen. And it was too much to take, when she had her own grief to deal with too. Jess needed someone to be strong for her: Felix. She wanted nothing more than to be protected, cherished. And if Louisa had come to live with Felix and Jess, wouldn't her butterfly-lovely younger sister have usurped Felix's care and attention in some way, required his admiration as she had required their father's – to belong to her alone?

Jess passed her hand over her eyes. What was she thinking of? What had she been thinking of back then? 'I hardly know her,' she whispered. She had left their forwarding address with anyone Louisa might contact in Sussex. But Louisa hadn't been back in sixteen years. Why should she come back now?

Rupert's eyes were sympathetic. 'If you ever need a friend, Jess . . . Well, I'm here.'

'I know.' She sniffed and smiled back at him. But it would be all right. She was fine and about to rebuild her life, Felix was simply caught up with work, Sophie was enjoying her new freedom at university, and coming to Cliff Cottage for the weekend. And Louisa was presumably having fun in Brittany.

'Or a hug.' He squeezed her shoulders. 'Whatever.'

'Thanks, Rupert, I'll remember that.' And then he was gone, loping down the stairs and out of her cottage, the front door shutting with a firm click behind him. She would go round to see him soon, she thought. She would thank him for being nice. Maybe she'd even get him to play his violin for her.

'I can understand why you wanted to stay here for the summer,' Stevie said as they strolled along the top of the dunes. 'It sure is a beautiful place. And you can see for miles along the coast.'

'It's the best.' Louisa felt full and strangely contented. After the longest lunch she'd ever had (even her grinning waiter had begun to look a bit pissed off by four o'clock) they had walked it off along the cliff path, found a place to have coffee – black and bitter espresso – and now they were back on Trégastel beach with the light already fading.

The beach was almost deserted, but from somewhere she heard a baby softly crying. And a few desultory strollers along the beach came into view from behind some boulders. They were not alone. Louisa zipped up her jacket. It was still mild for a December evening, but she could almost hear winter coming closer in the waves.

'When was the first time you came to Brittany?' Stevie caught her hand.

She looked down at the hand holding hers. Brown and confident like the man himself. 'When I was a kid.' She and Jess used to run over these dunes. Holding hands like this.

She took flight, pulling him along with her, over the dunes, brushing past the gorse (it had been bare legs then; now the thorns were useless against denim jeans). She laughed as his pace increased to match hers, until he was the one pulling her over the top, down the slope and on to the shallow sand beyond.

'What was it like then?'

'Heaven.' She spoke without thinking. 'Father said it was so perfect because it was like Cornwall only with better food, cheaper wine and fewer tourists.'

He laughed. 'Your father loved it too?'

'Oh, yes.' She shivered. He forgot to be cross in Brittany. The family became a family instead of one long argument. But she didn't want to think of that now.

'We should be barefoot.' Stevie sat down to pull off his heavy boots. 'We need to feel the sand.'

'In December?' But she followed suit.

They stood, boots in their free hands. The damp sand silted through the gaps between her toes, soft, scrunching and insinuating. In England you'd never do this on a December night, no way. Even here it was pretty mad; her toes were red and half-frozen already. 'And before you suggest it, I am not going in.'

But they walked towards the shadow of the sea, bruising the sand with their footsteps, slowly approaching the soft hiss and slither of the waves. 'And you said it was heaven . . .' He seemed thoughtful.

'Oh, it was.' There was more to Stevie Black than she'd realised. 'I suppose that's why I can't keep away from the place now.' She spoke, half to herself. 'But there are no answers here.'

'Answers?' His voice was almost lost in the sound of the waves as they stood at the water's edge. 'What were the questions?'

If she knew that, she'd be halfway there. She yelped as the first freezing tails of water curled around her toes before she could run. 'Bloody hell.'

He laughed. 'Chicken.'

'I suppose I'm not sure where I'm going, that's all.' Or even if there was a place to go. Why was she telling him this? He was a nice guy and she fancied him like mad, but he wouldn't want to know about the hidden corners of her past. Was it because, whatever she decided to do next, this was her last night in Trégastel – at least for a while?

She led the way, along the waterline towards the small island beyond the beach, only accessible by foot at low tide, where the rock formations were even more dramatic. It was the place where she and Jean-Pierre often used to sunbathe, not caring if they'd be cut off by the sea, because they could swim back to the shore in safety if necessary. But she wasn't drawn here by any memory. This was a desolate place, and she wanted to be alone with him. She didn't want this evening to end.

'Come to St Malo with me tomorrow.' He was very persuasive.

Louisa shivered. Maybe it was colder than she'd thought. Maybe it was just part of the meltdown. But they were walking in step, and she had the strangest feeling that Stevie Black had come into her life at just the right moment.

'Wouldn't the other guys mind?' she hedged. She hadn't taken to ginger-jaws and she didn't relish the prospect of a day in the van with him.

Stevie helped her over a small rock formation barring their path to the island. 'No, the other guys wouldn't mind. And soon you're going to run out of excuses.'

She smiled. That would be the day.

'What will you say then, Louisa?' He stopped walking. 'When you have to tell me what you really want to do? When you tell someone how you really feel?'

Louisa continued walking. He was teasing, but . . . was she so transparent? Did she wear her armour so blatantly on her sleeve? She turned back to him. 'I'll tell you when I know. Right now I'm still thinking about it.'

Ahead, the rocks on the island stood tall, skew-whiff and slightly crazy against the backdrop of the darkening sky. Louisa paused. They would have to put their boots back on to climb up these boulders. The pink granite – dark and volcanic-looking in this light – might be beautiful, but the barnacles and mussels were rough on bare feet as she knew to her cost. Even the granite, although smooth in places, could be grainy and sharp; if you stubbed your toe you knew about it, for sure.

'Shall we go all the way?'

She responded to the challenge in his eyes. 'Why not?'

They were out of breath by the time they got to the top of the formation known locally as the pile of pancakes. *'Le tas de crêpes,'* she told him. The same name as the café in which they'd had lunch.

He was looking around him. 'This is an amazing place.'

And he was right. The rocks that in daylight seemed to be made up of ever-changing shades of pink, red, orange and beige, had been worn over time by both wind and sea. She always saw something different here. Many of them even seemed to defy gravity, lurching towards ground level or reaching like misshapen giant wobbly fingers for the sky.

'Loads of them have been given names.' She showed him, pointing into the dusk: *'Les tortues* – the tortoises; *la sorcière* – the witch. And *la tête de mort—'*

'Death's head,' he said, with a melodramatic groan.

Louisa giggled.

'Let's see if we can get down here.' He eased himself into a narrow space between two overhanging rocks, and on to a flattish ledge that was protected from wind,

And completely secluded, Louisa thought, huddling on the rock beside him, hugging her knees. The moon was half-veiled by cloud. The sea was lurching like some drunken animal in the thin light. It was getting dark – and getting cold.

'You are a very unusual person.' He put an arm round her and kissed her, lightly, experimentally on the mouth. 'And this is a very unusual place you've brought me to.'

Her body turned to liquid. Meltdown completed. 'Mmm.' She kissed him back with passion. 'So much so that I think while we're here we should do something pretty unusual.'

'You do?' His eyes had been closed. Now, he opened them again, as he cradled her face in his hands, moved a fingertip along the line of her jaw.

Drown-in-me hazel. She caught her breath. 'Oh, yes. Unusual, at any rate, for the time of year.'

He chuckled. His hands were on her shoulders now, moving to her neck, looking for the zip of her jacket. 'Hey – I think you should explain exactly what you mean.'

'Well . . . it's not *that* cold.' She felt for the buttons of his fleece shirt.

'Sure?' He had already half-undressed her. She leaned against the rock. 'Aargh!' The touch of granite was like a cold slap on her back. She gasped.

'And about St Malo . . .' He kissed her again.

Did he never give up? She smelt the salt, the faintly sour whiff of stale water, earthy granite and the small rock pools below. She listened to the rush of the tide. It sounded as if it were coming from her own body, like the rush of her blood. 'Of course I'll come,' she said.

Afterwards, their arms crept round one another again and he pulled his fleece and her jacket on top of them to keep out the cold. Louisa was conscious of a sense of sadness, one that wasn't entirely unfamiliar to her. It had been nice; it had been good. But she and Stevie were just two people passing through, two people grasping a piece of warmth. It was pleasure, but it was still a one night stand.

At last Stevie jumped up. 'And after St Malo . . .' He pulled her to her feet.

'After St Malo?'

'Those answers you were talking about, Louisa.'

'Answers?' She watched him pull on his checked fleece shirt.

'Perhaps you should go further back than Brittany to find them.'

'Further back?' Why was she repeating everything he said? He would think her crazy, at the very least that she had no mind of her own.

'After St Malo, why not stick around for a while?' He took her hands. 'No strings. And if it doesn't work out . . .'

'After St Malo?' She stared at him. She was suffering from scrambled brain syndrome, that much was clear.

'Come back with me to England.'

To England? This time, she was unable to say a word.

Jess stood on the platform in Axminster, waiting for Sophie's train. She hadn't known until this morning that she was even coming for sure. Yesterday Jess had phoned the hostel and inevitably got Karin (who either had the nearest room to the phone or had been elected general receptionist by the other students). And she had been evasive, again. It was getting to be a habit, nudging Jess into concern.

And then later, it was Ruth on the phone. 'How's Sophie getting on? The weirdest thing – I thought I saw her this afternoon, in Brighton.'

Jess had laughed. 'Must have been a Sophie lookalike.' Although this was hard to imagine. At five feet eleven inches, with her dark frizz of hair, her father's striking blue eyes and – since last summer – a silver nose-stud, Sophie hardly melted into a crowd.

'Yes, I suppose it must.' Ruth paused. 'Honestly, Jess, I'm getting more like my mother every day, bless her.'

But Ruth hadn't phoned about Sophie; she had phoned to arrange a weekend visit. 'Me and Patti. She'd never forgive either of us if I came without her.'

Jess, Ruth and Patti. It would be just like old times in the Café Continental on a Friday lunchtime. Or sitting round Jess's kitchen table putting the world, and themselves, to rights. She couldn't wait.

The train drew into the station with a rush and a hiss. Jess began to scour the faces at open windows and doors. Where was she?

'Mums!'

'Sofe . . .' She didn't spot her until she was right in front of her and Jess was being enveloped in one of Sophie's bear hugs. Her daughter was home.

'Let me look at you.' She held her at arm's length; gazed into her face. 'You look tired.' There were dark shadows round her eyes. But the grin was infectious. Jess could feel her own smile threatening to split her face in two.

'I'm fine.' Sophie bent for her rucksack. 'Come on. I'm itching to see this dream cottage of yours.'

'You'll love it.' Jess wanted to hug her again already. But she contented herself with a kiss brushed against the dark mass of Sophie's hair. One hug was permissible; two would be way, way over the top.

As they left the station together, arm in arm, Jess added a quick squeeze of the arm she held. If there was anything bothering Sophie, she would get to the bottom of it this weekend. She would ensure that there was plenty of time for a good mother and daughter heart to heart. God, it was good to see this girl of hers. She was so proud of her.

On the way back to her mother's new home, Sophie felt herself bombarded by maternal questions. Mums didn't mean to go on; she was just being Mums.

How's university? Is it what you expected? What are the tutors like? Are they working you too hard? And, *Have you made any really good friends yet?* Unfortunately, all the questions were about university life. And Sophie hadn't seen too much of that lately.

'There's Karin,' she said, in answer to the last one.

'Ah yes, Karin. She sounds a nice girl.'

Sophie pulled a face. Even Karin wouldn't relish that description. Parents . . . If Jack the Ripper said please and thank you in the right places, they would call him a nice boy.

Of course, Karin was a bit on the conventional side. A bit of a boff too. Sophie had thought she could talk to her, that Karin would understand. But yesterday, when she'd been getting ready to go to Brighton to meet Nick, she had been a right pain.

'Again?' She had stood there, hand on hip, like somebody's mother.

'And why not?'

Karin had looked at her with what seemed suspiciously like sympathy. 'Because you're getting so behind with work, Sofe, that's why. I mean, really behind. You must be.'

Did Karin imagine she didn't know that? Her personal tutor had called her in two days ago to ask if she had any problems. Problems? The opposite. 'I'll catch up,' she said.

'When?'

'In the Christmas holidays.' She'd never be able to think up an excuse for not going to Dorset. So unless she could think of a good reason for a flying visit to Sussex while she was there, she wouldn't see Nick for six whole weeks. Purgatory. She'd have to improvise.

And what was it to Karin anyway?

Sophie sat in the passenger seat of her mother's battered Renault and listened to Jess burble on. She was full of all the things she'd done to the cottage. Hardly mentioned Dad at all.

'How's Dad?' she interrupted. Was it her imagination, or was there a long pause before Jess answered?

'Oh, he's fine. Busy with work, you know.'

Sophie knew. 'And Uncle Peter?' She still called him that. Since Sophie was a small child she'd had a special relationship with the man who was her godfather. Some of her happiest memories were of times when her mother had been needed to help out in the shop (before her Immaculate Interiors days). Sophie had gone in with her, been told to sit quietly. But she would creep into the back to the workshop, because it was her Uncle Peter she wanted to watch. She wanted to watch him as he sketched out beautiful pictures and patterns and created the most beautiful jewellery from dull raw old materials. How the stones sparkled when he polished them! It was like magic. And there she would stay until her mother came to take her home. *I hope you haven't been bothering Uncle Peter.*

'Never a bother,' he used to say. 'How could she be?' Sophie had liked that.

'I want to do something with my life,' Jess was saying. She was talking about some course she was enrolling on.

'Good for you, Mums.' But Sophie was thinking that Karin had said something similar yesterday morning.

'What are you doing with your life?' That had been it.

What did she think? Living it, that was what.

And then the hurtful bit: 'What's the point of it? I mean, he won't leave his wife, will he?'

Sophie had shrugged. 'That's not important.' Karin had no idea – because Karin hadn't been there, had she? She was involved with some acne-infested eighteen-year-old called Malcolm, for Christ's sake. Nick, the sort of man he was and the kind of world he lived in were beyond her comprehension. Karin could twitter on about Sophie being used, about her getting behind with work, about her being knackered all the time. But she could never see that it was worth it – every rushed second of it. Because Sophie was experiencing real life for the very first time. And loving it. If anyone deserved sympathy it was Karin, not Sophie. She didn't know what she was missing.

She glanced across at Jess as her mother brought the car to a halt outside a stone cottage with bay windows and an untidy front garden. 'So this is it?' Her mother didn't look in the least tired. On the contrary, she seemed positively bursting with energy, and knowing her this garden would probably be next on her agenda.

'Yes, this is it.' Jess turned towards her, and for one fleeting second Sophie saw something different on the face she loved. A touch of sadness; just the briefest of brush-strokes across the fine lines fanning from the corners of her eyes, a hesitation in the smile.

'Mums.' Maybe they both needed another hug. For all his charms, Nick tended to caress rather than cuddle, to demand rather than comfort.

So Sophie held her mother tight as if she could transfer some of her strength and youth. But she couldn't tell her, could she? Quickly, she jumped out of the car. 'Come on, then. How long do I have to wait for my guided tour?'

When she had finished showing her around, Jess said, 'We'll leave the garden and the cliff till tomorrow, I think,' and opened a bottle of white wine. It was kind of odd when you started drinking with your daughter – another boundary crossed.

'Deal.' They clashed glasses.

'Then on Sunday . . .' Their eyes met. Sunday was the day of Hilary and Bas's wedding.

Jess wondered how much Sophie knew. How much did anyone know? At times she thought maybe the entire company knew that Felix and Hilary had been involved (for how long, though?). And at other times, she wasn't even sure herself. Had it ever happened? She had no proof. She had never confronted him.

'Why the hell not?' her new friend Patti had asked her, when she'd confided in her five years later. But Patti wasn't married and so she couldn't understand. To confront him was to take a huge risk with marriage, with child, with home, with stability as Jess knew it. Honesty was all very well. But she had a marriage to protect – a marriage that, surely, was worth saving.

She had said *something*, of course, she had to say something. She asked him once where he had been, why he was so late, and another time, what was happening here?

Nothing. What had she expected? For Felix to crumple at

91

her feet, confess he was having an affair, beg for forgiveness, swear it wouldn't happen again? Of course he hadn't
done any of those things. He had merely been irritable and
evasive and told her nothing.

And that was what you wanted, some inner voice
reminded her now. So that she could shut the knowledge
away in that little cupboard and pretend she'd got it all
wrong. She could give him the benefit of her – oh, so
blessed – doubt. That way she wouldn't have to risk
marriage, child, home, stability. That way she could keep it
all.

'Why don't you want to go to the wedding?' Sophie asked
her now. 'What have you got against Hilary Buchanan, apart
from the fact that she's a snooty bitch, that is?'

'Nothing.' Perhaps rather it should be a cause of celebra-
tion. Hilary Buchanan as a single, attractive and
devastatingly efficient PA presented quite a threat, whether
Jess would admit it or not. Hilary Buchanan married,
perhaps even leaving to have children – although it was hard
to imagine Hilary either finding the time or sacrificing her
body image – had to be a better deal.

Sophie was frowning. She looked as if she were trying to
piece together the fragments of some memory. Children
always saw so much more than you thought. 'Not Dad—'

'Don't be silly,' Jess said briskly. 'She's the type of
woman who always makes me feel under-dressed, that's all.'

Sophie brightened. 'So what are you going to wear?'

'Oh, I haven't decided.' She'd been so caught up with the
restoration of the cottage, not to mention the interior design
course, that she'd hardly given it a second thought. Patti
would be horrified.

'You haven't decided?' Sophie too seemed outraged. She
raked her dark hair back from her face in a gesture that
reminded Jess of Felix. 'Mums, are you telling me you
haven't even bought a new dress?'

'I certainly haven't.' Jess poured more wine. 'I've got more interesting things to do than trail around shops looking for a new dress.' Oh yes, sure. Like redecorate the cottage ... Now she came to think of it, she couldn't imagine why she hadn't. There was nothing that created instant confidence like a new frock.

Sophie clicked her tongue pityingly. 'We'll have to go shopping tomorrow, then. Number one priority.'

Jess grinned. 'And what if I don't want to doll myself up in aid of Hilary's wedding?'

Sophie's eyes were fierce. 'Then you'll have to put up with Hilary bloody Buchanan looking down her shapely toffee-nose at you. Bugger that.'

University had clearly sent Sophie's language reeling downhill. Jess shrugged. 'Darling, I'm not sure that I care.'

'Then you should.' Sophie's eyes continued to flash fury.

'It's her wedding day.' Jess couldn't help laughing. 'Hilary will have plenty of other things on her mind.'

'I wouldn't bet on it,' Sophie growled.

'And if it weren't for your father ...' Where was he? It was past ten o'clock and his squash game must have finished by eight. 'I probably wouldn't even go.' She leaned heavily on the kitchen sink and stared out into the darkness of her back garden. She couldn't see a thing. But somewhere out there was the sea, the tide rolling inexorably towards the mouth of the River Brockle. She turned to face her daughter. 'To tell you the truth, Sophie, I'm not particularly interested in wishing Hilary Buchanan future happiness in life, whoever she's marrying.'

Rather to her surprise, Sophie giggled. 'But still you should ...'

'Should what?'

Sophie drained her glass. 'You should see her off.'

'Hah!' This idea rather appealed to Jess. Of course she should. Of course she should be there, with Felix, making her position plain, showing that she didn't care – if, that is, there was anything to care about. She should, as Sophie so neatly put it, see her off.

Sophie draped herself languidly over one of the kitchen chairs. She picked up last week's Sunday colour supplement. 'Let's have a dekko at the fashion pages to get some ideas. You know, what's in, what's out. And tomorrow we'll hit Lyme Regis.'

'Lyme Regis.' Jess lifted her glass. Thank God for Sophie.

Chapter 7

The next day dawned so bright and crisp that after Felix had left for work, Jess and Sophie decided to walk to Lyme along the cliff path. It wasn't far, Lyme Regis was impossible for parking on any day of the week, and Jess had already got into the habit of a brisk cliff walk before the interior of the cottage reclaimed her for the rest of the day.

Mother and daughter put on boots and warm jackets and set off. They stomped through the garden, trampled the nettles down to the path, and headed west.

'Mary Anning used to roam these cliffs,' Jess informed Sophie, shoving her hands into the pockets of her old waxed jacket, and setting a brisk pace. It had all been very different then. No golf course – she turned to her right; the first golfers in their silly caps were teeing up on the green, but it was still too early for most of them. No, Mary Anning would have been free to wander around this rock formation – the Spittles – without fear of being observed or knocked senseless by somebody's golf ball.

'Mary who?'

'Anning. Only the most famous fossil collector of all time.'

'Really?' Despite the fact that she was studying history, Sophie seemed unimpressed.

So how could she lead into asking Sophie what was really bothering her? So far she had fielded every question about college and friends that Jess had batted in her direction. She had found out precisely zilch. So back to Mary Anning – for now. 'She found the first complete skeleton of a pterodactyl along here somewhere.' Jess waved at the rusty cliff face beneath them, the granite and sparse clumps of grass that had not yet died back for the winter. 'In eighteen twenty-eight.'

She was conscious of Sophie's curious gaze. 'You're not thinking of taking up fossil hunting, are you, Mums? You seem very knowledgeable all of a sudden.'

'No.' But it was important, wasn't it, the sense of history embedded in these rocks and sandstone and granite cliffs? In West Dorset the cliff face changed from red to grey to brown, then back to grey and red again with the East Devon coastline. She'd made a beeline for a book in the tourist information office in Lyme that could fill in some gaps. 'The most important fossil discoveries have been in this area,' Jess told Sophie. 'Especially down there.' She pointed. 'Where the old path used to be.'

'Why was it moved?' Sophie peered tentatively towards the cliff edge.

'Landslip. Erosion.' Parts of the old path had disappeared completely into the sea and probably a lot of ammonites had gone with it. But there was still an interesting nature trail which Jess had walked only a few days ago.

'Let's hope they don't want to move *you*. Cliff Cottage is a bit of an ominous name.'

'Not as ominous as Sea Cottage. But your father assures me,' Jess laughed and took her daughter's arm, 'that we are too far back from the cliff edge to have anything to worry about.' She mimicked his tone, the slight Australian accent in his voice.

Sophie grinned her famous grin. 'So now you're terrified, right?'

'Right.' Whatever her problems might be, Jess was glad that Sophie was here; especially glad for the moral support she would provide for tomorrow. She couldn't say anything to Felix. Although equally she couldn't help wondering how he felt about Hilary getting married.

Sophie was looking around her as they walked on. 'It's pretty obvious that you don't miss Sussex at all,' she said.

Didn't she? Jess realised it was true. She missed Patti and Ruth, and in a strange sort of way she even missed Sandra Slattersly with her orange hair and lipstick and little homily for every situation under the Interiors sun. She could just hear her now. *Co-ordination is the key, my dear* . . . (Sandra had lots of keys). *If our houses are co-ordinated our lives will be lived in harmony.* Perhaps Sandra should go in for feng shui, Jess thought, as the path twisted to the north and a sudden shaft of wind took her by surprise, scoring into the skin of her face. Harmonious Interiors had more of a nineties ring to it; who wanted to be Immaculate in this day and age?

But no, she didn't miss Sussex, venue of her disastrous childhood. In Sussex the hills were gentle and the coastline flat. Sussex held the wrong kind of past and the wrong kind of countryside. Perhaps that was why she felt such a sense of potential liberation, here in Dorset.

But what about Sophie? 'Do you miss it?' she asked her. They paused for a moment to look out to sea. The wind gusted Jess's hair into her face and she held it back with her hand as she stared towards the grey horizon.

'What? Oh . . .' Sophie blew on her fingers. 'A bit, yeah, I suppose I do.'

They walked on. Was that it? Jess was surprised. 'But you do like it at Bishop Otter?'

She glanced across at Sophie tramping the path beside her. This morning she had pulled the wild frizz of her hair into a rubber band, and to Jess she looked about twelve.

Vulnerable. It was a temporary tease – this apparent flash-back to childhood – but she still cherished it.

'It's just . . .' Sophie didn't seem capable of finishing a sentence. Was she so hard to talk to?

'Just?'

Sophie scuffed her boots across the dry mud ridges of the path and smiled.

There was a dreamy expression in her daughter's eyes, half mystery, half sensuality. And suddenly Jess knew what had happened. A man. Not just some casual boy/girl friend-ship of the sort Sophie had experienced so far. But the biggie. The four-letter-word stuff.

'Have you met someone?' she asked casually, leading the way down the hill. She mustn't panic. It was perfectly natural. Sophie was eighteen years old, for heaven's sake. She climbed the stile into the meadow and waited for her to follow.

As she jumped down from the stile, Sophie seemed to come to a decision. 'Yeah, I have actually.'

'Oh.' Jess realised she'd been holding her breath. Now, she let it out. What was wrong with meeting someone? Nothing. Only, love had this irritating heartbreaking habit of bringing pain. And she wanted to protect her daughter from pain, at least for as long as possible.

'What's his name then?' Jess resisted the urge to tease her for being secretive. What was the big mystery? Why hadn't she told them before?

'Nick.'

They reached the bottom of the hill and the car park, and turned left to walk down into Lyme. Had she mentioned a Nick? Jess reminded herself that Lyme Regis too was slip-ping. She had a vision of them all being dumped unceremoniously in the sea. 'How long have you known him?' She didn't want this to sound like twenty questions, but she ached for the details, for any clues she could connect to her daughter's well-being.

'A few months.' Sophie's eyes had become wary now, but Jess sensed she would open up if she only said the right things. Didn't everyone in love want to talk about it?

'What's he reading?' And is he the reason you're looking so tired? But of course she didn't say this. That was not the right thing. Teenagers needed to be coaxed, not bullied, into communication, as she knew only too well.

'He's not.'

'Not reading anything?' Jess was confused. They passed the parish church on their left, and were fast approaching the bottom of the hill and the Guildhall. Her mind raced. 'He's not—'

'What?' Sophie turned to face her. There was no mistaking her expression. She was paralysed with guilt.

Jess grabbed her arm. 'He's not a tutor?'

'Oh, no.' Visibly, Sophie relaxed. 'He's not at university at all, Mums. Life doesn't entirely revolve around Bishop Otter, you know.'

'It doesn't?' Jess had rather thought that was the idea. 'So where does he live? How did you meet him?' Oops, two questions without waiting for an answer. But Sophie didn't seem to notice.

'In Brighton – at a party. Amy's party actually.'

'In Brighton?' Jess struggled to recall the day. But as they turned right towards the main shopping centre, all she found were several separate items floating around her mind. The difficulty was in getting them to form a logical chain.

Sophie was in love with a man who lived in Brighton. Sophie was exhausted. She felt guilty about something. She was being cagey about university. And the item that linked all four? Ruth had thought she saw Sophie in Brighton last week.

'Sofe – we need to talk.' She remembered that her daughter had also been rather pleased about their move to Dorset. And she was never there when Jess called . . .

99

But Sophie was pulling her across the road. 'Later, Mums. Right now we have to shop.' She rolled her eyes. 'We're here on a mission, remember.'

'*Questo . . . questo . . .*' As he drove towards Brocklemouth, Felix sang loudly along with Placido Domingo. He had never learned Italian, but this was stirring stuff, perfect driving music. And he was in the mood. Why shouldn't he be cheerful? He was returning to Cliff Cottage to take the two women in his life out to a surprise lunch. '*Questo . . . questo.*'

Jess's Renault was parked outside the cottage. He drew in behind it, jumped out of the Audi and took the broken flagstones in three strides. '*Questo . . . questo.*' Key in the lock. 'Jess! Sophie!'

No reply. Surely they weren't sitting in the garden in this weather? But with Jess you never knew. He remembered the day they'd moved in and he'd found her sitting on a bench halfway along the cliff path, brooding. He smiled to himself. She was a bit mad and a bit sad, and that was why he loved her. He *did* love her.

Felix was still humming the aria when he saw the note in Jess's looping scrawl. It was on the kitchen table between two mugs half-full of coffee dregs. *Dear F . . .* F? Wasn't there something vaguely insulting about being denied your first name – as if she hadn't quite had time for it? *If you get back before us (but you probably won't) we've gone to Lyme. Shopping! Love, Jess.* But you probably won't? What did she mean by that? Was she making some comment on the number of times he'd been working late? But damn it, what did it matter when they weren't here?

Felix felt deflated. He scrunched the piece of paper into a ball and threw it towards the bin. It missed. He'd been looking forward to this lunch for the past hour. Why hadn't they told him they were planning to go out? What had they gone shopping for? There was no time written on the note (typically disorganised Jess) so no clue as to whether it was an afternoon-only expedition or not. But it was only twelve. And her car was outside. So how had they got there? They wouldn't have walked, surely?

He considered going to look for them, but they could be anywhere; probably holed up in one of Lyme's fancy gift shops, spending a fortune on nothing in particular. It would be hell to park, and he had no guarantee of finding them anyway. 'Damn.' He left the house, got back into his car, ejected the CD because he didn't feel like singing any more. He had wanted their company, needed to see Jess . . .

Nothing had happened. Felix performed a screeching three-point turn and headed back towards Abbotsbury and work. He might as well grab a sandwich and work through. Nothing had happened with Marilyn Beck. He didn't want it to; he wouldn't get involved, he wouldn't slip into this yawning great pit that spelled desire, sex, power, revenge and disaster, all at the same time. He would not, although every time the phone rang he half-expected to hear her gravelly tones on the other end of the line.

Of course she had only hinted. And he knew better than anyone that women loved to play games. But Felix didn't want to play this game. On second thoughts he selected another CD and flipped on to Puccini's 'E lucevan le stelle' from *Tosca*. Solemn stuff. Felix didn't want to play this game, because this time he was playing with fire. Normally he enjoyed the risk of getting his hands burned, he loved it when the stakes were high. But not now. He wanted it to be just him and Jess, Jess laughing like the old days. This was supposed to be a new beginning. But instead of that, he felt himself slipping, slipping into that pit. And he had this crazy feeling that only Jess could pull him out.

But there was a problem. Jess was involved in her own life in a way he'd never seen before. He had tried to sound enthusiastic about this design thing, he had tried to be unselfish. But all the time there had been this nagging feeling. *She's moving away from me.* He knew it was true, but he didn't know what the bloody hell to do about it.

In Trégastel, Brittany, Louisa was having a farewell morning coffee with Claude. On the floor beside her was the rucksack that held all her personal possessions. One of Scarlet's battered blue ears poked out of one corner.

She raised her glass. 'I'll miss you, Claude.'

'Me too. I am green.'

'Green with envy,' she said automatically, before realising what he'd said. 'Green with envy? Is that what you mean?'

'Oh, yes.' He nodded furiously.

'But why?' He wasn't still stuck on Stevie, surely?

'No, no.' Claude apparently knew what she was thinking. 'You are going to England.' His rather striking and almond-shaped brown eyes took on their habitual dreamy expression. 'England, land of the green fields and the wonderful cities and . . .' Here his imagination began to fail him. 'And the English pubs. The . . .'

'English men?' she suggested.

'Ah, yes. The men.' Claude could be poetic, but his views were also limited, even jaundiced at times.

As a matter of fact she thought Englishmen vastly over-rated. They were neither sexy nor romantic, they thought more of beer and football than they did of their women, they told jokes that weren't remotely funny and they farted in bed. All she could think was that gay Englishmen must be a hell of a lot nicer.

'But I don't even know if I'm going to go back to England,' Louisa wailed. Stevie had taken her completely by surprise. And while it had been pleasant to discover that their liaison might not be just a two-night affair, it was also awfully scary. She hadn't been to England for sixteen years.

'You will go.' Claude said this with utmost confidence.

'*If* I do,' she smiled at him with affection, 'I'll be back before you know it. You know I can't stay away for long.'

'Per'aps.' Claude wagged a finger at her. 'But if you don't come, then send me your house—'

'Address.' She laughed.

'Address. And I will come to you.'

'Deal.' They shook on it.

'And *if* you go . . .' She realised he was humouring her. 'Will you see the family?' Claude sounded as if they shared one.

'I very much doubt it.' Louisa wasn't sure she would even let Jess know she was in the country. What was the point? With their parents gone they had nothing in common. If they were to meet it would only be embarrassing – they wouldn't know what to say, and the past would always be there between them. Resentment. Betrayal.

Claude looked over her shoulder. 'And 'ere he comes.'

Louisa turned to see Stevie jumping out of the black van parked outside the café. Usually she was excited at the thought of travelling. Today there were butterflies doing a war dance in her stomach.

'*Bon voyage, chérie.*' Claude's eyes misted as he lapsed into his native language.

Louisa tried to smile. She would miss him. 'Goodbye, sweet thing,' she said, providing Claude with a useful phrase to remember her by.

They kissed. '*Non. Au revoir.*'

Louisa headed for the door. There was no mistaking it – she was nervous all right. She hadn't decided whether or not to return to England with Stevie. Had she? And she had told herself once that she would never go back there again. So why the heck did she feel as if she were going home?

'How about this one?' Jess picked up the hanger and twirled

103

it experimentally in front of her. The blue dress shimmered in response. It was pretty; the right kind of dress for a wedding. But why didn't she feel more enthusiastic about it?

Sophie pulled a face.

'At least let me try it on.' This was the fifth shop they'd been in and Jess was getting more than a little fed up.

'It wouldn't suit you, Mums.'

'I like blue.' Jess was becoming mutinous. She was reminded of past outings with her daughter in Sophie's early teenage years when the roles had been reversed. It hadn't been too easy then, either.

'It's not the colour.' Sophie moved with purpose over to a different rail. 'It's the style that's all wrong.'

'But I like floaty dresses,' Jess protested. Actually she rarely wore dresses at all. Sandra had insisted on black suits and white blouses for all employees at Immaculate Interiors (*We don't want to clash with anything, do we?*) and at home Jess found jeans more practical, with tailored and baggies for other occasions. Of course she owned the must-have little black dress and a few outfits for dinner parties. But on the whole dresses and Jess's lifestyle did not complement one another.

Sophie held up a chocolate-brown jersey dress that was little more than a tube.

'Hmm.' Her daugher's tastes had come a long way since she'd expected Jess to collect her from school wearing Barbie-pink from head to toe.

'The bride will be floaty,' Sophie said. 'For you, Mums, we're looking for—'

'Total transformation?'

'For class.' To Jess's horror her daughter advanced with the brown dress.

'I don't even like brown,' she wailed.

'OK.' In one movement, Sophie had swapped the dress for an identical one in deep forest-green.

Almost against her will, Jess reached out. The fabric was soft to the touch. And she loved the colour. But this was the kind of dress that clung to the curves and revealed all. 'I can't wear a dress like this,' she said. For although she did a lot of walking – and even more running up and down ladders painting ceilings and walls – her curves included a few too many bulges in the wrong places. 'All my bad bits will show.'

'Rubbish.' Sophie became more forceful still. 'You have a lovely figure.'

'But—'

'And any slight . . .' tactfully she paused, 'blemishes, will be disguised by the cut.'

'The cut?' The dress didn't seem to have a cut so much as a continuous flow.

'Of the jacket.' Sophie wore a long-suffering expression. 'Try it on, Mums, please.'

The dress was totally unlike any Jess had worn before. It wasn't *her*. 'Oh, I don't know.'

'Mother . . .' Sophie's dark blue velvet eyes, much too much like Felix's eyes for her liking, looked so fierce in the moment before Sophie swept over towards the jackets and separates section that Jess could only withdraw into the changing room.

She would try it on to please Sophie. But it wouldn't suit her. She knew it wouldn't. She never wore this kind of thing.

She eased it over her hips, smoothed the fabric, stood back and stared at herself in the mirror. She looked entirely different. How come? And although it clung to the curves the dress didn't make her look fat at all as long as she didn't breathe. In fact it made her look . . .

'Wonderful,' Sophie murmured as she drew the curtain. 'You look absolutely great, Mums.' She looked her up and down and whistled between her teeth.

105

Jess continued to stare into the mirror, trying to think of objections. The dress felt like a second skin. It almost scared her how much she loved it. 'It isn't really me,' she said. But she wasn't sure. The dress had somehow transformed her into an elegant woman. A sexy woman. A row of tiny buttons went from neckline to sacrum. And not only did it cling, but it was slashed at the back – a deep slit that reached almost mid-thigh, revealing a lot of leg, but only when she moved in a certain way. 'Mmm.' Maybe it was a different Jess, but she could get used to her. It wouldn't do any harm to be that Jess, would it, just occasionally, and especially for Hilary's wedding?

Sophie only clapped her hands. 'Class,' she said, handing her a dark jacket, beautifully cut in the softest suede.

Jess slipped it on, and had to admit that once more her daughter was right. She turned to gaze at her with a new admiration. When had Sophie, who dressed as most students dressed and who had never had the money to indulge a taste for fine clothes, managed to acquire this much dress sense? She thought of this Nick, whoever he might be. Was this another part of Sophie's life she knew nothing about?

'All we need now is a new bag and shoes and you'll be drop dead gorgeous,' Sophie said.

'Whoa.' Jess turned resolutely from the mirror. She'd done quite enough body-gazing for one day. 'How much is all this going to cost me?' She glanced at the price tag on the jacket; usually she did this first, but Sophie had overcome her customary caution. Her jaw dropped. 'Oh, my God.'

Sophie peered over her shoulder. 'And worth every penny.'

But Jess was already taking off the jacket, and no sooner had she done that, but she had one arm over her left shoulder, scrabbling around for the price tag of the dress she had fallen in love with. She craned her neck to read it. It wasn't good news. Apparently you had to pay for class.

Sophie stood outside the changing room as Jess replaced the dress with her jeans and sweater. 'Mums, you never spend any money on clothes, you know you don't.'

'Right now I don't *earn* any money.' Suddenly Jess felt fiercely independent.

Felix had made the right noises when she'd told him of her career plans. He had said, 'Yes, do it, Jess, if that's really what you want.'

Not quite the wholehearted enthusiasm she would have liked. But she couldn't blame him. The company wasn't making a fortune. And she – who had always prided herself on her healthy contribution to the family coffers – was conscious that the design course she was planning to enrol on would be a drain on their resources. In a year or two she would be qualified and earning, but before then it would cost, in materials, in her time, in her inability to contribute hard cash. What was the answer? How could she find a way of doing both?

'You look after the house, don't you?' Sophie was indignant. 'You look after Dad. You go and help out at Beck and Newman when they need someone.'

'Mmm.' Jess stroked the dress lovingly. She was reluctant to relinquish it to the rail; ready to be persuaded.

'And Dad will love it.'

'He won't love what it cost.' Although Felix had always been generous. Would he love it? Would he love her in it?

'And it'll show Hilary Buchanan what you're made of,' Sophie said – a master-stroke, if Jess had ever heard one.

Yes, it would. She thought of a night long ago, and she thought of Felix's white lilies. 'I'm going to buy it.'

'Attagirl.' Sophie grinned. 'And the jacket?'

She might as well go the whole hog. 'Of course we'll have the jacket too.' She grinned back at Sophie. 'D'you think I don't know a classy outfit when I see it?'

*

107

She had been looking out for it as they walked back down the street towards the Cobb, but Jess still almost missed Rupert's shop. It was small and tucked away between a fossil shop and a baker's. But it had an *open* sign stuck on the door, so she said, 'Come on,' and pulled Sophie inside.

'Oh, hi.' Rupert unwrapped himself from his semi-prone position on the floor, where he was apparently examining the leg of an upturned oak table. 'I'm restoring the moulding,' he said in explanation. 'You found me, then?'

'It wasn't easy.' Jess flopped into the nearest chair.

'Not that one.' He winced, pulled her unceremoniously out of it again and indicated a chaise longue upholstered in black velvet. 'If you're clean you can sit there.'

'Very gracious of you.' Jess sat. 'Do we get coffee or do we have to make it ourselves?'

Sophie was looking from one to the other of them. 'And do I get an introduction?'

'Oh, sorry, love.' Jess did the honours. 'Rupert's our next-door neighbour.' She looked round the shop. It was bigger than she'd thought, going quite a long way back, but not huge, and crammed with enough furniture to fill twenty houses. Rocking chairs sat side by side with upholstered diners and a battered chesterfield; there were small round tables, large rectangular tables, a couple of dressers, a huge mahogany glass-fronted bookcase and various coat stands, footstools and writing desks. It was mind-boggling. 'Where on earth do you get all this stuff from?' she asked him.

'Oh, from dealers, from people who have inherited Aunt Jane's Victorian washstand and discovered it's got woodworm. All sorts.' He shrugged. 'Sometimes dealers sell pieces on to me from house clearances; sometimes I restore to order.'

'Hmm.' Restore to order? That was in interesting thought. It would be rather nice if people could undergo a similar process. 'But do you ever get to sell any of it?' She tried unsuccessfully to stretch out her legs. 'I mean it's a little cramped in here, if you don't mind me saying.'

'I need bigger premises.' Rupert disappeared behind a bookcase, presumably to make the coffee. 'So I can have a showroom area.'

'You certainly do.' And he was in the right place to do it; Lyme Regis was upmarket enough and popular enough for any antique dealer or furniture restorer to do pretty well.

Rupert reappeared with the coffee. 'I keep meaning to get around to it. But I always seem to have too much work on.'

'First thing,' Jess advised. 'Make an appointment with your bank manager. You need to grow.' Although not literally. As it was, his cropped head was almost touching the ceiling.

Rupert shot her a strange look, seemed about to say something and changed his mind.

'But what made you start doing this in the first place?' Sophie asked him, looking around her in fascination.

'These.' Rupert held out his hands. 'They were never meant to pen-push. And furniture has such a nice feel to it, don't you think?' Lovingly, he stroked the smooth surface of the table.

Jess smiled. They were definitely an artist's hands. The fingers were long and slender but these hands were also used to hard work.

'Before I did this, I was studying psychology at Leicester.'

'Really?' Jess was surprised. She hadn't known that.

'But I didn't want to spend my life delving around in the human brain. I wanted to *do*.' He flexed his knuckles. 'I wanted to use these.'

Sophie nodded as if she understood. 'Like Mums,' she said.

'Only I need a job as well.' Jess poked the carrier bag with her toe. 'Especially now I'm so racked with guilt.'

109

They laughed. Clearly, she didn't look racked with guilt.

Slowly, Rupert cradled the leg of the old oak table inside the palm of one hand. 'You should decorate other people's houses, then.'

'Huh?'

'Offer your services as an amateur designer and decorator. You don't have to ask top money – until you're qualified.' He grinned. 'But you'll be doing what you like and establishing your reputation.'

Jess stared at him. He had a point. She could do it in her spare time and use it to consolidate all the methods and practices she'd be learning on the interior design course. It was nothing short of brilliant.

'You can stick a card in my window if you like.' Rupert pulled a cloth from the drawer and began cleaning away the dust from the moulding. 'I'm always getting people in moaning about how they've got to do up Aunt Jane's house before they can sell it on or move in.'

'Rupert, I love you!' Jess jumped to her feet. 'Come on, Sofe, we should be getting back.' He had cracked it. It was so blindingly obvious that she couldn't believe she hadn't thought of it herself.

'Nice guy.' Sophie eyed her curiously as they made their way back to the car park.

'Yes, he is.' Jess saw her chance. She had waited long enough. 'But what about *your* guy?'

'My guy? Well ...' The different light came into Sophie's eyes again. 'He's a few years older than me.'

'A few?'

'Nine.' Sophie at least had the grace to look away.

Jess coughed loudly to stop herself yelling, '*Nine*?!' in absolute horror.

'Dad's seven years older than you,' Sophie said, as if Jess had actually voiced her objection.

'I know that.' As if it made any difference.

'He's kind and generous and absolutely gorgeous, Mums, he really is.'

Oh, God, it was much worse than she thought. And it wasn't just his age. 'Sophie darling,' she said as she caught hold of her daughter's arm, 'you won't throw everything away, will you?' She meant university.

'Of course not.' But Jess felt her withdrawal.

'And you will take care?' How could she possibly tell her not to get too involved? Quite clearly, she already was.

But Sophie stopped in her tracks. 'I don't understand what you're so worried about, Mums. When you were my age you were already married to Dad.'

Ah, but it had been very different for Jess. At seventeen she had lost her parents and she had turned to Felix as . . . as what? Surely not as some sort of replacement father figure? But certainly as a man who would love her, value her, look after her. *As her father never had?*

'Just because I did it,' Jess spoke carefully, 'is not to say it was the right thing to do.'

Sophie stared at her. 'Is everything really OK between you and Dad?'

'Yes, of course it is, darling.' Jess tried to sound more confident than she felt.

'And this guy Rupert?'

'Is just a friend.' Firmly, Jess took her arm and they walked on, back up the hill and towards Brocklemouth and Cliff Cottage. She had been outmanoeuvred by her eighteen-year-old daughter yet again. 'So don't worry,' she said. 'Everything is absolutely fine.'

Sitting on the bar stool, Louisa closed her eyes for a few moments to allow Stevie's bluesy voice to wash all over her, and thought of England. Of course she would go. How could she not? It was sixteen years since she'd climbed on that ferry, but sometimes it felt as close as yesterday.

She opened her eyes to see Stevie staring straight at her; he might have been singing for her alone. And it seemed like fate. She would go back to England. But she didn't have to stay . . .

Chapter 8

Louisa was just ordering herself another drink when she heard it.

'I wrote this song for my daughter, Suzannah.' His voice was unmistakable. Brown sugar and cinnamon with just a hint of lemon.

She looked up.

'So then, of course, I was immediately doomed.' He was staring straight at her. 'I had to write one for Izzy and then another for Justine.'

Louisa almost fell off her bar stool. How many?

'How many?' she demanded of him later, when they were in bed in the St Malo equivalent of B&B.

'Three. I thought I'd better mention it before you agreed to come back to London with me.'

Too right. Only, she'd already committed herself to England, hadn't she – with or without Stevie. 'Do they live with you?' Horror. With her fingertip she traced the outline of the blue rose on his forearm.

'No.' He made a lunge for her but she pushed him away. 'They live with their mothers.'

'Mothers?' It got worse. 'How many mothers?' Some sort of harem, was it?

'I was married to Suzannah's mother for two years.' Stevie kissed the corner of her mouth, but she didn't smile, not yet. 'We got hitched when she found out she was pregnant.'

'Oh.'

'Seemed like a good idea at the time.' He sighed and looked up at the ceiling. 'Izzy and Justine's mother ... Well, let's just say it didn't work out.'

Not exactly a blisteringly good track record, Louisa reflected as he began to make love to her. But then again, she didn't want Stevie for his ability to maintain family commitments.

He emerged for air. 'Does it matter? Have I put you off?'

'Heavens, no.'

But when Louisa finally drifted off to sleep, she dreamed about a thatched cottage in Sussex. There was a yellow and red honeysuckle growing up the flint wall in the front, and in the back was a huge and horrific playground made entirely of Lego. Stevie lived there with his three daughters, and there was a queue of other women stretching out of the front door, women whose goal in life was five minutes of his attention. And Louisa was in the dream too. She wore a plain black dress and no make-up. Good God. She woke in panic, her skin hot with a film of perspiration. Louisa was the original wicked stepmother.

Jess could not complain at the effect her new dress had on Felix.

It was the following morning, they were getting ready for the church ceremony and he was da-dee-dumming in his usual manner and volume along to a tenor singing something from *Tosca*. Very uplifting, probably very suitable for horrible Hilary's wedding.

'"Recondita armonia",' he informed Jess, though she hadn't asked. Sounded like lavatory bleach to her. Then he did a double take, looked her up and down and whistled through his teeth in much the same way as his daughter had done yesterday. 'You look bloody marvellous,' he said. It must be true. Puccini was almost forgotten.

'You like it then?' Jess did a twirl. She wouldn't tell him how much it had cost.

'I love it.' He came closer, put his hands on her shoulders and kissed her cheek. 'I love you.' His hands moved very slowly past her breasts, her waist and down to her hips, their pressure easing her body closer to his. 'You're beautiful,' he whispered into her ear. 'And you're all mine.'

She arched her back and drew away from him. 'Is that what you reckon?' she teased, putting on a Dorset accent.

He pulled her close again. 'That's exactly what I reckon.' This time his lips were on hers.

Her mouth opened under his, she felt the warm wetness of his tongue exploring and insistent, the heat of his hand as it crept round to the curve of her buttocks. And despite the fact that they were already late, Jess felt herself wanting him, here and now. It had been a while. For two pins she would have ripped off the dress and made love with him in their brand new Larsson-style bedroom. But they were already late. And the thought of Hilary Buchanan was just a little too close.

Gently, she pushed him from her. 'Felix, I'll have to do my lipstick again – it's all over your mouth.'

And then Sophie called up the stairs. 'Come on, you two, the taxi's here.'

'Bloody awful timing,' Felix grumbled, but he smoothed his hair, brushed an imaginary fleck of wool from his suit, and licked the end of his handkerchief to remove Jess's Sunset Boulevard lip colour from his face.

The wedding ceremony itself, which took place in a nearby village church, went off well enough. Sophie had been right,

115

Jess observed, the bride had chosen floaty. But the no doubt hideously expensive creation of taffeta and lace didn't sit right on Hilary, who, when push came to shove, was neither young nor virginal. In fact the only blushing was done by the bridegroom, Bas, who also smiled a lot.

'He looks as if he can't believe his luck,' Jess whispered to Sophie.

'Perhaps he hasn't known her very long.'

Jess giggled. Sophie, wearing a black mini-dress, tights and platform boots, was making her feel glad she came.

At the reception, Felix moved smoothly into matey mode with Bas, while Hilary's cool glance took in Jess's outfit and betrayed – yes, there it was – more than a hint of surprise.

'Good luck, Hilary.' And wouldn't she need it? Jess felt confident and serene. As Sophie had so rightly pointed out, a new frock could do wonders when you wanted to see someone off.

After the harp music, a seemingly endless river of champagne, photographs, wedding luncheon and inevitable speeches, came the dancing, to a six-piece band that veered dangerously between ballroom, blues and disco in a valiant effort to cater for all tastes.

Sophie was asked to dance by Tom, one of Peter's assistants at Beck and Newman; Peter whisked Marilyn on to the floor, and Jess watched Hilary, as the bride weaved a rather unsteady path over to their table.

*

Up until that moment, Hilary had experienced no doubts about marrying Bas. Bas Nicholson was not like Felix at all – a point in his favour since Felix was not the marrying kind. Absolutely not. Hilary had seen it the very first time she sat opposite him at her interview for the secretarial job that had led as the company expanded into the post as personal assistant at Beck and Newman. Personal assistant?

116

She as good as ran the place. But she had known several things by the time she left Felix's office that day. Almost certainly she would get the job. She had all the right qualifications plus a certain quality that made her special, that Felix Newman would recognise too. Added to that, she would have an affair with Felix – Hilary had never been wrong yet. And thirdly, she knew that he was not the marrying kind.

When she found out that he *was* married it had been a shock, but pretty soon she proved to herself that she'd been right all along. Felix was married, yes, but he should never have done it. This left his wife in an unenviable position. One that Hilary certainly wouldn't want for herself. He was good-looking, sexy, and oozed Hilary's favourite aphrodisiac: power. But he wasn't rich enough and his craving to be the centre of attention was a childish quality that she could live without.

Bas, on the other hand, was excellent marriage material. What he lacked in the looks department he more than made up for with background. He was reliable and loyal, while a career with the family firm ensured a high profile and an even higher income. It was an irresistible package. And love? Love meant weakness, and Hilary had no space for that in her life. If she wanted to have fun she would have a discreet affair. That was what men like Felix Newman were for.

But five glasses of champagne at her own wedding led to Hilary's first niggling doubt. Felix looked so gorgeous and yet she couldn't touch him. And Jess Newman didn't seem as scatty and dreamy as usual. She was very much on this planet and looking bloody good in an outfit that simply wasn't her style at all. Felix kept touching her hand – not exactly the sort of behaviour Hilary would expect from a man who'd been married for almost twenty years. And especially not from a man with whom she had made

117

love on his office desk not so long ago. Felix and Jess, on top of all that champagne, were making her feel slightly sick. They looked almost as if they were still in love, for God's sake.

Hilary couldn't help feeling Felix had been a little casual that last time, not quite as grateful as she'd expected. They were so good together and she knew him so well. Well enough to know there was someone else on the horizon. She sensed it. Not his wife. Someone else who was making him distracted, vague, making him jump every time the phone rang. And *that* had not been on the game plan either. Hilary could feel herself being pushed out, and she didn't like it. If anyone was going to end the relationship, it would be Hilary. And she was damned if she was going to let him just walk away.

'Come and dance with me, Felix, darling,' Hilary said when she reached their table.

Jess saw him hesitate. It was obvious that Hilary had been hitting the champagne; she leaned over towards him, half-draping herself across his lap, decidedly squiffy.

'Go on,' she urged. If he refused the bride, Hilary would go ballistic. And it was her day, so she could be as outrageous as she pleased and no one (at least not Jess) could object.

'My pleasure.' Looking daggers, Felix took her hand and led her off.

Jess watched them move on to the dance floor. How could she tear her eyes away? They looked like the perfect couple, one so dark, one so blonde, two of the beautiful people. It was another slow song and Hilary snaked in close to him. Too close, too intimate. Jess looked around the room for Bas. Because anyone watching would know these two had been intimate once – or would be very soon.

Jess wanted to turn away, she wanted to slam shut that

118

door in her head that would keep slipping open; she didn't want to let any of it spill out.

But she found herself thinking back to the night when Sophie was born and try as she might, she couldn't make it go away this time.

Felix had been marvellous throughout her pregnancy. He never minded nipping out for the chips she liked to dip in horseradish sauce before she went to bed, he did more than his fair share of housework, and his back massages were out of this world. Also, to her surprise, sex was still good between them. In fact it was better than ever. Felix always seemed to know instinctively just how to please her, when she was tired and wanted only to soak in a hot bath, when a massage would send her to sleep or when it could be a prelude to sex. The sex they'd enjoyed during her pregnancy had been some of their best.

Jess could see herself now with tangled hair, swollen belly and engorged breasts, sitting on top of him like some wild mother earth; the baby inside her another part of their love. He shared as much of it as he could. He learnt the ante-natal exercises, he came to the clinic, he joined in the breathing. He loved to feel the baby kick and he would often rest his head on her lap, immersing himself as far into the experience of pregnancy as he could possibly go.

Now Jess watched Felix dancing with Hilary, saw Hilary's thin smile, saw the whiteness of her hands inside the fingerless lace gloves, as those hands rested on his shoulders.

When she went into labour she had held out for as long as possible, knowing he was due back from work. At last when he didn't come, she phoned the office, but there was no reply. And when it became clear that he wasn't on his way back, she phoned the hospital. She wasn't worried; Felix often had house calls to make when he was buying or valuing jewellery. She trusted him. He would get to her in time.

On the dance floor she saw Felix bend to whisper something into Hilary's ear. They turned. His hand was on the small of Hilary's back; Jess knew exactly how it would feel.

She asked the hospital to keep trying, but it was a quick labour – not much more than two hours – and Felix arrived with flowers five minutes after Sophie was born. White lilies. Felix always chose lilies. He knew how Jess loved them; she adored their stateliness, the way they preferred to stand alone.

'How could I have missed it?' She would swear there were tears in his eyes. 'How could I have not been there? How could I?'

'It wasn't your fault.' She was quick to reassure him.

'I was listening to some silly old bag. She was showing me her gold brooches. Bloody Victoriana.' His eyes were mournful. 'While you were all alone.'

'It doesn't matter.'

'What a shit I am.'

Jess remembered how he had thumped his chest as he said this. And even then, in the high emotion of the moment, she had thought: *There's something wrong.* Then the misgiving disappeared as he picked up Sophie with the gentlest of hands, as he admired her, loved her, and said to Jess all the right things.

'I'm sorry, love.'

'It doesn't matter,' she said again. But it had.

As the music ended, Jess saw Felix make a move to return to their table; she saw Hilary put her hands on his arms; saw them laugh; saw Felix's shrug. She couldn't see Bas Nicholson at all. Was he watching them too? Could he tell that his wife was in love with Felix Newman, the way that Jess could tell?

'Trust old Felix to be working late the night you went

into labour.' Teddy from the workshop had come round a few days later to see the baby. 'Sometimes no one can get him out of that office.'

'Oh, he wasn't in the office. He was ...' Jess's voice trailed to a standstill. She had phoned the office. Instinctively, she picked up baby Sophie and held her close to her breast.

'But I saw him and H.B. as they were leaving.' Even as he spoke, Teddy must have realised the implications, because he tried to get the words back. ''Course, I could be wrong, it might have been a different day.'

She knew it hadn't been a different day; she could see it written all over his face. Teddy was a simple lad. He wasn't a master of disguises like ... like Felix? 'What time was it, Teddy?' she asked.

Dumbly, he stared at her.

'What time?'

'Seven thirty.'

'Thank you.' Jess put Sophie back in her cot. At seven thirty she had been giving birth to their baby. Before that she had tried to phone Felix. But he had been with Hilary Buchanan. He had simply let the office phone ring. Now why should he do that and then lie about it?

Fool. She had imagined herself to be living a perfect life, that was where she had gone wrong. Only a fool thought life perfect; there must always be flaws.

Jess sat for a long time that afternoon, wondering what to do. Her first instinct was to confront Felix, but she still felt so hopelessly vulnerable after the birth that she couldn't find the energy to do it. And as time went on ... She had closed her eyes. It hadn't stopped there; it had been a while. It had gone on between Felix and Hilary, and apart from a few silly questions, she had closed her eyes.

Peter and Marilyn had returned from the dance floor now. Marilyn was watching Hilary and Felix. 'Jesus.' She lit a cigarette, the flame of her lighter illuminating the mahogany of her dark hair. The bob swung dangerously close to the flame before she clicked the lighter shut with one red fingernail. 'How do you stand it?'

Jess was shocked. It was the first time anyone had directly referred to Hilary and Felix and what might have gone on between them. And Marilyn seemed more angry about it than she. 'It was over a long time ago,' she said.

It was the first time she had actually admitted to herself that it had happened, the first time she had said it aloud. And the sense of release amazed her. She had kept the cupboard door shut for far too long.

She didn't know how long it had gone on for – and now was hardly the time to tap Hilary on the shoulder and ask her, *By the way, how many times did you have sex with my husband*?

But it didn't matter. Jess turned to watch them. It was high time she faced up to it and put it in the past. It was one woman, one lapse of fidelity. But wasn't her marriage worth more than that? What was Hilary Nicholson to her? She felt the strength surge through her. She knew it was over. And in this dress, she could defeat the other woman with her eyes closed.

'Jess.' She could hear kindness in Peter's voice. 'Dance with me?'

'I'd love to.' Jess liked Peter a lot more than she liked his wife. And she sensed support rather than pity in the man who held her on the dance floor. He wasn't a great dancer, but who needed to dance when you could make jewellery like Peter did? Slowly, she began to relax and enjoy the music.

She had encountered the flamboyant Art Deco jewellery that Peter Beck designed before she met the man himself, and it had been hard to reconcile the two. Peter seemed the most ordinary and unassuming of men, yet he lovingly recreated elegant panelled bangles in the white gold and platinum of the nineteen twenties, brooches using the famous nineteen thirties' 'tutti frutti' effect from carved rubies, emeralds and sapphires and pendants featuring exotic images in the tradition of Fouquet, Lalique and Cartier that took her breath away. Jess had been interested enough to delve into some of his reference books in the days when she often helped out at Beck and Newman, and it had been fascinating stuff. Peter and Marilyn's present to her on her twenty-first birthday, when Sophie was two, had been one of Peter's pendants: silver, set with a teardrop rock crystal, moonstones, pink coral and pearls. It was perhaps, her favourite piece. So long ago . . .

Felix and Hilary had stopped dancing. Felix had returned to their table and Hilary had disappeared in the direction of the Ladies.

'Are you all right?' Peter was watching her with concern in his grey eyes. 'Is Felix . . .?'

'Everything's fine.' It was exactly what she'd said to Sophie.

As the music came to an end they returned to their table where Felix was talking to Marilyn. His blue eyes were intense; they always were. She didn't know why he had been distracted lately. But now, with this new strength, maybe she could ask him.

Felix got up as they approached. 'Perhaps we should go?' His arm was round her shoulders. He was looking about for Sophie. Why did they all think her so fragile?

'But I'm having a good time.' And she realised to her surprise that it was true. She didn't even mind about Hilary, and how she had been looking at Felix. What mattered was that he most certainly did not feel the same way – not any more. And that now, her eyes were open.

123

Chapter 9

Louisa stared moodily at Stevie's back as he ambled towards Michael's Monkey Village. Skipping along beside him were his entourage clothed in a variety of leggings, padded jackets, scarves and hats in every shade of pink from a toy shop. Louisa groaned. My Little Pony pink meets Barbie candyfloss, with a dash of Anastasia purple thrown in.

It honestly wasn't that she didn't like kids. It wasn't even that she didn't like *his* kids (although she had doubts about Suzannah; at seven she seemed far too adult for her own good). It was, she reflected as she followed them into the monkey-screeching mayhem, just that she didn't feel she remotely *belonged* with them.

'What're they doing Daddy? Why has he got his fingers up his—?'

'Sssh.' Stevie laughed.

'Up his bum? And what's that one doing to the hairy one? Is that a banana? And . . .'

Louisa switched off. The nonstop demand for information came from four-year-old Justine, a blonde bombshell of a child who hadn't stopped asking questions since they'd picked her and her sister Izzy up two hours ago. Questions, questions, more questions. Didn't she ever get tired of asking them?

Who's she? had been Justine's first, the day they returned to England, bleary-eyed and in Louisa's case ready for a bath, a long sleep and other nice bits connected with bed. Not a barrage of child-interrogation. *Who's she?* followed by, *What's she doing here?* were directed at Louisa with barely veiled hostility slap bang in the middle of the first Daddy-hug. And they hadn't looked back.

'Why do you wear all that stuff round your eyes?' Justine asked now, switching her attention from monkey-mania to Louisa in one fearless bound.

'I like to look colourful,' Louisa snapped. And instantly regretted it.

Justine was gathered closer to her father. She's only curious, Stevie's eyes accused. She's only asking.

'Like a parrot,' Suzannah said nastily. She could teach her half-sister a thing or two about cruelty. At seven, Suzannah, with her black curtain of hair and distanced eyes, had it down to an art form. She even stood, weight on one leg, hand on one hip, looking bored yet interesting at the same time. 'My mummy doesn't wear make-up,' she continued. 'She says she doesn't want to look like a tart.'

Stevie roared with laughter as if this were the funniest thing he'd heard all day. 'Kids!'

Kids? More like apprentice heartbreakers.

'What's a tart?' asked Justine.

Suzannah rolled her eyes heavenwards. 'Don't you know anything? A tart is—'

'Better than ice cream.' This was from Stevie. He reached out the free hand, the one that wasn't preventing Izzy the terrifying two-year-old from leaping into the penguin enclosure, towards Louisa in a gesture of conciliation. 'Don't take any notice. They're only—'

'Kids. I know.' Louisa tried to smile and wondered if it looked as unconvincing as it felt.

But Suzannah hadn't finished. 'Actually,' she began. 'My

125

mummy says she's buggered if she's going to make that kind of effort for any man. Not any more.' She shot her father a significant, though forgiving, look. 'She's got far better things to do with her time, she says.'

Louisa bet she had. And it wouldn't be anything remotely connected with her children either. Since they'd been in London she and Stevie had also been practically full time babysitters for his children. Surely access didn't mean this?

She had envisaged the odd Sunday afternoon in the park, even pictured herself pushing the swing, exchanging the occasional intimate smile with Stevie as he operated the roundabout for the little darlings. But she hadn't envisaged trailing around a zoo walk which ranged from Pamela's Prickly Porcupines to Boris Beaver-land. And she had never dreamed that the children would be there almost every evening that Stevie wasn't actually working, presumably so that one mother or the other could go partying. Neither had she expected these anonymous mothers (Stevie seemed to want to keep her apart from them, as if afraid they'd ruin his credibility in one fell swoop) to ring at eight in the morning waking them with phrases like, *Could you just watch her for a few hours*, followed by a slug of emotional blackmail. *She wants to see her Daddy so much.* Worst of all was this weekend – a Friday to Sunday marathon that had already left Louisa drained. And there were thirty hours to go.

'I don't wear make-up for the benefit of men,' she said to herself, since the others had clearly lost interest and were heading for Freddie's farmyard. 'I do it for me.'

'Pingy, pingy,' Izzy chanted. 'Nappy pappy.'

'What, darling?' Stevie clutched her more tightly. Every time he loosened his grip she had a habit of whizzing like elastic towards whatever caught her two-year-old eye – usually something potentially hazardous. But the problem was that, unlike elastic, she wouldn't come back unless dragged.

'She wants to see the penguins,' Justine translated. *'Pingu's* her best programme.'

'And nappy pappy?' Louisa held her breath. Michael's Monkey Village had stunk to high heaven; she hoped Stephanie's Skunk-land wouldn't be on the agenda.

'She's just done a pooh.'

That explained the unpleasant whiff in the air. They retraced their steps back to the toilets.

Stevie shot her a beseeching look, but Louisa pretended not to notice. No way. Izzy's nappy was not her responsibility; Izzy was not her responsibility. If Louisa ever had children she'd have them toilet-trained within a year.

Stevie was therefore forced to resort to the mother and baby room, muttering, 'Bloody sexist places,' under his breath.

He emerged five minutes later, red-faced and apologetic. 'Breast-feeding,' he hissed to Louisa in explanation.

From here, Stevie and his shadows, with Louisa trailing in their wake, went in search of pingu at Paula's Penguin Bay. They progressed to Oswald's Otter Valley by the riverbank and Mr Frosty's ice creams, although Louisa found it hard to believe that children could want to stick something freezing in their mouths and stomachs in this weather. Not much of Mr Frosty reached Izzy's stomach though – it was deposited equally on to her face, her hair, her hands, her pink padded jacket, and Stevie's jeans.

The tots' indoor adventure playground (huge brightly coloured balls in a see-through plastic tunnel) claimed Izzy for a while, at which point Louisa threaded her fingers through Stevie's and tried to take advantage of a quick snog.

For the first time ever he brushed her off. 'Not in front of the kids, sweet-pie,' he muttered, blushing under his tan.

'Why not?' she whispered back. 'They know we sleep together.' Although sleep had been hard to come by with Suzannah getting up to sleepwalk at midnight (Louisa would swear she'd done it on purpose because she'd heard them attempting to make absolutely silent love); Justine having a nightmare at three in the morning and Izzy bright and early at five am demanding chocolate wheaties and milk *NOW.*

'Because it's confusing for them,' was all he said.

That was no joke. Surely the entire scenario was confusing for them. How many mummies did a girl need? Louisa groaned, sank lower on the wooden bench and closed her eyes. She was confused herself – about being back in England.

In one way, as the ferry had docked at Portsmouth, she'd had the strangest feeling, as if she'd pulled on a familiar glove on a cold winter's day. And in another way . . . she wanted to run. While Stevie wrote new songs, rehearsed and children-sat, Louisa spent the days sightseeing.

Childhood visits to London had been rare – once to the Natural History Museum and once to Madam Tussaud's and the changing of the guard outside Buckingham Palace. Now, she visited the Tate and the National galleries, the Tower, the V & A, becoming more adventurous each time. She roamed the streets and the Tube, she caught red buses and let their destination be hers. And she kept thinking about Jess, but couldn't bring herself to call her.

And then she would return, usually to find at least one child in residence.

'I like to see a lot of the kids when I'm in the country,' Stevie had said on the day of their return, the same day that the onslaught from the three female Black juniors had begun.

Louisa tried to stifle her natural anti-children hysteria. He had done his best to make her feel included in the family fun. It was the Christmas holidays – it wouldn't (couldn't?) be so bad when they were back at school.

But did she want to be included in the family fun? She'd never been much of a one for families, even her own. And

128

fun was hard to connect with them somehow. Family pain seemed more appropriate.

So when Stevie kept saying, 'They'll get used to you, they'll learn to love you,' and other platitudes, she found herself wondering if she even wanted them to; if she even cared.

Louisa opened one eye to watch Stevie preventing Izzy from burying a small boy under red and yellow plastic balls. What it came down to was: did she love this man enough to take on his unruly children? And would it be so very selfish to say, no?

Later, they drank hot coffee to warm themselves up, and had a few rare minutes alone while the girls played on a slot machine with the fifty pence each that Stevie had given them.

'I'll have to get a job,' Louisa said, realising that she was almost broke. So much for saving a stash for the winter. Hers had been decimated by travelling expenses, endless sightseeing and too many nights sitting drinking in the pub where Stevie played.

He touched her fingers – the closest he'd come to showing affection all day. 'It should be easy enough around here.'

Yes, there were plenty of pubs, restaurants, cafés. It wouldn't be difficult. But . . . 'I'm not sure how long I'll be staying.' She didn't want to look at him. No promises, they had said, no commitment. So why did she feel like she was stabbing him in the back?

'Is it the kids?' Stevie's drown-in-me hazel eyes barely flickered. Love me, love my kids, she thought. 'Because we're doing another tour in the spring. Germany. It would be great if you could come too.'

She hesitated. The moment, her silence, hung heavily between them. She fiddled with the vinegar bottle on the formica table-top between them.

'Will you?'

Louisa pulled her coat closer around her. Was that what she wanted? To spend her life following Stevie around the world? To spend their time at home base looking after his kids? 'I don't think so.' She tried to make the words sound gentle. But rejections didn't work that way, did they?

'I see.' With a scrape of his chair Stevie left the table, moved over to where the girls were playing the machines.

Shit. She stared at the grey walls and even greyer ceiling of the café. This place was a dump. But it wasn't Stevie's fault, and she hadn't meant her words to come out in quite so negative a way. She hadn't meant to hurt him; she really liked him. When he played and sang he had as much instant impact as that very first day. He was kind and he was gentle; she had even thought it could work out between them, at least for a while.

When he came back to the table he grabbed her hand more forcefully. 'What is it you want, Louisa? Do you want kids of your own, is that it?'

'Bloody hell, no.' But he had a point.

She thought about it as he gathered up the protesting children, as they left the café, walked out of the zoo, located the black van in the near-empty car park and piled in. For the very first time in her life she could almost hear her biological clock ticking and it scared her to death. She wanted to chuck it out of the van window and watch it smash to pieces on a London pavement.

After all, Stevie's travelling lifestyle should be perfect for a girl like her, a girl who preferred to keep moving, a girl like she had always been. Even the kids weren't *that* bad. She had never in her life looked for a man she could settle with, marry, have children with. And didn't she have her reasons? No, she had never wanted any of that; that sort of life was for women like Jess, it was stifling, claustrophobic, scary as hell. She stared gloomily out of the window. It was starting to rain – again – and the London streets looked particularly damp and depressing, the buildings as bloody grey as the café they'd just come from. But coming back to England like this made her feel lonely, yet still close to home.

'Daddy, can we have dinner at Mcdonalds?'

'Louisa?'

She had been thinking more in terms of a pasta sauce, green salad and huge quantities of red wine. She shifted in her seat, aware of Suzannah's eyes boring into the back of her neck. 'All right.'

She was going doolally, that was it. She was being influenced by the unaccustomed and unwanted presence of children in her life. She had never intended to get too involved with Stevie, and now she was rejecting him because he already had a family and wouldn't want another. Families . . . She had finally lost her marbles. She was treading the slippery slope. Louisa was beginning to wonder if she should ever have left France at all.

Felix Newman paused at the traffic lights to admire the emerald necklace he had just purchased for a song. Peter would disapprove, but if the old lady was happy it didn't matter.

And she was happy. He had drunk her tea, eaten a slice of her soggy fruit cake and left her happy as Larry to think that her necklace was going to a good home. For Felix had omitted to tell her that he represented a company called Beck and Newman, jewellers of repute. He had found this necklace through a touch of cold calling – he used to do that a lot and it was good to keep your hand in – and on impulse had pretended to the old soul that he wanted it for his wife. It was foolproof on the sentimentality front.

From the stereo, Domingo wasn't half doing justice to Verdi's 'Celeste Aida'. Felix tapped the steering wheel keeping pace with the fanfare section. Jess wouldn't like the piece, of course; her taste in jewellery was a bit off. Rather than seeing the lasting class of the traditional styles, the classics, the precious stones that Felix admired, she inclined to the downmarket, preferring the semi-precious like amber, a very blowsy stone; or like Peter's stuff, some of which was downright tatty.

Even Marilyn, bless her heart, had been scathing about the rhinestone earrings of Peter's that she'd worn at Hilary and Bas's wedding.

'But they go with your hair,' Felix had told her, admiring the sleek black bob, that was always tidy, that would be smooth to the touch, and whose stark, geometric lines set off the Deco earrings to perfection.

'Tat,' she had said, without a flicker of disloyalty. 'But Peter does tat so bloody well.'

Felix took the road towards Abbotsbury. He was tempted to do a detour to Litton Cheney, but that wouldn't be a good idea. Look at what had happened with Hilary. He braked and took a left-hand bend too fast; he hadn't yet got used to these roads, all twists and turns when you least expected them. Yes, Hilary had been little more than a silly bitch at her own wedding, and now she was back from their honeymoon, she was still acting a bit suspect, as if she were likely to go all soppy on him at any moment. And he didn't want that. He wanted . . .

Felix sighed. He wanted Jess. But at the same time it would be nice if Jess were a bit different. More like Hilary say, with a bit of Marilyn thrown in. Marilyn was a bloody minefield of sexual promises – even at the wedding with her own husband only yards away, she had batted those sooty lashes at him, every word spoken in that husky voice a come-on. And it was tempting.

Peter had got stroppy at yesterday's meeting, accusing Felix yet again of not giving him enough time to create.

132

Felix pulled a face. Bloody prima donna, playing the same old record. So yes, it was tempting. Undeniably, it would be good to have a bit of what Peter treasured the most, regarded as his alone. Not to mention a boost to the old ego. He could always do with that.

Felix braked as a tractor loomed in front of the Alfa Romeo. But it would also be a guilt trip, and he didn't relish that so much. Jess had been different since the wedding, more alive; all keyed up. But if something apart from this design thing was going on then he didn't know what it could be. He did know that sex was good between them again, and what was most confusing was her reaction to his apology after the wedding. Well, he'd felt compelled to say something, what with Hilary pouring herself all over him like that. A bit embarrassing, to say the least.

But Jess had laughed. 'More fool Bas,' she'd said, a smile on her face as she'd squeezed his arm. And, 'It's all in the past.' Almost as if she knew. But if she knew, wouldn't she have said something before?

What did Jess expect of him?

Sometimes, Felix thought, as he increased his speed and overtook the tractor, his wife confused the hell out of him. Sometimes he was unsure of her, often she seemed on another planet, at other times he wondered how well he really knew her, even after all these years. She wasn't like other women. She rarely made an effort over her appearance, her paint-pots were more important to her than her oven, she had an on-off switch that operated like lightning . . .

Felix thumped the dashboard. It was about time he surprised *her*. It was about time he did something to show her how much he loved her, how much he appreciated her. He grinned. And he knew just the thing. He would stop off in Bridport on his way home. And he would buy his wife an early anniversary present. The kind that was unforgettable.

In the cinema Jack Nicholson turned round to a group of patients awaiting psychoanalysis and said, 'Maybe this is as good as it gets.'

What an unbearable pessimist. Sophie sniffed and gripped Nick's hand harder. Several days ago he had broken their first date and she wasn't prepared to forgive him – yet. Who cared if Barbara had arranged a dinner party without checking with him first? Whose fault was that exactly? His for not knowing about it? Sophie's for being the other woman? No, it was clearly the fault of the still anonymous Barbara.

Sophie stared at the screen. Still anonymous, though lately Sophie had felt the urge to find out what she looked like, wanted to lurk outside their house like a Peeping Tom and see if Barbara really was the frump she liked to imagine. It was Barbara's fault for blithely assuming that Nick's time was free for her to arrange. It wasn't. And he should tell her so.

When Nick had not turned up at the flat, Sophie grew worried about him. She gnawed her nails to the quick, reapplied her make-up three times, and jumped out of her skin as the phone rang.

After their conversation – both whispered and brief on his part, full of *I can't talk now*'s and *I'll make it up to you soon*'s, she slammed down the phone and out of the flat, furious that she had skipped another afternoon from college for nothing, hotly resenting the fact that a dinner party with *family friends* came before her in priority.

Karin, predictably, had no sympathy. 'It's always on his terms,' she said. 'And who can blame the guy? You make it so easy for him.'

Did she? Had she? 'I hung up on him,' she wailed.

'He'll call again soon.' Karin had grabbed her bags and given Sophie one of her pitying looks. 'When he's feeling horny.'

134

'Karin!'

But her friend only shrugged. 'Test him out then. Have a sexless date.' She paused in the doorway, laughing, no doubt at the stricken expression that must be drawn in bold on Sophie's face. 'And make him come here for a change.'

Sophie laughed as Jack Nicholson once more performed his trick of not walking on the lines of the pavement. Bloody weirdo. What girl in their right mind would get involved with that? She sneaked a glance at Nick's rather aristocratic profile – high cheekbones, slightly hollow cheeks, long straight nose, and neat layered fair hair. Any girl would be tempted by him.

And Karin had been spot on. He had phoned the following day; she was cool, but not too cool.

When he suggested they meet up at the flat on Friday afternoon her lip curled. He was so predictable. She knew he could leave work early on Fridays and tell Barbara a convincing lie about going out for an end-of-a-hard-week drink with the guys at the estate agent's.

'I'm not free until five,' she said, consulting her timetable. 'And I won't have time to come to Brighton.'

'No go then?' The disappointment in his voice made her gloat. It was her moment.

'Why don't you come here?'

'What, to Chichester, you mean?' She could almost hear him making the calculations. But it wasn't far. Perhaps Karin had a point. For too long she had done all the running around.

'About time you put in a bit of effort,' she teased, keeping her voice low and level, in a way that she knew turned him on. Karin would be pleased with her. 'It's less than an hour's drive.' And then just to persuade him a little more. 'I'll be going back to Dorset for Christmas. So we won't see each other for ages otherwise . . .'

She had waited until he agreed before suggesting a movie;

135

by then he couldn't get out of it. And OK, he hadn't exactly been burning with enthusiasm, but with Karin's voice ringing in her ears. Sophie stuck to her guns. Because she didn't want this to be as good as it ever got.

When the lights went up she caught his surreptitious glance around. Even here, for God's sake. But he leaned closer and planted a house-lights-up kiss right on her mouth.

She wound her arms round his neck. 'Good, huh? Isn't it nice,' she snuggled in closer, 'just to do normal things sometimes?'

'Yeah.' He pulled her to her feet. 'But where shall we go now?'

'Now?' She pretended not to know what he meant. 'How about a pizza? I know a good place.'

He laughed. It was OK, she saw that. Karin was wrong. This wasn't just about sex, and this was going to get a hell of a lot better. 'And after that?' he teased.

'My room?'

'With all those students?' He scratched his chin. 'I'm a bit old for that sort of thing, angel.'

What rubbish. 'And Jack Nicholson,' she said as they walked out arm in arm, 'was way too old – and barmy – for that woman.'

'At least he wasn't married.' He sounded so serious.

She stopped walking, slipped her arm from his, and turned to stare at him. 'What are you saying, Nick?' Her stomach was suddenly a mass of collywobbles. And she didn't like the look in his eyes.

He sighed. 'Just that some women would think you were getting a raw deal.'

Some women? She took his arm once more to stop herself from stumbling. Like Karin. And her mother would certainly say the same as Karin if she knew the situation. As it was, Sophie had been subjected to yet another maternal cross-examination on the way back to the station after her weekend in Dorset. But she had been prepared, ready with protestations that yes, she was working hard, yes, Nick lived in Brighton but she hardly ever saw him, yes, she was OK for money (true enough since she'd cadged fifty quid from her dad the day before) and no, there was absolutely nothing for her mother to worry about. They had covered everything.

'Have you heard me complaining?' she joked to him now. A bit of Nick was better than all of some prat her own age with spots and an ego the size of a house.

'No, but . . .'

'It won't always be like this. Will it?' He didn't answer and the collywobbles increased. She turned to face him. 'Nick?' *Tell me.* She wanted to be told it would get better, she wanted some sign she was important. Important enough to leave his wife for?

They got to the car and she slipped thankfully inside, though he still hadn't replied. He looked serious and rather silly – with that tolerant-parent expression on his face that she'd noticed several times before. But he would leave Barbara one day, of course he would. Otherwise what was the point in seeing Sophie, in loving her?

'When you say it won't always be like this . . .' He didn't start the car. He just sat there staring in front of him, refusing to look at her – a bad sign. 'I don't know that I could ever bring myself to leave Barbara.'

'Oh.' The collywobbles gave way to a nasty numb stone-weight in her belly. He couldn't put it plainer than that. 'Why not?'

Nick put his hand up to his perfectly layered hair and patted it. 'Because it would crack her up, I know it would. She wouldn't be able to take it, angel. God knows what she would do.'

Was that his arrogance, or was he just being honest about

Barbara's weakness? Sophie sat up straighter. She sounded a right wimp. How could a man like Nick possibly be attracted to a pathetic specimen like that? 'Well, if you want to knock this thing with me on the head, Nick,' she said. 'I might as well tell you right now that it won't crack *me* up.'

He sneaked a glance at her. 'No?'

'No.'

The next moment he practically flattened her with a kiss that was violent, but otherwise pure heaven.

'Wow.' She emerged for air.

'Let's drive somewhere.' The passion was still fizzing between them as Nick started the car. 'Where?'

And this time she didn't bother to tease him. She knew exactly what he wanted, and Karin could go take a running jump. Because the simple fact was that Sophie wanted it too.

Chapter 10

What should she call herself? Jess frowned. Amateur designer? Did that sound too pretentious? Painter and decorator, on the other hand, had a definite white overalls and right-said-Fred ring to it. Design and decorating student, how about that? She scribbled in the words.

Is there a room in your house in need of a face-lift? Which reminded her. She looked around the room in which she was sitting hunched at the kitchen table. Her own kitchen was number one priority; it would be nice to get that done first. Terracotta and fennel perhaps? A splash of paint, some different lighting, a little rearranging of furniture and a new plant for the dresser, and the kitchen would be a new room. Not particularly ambitious, perhaps, but she would leave the ambition until someone else was paying for it.

After searching under the table, Jess relocated her drawing pen from where she'd slotted it behind one ear, and completed the simple illustration of a paint-pot and brush that went with the ad.

She then grabbed her bag and the keys to the battered Renault and headed out of Cliff Cottage. But as she flung open the front door, she encountered Felix about to put his key in the lock.

139

'Hey!' His face was lit up by a huge grin.

'Hi.' Jess reached up to kiss him. He smelt of fruit cake.

'Are you skiving?'

'No. And you're going the wrong way.' He turned her around and propelled her back inside.

'What?' She laughed. He was so bossy sometimes. But call it dominating and sometimes she could succumb like all the rest.

'I've got something to show you.'

'I bet you say that to all the girls.' But he looked excited, she observed, and it wasn't just the big smile. His face was slightly flushed and his spiky hair was ruffled. Felix might be seven years older than her, but for Jess he had never lost his little-boy charm. It was there in the teasing blue of his eyes and in the sulky droop of his mouth when he didn't get his own way. And how could you help it? You wanted to please him. 'What is it?'

Felix dipped his hand into his breast pocket. 'Ah hah, wouldn't you like to know?' He extracted a long slim envelope and waved it above her head.

'I might.' Jess watched him. One more second and then . . .

She jumped, lunged and made a grab for the envelope.

'OK, OK, you win.'

Smiling at her success, Jess ripped it open. He was waiting for her reaction. He looked almost nervous. Travel tickets. She read them quickly. 'Venice!'

Felix looked smug now. 'A nice and romantic long weekend. A dreamy hotel overlooking the Grand Canal. Just the two of us. What do you think?'

What did she think? 'Oh, Felix . . .' She had always wanted to go to Venice. 'How lovely.'

His hands were light on her shoulders. 'I thought we should see it, before it sinks for ever.'

'Oh, Felix.' She was beginning to repeat herself now. But sometimes Felix's timing was nothing short of impeccable.

His fingers moved to her face. He caressed her cheek with the back of his hand. 'Are you pleased?'

'I'm ecstatic!' She threw her arms round his neck. 'It's a perfectly wonderful idea.' It was at times like these that she remembered why she was married to Felix. OK, he had made a few mistakes. He had not *always* been entirely honest with her. But that was in the past. He had also looked after her, given her the love and security she craved when she lost her parents, and more importantly he could still bring a blast of sunshine, a touch of magic into her life. If he could bring home such a marvellously unexpected surprise, wasn't that a sign that their marriage could work, that the trust she'd lost could be reclaimed in time?

He kissed her. 'Should we go out to dinner to celebrate? Maybe we should shop till we drop in Lyme on Saturday, and then spend even more on a slap-up feast. What d'you think?'

Jess frowned. It wasn't like Felix to suggest a shopping expedition. 'Shop?'

'You're in another world, aren't you?' He pushed her hair from her face and kissed her nose. 'You've been so caught up with your paint-pots and your sketchbook that you haven't even registered it's the last weekend before Christmas.'

'What?' Jess noted the tolerant smile. Felix thought it a daft idea to base a career choice on a passion like hers, a passion for changing the colours and spaces of a room in order to alter its entire character. So she would just have to prove him wrong. But, 'The last weekend before Christmas?' she echoed. That meant something else to her too.

'Yeah, you know, time of chaos and complaint in every household. Mad vacuuming, cooking, ordering the turkey time. Not to mention the Christmas shopping.'

'Ah.' Jess was beginning to see what he meant. And it was true – she had been so caught up with plans for the

141

course, and plans for the cottage, that the preparations had almost passed her by this year. 'I haven't even made a cake.' She put a hand to her mouth. Birthdays and Christmas were the only times she ever got round to it; but since Christmas cakes were supposed to mature for at least three weeks, she appeared to have missed the boat.

'Buy one.'

'And that's not all.' Jess slipped out of his embrace and consulted the calendar by the phone. 'I did put it on here. We thought it was a good idea at the time.'

'Put what on?' Felix peered over her shoulder. 'PR. What's that?'

'Um . . .'

'Public relations? Partying and raving until you drop?'

'Patti and Ruth.' Jess turned to face him. 'We arranged it a while ago. I did tell you.' She watched his face fall.

'Bloody hell. Are they coming for the whole weekend?' He moved away, raked his fingers through his hair. '*This* weekend?'

'Uh huh. We wanted a Christmas get-together.' At the time it had seemed a great way to combine festive celebrations with Patti and Ruth coming to see the new cottage. 'I suppose I could cancel it.' But she didn't want to. She was longing to see them, itching to bring them up to date with everything that was happening. And she didn't really care that Christmas was looming around the corner; it would only be herself, Felix, Sophie and maybe Rupert for Christmas dinner anyway.

'No, no, let them come. Shopping can wait. Dinner can wait.' His mouth twitched into a smile, but Jess knew his mood had swung and that she'd ruined his lovely surprise.

'How about dinner tonight?' she wheedled.

'I'm working late.' He plucked the piece of paper poking out of her bulging bag. 'What's this?'

It was her advertisement. 'I'm putting one in the local rag. What d'you think?'

142

Felix shrugged. 'You don't have to work.'

'I want to work.' She grabbed it back from him. He could be so damned patronising. But she knew it wasn't work that he objected to, so much as *this* work. He might have pretended an enthusiasm for her design project, but it wasn't safe, was it? Not like working in bloody Immaculate Interiors when he always knew where she was nine to five and *she* always knew what she'd be doing. *Guiding (not pushing,* Sandra would say, *never pushing, customers don't like to be pushed)* people into buying furniture and fabrics that half the time she didn't even like. Being ever so careful what she said to them in case she lost the sale and Sandra got to hear about it. *Having respect for their opinions*, or lying – which was what it often amounted to. Never being able to create an entire look; having to be content with half a look, which was often more frustrating than no look at all. Oh, hell . . .

Jess sniffed. And advertising her design service wasn't safe either; far from it. At least not safe enough for Felix. Jess hitched her bag higher on to her shoulder. But this wasn't the time to be getting cross with Felix. He had been spontaneous and charming and thoughtful. And she probably wasn't being in the least fair.

'Do what you like.' Felix was already making for the door. 'You usually do.'

Damn. 'Felix, don't be like—'

But he had gone, with a face like thunder and a slam of the door. And if she wanted to get this ad in before the deadline she must go too.

So with a last lingering look at the tickets for Venice still sitting on the kitchen table, Jess followed Felix out of Cliff Cottage and stood there staring after him as the Alfa Romeo whizzed off down Jupps Lane.

On his way to the cottage half an hour ago, Felix reflected, his mood had been very different. He had been immersed in 'Questo o quello' from *Rigoletto*, a raunchy little number that involved plenty of gutsy laughter and which invariably made him think of sex. The tickets for Venice had been safely tucked in his jacket pocket, and he was so desperate to see Jess that he hadn't been able to wait until after work to give them to her. Even an afternoon quickie wouldn't have gone amiss.

He ejected the CD. And now he felt like shit.

At Bridport he took the B 3157, the coast road, which took him every working day through some of the most spectacular scenery in Dorset. From the picturesque village of Burton Bradstock through green hills and valleys, up Limekiln Hill past the tumuli of Tulk's Hill that were so often hidden by mist or low cloud. Before swooping back through the Abbotsbury Plains down to the coast and the village itself with its famous swannery, gardens and chapel. But Felix saw none of it. His mood was getting blacker by the minute.

Arriving at the premises of Beck and Newman, he parked in his reserved space, noted the presence of Peter Beck's Range Rover, and instead of going up to the office, stalked into the shop. He nodded at Ralph who was behind the counter, and marched past the small team hard at it in the workshop, through to Peter's personal studio space. He was itching for a fight.

Peter Beck's fair hair was standing on end. Since he continually pulled his fingers through it when a design wasn't going to plan, he usually ended up looking like a big, crazy scarecrow. He was immersed in the tracing of a sketch that Felix knew would later be transferred on to metal that had been rubbed with Plasticine to leave a coating to show up the marks. And later, Peter would score the pattern with a scriber. The whole was a painstaking process. Felix pulled a face. Rather him . . . And yet Peter was so absorbed in it he barely glanced up.

'Peter.' Felix knew his voice was more assertive than necessary. He hated to be ignored.

Peter's grey eyes flickered. 'Felix, hello. What are you up to?'

'Not a lot.' He didn't bother to elaborate. He and Peter had very separate responsibilities in the company, and both preferred to keep it that way. 'How about you?'

Peter indicated the design he was working on, but reluctantly; Felix knew he hated being disturbed at such times – this being part of the reason that he had chosen to do so. There were sketches of a plan, a side view and a detailed perspective, painted, mounted and probably already approved.

'Art Deco meets Egypt,' he said.

Felix snorted. He couldn't make it out at all. 'Where are they meeting exactly? In the pub down the road? They look pretty pissed to me.' It was too easy, especially in his current mood, to put Peter down. How could he not? His position in Beck and Newman would always be subordinate to Peter's, and this always pissed him off – some days more than others. His partner wasn't a bad sort of guy, but he was a plodder. All right, he was creative, but he lacked Felix's business vision.

'It's a gold bracelet. See the Deco lines?' Peter pointed with his pencil. Felix shifted uneasily. He loathed the talented artist routine.

'I'm not bloody stupid,' he snapped. 'I can see it's a bracelet.' Hadn't he spent years working his bollocks off trying to buy the stuff from unsuspecting punters?

Peter ignored the tantrum. 'Well, then, this . . .' He pointed again. 'Shows the birth of the sun god from the lotus flower. Flanked by uraeus serpents.'

'I should have known.'

'A popular Egyptian motif.'

145

'And commissioned, I hope.' Felix couldn't imagine anyone buying such a monstrosity for the kind of money Peter would be asking. Give him a good set of pearls any day.

Peter's mouth tightened, and a nerve just under his right eye twitched. 'It is commissioned as it happens. It's for Martha Hunter. She wants it for a New Year bash.'

'It won't make her any prettier.' Martha Hunter positively dripped money and she *utterly* adored Peter, as she took care to inform Felix every time they met. But she was an old hag. She lived in Dorchester and was one of Peter's few local clients, having discovered his talents when Beck and Newman were still based in Sussex, and Martha had come to Worthing to visit her sister.

'Felix.' Hilary Nicholson appeared in the doorway, a swish of blonde hair and cool blue eyes. 'I've been looking everywhere for you. You were due back hours ago.'

Felix scowled. 'And the place can't exist without me, is that it?' Sometimes, he even did get to wondering if he could manage the business without Peter Beck. But how could he, when for far too many people, Peter and his flashy Art Deco creations *were* the business; all Felix's hard slog buying and selling antiques, offering insurance and pawnbroker facilities and getting their stuff into retail outlets merely a sideline.

'No.' Hilary slid him an intimate look that Felix just knew Peter had intercepted. 'But I like to keep tabs on you, you know that. You're always in demand. And there's some post that should be dealt with today.' She paused. 'So are you coming through?'

'In a minute.' He supposed he should be getting on, but Peter put a hand on his arm to prevent him from following his PA through to the office. 'What?'

'Watch yourself, Felix,' he said.

'What are you on about now?' Irritably, Felix shook off the hand.

146

Peter waved at the empty doorway. 'Much as I value her services to the company – why is Hilary still working here? It must take her an hour to do the drive. And then there's Bas . . .' He let this hang in the air.

Felix remembered Jess's words this afternoon. It had been an attack. 'Women *want* to work these days, Peter. It doesn't matter how loaded the old man is – they want their independence, their own career.' His words sounded bitter even to his own ears. 'And lots of people commute much further than Hilary does. You're way out of date, pal.'

'And you're not fooling anyone.' Peter stood up, straightening to his full six feet whatever-it-was.

Felix hated that. He moved away a few paces. 'What are you trying to say?' The man was talking in riddles.

'That you'd better sort it out.' Peter's voice remained calm, but his freckled face seemed to darken slightly and there was no mistaking the flash of venom in his light eyes. 'Whatever's going on with Hilary Nicholson. I mean it, Felix.'

What right did he have to speak to him like that? Who the hell did he think he was? 'Hilary and I have been finished for a long time,' he muttered. He might have been spoiling for a fight, but this wasn't exactly what he'd had in mind.

'It didn't look like it at her wedding.' Peter sat down again and gazed at him thoughtfully. 'And she's making it increasingly obvious that it isn't over as far as she's concerned.'

'And that's my fault, I suppose?' Felix kicked a leg of the nearest stool and watched as Peter licked the tip of his pencil.

An irritating habit – and a pity pencils weren't made of lead any more.

'Jess is a lovely woman,' he said, as if Felix hadn't noticed. 'You wouldn't want to lose her.'

That was way below the belt. Maybe Peter should look to

147

his own marriage before he started picking on other people's. 'I'm not going to lose her.'

'I wouldn't count on it.'

'And is it any bloody business of yours?'

'When it affects my company, yes.' Peter's voice grew cold.

My company, Felix noted.

'And when it affects my friends.'

'Your friends?' Felix was flabbergasted. Now Peter was really going too far.

'Jess is my friend.' Peter looked up at him. Now that he was sitting down again Felix felt more sure of himself, but the reversal of their body language had not apparently made Peter feel more ill at ease. He was regarding Felix with perfect equanimity.

'I see.' Felix felt a wave of jealousy. 'Is that all she is?'

'Oh, don't be bloody ridiculous.'

Yes, Felix realised. It was ridiculous. Jess wouldn't look at a man like Peter Beck. 'And what makes you qualified to act as a bloody marriage guidance counsellor?' he demanded. 'Personal experience?'

It had been a shot in the dark, but to his surprise he saw that the shot had gone home. Peter's face turned red, puce, then red again. What was going on here? He'd have to quiz Marilyn about this.

'That woman you married,' as if dismissing him, Peter made a few strokes with the pencil on the sheet of paper in front of him, 'is worth fifty of the Hilarys of this world.'

Did he imagine that Felix didn't know that? 'Shut the fuck up.' He mouthed it through clenched lips, turned on his heel and left the studio.

'Shut the fuck up,' he said again as he charged through the workshop, not caring who heard him or what they might think.

He slammed the door of the shop behind him, ignoring

Ralph's look of surprise, got into his car and began to drive. Anywhere would do. He could face neither Hilary nor the office right now. He was fed up with the lot of them.

As he drove, he replayed the conversation with Peter in his head. This time his partner remained seated, Felix towered over him, looking scathingly at the design Peter was working on. And he had all the right answers. When Peter mentioned Jess he merely told him to mind his own bloody business and left the room. That was what he *should* have done. The next day Peter came through to the office and grovelled, apologising profusely for having dared to interfere. He reminded Felix how much he respected him, admired him, how grateful he was for the way Felix had built the business up to the success it was today. He told Felix that he needed him. That was what *should* have happened.

'In your dreams, boy,' Felix growled.

Still, the next track he chose was wistful and slow; Placido Domingo – his favourite tenor – singing 'Una furtiva lagrima' from Donizetti's *L'Elisir d'Amore*. It was sad; the strings of the London Symphony Orchestra had a way of making it more plaintive than ever.

And then the music was disturbed by the ring of his mobile.

'Felix Newman.' For a brief moment he thought it was indeed Peter calling to apologise.

'Hi.' The female voice sliced into his fantasy.

'Hi.' Absent-mindedly Felix caressed the steering wheel of the Alfa.

'Can you come over? I want to see you.'

He liked the way she didn't announce her identity and didn't feel the need to. Felix turned the volume of the music down. 'Why did you move to Dorset, Marilyn?'

To give Marilyn her due, she didn't even hesitate. 'I was screwing the guy next door, darling. Had been for yonks.

Peter found out.'

'And?'

'He'd been on about moving for a while anyway. Mother was here. It seemed the obvious solution.'

'And how did you feel? About leaving this guy?' To his surprise Felix felt another twinge of jealousy. It had never occurred to him that Marilyn might have screwed around in the past, let alone that it would all be so casual and matter of fact to her. But when he thought about it – why had she suddenly given him the come-on after all the years he'd known her?

'It was already burned out. Peter made it a condition to move. I had no choice if I was going to stay with Peter.'

'I see.' He wondered why she *did* want to stay with Peter. Clearly, she had never been faithful to him. 'Was he married? The other guy?'

'Darling, everyone half-decent is married. But he was getting boring. He couldn't just have a laugh any more; he wanted to do the guilt thing too.'

'Hmm.' He could see how that would cramp her style. 'So you blew him out?'

He could almost hear her shrug. 'It wasn't painful in the least. Maybe I already had half an eye on you, darling.'

'I bet.' But he was feeling more cheerful already. It was flattering. What with Jess, her bloody painting, and even bloodier friends, and then Peter warning him off Hilary, Felix had just about had enough.

'So are you coming?' She sounded beautifully restless, and the sexual invitation was unmistakable.

He hesitated. But how could he resist? He didn't even want to resist. It was a risk; but he'd always loved living on the dangerous side of the tracks. 'I'm on my way.'

'I'll be waiting.'

Felix felt the tremor of sexual desire as he replaced the mobile, swung the car round and made his way back towards

150

Litton Cheney. He would show Peter Beck what kind of a man he was. Nobody could tell Felix what to do and who to see. He would see and sleep with whoever he bloody well chose. Nobody made Felix Newman feel small.

He replaced the tape with *Rigoletto*, which reflected his mood as precisely as it had done earlier that day, made another call on his mobile to Ralph at the shop to fix up a game of squash for later – he might not need the exercise but he would sure need the shower.

And as he drove to Litton Cheney, Felix sang along loudly with Alfredo Kraus. Sex and squash would make him feel strong again. Sex and squash would stop him worrying about Jess. Sex and squash would make him forget every single word that Peter had said.

Chapter 11

Louisa held Scarlet against her face and kissed his torn ear. 'Let's face it,' she told him. 'We should never have come back.'

Scarlet gave her one of his *I told you so* looks.

'I know you did. And I took no notice.' She shivered. London was so bloody cold. She'd forgotten this, but Stevie's electric fire had soon reminded her. It ate electricity so fast. It might even be cheaper to be with Stevie down the pub.

But hardly appropriate, since last night she had told him she was leaving. Louisa pushed her hair behind her ears. She would get it cut tomorrow; she liked the feel of it when the hair was hardly a bristle on the back of her neck. Ah well. She knew when something wasn't working; it was pointless prolonging the agony – better to move on.

Perhaps it would never work out with any guy – because she was too scared of losing a good thing, because trust came so hard. Who could tell? Maybe she was destined for a string of glorious failures. But as far as Stevie was concerned, she was a square peg in a round hole. She didn't belong; she didn't want to have to compete with his kids for his attention, she wanted something different. But what?

For a moment, Scarlet's mournful brown eyes looked a bit like Stevie's.

'He'll get over it,' she told the bear. 'You know he will.' The guy was drop-dead gorgeous. She'd seen the way girls looked at him in the pubs and clubs. The addition of three children would probably just be a challenge to some of them.

'But where will you go?' he'd asked her last night. 'You won't leave the country without seeing your sister, will you?' Did he think her a hard bitch? And what did it matter now?

'Haven't decided.' It had been easy to sound casual, better for him to think of her this way. And she would leave soon. It was, after all, bloody awkward sleeping in the same bed as someone you were leaving behind you; particularly such an attractive someone. Awkward and unfair.

Louisa propped Scarlet up on the couch, took a deep breath and reached for the phone. She knew the number off by heart. Stevie was right. It was ridiculous to come all the way back to England, and not even phone. She had put it off too long.

Her hesitating fingers hovered over the push buttons. Jess would ask her to go to Sussex. She would expect her to go to Sussex. But how could she? How could she bear to see what a success her sister had made of her life with an adoring husband, a house to die for, a daughter who completed one compact and happy family. . . If she went, there would probably be bread baking in the oven, a pot of fresh coffee on the go and an adorable labrador puppy racing out to meet her. Jess might even have a grandchild by now, oh God, a son-in-law, crystal glasses and a porcelain plate collection. Her life would be well ordered, secure, complete. . .

And how would that make Louisa feel? Bloody awful. She would phone Jess. And then she would go to Spain instead.

153

She pushed the buttons, nerves twitching at her stomach muscles, making them contract until she thought she'd have to dash for the loo. The number was unobtainable.

Irritated, she tried again. Nothing. She didn't need to check her address book because the number was branded into her head. She pressed the buttons again, slower this time. Silence. She replaced the receiver.

Where was she?

Louisa picked up Scarlet and held him tight. It was something she'd never conceived of, that Jess wouldn't be there, always available. But available for what? For help? To be there, simply for Louisa to turn away from, time after time? Just because Jess had turned Louisa away twenty years ago . . . She didn't need to look at Scarlet to know that she had given her sister no choice. Jess had no idea where Louisa was living; how could she have let her know if she was leaving Sussex, if the phone number changed, whatever – even if she'd wanted to?

Louisa glared at the phone. She had barely kept in touch. Jess was so often in her head that it didn't seem like that. But that was exactly how it was.

'Shit.' What if Jess were in trouble, what if Jess had ever needed *her*? She would never have been able to find her; she would have been alone. And Louisa didn't need to look at Scarlet's face to know what she must do.

Jess refused to feel deserted. Why should she? She had plenty to do. Felix had told her he'd be late (because Patti and Ruth were coming for the weekend? Because she was advertising her services as an interior designer? It had rather seemed that way this afternoon.) But it was now after nine, which surely was a bit much for one of Felix's yah boo sucks numbers.

Mustn't be mean to Felix. She poured herself another large glass of wine, stuck a frozen pizza in the oven and then changed her mind and took it out again. Mustn't be mean to Felix – he couldn't help behaving like a child on occasion. Or could he? Patti said that men never really grew up, they just pretended sometimes; at heart they still cared most about what gave them the biggest and simplest kicks. Football? Fast cars? Sex? Jess sipped her drink. With Felix it was attention and sex tangled and rolled into one. He must be aware that her new course and friends coming for the weekend would deprive him of the first if not the second. And neither was safe. So, like a child he was making his point as effectively as having a tantrum or slamming a door. *And* as childishly.

Jess put her glass down on the drainer and peered out of the kitchen window into the darkness beyond. Nothing. She could see bugger all. She rubbed the glass but it misted right up again from her breath. She put the lights out and squinted, nose up close. Now she felt a twit, but she still couldn't see a thing. Where had her garden gone?

In frustration, she stomped out of the kitchen door and into the workshop. The brushes were all soaking in a wiggledy line of assorted jars and trays on the surface of the old pharmacy cupboard. Her kitchen was mid-transformation; she could do nothing until the last coat was dry. She could wait for Felix, eat pizza and get drunk or …

Jess pulled on gumboots and her old waxed jacket, and let herself out of the back door into the garden. That was better. Fresh air. She shivered, pulled the jacket in closer. Not that she could see much of the garden even now – it was far too dark. But she stepped hopefully through the long wet grass towards the pond, peered into the murky depths peppered on the surface with duckweed, and prepared to fish-spot.

Five minutes later there was still nothing forthcoming, but there was too much blanket-weed to see very much even in daylight. She hadn't done much algae-clearing, and the

155

rockery consisted only of a piece of granite she had lugged home from the salvage yard the other day. But at least she had done some of the pruning and cut down a load of nettles. In the spring the pond would come good. The warmer weather would draw her outside; she would buy more fish and a beautiful pure white water lily. She smiled, almost feeling the warmth and hope of spring on her skin already.

The air was damp, but it wasn't as cold as she'd thought, or maybe she was getting used to it after the first shock of leaving the centrally heated cottage behind her. But as she turned towards the back garden gate, the sea breeze swept her hair from her face, as if intending to tug it right off her scalp. It was a delicious shock. She stood, holding her face up to the night, wanting to drink it in – this soft darkness, the salt abrasions on the skin of her face, the distant thud and splash of water on rocks and shingle. And once more, she slipped through the gate, trod down the remaining nettles and was striding along the path towards Rupert's back gate before she had even decided to do so.

Would he be in? She was tempted to go and surprise him, but when she peered over the fence his cottage was in darkness. Down the pub probably. She sniffed. There was rain in the air, and the slightly musty smell was reminiscent of mornings after firework parties, when soggy, empty cardboard packages were picked up from wet lawns and sodden earth.

Night-time on the cliff . . . It was almost surreal. She dug her hands deep in the pockets of her jacket and walked on along the path. The ground was wet and slippery under her boots. It was surreal because it was other-worldly: the dense shadows of sea and cliff, of the rocks down below, of the trees and gorse bushes bordering the path, held a starkness that was a million miles from the blurred edges they offered to daylight. She knew Felix would say that she was bloody

156

crazy to walk along the path at night, alone and unarmed. He'd give her surreal.

But it was hard to say no to the cliff path. And it seemed unlikely that anyone else would be here. No one else would be crazy enough. She really seemed to be entirely alone. She held her breath. It felt kind of thrilling to be at one with the sea and the cliff like this.

She walked on for ten minutes until the path began to dip down into Brocklemouth, a stretch of sandy bay bordered by rocks and inundated with tourists in the summer. She rounded a blind bend, registered a tall dark figure not ten yards away, stopped, gulped, swallowed and turned to run.

What a bloody idiot – Felix was right; Jess puffed her way back up the path. She should have brought a weapon with her (what? an umbrella? a big stick?). She shouldn't have gone so far. She shouldn't have gone out at all, not in the dark, not on her own, not on the cliff path.

What if the figure were a maniac, a pervert, a rapist, a murderer? Which was the worst? Did it even matter? She turned her head to see how far away he was. Only twenty yards! God, he was tall and walking with a long loping stride that seemed to be equalling her own short, fast, increasingly desperate steps. He might even be gaining on her. She searched her experience for good advice. *Don't look as if you are running away.* But if you didn't run you were more likely to get caught, get grabbed, get raped or murdered. And how could you run and yet not look as though you were running? *Don't look scared.* A bit late since she'd fled at first sight of him, racing back the way she'd come.

'Jess!' the figure seemed to call.

But at least she was heading the right way for safety – back to Cliff Cottage and a few heavy bolts. If she could find her key . . . What was that noise? Was that the sound of her heart thudding against her chest cavity in double time?

Or was it . . . ? God, no. Her heart did a nose dive into her stomach. It was the sound of his bloody footsteps on the path behind her. Her half-jog, half-walk increased dramatically, but it was slippery. And he was running too. Bloody hell.

'Jess, is that you?'

'Help!' she squeaked. Her throat was dry as dust. All her worst nightmares were realised. When she was being chased she couldn't yell and she couldn't run.

She spun round. Maniacs, perverts, rapists and murderers wouldn't know her name – she hoped. And she'd seen that long, loping gait before. 'Rupert!' She was totally out of breath, badly winded, and had probably wet herself into the bargain. She bent double trying to recover, too knackered to give vent to her anger.

'Jess. Did I scare you?' He was beside her on the path, his eyes looking not so much hungry as concerned.

'Well, I wasn't playing catch me,' she growled, when she finally got enough breath together to speak. 'What on earth are you doing out here?' Now that her terror had receded she was cross that she'd been mistaken. It hadn't been just her, the sea and the cliff out here tonight. And all that stuff about surreal night-time just seemed plain batty with Rupert standing here grinning at her.

He shrugged. 'I could ask you the same thing.'

Jess snorted. Trust him to twist things. 'I was walking down to Brocklemouth Bay,' she said, as if it were the most natural thing in the world to be doing in the dark of a winter's evening.

'Fancied a dip, did you?'

'No, I was hoping to play a game of Frisbee. And you?'

He laughed. 'I often go walking at this time of night. When I want to be alone.' She caught his speculative glance. 'But I don't mind being disturbed by you.'

Damned cheek. 'Well, that's too kind of you,' she

retorted. 'But I'm going home now that I've been half-scared to death.'

'Sorry.' He held out his arm and part-gratefully, part-crossly she took it. She felt emotionally zapped, in need of another drink if not a frozen pizza.

'That's what it's like for women,' she felt compelled to explain to him. 'We spend our lives trying to be independent and it only shows us how vulnerable we are.'

'Where's Felix?' He glanced around, as if expecting Jess's husband to leap out from behind a gorse bush. But if she'd followed his train of thought correctly, then he'd missed the point. Women wanted to feel safe to go out *alone* without worrying they were about to be clubbed to death or flashed at in the process.

'Out. Anyway, night-time cliff walking isn't his thing.' *That's why we bought a house on the cliff*, he had said. *So in winter we can look at the view and still stay warm inside.* Jess smiled. But that wasn't enough for her.

They reached his gate, and she glanced at him curiously. 'Did you never want to get married, Rupert?' He seemed so self-contained somehow; she couldn't imagine him needing another human being for anything.

'It was never one of my burning ambitions, no,' he said dryly. 'I've seen what it does to people.'

'Oh?' What had it done to Jess and Felix?

For a moment, his eyes burned with a strange sort of passion. 'People say they get married because they want to make a commitment to a person, right?'

'Right.' Jess watched him. Although it was often more a case of need.

'And then they go about trying to change that person, trying to trap them into being what *they* want, what's best for *them*, what's safest. Trying to tie them up so they can't escape. Stifling them.' He paused for breath. 'Making them dependent so they can't take a step away, so that if they did

159

happen to meet someone new they wouldn't be able to just go for it, because society – not to mention their own conscience – would make them feel such a shit, that they wouldn't have the guts to go through with it anyway.'

Wow. Jess stared at him. 'So you've never been in love, then?'

He climbed over his gate without bothering to open it. 'I never said that. Love is something else entirely.'

'I see.' She watched him as he walked up the path, a tall figure with cropped hair, and arms that somehow seemed too long for his body. He was scuffing dead leaves with the toes of his heavy black boots. 'And of course, you're not bitter?'

He turned, but she couldn't make out his expression. 'Not bitter,' he said. 'But I know when I'm beaten.'

It would be a relief, she thought, as she walked the fifteen yards to her own gate, slipped the catch and shut it with a satisfying click behind her, to have Patti and Ruth here this weekend. Rupert was lovely and without doubt an interesting man, even if he did make a habit of wandering around in the dark and scaring women to bits. But with women you were left in no doubt of what they really felt – they made damn sure you knew it. Female friends were for confiding in. Rupert, on the other hand, seemed to make himself more a man of mystery by the second.

She was about to let herself in at the back door when she heard it. The sound of a violin playing, so faint she could hardly make it out. But she sensed the melancholy nature of the music he was playing. And she knew it was Rupert. 'So just who,' she said to herself – and to her absent neighbour – as she replaced the frozen pizza in the oven, 'would you have liked to marry, I wonder?'

Jess was half-asleep in the armchair, the uneaten pizza on the coffee table beside her, when she heard Felix come in.

160

She hadn't been able to get what Rupert had been saying about the state of marriage out of her head. And it had made her think uneasily of what marriage meant to her. Were she and Felix guilty of trying to mould one another into what they needed? Were they restricting one another rather than letting each other find a sense of self? And – worst of all – would they always stay together simply because it was the easiest option? She sensed Felix standing in the doorway, watching her, but didn't open her eyes.

'I love you, Jess,' he whispered, half to himself. 'I'm sorry.'

She heard him go into the kitchen, heard the chink of cups and the kettle being filled as he made coffee. He would bring her a cup, wake her and they would go to bed as if nothing had happened. Only what exactly was he sorry for?

Chapter 12

'It's so good to have you both here.' Jess beamed across the table at her two friends.

They had arrived late on Friday, spent Saturday in Lyme Regis with Jess and Felix, and were now having dinner at Picasso's, a trendy Spanish tapas restaurant just outside Lyme. Felix had also been invited along, but he had suggested (surprisingly good-humouredly) that he might cramp their style.

Privately the three women agreed. His presence would certainly limit the conversation.

'All girls together then,' Patti said, and grinned.

Jess wasn't complaining. She felt as if she had re-established her female connections over this weekend and boy, did it feel good.

'We've missed you, darling.' Patti swung back her curtain of raven-black hair, sipped her wine and caught the eye of the waiter, a skill that Jess had watched her hone to perfection over the years. It was especially useful, Jess thought, when she fancied the waiter like mad, as she obviously did tonight.

'Another bottle, please,' she told the young Spaniard. 'Thank God for house Rioja.' She smiled seductively up at him.

'My pleasure, madam.'

And he looked as if it was. Ruth and Jess exchanged an amused glance. Patti would never change. Thank goodness. 'And what exactly does madam have on the agenda for tonight?' Jess teased.

Patti regarded the receding figure (or more probably his bum in tight black trousers) with gleaming eyes. 'Not that one. In fact no one; I'm having a celibate weekend.' She sighed. 'Although he's rather beautiful, you have to admit.'

'And very young,' Ruth said.

'Even by your standards,' Jess chipped in.

She watched Patti as she sat back in her chair. Her body was long and languid; she looked quite simply as good as ever. Jess had no idea whether it was her lifestyle that kept her friend looking young – twenty fags and a bottle of plonk a day, lots of salad and seafood, a string of lovers, and the stress of running her own boutique – but whatever it was, she wouldn't mind some. Tonight, Patti was dressed in a rust crepe figure-hugging little number, with a pair of huge black jet earrings representing her only jewellery. She didn't look as if she were wearing a scrap of make-up, although she was; an effect that would take Jess hours to achieve, instead of the fifteen minutes in the bathroom that Patti had required.

Jess had also dressed up for tonight in a blue silk wrap-around skirt teamed with a favourite sheer top, and Ruth was elegant as always in soft and clinging green jersey. Together they looked rather splendid, she decided. No wonder the young waiter was impressed.

'The libido of the forty-year-old woman,' Patti leaned forward in her chair and tapped rust-tinted nails on the linen tablecloth, 'is at—'

'Hang on a second.' Jess rapped her knuckles on the table in response. 'I'm not there yet, remember. I've got three years to go. For heaven's sake don't age me before my time.'

163

Patti eyed her sympathetically. 'The libido of the forty-year-old woman,' she repeated, 'is at its peak.' There was an unmistakable hint of victory in her tone. 'Never mind, darling.' She patted Jess's arm. 'You'll be joining us before you know it.'

'Thanks a lot.' Jess popped a piece of deep-fried potato dipped in garlic mayonnaise in her mouth. She could always rely on Patti to make her feel good.

'And what about the forty-year-old male?' Ruth asked, always able to see both sides of any argument.

'Not a chance.' Patti dismissed the lot of them. 'They had their peak in their twenties, darling. The perfect match for the forty-year-old woman,' she watched as their young and dashing waiter returned with another bottle of wine and a very big smile, 'is the twenty-year-old man.'

'I can't wait for my time to come, then.' Jess thought of Felix. He didn't show much evidence of a diminishing libido and he'd passed forty over four years ago.

'But they haven't seen anything of the world,' down-to-earth Ruth objected. 'Some of these young blokes may be pretty, but they don't have much in the way of conversation. And most of them don't have a lot up top either.'

Patti's expression indicated that what was *up top* wasn't at issue here. 'Anyone could tell you've just done a degree.' She lifted her glass to her lips. 'Who needs conversation when you've got a willing young body – who also happens to consider you an incredibly sexy older woman – in your bed? Conversation you can get from friends.'

Jess smiled. Patti was incorrigible. But how much of this was for real? She had seen Patti cry over a man. She had heard her bemoan the fact that every guy she fell for was either married or stupid, on the breadline or mean as hell. Patti often said she preferred her single lifestyle, but she often complained about it too.

'I would need at least a smattering.' Ruth laughed.

164

'Degree or not. At least after a week or two.'

'Ah . . .' Patti fished a king prawn from the garlic sauce and began peeling. 'There you have it, darling. I'm thinking short-term, you see, that's the difference. Or at least,' she sucked the juice from her fingers, 'the kind of relationship that lives off a bit of fun twice a week instead of a man moving in lock stock and whatsits.'

'Whatsits?'

Patti didn't deign to reply. 'And you know what happens next?'

They did, but both shook their heads obligingly.

'The bastard expects you to do his washing and become the underpant fairy twice a week.'

'Underpant fairy?' Jess was confused.

'Brings clean ones to the drawer as if by magic.'

'Ah.' Jess giggled.

But Ruth was frowning. 'Still, there's a lot more to a relationship than doing a man's washing,' she objected. 'And these days I thought men were supposed to be capable of doing their own.'

'Hah!' Patti clearly wasn't convinced. And Jess had some sympathy. It was somewhat easier to locate the man who was into creative cookery than it was the man with a flair for ironing. Cooking wonderful food could be inventive – sensual, even. But it was hard to see how ironing five white shirts on the trot could reach such dizzy heights.

'And what happens when you're lonely? What happens when you've got too many lines and saggy bits to attract young lovers any more?' Ruth demanded.

'There's no guarantee any man will stick around for that,' Patti shot back. She turned to Jess. 'What do you think, Jessie? Will you and Felix love one another for ever? Has it been worthwhile or do you sometimes wish you'd played the field a bit first?' The roll of Patti's green eyes and the slight rise of the perfectly plucked eyebrows left much unsaid, but all perfectly clear. *Is Felix behaving himself?* she meant. *Is he playing around?*

'Patti . . .' Ruth was about to object once more but Jess stopped her. It was a fair question. And Patti knew of some of Jess's past doubts in the Felix department. She might seem hard, but it was all on the outside. In reality, Patti was more soft-hearted than any of them. She wouldn't want to embarrass Jess, but this was probably her roundabout way of enquiring after the health of her friend's marriage.

'Everything is fine.' Jess selected a clam, split the shell and dipped it in the delicious oregano and tomato sauce. How many more people would she be saying this to? Was it becoming a case of protesting too much? And what about this nagging sense that she and Felix weren't being entirely honest with one another? But then again, she had invested an awful lot of emotion in her marriage; an awful lot of years too.

'Everything?' Patti looked sceptical.

Jess leaned closer over the table. 'Well, the sex is pretty good for an over-forty-something,' she teased. It would need to be after all this garlic. 'And the firm seems to have taken the move in their stride.'

'And?' Patti narrowed her eyes. 'This dreamy look keeps appearing on your face and although once upon a time I would have said you were just mentally redecorating the restaurant . . .' She paused as they all laughed. 'It's not that, is it? You're all pent up and excited. Surely it isn't your husband of almost twenty years making you feel that way?'

'Ah . . .' Trust Patti to notice. Jess tapped her nose. 'I'll tell you later.' She helped herself to some chicken and chilli. 'But as far as Felix is concerned, I get quite a good deal, you know.' She thought of Venice. How many husbands would present their wives with a wonderful surprise like that?

'Of course you do.' Ruth nodded, but Patti looked unconvinced.

166

'And *that* is precisely why I never got married,' she said.

'Because you didn't want a good deal?' Ruth smiled.

'Because it all gets so bloody stale and comfortable. I mean,' she sighed. 'who wants a *good deal*?'

Jess took a slug of wine to help her mouth recover from the chilli. 'We've never been comfortable,' she protested. That was definitely not the word she would have chosen.

'But you're happy with a good deal.' Patti's eyes were challenging. 'You don't want more?'

Why were all her friends so anti-marriage? Had she gone out of her way to collect them? Rupert had given her a mouthful against the married state the other night, Ruth was forty and more attached to her mother and her cats than any man, and Patti . . . well, Patti never let a man stay for long inside her door. Perhaps Jess should have fostered more friendships from her waiting-for-Sophie-in-the-playground days. It might have brought at least some balance to her life.

Ruth was frowning at Patti. 'There's nothing wrong with that,' she said. 'I'd settle for a good deal.'

'Huh.' Boring as hell, Patti's expression told them.

'What about having some security in your old age?' Ruth managed to make it sound more boring than ever. 'What about having someone to grow old with?'

Heavens. They would be discussing pensions next. Whatever had happened to love?

Patti scowled. 'I'll come and move in with *you*, darling.' She grabbed Jess's hand. 'Ruth's bloody cats give me asthma.'

'And my cats,' Ruth laughed, 'hate your bloody cigarettes.'

Jess speared a prawn. She loved these two women. However had she managed without them?

Two hours later they lurched out of the taxi and gathered on the roadside as Jess searched for her keys.

'I don't have anyone to go to lunch with any more,' Patti

was moaning. 'And even the Café Continental has changed hands. The prawn salads have gone way downhill.' She tensed. 'God, these shoes are killing me.' She proceeded to take off one shoe and lean heavily on Ruth's shoulder in order to light another cigarette.

'You have masses of people to lunch with,' Ruth corrected. 'Whenever I phone, you're never free.'

'But I miss collecting Jessie from Immaculate Interiors. That awful place ...' Patti hopped up and down on the pavement, rubbing her foot at the same time. 'And I miss seeing that woman's face.'

'You could always go there to buy a cushion cover.' Jess laughed. She was down to the bottom layer of her bag and still no keys. 'If you miss her so much.'

'Yeah, brilliant.' Patti sat on the wall by the buddleia tree and took off the other shoe. 'I could ask Sandra Slattersly's advice about whether delicate plum goes with grunge-green or—'

'It is a *glorious* clash, madam.' Jess waved her keys triumphantly in the air. 'And I can *quite* see the appeal. But ...'

They all laughed and Jess tripped over a paving stone.

Ruth grabbed her. 'Steady.'

'How did you put up with that woman?' Patti squealed. 'She was perfectly dreadful. Not only bossy – but so bloody superior.'

Drunkenly, Jess made her way up the path. 'But you should have seen her with her husband,' she said. She held the key out in front of her like a talisman. 'She was so scared of him, honestly, and he was such a tiny little man—' She stopped abruptly in her tracks as Felix threw open the door.

'Hi, darling.' Gosh, he looked cross. Were they very late or just very drunk? Rupert's words came back to her. *They tie one another down.*

'Felix!' Patti flung herself through the doorway, thus saving the situation. 'Take that peeved look off your face

168

right now and kiss me.' She puckered her lips.

Ruth and Jess collapsed into a further fit of the giggles as Felix's lips twitched into a grin and he planted a chaste kiss on Patti's cheek. 'Been having fun, have you, girls?'

'Wonderful fun.' Patti pouted. 'Do you think he doesn't fancy me?' she hissed over her shoulder to the other two.

'He thinks he'll put some coffee on.' Felix disappeared into the kitchen. 'Very black and very strong.'

It wasn't until the next morning that Patti and Ruth cornered Jess in the kitchen, taking full advantage of her hangover from hell.

'You never told us,' Patti accused. 'What's it all about?'

'Huh?' Jess groaned. She couldn't face riddles when she was in this state.

'What you're so pleased about,' Ruth said.

'Oh yeah, well . . .' She had told them about the course she was starting after Christmas and they had both been suitably pleased for her. And she had even mentioned her ad – in passing. But she had omitted to tell them of the latest development. 'I've got my first client lined up.' She looked surreptitiously around as she hadn't actually told Felix, not yet.

'First client?' Patti was speaking much too loudly.

'Sssh.' Frantically, Jess waved her arms. 'Felix doesn't know yet.'

Patti shook her head in mock-despair. 'And she says everything's hunky-dory.'

'It is, only, he doesn't understand why—'

'Why you're so bloody excited about it?' Patti grabbed her hands and swung her round. 'Well, we do, so tell us who it is.'

And for some reason Jess found herself blushing as she replied. 'His name's Matthew Hill. He's a doctor. And he lives on the other side of Lyme.'

169

Sex, thought Felix, as he played the first gentle bars of Puccini's 'Nessun dorma' in his head, was very much like music. There was variation of tone, rhythm, pitch and volume; various instruments at the lover's disposal; a collection of bars and phrases that needed to be carefully constructed from tiny interlocking touches and moments, for the thing to work. And it must be formed lovingly into a whole – with a fitting climax, of course.

Sometimes the tone was predominantly wistful ... He stroked her eyebrow with a tender fingertip, like 'Una furtiva lagrima', for example. Sometimes it was dramatic ... he bent and kissed her firmly between the shoulder blades, like Giordano's 'Come un bel di maggio'. Sometimes it was stirring like so many of the pieces from *Tosca*, sometimes downright funny. In sex, rarely was there the kind of emotion to be found in 'Nessun dorma'. But there was, with this woman.

She turned around to face him, lying half beneath him, moving first her neck and then her whole spine, her breasts bending towards him like some delectable fruit.

Delicious. He allowed his tongue to flick across each in turn – just long enough – wetting the nipples, feeling them harden into the tightness that only increased his desire. Christ. His tongue circled back around them, an ever-increasing arc, moistening the white flesh, before moving sharply back to the centres.

She gasped, and that was his pleasure.

He could feel her hands on his buttocks, pressing into the clenched muscles, bringing him closer to her, but it wasn't time, the music had barely begun. Wistful at first, it began its teasing melody, as Felix caressed her breasts, her belly, her thighs, with his fingers, his mouth, his lips, his tongue. All in turn. Slowly and with tension mounting, in turn.

Unlike other women, she did not smell of flowers, musk

or some exclusive scent with a price tag to match. Felix recognised most of them, and he knew how worthless they could be. No. He sniffed her skin, rolling the fragrance around his senses as if he could keep it bottled in his memory for later. This woman smelt of herbs from a kitchen garden, slightly sweet, slightly damp from rain, very tempting; marjoram and rosemary mingling with melons, soap and the saltiness of the sea. She didn't smell of chemicals, she smelt of life itself, of whatever she had been doing today and however she had washed it off.

She parted her legs for him, just a little, showing how she wanted him, and the volume in his head rose in a crescendo.

He put his hands underneath her, raised her up, and eased into a rhythm change – not too abrupt, not too fast, very slow, very smooth, each thrust echoed by some element of the London Symphony Orchestra in his head. He looked into her eyes but they had become unfocused, not with him, not with this. Part of Felix wanted to bring her back, and part of him wanted her to go further into her secret pleasure, a place where he could take her but never come to know. And yes, there was some part of this woman he never could reach. He even wondered if she had found it herself. But that was how it was with all the best music.

'Oh, Felix,' she moaned.

'Ssh, darling.' The sound of her voice could make him come too soon. He was poised on the edge, the emotion was rising, and he wanted to stay there just as long as he could.

But this woman who always had the power to move him, didn't always play the game as he would like. 'Mmm, Felix.' He felt her hands move across his shoulders, along his back, lingering on the crease of his buttocks. And she had perfected a way of arching into him, of gripping and arching with him and into him that was pure joy.

Since his first sexual experience at the age of twelve, with

171

the woman who ran the bar at the end of the street and who Felix suspected had initiated a large proportion of young men of the neighbourhood, this woman on the bed with him right now had been the best.

'Nessun dorma' reached its point of climax, Felix looked down at her, at the closed eyes, the slope of her shoulders, the gentle outward curve of her stomach, the wild tangle of her hair. And he came just as she did once more, muttering his name, her fingers wound into his hair.

Jess padded into her almost completed fennel and terracotta kitchen to make coffee. Only two ivy stencils to go. She was pleased with it, but already her eyes were wandering; she was itching to start a new project. The hall?

She glanced back in the direction from which she'd come. It was so dark. Like stepping into a dungeon some-times when you walked through the front door. It *should* merge with the kitchen so that on walking from one space to another there would be no jarring sensation, no sense of ending and beginning, but a continual flow of experi-ence, of colour. She paused, kettle in hand, deep in thought. It would be easy, of course, to simply repaint it in a light, bright shade. But that wouldn't be enough, and it wouldn't tone in. Her hallway needed an illusion of the width it did not truly possess. Jess wanted to make an entrance with style.

She wandered back through. There was a small alcove by the stairs that needed more than a paint job. Wrought iron would make a perfect coat stand as it took up so little solid space, with variegated ivy perhaps, and maybe a huge mirror reflecting a picture on the other side. An abstract? Cubist to prolong the optical illusion? She'd have time to at least make a few tentative plans and sketches over the Christmas break. Jess shivered. Before she started thinking about the house of this Matthew Hill, something which really did give her goosebumps; she became a nervous wreck just contemplating it.

'I have a house that needs a face-lift,' a male voice she hadn't recognised had informed her on the phone two days ago.

'Oh?' It was an odd way to begin a conversation. He had caught her mid-coat, and she was anxious to return to the fennel wall as soon as possible before it went patchy.

'Could I speak to the interior designer?'

'Who?' Jess attempted to tuck the frizz of her hair behind her ears, but it sprang back again. That was all she needed now, some weirdo.

The voice had sounded very patient. She kept remembering that now. She remembered, and it made her giggle. Surely he must have had her down as a complete amateur right from the start?

'The person who is advertising their services as a designer and decorator?'

'Oh.' She was ashamed at how long it had taken for the penny to drop. 'That's me.' What an utter twit. Jess shifted the receiver to the other ear. She hadn't expected anyone to reply before Christmas. 'I'm female, I'm afraid,' she added, conscious that she hadn't made this clear in the ad for fear of putting prospective clients off. If you wanted heavy lifting and that right-said-Fred approach, then she wasn't your man.

'I'm glad to hear it,' the dry voice remarked. 'And are you busy right now?'

'Now?' Jess glanced at the calendar. Someone (her) had scribbled all over it in red Biro and it was impossible to make out what she was doing when. No wonder Felix hadn't spotted the PR last week.

'When I say *now*,' nice voice, she registered, 'I was thinking of having this place decorated after Christmas. If you're not too busy, you might like to come and have a look at the house first? We could discuss your terms.'

173

Terms. She hadn't even thought about terms. For the first time the magnitude of what she was taking on struck her between the eyes. She would have to go round to strange people's houses; she would have to be business-like and professional or they would run a mile. And she would have to decide what to charge. 'That would be fine,' she said smoothly, reaching for her bag, scrabbling in its darker recesses for an ever-elusive pen. Her sketchbook fell out with an uncompromising thud. 'What's the address?' Help. 'And when would be convenient?'

They had made an arrangement to meet, and had even chatted for a few minutes about her prospective client's requirements. He was a busy GP, he had told her, with no time for decorating. He knew the house needed something, but he didn't for the life of him know what. But the question was – would she?

'The whole house?' Abruptly, she sat down.

'The living room certainly,' he said. 'The rest can wait, at least for a while.'

Phew. For a minute there Jess had wondered if she had bitten off more than she could chew. But she had to do this to prove her independence both to herself and to Felix. It was part of her new future and this time she alone would make it happen.

Meanwhile, in the kitchen, the kettle had boiled.

She made tea for herself and coffee for him, and took it upstairs. Felix was in the bathroom, taking a shower; she could hear the rush of the water and the sound of him singing 'Nessun dorma', putting a lot of volume into it too. Smiling, recalling their passion of the last hour – not at all bad for an old married couple – she straightened the sheets, unwilling to change them immediately, wanting to keep awhile the flavour of their sensuality, the smell and the touch of Felix. It had been so good. But why did she get the feeling that Felix had been trying so very hard?

174

She took the coffee into the bathroom and broached the subject of the hallway. Post-sex generally guaranteed a good mood.

'So I thought a kind of parchment effect.' She finished off her explanation as Felix emerged, dripping wet, from the shower.

He grabbed her by both arms.

'Felix, ugh!' she shrieked.

'That's a fine way to talk to your husband.' He kissed her, long and hard, and she felt the desire all over again and twice as strong. What was going on here? There was a kind of desperate tension between them that almost scared her.

She clutched his wet shoulders until they emerged from the kiss, both a little surprised perhaps at the extent of their passion. 'You've soaked me,' she whispered.

'You deserved it.' Felix picked up his coffee and stood stark naked drinking it, eyeing her over the rim of the mug. 'You haven't even drawn breath since you redecorated the kitchen. More paint and dustsheets already? It's like living on a bloody building site.'

'The cottage needed decorating, you know that.'

'Not all at once.'

Jess avoided his eye. She knew that the only time she felt completely herself was when she was changing a room. It was daft, wasn't it? And it would certainly sound daft to Felix. 'Then you should be glad that I'm planning on moving the building site elsewhere.'

Deadlock. Their eyes met. He wasn't glad of course, but at the same time, what right did he have to complain about it?

The phone rang; the connection between them relaxed. Jess went into the bedroom, picked up the extension. 'Hello?'

Felix followed her, coffee in one hand, towel in the other.

'Jess? How are you?' It was Marilyn.

175

'OK.' Jess wondered if Marilyn could tell by her voice what she'd been doing and how good it had been. 'You?'

'All right. Fed up with the thought of another bloody Christmas.' Marilyn sounded depressed and slightly weird. 'I swear when Mother's gone I'll take off to somewhere hot and un-Christmassy until it's all over.'

'Hmm.' There seemed to be no purpose to her call. Jess sat on the bed and rolled her eyes at Felix. But Marilyn went on and on. Perhaps she needed someone to talk to. Perhaps she was lonely.

'And I haven't even seen your cottage yet,' her husky voice drawled.

'Then come over, Marilyn.' Jess ignored Felix who had suddenly begun shaking his head and waving his arms energetically. *Why not?* she mouthed.

He shrugged, pulled an expressive face and yawned dramatically.

Jess grinned, deciding to teach him a lesson. 'Come over for dinner.'

Felix's expression changed to alarm. *No!* he mouthed.

Marilyn didn't hesitate. 'When?' she asked.

'Boxing Day, if you're free. We can all slob around and recover from the day before.'

'Bliss.' She heard Marilyn draw on her cigarette. 'We've got Mother all Christmas Day, but they're being entertained and fed turkey leftovers on Boxing Day. At least it will give the poor old relatives a break.'

Jess felt a stab of sympathy for Marilyn's mother, who she hadn't even met. She wouldn't mind having a parent around for Christmas. And she especially wouldn't mind having a sister around . . . 'No turkey leftovers, I promise.' Jess smiled. Felix was doing a war dance on the bedroom carpet.

'Does Felix know?'

Jess watched him. 'We haven't exactly discussed it. Why?'

176

Marilyn's voice dropped in tone to a low purr. 'Oh, it's just that he and Peter have had a bit of a barney. Didn't he tell you?'

That explained Felix's reaction then. 'No, he didn't tell me.' She glared at him. 'It's not serious, is it?'

Felix's jaw and the towel he was using dropped at the same time.

'I doubt it.' Marilyn laughed her husky laugh. 'Boys will be boys, won't they?'

'And boys can be bloody childish,' Jess said pointedly. 'See you about eight thirty then? 'Bye.'

'All right, all right,' she said before Felix had a chance to speak. 'I know why you don't want them to come.'

'You do?' He blinked at her.

'But it's so short-sighted to let a silly argument get in the way of a flourishing company.' She turned to consider her wardrobe, pulling jeans and her favourite sweater from the shelf. What would she wear on Boxing Day? She lifted a black satin skirt with Christmas roses on from its hanger. No dubious stains from last year; it was certainly a possibility. It was pretty, but she only wore it at Christmas. The trouble was, she seemed to wear it every Christmas. Perhaps plain black would be making less of a statement? By the time she'd finished considering this, Felix was dressed.

'So what was it about?'

'What?'

'The row with Peter.'

'Oh, nothing important.'

Evasive again. Jess sighed. 'Felix . . .'

But he only kissed her nose, left the room and thundered down the stairs. Jess frowned. Why did she always get the impression that the only bits she had of Felix, the only bits she knew of Felix, were the bits that happened when they were together? The rest of the time, most of the time, he was in a world that seemed to have no space in it for her.

Chapter 13

'Hi.' Jess smiled at the man who opened the door to greet her. He was slightly older than herself, she guessed, of medium build and height, and dressed casually in green corduroys and a baggy Aran sweater. 'Jess Newman.' She held out a hand.

'Matthew Hill.' He smiled.

He had nice eyes, a friendly smile and a rather careworn expression. Jess decided that she wasn't in any immediate danger.

'Come on in.' He led the way inside.

She couldn't help wincing at the sight of the garish red and black hallway. Someone had tried to bring it into the nineteen sixties and produced something more like a badly decorated Indian restaurant.

'I know.' Apparently he had read her expression. 'And I should tell you straight off,' he let out a rueful sigh, 'that I've changed my mind about the living room.'

'Oh?' Then why had he bothered to invite her in? Jess prepared to walk straight out again.

'I think the hallway is crying out for attention . . .'

'Hmm.' She wouldn't disagree with that.

'Just that little bit louder.'

She smiled. 'So you want to think about the hallway *first*?' Was that what he was saying? She repressed a shiver of apprehension.

'Are you game?'

She shrugged. It was his house. 'It is the first bit you see.' Which was exactly the kind of thinking she had been applying to her own cottage.

'Precisely. And as it stands right now, it's a very weird welcome.' He ran his fingers along the red paintwork. 'Is it redeemable, do you think?'

'Everything is redeemable.' She gave it her closer attention. The hallway was large but had been made to seem cramped by the positioning of the antique telephone table and bench to the right of the front door. The stair carpet was dark red and well worn, the balustrade was black. Someone had spray-painted the radiator silver, perhaps in a misplaced attempt to make the space less dingy. It hadn't worked.

Jess was examining the hallway; she glanced at Matthew Hill and realised that he was examining her.

'How do you usually work?' he asked.

She wondered if she should admit that this was a first. Probably not. 'I charge for my time by the hour,' she said instead, naming a conservative figure. She wasn't exactly a professional, and despite what Patti had said on the phone last night about not underselling herself, she didn't want to put her first client off. 'With all materials on top,' she added.

'Sounds reasonable.'

'You agree to the terms?'

'I certainly do.' His mouth twitched. 'What do we do next?'

'We talk.' Jess began to suspect that he knew only too well that he was the first. And that for some reason he found this amusing.

'About anything in particular?'

'About your own ideas.' Was he winding her up? 'About what you like.'

His eyes gleamed. They were a light blue with a darker ring around the outside of the iris. Rather appealing; and his brown hair had a way of flopping over his forehead, that was, she had to admit, attractive.

'And what you dislike,' she said tartly, now on her guard against him. An attractive face and a hint of charm was about all it took. She was Felix's wife after all, and she knew enough about charm to fill a book. 'I'll draw a few preliminary sketches, then we'll talk about colour, theme, style and so on.'

'Over lunch?'

'Pardon?'

'Can we talk over lunch?' He glanced at his watch. 'I haven't actually eaten yet, have you?'

'Well, no.' In fact, Jess had been far too nervous to think about food. This could be her very first commission, the start of a new and exciting career. Help! But now that she'd actually met the man and the house and found them both to be relatively harmless, she realised she was ravenous.

'Good.' He led the way through another door. 'Come and criticise the kitchen.'

'It's . . . nice,' Jess said carefully as she followed him. She glanced around. Although nice was hardly the word for the expanse of cool white floor tiles, fitted units and gleaming chrome.

'Don't bother to be polite.' To her amusement he donned a blue and white apron, grabbed a loaf of granary bread that was sitting on the tiled work surface, and started to saw. 'I've got bread, pickles, Brie and tomatoes. That do you?'

'It sounds lovely.' Jess began warming to him. His charm was not at all like Felix's – this man wasn't even trying. She sat on a kitchen stool. 'But I'm not being polite,' she told him. 'There's nothing at all wrong with your kitchen.'

180

Admittedly, it wasn't to her taste; the seemingly endless chrome and white was cold and uninviting and even the kitchen cupboards looked as if they had come from a science laboratory. But it was clean, slick and contemporary. Jess realised that a lot of people would admire it.

Matthew grinned. 'Nothing wrong with it perhaps, but do you like it?'

'No.' It seemed to be a test, so perhaps it was safer to opt for honesty.

'Good.' He grabbed pickles from the cupboard above. 'If you liked it I'd be seriously worried about our future together.'

Jess stared at him. He was certainly an unusual man. Surely people didn't normally have these kind of interviews with their interior designers?

'It's way too modern for my taste,' he added, ripping the wrapping from a huge slice of Brie. 'Like cooking in a tin can. Wrecks the creativity.'

Jess opened her sketchbook, wrote *anti-modern* in capitals. 'Do you like wood?'

'At least it's a bit warmer.' He shivered. 'And talking of warmth, let's take this lot through to the conservatory; I never eat perched on a bar stool if I can avoid it. In fact ...' He looked around the room and she panicked. Was he about to change his mind again and fling her in at the deep end? She didn't think she was up to redesigning new kitchens just yet. 'I spend as little time as possible in here. I prefer comfort as well as warmth. How about you?' He handed her a tray to carry, and Jess had the impression he was asking something quite different from the obvious.

'I used terracotta in my own kitchen,' she told him, refusing to be drawn. 'It's deep but not dense. It reflects the light in different ways – depending on the time of day, of course.'

'Of course.' He laughed. 'Come through and take a seat.'

181

In the conservatory, which was a tiny sun-room leading off from the kitchen, he put the tray down on a glass-topped coffee table and collapsed into a low rattan chair.

Jess tried to perch on the edge of hers, but discovering it to be impossible, she gave in to the inevitable and sank into it as he had done. Beside her on the table was a photograph. 'Your wife?' The woman had short dark hair, determined eyes and a neat appearance. Hard, Jess thought, without knowing why. She seemed an unlikely mate for this man who, by his own admission, wanted comfort and warmth.

'Ex-wife.' He helped himself to bread and Brie and motioned to Jess to do the same.

'Oh.' She wondered then why he should keep a picture of her by his side. In her experience, most divorcees removed every trace of what they called their *mistake* from their new lives. She sneaked a look at him. Perhaps he still cared.

'She lives in Wales with our two kids,' he said. 'Sean and Magda, sixteen and twelve.'

'You must miss them.' The cheese, Jess found, was delicious, at just the right point of ripeness. And it didn't seem odd to be talking in such a personal manner to this, her first client. In fact, she was beginning to enjoy herself.

'Yes, I do.' He started to attack the contents of the jar of pickles before passing it to Jess.

She leaned over with some difficulty to take it from him. 'Do you get to see them very often?'

'Whenever I can – once a month and for part of the holidays.' He sighed. 'It's part of modern life, isn't it, the broken home?'

'I suppose.'

'Perhaps the family unit is outdated.' She couldn't read his expression. 'Perhaps it's too much to expect a couple to stay together for more than a few years.'

'Perhaps.' Jess was conscious of a hidden agenda here. She didn't mind a *light* discussion on the personal side. But

182

she most definitely did not want to become involved in his marital problems.

He bit into a tomato and after a moment went on. 'The kids look at it the right way. They see it as having the advantage of two homes instead of one, and always having someone else to complain to when one parent gives them a hard time.' He chuckled.

No one could accuse him of sentimentality, Jess thought.

'And at least I escape most of the teenage traumas. You?'

She blinked back at him. 'One daughter, Sophie, at university. No extreme teenage trauma to date.' Sophie, as everyone kept telling her, had always been sensible. Moreover, she was, as people also told her, a big girl now. But she was still Jess's girl, and what's more she had been due back from university three days ago.

'She's probably gone to Brighton,' Sophie's receptionist, the enigmatic Karin, had told her the day before yesterday when she phoned. 'I'm not going home myself till Christmas Eve.'

Jess took another bite of the delicious bread. They didn't want to prolong the agony of home life with the parents, one presumed. She really shouldn't worry . . . Sophie was obviously grabbing the chance to be with this Nick chap of hers while she could. But still, she should have phoned.

'Lucky you.' He continued to watch her appraisingly.

'Hmm?'

'To have no traumas.'

'Oh.' Did he treat all his new contacts this way? Did his patients offer him tea and scones when he visited their houses? Was he lonely? She guessed not. Still, it was bizarre, sitting in a rattan chair talking families in a weird kind of shorthand to a rather attractive but also very unsettling man.

For a few moments they ate in silence. The sun-room was pleasant, Jess decided, although it could do with some decent blinds, muslin maybe, that would float in the breeze in summer, with some blackout overheads for when it got too hot. Lemon grass came into her head, goodness knows why. The sharp smell of it first. Then she could see a colour palette of yellows, taupe greens and ochres; shapes that were long and slender, slightly drooping. In the up-lighters perhaps, the fronds of palms and ferns, the subtle statement of a tall and elegant green glass vase. The picture began to build, as it always did when she was in someone else's house. Something bamboo stretching into that alcove over there – a screen, or a bookcase. The trouble came, she thought wryly, in trying to stop.

Abruptly, he put down his tray and got to his feet. 'I forgot the wine.'

'Oh, but I shouldn't . . .'Jess didn't make a habit of drinking at lunchtime, even when she wasn't working. And surely it wasn't professional to drink on the job?

'Just a small one, then?' He produced a South African red from a rack in the corner. 'Is this all right? The cheese requires it, don't you think? And this room tends to keep it at the perfect temperature.'

She laughed. Why not? 'Just a small one,' she agreed, taking the glass from him.

'Is your daughter coming back for Christmas?' he asked.

'Oh, I think so.' She realised how ridiculous that sounded. Surely she should know -- it was the day before Christmas Eve after all. 'It's important, isn't it, to be with your family at Christmas?' She babbled on, half-thinking of Louisa, half-wanting to prolong the conversation at any cost, rather than listen to her own munching. And she could hardly start discussing the hallway – let alone make notes and eat lunch at the same time – when neither of them could even see it from here.

'Families . . . That is what it's supposed to be all about.'

Sharply, she looked up. 'I'm sorry, I forgot.' Perhaps it

184

was a recent separation; perhaps he was still bitter, as well as still in love with his wife.

'Bloody hell, no.' He laughed. 'Don't imagine I miss family Christmases,' he said, 'because I don't.'

'Not at all?'

'Certainly not.' He sipped the wine, his eyes showing his pleasure. 'I'm not a churchgoer, I have faith in medicine not in God, and Christmas was never a time of joy for me.'

'Really?' Jess raised her eyebrows. But she had some sympathy for that line of thought. And anyway, whatever Christmas had originally meant had long ago been drowned in the commercial razzmatazz.

'I never got too much of a kick from balancing a living tree in a bucket with pieces of brick, nor from the realisation that however many they got, my children would always want more presents.'

Jess smiled to herself.

'I never asked to grapple with a turkey that was ten pounds bigger than we needed, and I certainly never wanted to listen to Pamela's . . . sorry.' He broke off abruptly and raised one hand in apology, as he caught sight of Jess's expression.

'Christmas does tend to bring emotions and greed to the surface,' she concurred. 'I complain about the preparations and the blatant commercialism every single year.' What a prig she sounded. And what exactly had she done in the way of preparation this time? 'But I always find myself wallowing in the nostalgia of it in the end.' That at least was true enough.

Matthew nodded. 'I know exactly what you mean.'

'So what will you do?'

'I shall phone my children to say hello; I shall go off for a very long walk in countryside guaranteed to be deserted . . .'

Jess smiled again at this; it did sound very appealing.

'And I shall be back home by three o'clock because I'm on call.'

'On call?'

'I mentioned that I'm a GP?' He offered her the last of the cheese, but she declined. She had already eaten more than she should.

'Of course you did.' Half a glass of wine and she was already losing her touch.

'People do have a habit of getting ill on Christmas Day,' he said. 'And you wouldn't believe the disasters. The accident and emergency department at the hospital is always chock-a-block.'

'Probably due to all those emotions flying around,' Jess murmured.

'Thanks to the vast amounts of alcohol consumed.'

'Not to mention the food.' They exchanged a strangely conspiratorial glance of amusement.

'Which is why I'm always busy and why I need someone to decorate my house,' he concluded, draining his glass.

Jess thought she could detect a hint. 'Shall we go back through to the hallway then,' she suggested. 'I can't do much from here.'

'Whatever you say.' His expression once again told her nothing. 'You're the lady in charge.'

What kind of doctor would he be, she wondered. Kind? Friendly? Probably, she guessed, a good one, and one who would not suffer fools gladly. She staggered to her feet with some difficulty due to the combination of a huge lunch and the low level of the rattan chair.

'It's good to be busy, though,' he said.

She noticed his eyes had dulled slightly, almost as if he were remembering some pain. Her gaze strayed to the picture of his wife.

He followed it. 'I keep it there to remind me,' he said.

'Of good times?'

186

But he only laughed with some bitterness. 'Work keeps me busy. Doctors don't have time for loneliness. Nor self-indulgence, believe me.'

Should she ask what was really troubling him or move smoothly on to the subject of the hall? The first option was too personal, definitely too intimate for an interior designer, so she chose option number two. 'Can you give me an idea of your budget?' she asked him.

He shrugged, naming a figure that seemed to have been chosen more or less at random.

'And what kind of look are you after?'

He frowned in confusion.

She tried a new tack. 'What do you want to keep?'

'None of the colours.' He pulled a face. 'The table and bench are OK.'

Jess made notes. She too liked the telephone table and the old mahogany bench, but they would need to be moved to create more space. She narrowed her eyes, imagining a certain cornflower blue for the main shade that would contrast well with the colour and style of this mahogany and somewhat formal furniture. It would also be a good colour for the carpet, if he wanted carpet rather than some of the more contemporary options. They would need something much softer to go with the blue, though; a raffia with just a hint of pale yellow perhaps? It was important, she felt, to consider the colour palette first, and then build, using clean lines, eliminating clutter.

She turned her attention back to the stairs. The very design of it was clutter at its worst. 'Would you be interested in my designing a new balustrade?'

He cast an odd look in her direction. 'You wouldn't make it yourself, surely?'

She shook her head. 'I'd do sketches, then I'd give it to a carpenter. He would do the drawings to scale and then he'd make it. Naturally, I would get your approval for the design.' She sounded pompous now, as well as a prig. Patti would roar if she could hear her.

'All right.' Matthew Hill seemed determined to leave the entire matter of his new hallway to Jess.

She walked slowly up the stairs. 'A runner might look good.' Traditional and flat weave would blend nicely. And then there was the lighting – that was a big problem in this hallway. 'We need a focus,' she murmured. Perhaps a piece of sculptural lighting. She loved the idea of discarding traditional base and shade and just selecting a shape, a glowing object that was an artwork in its own right. But a classic shape would be best, to blend with the existing furniture and mood.

'Do you reckon so?' For the first time she picked up on his Dorset accent.

'Oh, yes. And we might try the salvage yard for a new radiator.' She put her head to one side. 'Or we could do a disguise job on this one. Get rid of that awful silver that makes it look like a juke-box from the fifties . . .'

He chuckled.

'And maybe add a shelf, a mirror, or something organic.'

'Mmm. OK.'

'The staircase could do with a more classic feel.' Jess made another note. 'What's your opinion on colours?' He might hate blue. 'Do you prefer bold or neutral? Bright or muted?'

He frowned once more.

'Peacock green? Orange with purple spots?' It was probably because of the wine, and it wasn't exactly professional, but Jess was becoming exasperated. She couldn't help it. She wanted *some* input, for goodness' sake.

'Sorry.' He smiled again. 'You see, I realise that I need to update my life, but I'm not terribly good at knowing how to do it. What about you making a free choice?'

Jess chewed the end of her pencil. A disgusting habit,

Felix always said. This was something she had been avoiding, mainly because she was more than aware of her amateur status, and just plain scared she'd mess up his house. There was, after all, no guarantee that he would like anything she did. And his lack of input also meant that she had to act part-psychologist. In a way – as it was his house and his money she was using – she had to assess his personality and go for something slightly different to what he would choose himself (otherwise there was no point in her being here) and yet close enough to his taste for it to be acceptable. He had to live with it; she could walk away. It was tricky, something she'd never had to consider before.

'I'm sure it will be a marvellous improvement,' he said, as if knowing what she was thinking.

She wished she shared his confidence. 'But I want to be sure you'll like it.' She tapped her pencil on the sketchpad.

'There are no guarantees in life.'

Abruptly, Jess moved away. She knew *that* only too well. 'I'll bring some testers and some catalogues along for you to look at,' she said in a brisk voice. 'When would suit you?'

He went across to the telephone table and they checked diaries, making a date for the third of January.

'We'll do some test patches then,' Jess told him, moving towards the door. Perhaps she shouldn't have had lunch with him, let alone entered any discussion of such an intimate nature, but what the hell. She had enjoyed herself. 'And afterwards, I'll have to come back a few times so we can assess the colours in various lights.' She paused. 'Living space has to look good by day and by night,' she said. Bloody know-all.

'Fine.' She wasn't sure whether or not he liked the idea. Did he know how much time she would have to spend in his hallway before the job was done? He took a step towards her, but it was only to shake her hand. 'I'll look forward to it.'

Jess found to her irritation that it was hard to look him in the eye. 'And in the meantime I'll do some sketches,' she said, with a brief – hopefully professional – smile. His touch on her hand was warm, like the man himself.

'Keep in touch.' He smiled.

'I will. And thanks for the lunch.' She walked quickly down the driveway.

'And Jess?' he called after her.

She looked back, seeing an unusual man whom she was inexplicably drawn to. 'Yes?'

'Happy Christmas,' he said.

Back home, Jess found her husband in the sitting room listening to *Madam Butterfly* blaring full blast from four speakers, and her daughter's suitcase in the hall.

For a moment she leaned against the wall in pure relief. You knew they could look after themselves, but how could you ever stop yourself from worrying? So that would be three for Christmas dinner after all.

When the doorbell rang a little later, she peered out of the sitting-room window and thought she was imagining things, for the figure on the doorstep was another Sophie, quite tall and not very substantial, though with shorn hair.

She hardly dared hope . . . She ran out and opened the door to see huge green eyes and a wide grinning mouth set in a gamine face that she remembered very well. She thought it was a mirage, caused by unaccustomed lunchtime drinking or simply exhaustion. But mirages didn't burst into tears before sweeping you up into a huge hug. There would be four for Christmas dinner. It was Louisa all right. Sixteen years on and hardly changed a bit.

Chapter 14

'I must finish this blasted ivy.'

Jess was wearing a huge boiler suit and had – somewhat fiercely, Louisa thought – tied her dark frizz of hair inside a particularly unbecoming and paint-splashed chiffon scarf. Watching her, Louisa shook her head in disbelief. 'But it's Christmas Eve.'

'So?'

'So, shouldn't you be,' she was almost ashamed to say it, 'well, cooking or something?'

'Cooking?' From Jess's indignant tone, she might have said she should be having fellatio on the lawn. What was wrong with cooking, for heaven's sake? Louisa hadn't expected her first prodigal meal to be takeaway Chinese. And now, Jess apparently *had* to finish painting her kitchen. And with ivy. She was beginning to doubt her sister's sanity.

She narrowed her eyes as Jess carefully repositioned the stepladder by the west-facing wall of the kitchen and bit her bottom lip. Though Louisa couldn't complain about her welcome (and, *what did you expect?* some little voice whispered); she and Jess had hugged a lot and cried a lot, had a couple of big drinks and then Jess had glanced at her watch,

191

screamed in horror, ordered a meal from the takeaway and laid more dustsheets ready for the morning. This morning she had pleaded a headache, sent Sophie out shopping and promptly got out her painting gear.

'Or putting up decorations,' Louisa said hopefully. Felix and Jess hadn't been living here very long, admittedly, and she knew that moving house was meant to be the second most stressful experience after divorce (or was it the other way round? And where did death of a loved one and giving up smoking come into it?) but it wasn't exactly Christmassy in Cliff Cottage. This was hardly the picture she'd painted herself. No cosy log fire – only a central heating system that was so temperamental Jess had been compelled to literally kick it into action this morning. No tantalising whiffs of mince pies, cinnamon or mulled wine coming from the kitchen, only paint and the tang of white spirit on a musty cloth, and not a Labrador puppy in sight. No crystal, no porcelain. Jess and Felix hadn't even got a tree.

'Decorations?' Jess might never have heard the word.

'Oh, never mind,' Louisa shook her head. Her sister was not with it. Not with it at all. So much for traditional family Christmases in England; how could she have longed for one every single year?

At this point in the conversation Jess took a leap from the second rung of the stepladder and disappeared out of the kitchen.

'What?'

'Back in a mo.'

She returned, tossing something on to Louisa's lap.

'Huh?' Lots of brightly coloured books of sticky paper. What was she supposed to do with these?

'Paper-chains.' Jess wore a wicked smile as she approached the step ladder once more. 'Remember *Blue Peter*? And it's not my fault we're un-Christmassy. We didn't even know you were coming.'

Louisa licked a piece of gummed paper. Disgusting. But what Jess said was very true. She hadn't known herself that she was coming. It had taken her a few days to get it together, zoom off to Sussex and track down Jess's whereabouts. But when she'd got the new address and number tucked in her rucksack, she had known she wouldn't be able to leave it there. She had to come. She must make amends – or something.

What she had not known was that she would be expected to make the blasted Christmas decorations. Louisa pulled a face at her sister's back. But Jess was entitled to a little sisterly reproach, she supposed. After all, how could Jess hope to live up to Louisa's fantasies if the poor woman had no idea of what they were? The trouble was, Louisa was beginning to realise that these convenient fantasies she had carted around Europe and beyond over the last sixteen years had no basis in reality whatsoever.

'I only thought you'd be into all that sort of stuff,' she said mid-lick, flexing her dry and horrible-tasting tongue, 'because you've got Sophie.' Although the long-legged streak with the silver nose stud whom she'd met last night had been another revelation. 'Don't people do all the Christmas thing for their kids any more?' she asked innocently.

'Kids?' Jess's eyebrows shot towards the freshly painted ceiling that she'd referred to as Irish linen when she'd shown Louisa around last night (though it looked more like off-white to be honest). 'Sophie's hardly a kid any more.'

'I forgot. I didn't think.' Louisa winced at the taste of her fifth chain. It would take an awful long time and an awful lot of spit to make a chain long enough to stretch from one end of a room to the other. Any room; even the loo. But face it, she hadn't thought at all, about any of it. She had been so fond of imagining Jess in the midst of a calm domestic routine, husband at her side, child on her knee,

fresh coffee on the hob, that she'd entirely forgotten what
Jess was really like. She wasn't the calm child-on-your-knee
type. She was wild, she went her own way, and always had.
She was a little bit crazy, scatty as Larry and hated both
housework and coffee. Which must explain why she was
painting an ivy stencil on her pale green kitchen wall (what
had Jess called it? Fennel? Ye gods . . .) on Christmas Eve.

'Did Mum and Dad do any of that?' Jess had stopped
mid-sponging.

Louisa didn't trust herself to speak and she probably
wouldn't be able to anyway since her tongue was stuck to
the roof of her mouth with paper-chain glue.

'Maybe they did . . .' Jess seemed thoughtful. Then she
turned to Louisa with one of her wide beaming smiles that
lit up the room. 'I'm sorry we're not what you expected.'

'No . . . I—'

'But I'm so glad you came,' Jess said. 'I always hoped
you'd turn up like this one day.' She leaned back to assess
the effect so far. 'And I knew you'd manage to take me by
surprise.'

She was being too nice. Why didn't she ask her why she
hadn't kept in touch a little more efficiently; why she hadn't
been back in sixteen years? Louisa threw down the paper-
chains in disgust. She hated feeling guilty. 'You're really
into all this, aren't you?'

Jess blinked. 'Painting? Oh, yes.' Her expression softened
as if she were remembering. 'I got the bug after Sophie was
born and you left.'

'The bug?' And why didn't she already know all this
about her own sister?

'Changing colours.' Jess dipped her sponge into the paint
again. 'You know.'

'For fun?' Louisa had never decorated a room in her life.
She could see that it fulfilled a need. Some of the dingy
rooms she'd stayed in could have done with a bit of bright-

194

ening up, if only to hide the damp patches. But she couldn't see how breathing in paint fumes, covering yourself in wallpaper paste, and wielding brush or roller until your arm ached could actually be related to pleasure.

'Not just for fun.' Jess's expression was enigmatic. 'Sometimes the colour's the only thing you can change.'

I don't know her, Louisa thought. And she shrank from that.

'I did Sophie a tangerine nursery.' Jess was laughing now. The stencil half-forgotten, she had turned towards Louisa, her eyes bright, a big smudge of green paint on her nose. 'It was total transformation.'

'I bet.' Louisa was beginning to catch her mood. It had always been that way. They had sparked off one another once upon a time. 'Did it give the poor girl terrible nightmares, or did she just develop an aversion to oranges?'

'Neither.' Jess giggled. 'Of course it was offset by the royal blue stencilling.'

'Of?'

'Crescent moons.'

'Oh, my God. As in . . .?' They started singing together. 'Blue moon . . .' And then they were both laughing, real bellylaughing, clutching their sides. It probably wouldn't be remotely funny to anyone else. But Jess grabbed the top of the stepladder to stop herself falling. She had forgotten how easily they could make one another laugh. And the song had been a favourite of their childhood. It had been one of the few songs that made their father come over all romantic, take their mother in his arms, waltz her ceremoniously up and down the kitchen. He could be fun, Jess remembered. Though it seemed to need Louisa's presence to remind her of that fact.

'You are so weird.' But Lousia's face belied her words.

Jess smiled at her. The laughter was still there in her eyes, and she looked so young and beautiful without a trace of the weary mask that she'd been wearing on and off since she'd arrived, a mask that made her someone quite different from the sister Jess remembered. Her taste in clothes hadn't changed too much though. This morning she was wearing a lime-green top and baggy trousers in a parrot print of green, blue and yellow. And her face still looked child-like and still had its faintly bruised sheen that Jess remembered so well. *My darling child.* Their father's voice came back to her. Jess sighed. It had always been Louisa. She had never been his darling child, and never would be now. Lightly, Jess brushed her free hand across her eyes. But it wasn't Louisa's fault, was it, that she had been loved more than Jess? And it was too ridiculous, to think of such things now. She swallowed a lump in her throat, realised that Louisa had got to her feet and was standing beside the stepladder.

'What is it you really want to change?' Louisa asked her.

Jess stared at the south-facing wall, at her luscious and deep terracotta that did such wonderful things with sunlight. Change? My life, she thought. But, 'Nobody's perfect,' she said instead.

'Felix?'

Louisa had a way, Jess recalled, at prodding about in the messy bits of other people's lives until she came upon a truth. She had always been that way, only Jess had forgotten.

She couldn't simply say, *everything is fine*, as she had to the rest of them. It was different with Louisa. 'Felix had an affair,' she told her. She had to face it head on. Anyway, Louisa probably knew Jess's fears without her even voicing them. Maybe she had worked out long ago why Jess had never wanted her to come and live with them after their parents died. Louisa had always known the darker secrets, or so it seemed to Jess.

But now Louisa's eyes were wide. 'I thought . . .'

'What?'

'That you were so happy.' She stumbled over the words.

Jess sighed again. 'Most of the time we were.' What was it she had told Patti about being satisfied with a good deal? 'We are,' she said.

'When was it?'

'When I had Sophie.'

The eyes grew wider.

Jess knew what Louisa was thinking. Hesitatingly, making herself continue with the stencil purely because she needed something to do with her hands and eyes, she told her the story, just the bare bones, not bothering with the emotion. The cupboard door in her head might be left ajar these days, but the stuff inside could still make one hell of a mess on the carpet.

'And now?' Louisa asked when she had finished. 'Is it still going on?'

'I'm not sure.' Honesty still hurt sometimes. 'Not with her, but . . .' Was there someone else? Could there possibly be? There had been lilies, there had been nights of working late. Signs. Every woman knows about such things. There had been Felix's desperation, and there was a missing sense of truth – a truth and a trust that she longed for between them. But there was nothing she could recognise for sure.

Louisa nodded her head vigorously as if she understood. Her short dark hair fitted as closely as a skull cap; her eyes and her mouth seemed huge. 'Who was it?'

'A woman from work.'

More nods. It was so bloody predictable, wasn't it, to have an affair with your secretary.

Louisa moved towards the kettle and filled it with water. Jess allowed herself a small smile. She might be unconventional, but she still reached for the kettle, thinking of tea in times of crisis, like so many other women she knew.

'But why?' Louisa hadn't finished with the questions. And it might be twisting the knife, but no pain, no gain.

'You mean why did he do it?' Jess had often asked herself

197

this. After all, their sex life was pretty rampant by anyone's standards. It was silly to wonder, but wasn't she pretty enough, intelligent enough, what? Was she simply not enough?

'No.' Louisa's face hardened. 'Even if he loves you, he would do it because it's fun to play around and he probably isn't the faithful type, I know *that*.'

Ouch. Jess flinched. But at the same time it struck her that Louisa's characteristically tactless description had left *her* out of the equation. Felix did it because of the way Felix was, not because of Jess's shortcomings. And this idea, simple and brilliant as it was, took some digesting.

'What I meant was, why do you . . . why *did* you,' she corrected herself, 'put up with it? Why didn't you leave him?'

'Oh, Louisa.' Jess's arms were killing her. She sponged in the last leaf and gently peeled the stencil from the wall. 'It's not so easy to throw everything away.' Perhaps Louisa's life hadn't taught her about pain and compromise. She was working in black and white, while – in the pain and compromise department – Jess unfortunately had entire colour palettes at her disposal.

'But he hurt you.' Louisa reached up to touch Jess's arm.

'Oh, yes. He hurt me. But that was *then*.' Jess folded the stepladder up with a bang. 'I was young, I had a baby to look after. I'm older and wiser now.'

'Did you stay with him because of Sophie?' she asked.

'No.' It was never that simple. 'But when I had Sophie, I was vulnerable.'

'And he hurt you.' They stared at one another.

Louisa seemed to realise that this was supreme lack of tact even by her standards. She started to apologise, but Jess stopped her.

'Felix and I have been through a lot,' she told her. 'And I never wanted a saint.'

198

Louisa's expression was thoughtful as she waited for the kettle to boil, as if Jess's life were a tricky piece of algebra. Enough puzzling over it would solve the problems once and for all. 'But you still want to change him,' she said.

'Change *something*,' Jess corrected, wondering if it were true. Could a leopard change its spots? Would you want it to? Rooms, she concluded, were so much easier than people. And leopards.

'And there I was,' Louisa murmured, 'thinking you had everything. A man who loves you to death exactly as you are, total security, the whole caboodle.'

Jess smiled. 'What made you think such a crazy thing?' Only, wasn't that what every woman craved?

'I don't know. I stopped understanding you.' Louisa frowned, a small frown that Jess wanted to wipe from her face. Because she was beginning to see why Louisa had really stayed away for so long.

'When you had Sophie,' she said, 'it seemed like some great gulf opened up between us.' The kettle came to the boil and she made the tea, her movements slow and deliberate. 'I mean, I didn't have the same experience. You were a woman, I was a girl. What did I have without Dad? And Dad . . .' She faltered. 'You had Felix and then you had a child. I had . . .'

'We weren't as different as you thought.' Though they had never admitted it.

'Yeah, but having a baby.' Louisa's fingernails drummed on the work surface in front of her. Clearly she had decided that one confession required another. 'It seemed like you were Mrs Convention, Mrs two point four children and a semi, and I was . . .'

'Who were you?' Jess took her hands.

'I was Miss Nowhere.'

For a few moments they were silent. 'Hey.' This wasn't how Jess had envisaged their first meeting after sixteen

199

years. 'You're here now. Stay as long as you can. Please?'

Louisa's eyes strayed past Jess's shoulder to the back garden. 'I might,' she said, 'if I can get a load of that.'

Jess spun round. Rupert, looking particularly long, moody and interesting, was staggering up the back path, partly obscured by the blue spruce tree in a big red pot that he was carrying. Good old Rupert! Jess grinned. And Louisa had said that Cliff Cottage lacked the Christmas spirit . . .

Jess came to a decision. She climbed out of the boiler suit and grabbed an apron from the hook by the door. She had been too busy by half, but from now on she would make up for it. She would stick and hang paper-chains as if her life depended on it, then she'd start preparing stuffings for the turkey and brandy butter for the pud. She would get Sophie, Louisa and Rupert to decorate the tree; she would finish wrapping her presents, and do everyone a surprise stocking for the morning. She might even manage to vacuum the carpets, although that might be a little premature with the needles from the tree and all.

She yanked open the back door. 'Rupert, you're an amazing man.'

He dumped the tree on the kitchen floor and straightened up with some difficulty, his surprised stare moving from the top of Jess's head to Louisa's lime-green parrot outfit and back again.

Chiffon scarf. Jess pulled it off and pushed the frizz of her hair behind her ears instead. 'This is my sister, Louisa,' she said, as she began to pull down all her recipe books from the top of the dresser. She had work to do. It was Christmas Eve and she was going to give them what they wanted. She would make Christmas special if it killed her.

Felix was in bed with Marilyn and thinking about Jess. He could lose her if he carried on with this; he could lose everything. He knew he should sort it out before it was too late. He must. It had been a bloody stupid, spur-of-the-moment, risk to take. One that he should have resisted; would have resisted if it hadn't been for bloody Peter thinking he could run his life and then Jess – too busy with her friends, with her life, with her new bloody career.

And then . . . OK, so he had given in, taken Marilyn Beck up on her offer. And the sex had been as good as he expected. Still, it should have been a one night stand; or in this case one very long and intimate afternoon. And afterwards, he knew what he should have done. He should have come over the guilty husband, made it clear that this wouldn't be happening again; he should have returned to his wife and his promises. Because only once wasn't too bad, was it? Only once said minor indiscretion. More than that said you wanted what was on offer.

So, why hadn't he finished it? Felix kissed the olive-skinned shoulder by his side. He wasn't entirely sure. He only knew that when he was with her he longed for Jess, and when he was with Jess he wished she could make him feel just a little like Marilyn made him feel: strong, powerful, more of a man. Litton Cheney continued to beckon, and the woman who lived there didn't like the word no.

Surreptitiously, he glanced at his watch. 'I'll have to be making a move . . .'

This was always the difficult bit. Women – for some reason that was totally beyond him – expected the post-coital time (cuddling, non-sexual caressing, lovey-dovey stuff and in Marilyn's case a fag) to go on for ever. Less than fifteen minutes and you were accused of jumping out of the bed *as soon as you'd got what you wanted*. Well? So what? It was what you were there for. You knew it, the lady knew it. Why bother to pretend otherwise? And women said that men weren't honest . . .

'Peter will be ages,' Marilyn reassured him. 'You can stay and have some coffee at least.'

201

But coffee would take too long. 'It's Christmas Eve,' Felix reminded her. 'I've got things to do.' Not that he felt very much like doing them. And he was certainly not looking forward to Boxing Day. He hadn't forgiven Marilyn for agreeing to that, nor for phoning Cliff Cottage in the first place. She could be a bitch; he would swear she had only accepted the invitation because Jess had sounded all sleepy and saturated on the phone. *Were you screwing her?* Marilyn had asked, as if he shouldn't be making love to his own wife. No, it was Marilyn he was screwing, Jess he was loving.

Marilyn pouted and leaned herself up on one elbow. 'God, I'm not looking forward to tomorrow.'

Felix took advantage of this movement to leap out of bed and pull his clothes on. The arm that had been round her had gone to sleep. He shook it angrily, waiting for the feeling to return.

'Don't you want a shower?'

Oh, sure. He could just imagine Peter coming home to catch him wet and dripping on his bedroom floor. At least if they were in bed he could – if pushed – make a getaway if he heard the car; not ideal, but the bedroom faced the road and he knew the sound of the Range Rover. But in the shower he wouldn't have a chance in hell. 'I'll have one at the Sports Centre,' he told her.

'So you don't smell of me?' Marilyn rolled on to her stomach.

What did she think? 'It wouldn't do us much good if Jess found out. Or Peter.'

But Marilyn only shrugged herself deeper into the pillow. 'He knows I need someone else.' She curled up her legs and turned her face towards him, eyeing Felix hungrily. 'Someone bigger, someone better.'

Despite his recent resolution, Felix felt himself getting another hard-on. He knew it was bloody silly, but the woman made him feel good. She said the right things.

But there was no time for that. He must get back to Cliff Cottage, Jess, Sophie and now Louisa. And wasn't she a turn-up? It was good for Jess, he supposed, to have her sister there. And it gave him some breathing space that he should be using to sort things out.

But she was certainly a surprise. Jess's sister had changed from the gawky schoolgirl who had left Sussex all those years ago. In another life, if she were someone else's sister, he might even have found her attractive. Mind, her way-out clothes were a turn-off – he could have done with sunglasses when he faced that green sweater she was wearing this morning.

But there was nothing wrong with what was inside the sweater. Slimmer than his usual taste, slimmer than Jess, even slimmer than the woman in the bed over there. If Louisa Parris weren't such a beanpole, she'd be a beauty, for sure. But despite all that, she didn't have half of what Jess had. What she *did* have was an attitude. Oh, yes. She had one hell of an attitude. And attitude, as he had learned in the past, could be bloody dangerous.

Chapter 15

Despite her mother's valiant efforts, Sophie Newman was not having a happy time.

She sighed. Happy time? Christmas was an utter con. It started in childhood, and was entirely based on deceit. What hope for happiness then? Parents lied, encouraged a belief in an unlikely being called Father Christmas (part man, part other, be it of the bat, spider, wonder, or flashing variety). Literally here today and gone tomorrow; a man not given to sticking around. A man... Involuntarily, she thought of Nick. But FC entered young lives on Christmas Eve for only a fleeting visit. And not only did he enter young lives – which was bad enough, because he was scary-big with a white beard and red cloak – but he entered young bedrooms, for Christ's sake. When the young were asleep (and probably parents were too, so they wouldn't be around to do any defending).

Sophie stretched out her legs and tasted the unusual silence of Christmas afternoon, broken only by the noises coming from the kitchen. Was her mother asleep? Her eyes were closed. Probably out of sheer exhaustion, since she'd been running around like a blue-arsed fly all yesterday. But why? Christmas today was as incomprehensible as

Christmas then, with its threat of FC and what he would or wouldn't do. What girl needed the promise of a man creeping up on her with a sack when she was at her most vulnerable? Was that supposed to make a girl happy??? All Sophie remembered was the fear.

She swirled thick red glutinous cherry brandy around the sides of her glass. Going to sleep, knowing some huge, male stranger would come to her bedroom – but it was OK, he had presents, forget all that stuff about strangers and sweeties and not getting into people's cars.

She took a sip. Yuck, but preferable to the tea her mother had made. It was wind-down time – four thirty in the afternoon signalled a temporary lull in alcohol consumption. Her father and Rupert had been dragooned into clearing the table and washing up everything that wouldn't fit into the dishwasher, Mums and Aunt Louisa were flopped side by side on the sofa. And Sophie? She was torn, just as children were torn at Christmas between the magical fairytale bits (FC was on the blurred edge of this; you just hoped it would be all right) and the story of the Christ child, which was apparently *what it was all about*, despite all evidence to the contrary.

She shifted in the armchair. Another cushion, just here, in the small of her back... So – just as you began to accept it, love it and long for Christmas all year round, what happened? You discovered none of it was true, that your parents (whom you used to trust) had lied to you for years. It was all one big con.

Sophie glanced at her mother as if this were her fault. Well, she was part of the deceit. And then you were reduced to this. A glass of cherry brandy and a ridiculous longing to phone Nick, and to hell with the consequences. To hear his voice, to get something – anything – from him today.

Her Aunt Louisa, who didn't seem too bad, though she wore weird clothes that made her mother look almost

205

normal in comparison, yawned loudly. 'I remember when we used to play charades at Christmas.'

Please, no. Mums had certainly gone all out to make the day swing, but you had to draw the line somewhere when parents threatened to get too silly and embarrassing.

'Charades.' Her mother's eyes remained closed. 'I remember that too.'

Sophie eyed her with pity. Nostalgia, she could live without. There was only one place she wanted to be, and it wasn't here with her parents, her aunt and the man next door. Rupert was OK – obviously in love with Mums, which was rather romantic, although a waste of his time since she'd never leave Dad. Earlier, Sophie had asked him why he didn't spend Christmas with *his* parents and his answer had quite impressed her. *Because I don't want to.* Brilliantly simple. Couldn't be faulted, really.

'How long have you got off, Sophie?' Louisa asked, probably in sympathy with Mums, wondering how long her mother would have to put up with her.

She thought of Nick. 'Ages.' Too, too long, although maybe that was a good thing since she had so much work to catch up on.

'And you're enjoying it?'

'What?'

'University. Studying history.'

Suddenly, Sophie was fed up with it all. With the gentle nagging for info from Mums, with Louisa trying to be an interested aunt after all these years. With Nick for not being here, not being with her, at a time that was supposed to be special. 'I hate it,' she said. 'I hate university, and I hate history even more.'

Jess's eyes blinked open. 'Sophie!'

She didn't have to look at her to gauge her reaction. Horror... OK, all this booze had loosened her tongue, but she was glad she'd said it, relieved to be honest about it for once. 'It's true.' She looked up in defiance. Her mother's expression made her shrink with guilt, but Louisa's sympathetic half-smile encouraged her to elaborate. 'University is a waste of three years,' she said firmly. Three years that felt like a lifetime. 'And history is complete and utter bunk.' Someone (she couldn't recall who) had said that once; someone else had called history a dust-heap and little more than rumour. All descriptions were pretty accurate.

'Bunk?' Jess echoed.

'Because you don't know for sure that any of it's true?' Rupert, entering the room from the kitchen, where his brief alliance with her father against the washing up was apparently at an end, lost no time in joining in with the philosophical spirit of the conversation.

'But there's evidence to support most of it,' Louisa objected. 'Apart from way back.'

'Possibly manufactured,' Rupert said. 'Most probably biased.'

Sophie was beginning to like him even more.

'You can't discount all of it.' Louisa frowned. 'And surely it's worthwhile to study the way things were? Even if every little detail isn't exactly spot on.'

Sophie looked down at her lap. Better than looking at her mother, who seemed to be in shock.

'I never knew you hated it,' Jess whispered. 'Why didn't you tell me before?'

'Oh, because...' She didn't want to go on. Because her mother would be upset, because she had been so proud, because she would see it as a failure, Sophie's failure.

She saw her take a deep breath, one of Mums's, *I am searching for patience from deep within*, sort of deep breaths. 'It's important for you to get your degree, darling,' she said.

But what if Sophie didn't want a silly degree? 'Why?' she demanded. 'What use will a history degree ever be to me?'

'It will give you the opportunity to make choices.' Jess slammed her mug down so hard on the coffee table in front of her that the remaining tea slopped over the sides. 'Having a decent degree gives you a say in your own life.'

'A say in your own life?' Sophie heard her own voice rising and petulant. 'Writing off three years in some silly institution, rather than earning and living in the real world does that?'

'No—'

'Throwing the certificate they give you in the waste bin, because you've decided to do something worthwhile – does that give you a say in your own life?'

'No.' Jess was flushed, though her voice was still calm. 'But you'll get the chance of a better paid, more challenging job that will give you a higher standard of living, more choices, more personal fulfilment—'

'That's utter crap!' What did her mother know? Only what she'd heard from people her own age – friends like their ex-neighbour Ruth, who had missed out on her education the first time around. Her mother had chucked away *her* education to get married. That was a choice, a real choice. Why couldn't she have the same?

'It isn't crap,' Jess said.

'But it isn't the real world either,' Sophie retorted, half-apologetic, telling herself to be nicer to her mother on Christmas Day. And thinking of Nick, who would be on her mother's side in all this. 'It hasn't got any meaning.'

But she wasn't to be diverted so easily. 'It's the only way to get a good job, a job that requires a qualified graduate,' she said. She shot a swift glance towards Louisa and Rupert, as if warning them not to revert to the theory of the thing. 'And you *wanted* to do history.'

Sophie shrugged. If she had, she couldn't recall it being a passionate ambition. In truth she hadn't known what she wanted to do. And apart from being with Nick, she still didn't. 'Maybe I don't want a *good* job.' She was scornful. 'Not if it means spending three years learning about a past that's dead and buried and no one bloody well cares.'

Her mother was still staring at her. 'Is all this to do with Nick?' she asked.

'No.' Sophie's cheeks were burning. Although the education he'd given her had certainly made her see things in a different light. She finished her drink and got unsteadily to her feet. 'It's what I think. It's what I feel.'

'Because you could have asked him here. He could have come for Christmas.'

'He couldn't.' That wasn't it at all. Couldn't Mums even try to understand?

'But why not?' Her mother looked genuinely baffled. 'Is it his job? His parents? Doesn't he want to meet—'

'He's an estate agent.'

'Bloody hell.' Felix, who had walked into the room, promptly walked out again.

What was wrong with being an estate agent? She noticed Jess and Louisa exchange a glance. It absolutely infuriated her. How dare they sit in judgement? 'And besides,' she said as she flounced out of the room. She would show them. 'He happens to be married.'

Jess looked at Louisa in consternation. 'Married?' She groaned and put her head in her hands. What next?

'The decent ones always are married,' Louisa said gloomily, helping herself to an olive. She sounded like Patti on a bad day.

'But Sophie's only eighteen,' Jess wailed. They weren't all married at eighteen. At eighteen you played the field and went out with students from your university, not with married estate agents who lived back in your home town.

'Would you let me talk to her?'

Could Louisa help? Who could tell? But Sophie seemed irretrievably lost to her already. She could see the pain ahead for her daughter, she sensed what it was doing to her studies and at the same time she knew, damn it, after all she'd been through, that her own daugher was now the other woman. It was horribly ironic. 'Well, if you really want to.'

'I do.' Louisa's arm was round her shoulder. Lending support. 'Besides, I'm not so involved. You know teenagers. Maybe she'll talk more easily to me.'

Jess glanced at her in surprise. What did Louisa know about teenagers? But it couldn't do any harm. 'Go on then. See if you can talk some sense into her. Tell her for God's sake to think about what she's doing.'

'The other woman never wins,' Louisa said with feeling as she left the room.

'But neither does the wife.' And Jess could vouch for that.

'The other woman never wins,' Louisa said to Sophie as they stood in the garden by the fish pond. It was a typically grey and damp Christmas Day; privately Sophie considered that Christmas should be moved to late January so there was at least a faint chance of snow.

'You don't even know him.' And Louisa hadn't been here five minutes.

'True.' Louisa shrugged. 'So tell me about him.'

She knew it was bait, but Sophie couldn't resist. 'He's gorgeous. Tall. He's got lovely eyes. And he dresses dead smart.' She smiled. 'He knows about things. Not university stuff, but real things.'

'In the real world.' Louisa nodded.

'Yeah. And he's exciting. He makes me feel...' She hesitated, but this was how it was. 'As if I'm living. You know?'

Her aunt didn't seem to be sitting in judgement. She was nodding and smiling as if she understood. 'And what's his wife like?' she asked.

'How should I know?' But Sophie glanced at her from the corner of her eye. Was her aunt aware that the only reason Sophie hadn't got back here till two days ago was because she had hot-footed it to Brighton? The thought of not seeing Nick for four whole weeks had been too much, and she had kind of hoped...

OK, so he had told her not to come (the last night she'd seen him, in the car, in a lay-by off the main road of all places; her mother would die if she knew) but she had phoned Amy, the original connection between the two of them. And Amy had said of course she could stay, and how great it would be to see her, and how was uni? Clearly, Amy knew nothing about Nick, but the connection was there, so Sophie might at least be able to phone him, see him, might even get a glimpse of the woman *she* thought of as the other woman, might get some inkling of what his other life was like.

'I assumed you would want to know where he goes when he's not with you,' Louisa said. 'It's natural, isn't it, to be curious?'

'Um, yeah, I s'pose.'

'And you don't have that much of him, do you?'

Sophie bristled into defence. 'I have enough.'

Louisa's expression told her she didn't believe her, no way. 'But you still need to know, don't you? What the rest of his life is like?' She had, of course, hit the nail on the head.

'Not specially.' Sophie moved one step away from the pond. She had thought it unnecessary at first, she had blithely assumed that Barbara was unimportant, that Nick's other life was unimportant. But it had happened, hadn't it? She wanted more of him. And so she needed to know the exact nature of what was keeping him away.

Louisa folded her arms. 'Go on... You haven't ever phoned him at home? Though I presume he's told you not to?'

'Why should I have?' This aunt of hers was too clever by half. While staying at Amy's she had phoned – twice – and got his wife both times. Worse, when Barbara picked up the phone, Sophie had waited for a good ten seconds, listening to the other woman's voice, trying to see a face, a body, before replacing the receiver. Nick would be furious; surely he would guess who it was? But if he said anything, she'd just deny it.

'Don't give me that, Sophie.' Louisa moved in closer. 'I know what it's like. I've done it myself.'

Now she was interested. 'Done what?'

'Had an affair with a married man, of course.'

'Oh.' Put like that... 'This isn't an affair.'

'What would you call it then?' Her aunt's eyebrows rose towards the neat black line of her hair. 'A casual friendship? A schoolgirl romance?'

'Well, all right, but with Nick it's—'

'Different?'

Sophie gazed into the pond. 'Yes, it is different. How did you know?'

'I know because it's always different, you daft girl.' Louisa grabbed her arm. 'You're freezing. Do you want to get a coat and come for a walk?'

Sophie hesitated. She wasn't sure she was ready for whatever her aunt had in mind. She liked her, she was direct and honest. But she also seemed able to see right through her. Mums had always told her they were alike, maybe that was it.

Louisa laughed. 'I know you'd rather be with your Nick, but he isn't here, so will I do?'

'I suppose.'

'Because you see...' Louisa held her by the shoulders and looked into her face. 'He'll never be here for Christmas and birthdays – they never are. They're elastic, always springing back to the family for anniversaries and a dose of nostalgia.'

Sophie smiled. 'He doesn't have a *family*, exactly.'

'No children – that's good.' Her aunt sounded brisk and practical. 'But he has a world separate from you, right? Wife, parents, brothers, sisters, in-laws.'

'Ye-es, I suppose.' And that was why she couldn't stop wondering what Christmas was like for him, what he was doing, whether or not he had told Barbara, whether Barbara had actually found out.

Sophie watched Louisa disappear into the workshop. Please, let Barbara find out, she thought. In her wilder moments, how she longed for that. Something had to change. Barbara might throw him out, straight into Sophie's arms. That was part of the reason for the phone calls, but she'd chickened out. She would never, could never, do such a thing to Nick.

'And if he has a whole world without you,' Louisa re-emerged from the back door with two coats, 'then you might wonder what he comes to you for.'

Sophie tensed. She knew what Louisa was saying. 'It isn't only for sex.' She had said this to Karin already. And it wasn't anyone's fault that the sexless date had gone wrong; she had wanted it quite as much as he had, although not expected it to be like *that*.

She shivered, despite the warm coat, as they set off for the cliff. Not like that, careering down the dual carriageway, his hands fumbling between her legs. Not like that in the lay-by with him so quick to start that he tore her blouse, and so quick to finish that she was still smarting from the pressure of his hands on her breasts and shoulders, when he came with a sharp and violent thrust inside her. Rough... yes, it was rough. But exciting, new. It was living, wasn't it? A passion that hit hard, that made you feel alive.

'Did you like it that way?' he had asked her afterwards as they careered back up the dual carriageway in the opposite direction, both his hands firmly on the steering wheel this time.

'Oh, yes.' With him, any way was the right way.

'Nothing wrong with sex,' Louisa said, as if she were tracking her thoughts. 'So long as you're careful.'

Condoms, she meant. Sophie wanted to laugh. As if Nick would ever forget his. Even that night he had paused for the obligatory condom-grope. Of course she didn't want any accidents any more than he did (pregnancy was the only risk with Nick, he wouldn't go near someone who wasn't clean as clean) but it was rather nice to fantasise – that one time he might want it all, her and the family stuff, all of it from Sophie, not Barbara. No more separate worlds. One day...

Inside the cottage Jess realised that she was alone. Rupert had gone back next door, probably thanking God that he rarely saw his parents and didn't have children; Felix had gone down to the village where one of his new buddies from the pub had installed a pool table in his garage, and Sophie and Louisa had disappeared. She was deserted then, all alone on Christmas Day. But it wasn't at all depressing – actually it opened up a whole lot of opportunities. She could take a walk along the cliff path, she could take a nap, she could curl up with a good book or she could watch some truly awful Christmas TV. It was liberating.

But instead of doing any of those things she moved instead towards the telephone, checked a number in her address book and dialled. She couldn't say why, but she had an urge to speak to Matthew Hill, the man who was also spending Christmas alone.

Jess heard the phone ring on and on, before his answer-phone clicked into action. She listened to his perfectly calm, perfectly matter-of-fact voice (he must be a reassuring doctor, she decided, the kind who stopped you from worrying unnecessarily) but at the sound of the tone, she balked, and replaced the receiver without leaving a message. What could she say? Would she make a joke about Christmas and

214

emotions and tell him that teenage trauma had now hit their household too? How could she explain that she had felt the need to talk to a stranger, a man who was only her first client, a man who just happened to be alone on Christmas Day?

It was, she decided, a mercy that he hadn't been there. He would be on call, he had said, and people very often became ill on Christmas Day. If he *had* answered, what on earth would she have said to him? He would have thought her quite crazy. Rather a good thing then, that he wasn't there, not witness to a moment's madness.

Chapter 16

'You'll spoil your dinner.' Jess heard herself speaking to Louisa as she must once have spoken to Sophie. Like her daughter often did, Louisa was munching her way through a packet of crackers, although dinner would be in an hour. And like Sophie, Louisa took no notice of her whatever.

'So what are they like?' she asked instead. Of course, Jess knew who she meant.

'Peter's lovely.'

'And his wife?' She looked up, eyes on red alert.

Jess smiled. Her sister was wearing a leopard-print minidress and a pair of high black boots. Quite outrageous. She was making a small protest against the predictability of middle-class dinner parties, that would probably be wasted on Marilyn.

'She's all right.' At one time she had thought Marilyn Beck might become a friend, but although Marilyn could undeniably be funny, it was a frosty, cruel kind of humour that didn't appeal to Jess. What had been the attraction for Peter? Marilyn was quite a vamp, but Peter was hardly the kind of man to be drawn to looks alone. 'They make rather an odd couple,' she elaborated. 'You'll see.'

'And Rupert didn't mind making up the numbers?' Louisa

rose from the chair, where she had been sitting, legs crossed, revealing a considerable amount of stockinged thigh that would no doubt recompense the man in question. She started rummaging around in the bottom of the dresser. 'Where's that photo album you were talking about?'

'Oh, not now, Louisa.' Jess cling-filmed the chopped peppers she'd prepared for her sauce. The rest was last-minute. 'No, he was delighted to make up the numbers.' Though perhaps delighted wasn't quite the right word. He too had growled something about not being into dinner parties, before pronouncing that he supposed it would be worth it if he got a decent meal out of the evening. Rupert's idea of cordon bleu was putting grated cheese on top of his baked beans on toast.

'Do you like him, then?' she asked her sister. Nothing would please her more. If Louisa were to get involved with a man (not any man, but someone as nice as Rupert would be perfect) it would guarantee her staying around, at least for a while. But then again, Jess reminded herself as she got the mushrooms out of the fridge, Rupert could be very touchy about the opposite sex, and she still hadn't found out exactly what – or who – had hurt him.

'Like him? I think he's drop-dead gorgeous. But the point is, has he noticed me?'

'Probably.' Jess didn't bother to add that given Louisa's predilection for jungle prints and shades of lime-green and fluorescent orange, he could hardly fail to.

'Ah, here it is.' With a small cry of triumph, Louisa pulled out a dusty album, and despite herself Jess wandered closer, wiping her hands on her apron.

'What about Stevie?' she asked. Louisa hadn't told her much about the man who had brought her back to England.

'Over. Too many kids.'

'Oh.'

'And before that was Jean-Pierre...'

'Yes?'

'Too many wives. Well, one anyway.'

Jess drew in breath. 'I see.' Louisa too. Did every unattached woman she knew become entangled with a man who was married to someone else? Upstairs, Sophie was working – she had said very firmly that dinner parties were not her thing, thank you (although her eyes had looked suspiciously smudgy) which made three antis. Why was she bothering? Even Felix hadn't wanted them to come. Sophie had also said that she had tons of work to catch up on (because of Nick? A married estate agent... Her Sophie?) and that if she could only have a little *space*, she would be just fine, thank you. So Jess had given her what she wanted, though tonight, space would be at a premium round here.

She looked at Louisa, whose leopard-print dress had shoestring shoulder straps and a very low neckline. 'So many different men,' she said. Not that she disapproved. She merely wondered what it was like. For Jess there had only ever been Felix, after all. She wandered back to the drainer to wipe mushrooms. How did other men make love? She couldn't imagine. She could hardly even hang on to the thought of another man's body. Rather pathetic of her, really.

Louisa glanced up from the album. 'You haven't lived,' she said.

'No.' Jess set the mushrooms aside. She loved the pinkish fawn of their skin, the delicious contrast with the dark fronds beneath. 'I probably haven't.'

'God, Jess!'

She swung round. 'What?'

'I can't believe you kept all these pictures.' Louisa had spread the album out on the pine table and was poring over them, another cracker in her hand. So how come she was whippet thin? Jess pulled in her tummy muscles.

'Of course I did.' How could she have thrown out the

218

most precious part of her past? Once more, she wandered closer. 'Has Brittany changed much?' She envied Louisa that too, that she had been able to return year after year, while Jess had never quite found the courage to go back. All she had of the pink granite coastline was upstairs...

'Trégastel has a few more cafés.' Louisa smiled, remembering. 'Oh, and a cute little aquarium built into the rocks – I don't think that was there before. Lots more shops selling postcards and ice cream, of course. But basically it's still the same. Still the best place for rock-hopping in the universe.'

'Do you remember as we drove there?' What Jess had loved most was the way in which her father's irritation turned to good cheer like the flick of a camera shutter capturing a smile, at his first sight of their campsite by the sea. And the way in which sisterly battles became shared camaraderie. 'Remember him singing as we drove down the coast road? *"Oh, I do like to be beside the seaside..."*'

'In France,' they sang together; that was how every line of the song had ended.

His great voice had bellowed out of the open windows of the car, leaving the girls inside not sure whether to laugh or curl up in embarrassment.

'Oh, yes.' Louisa's eyes grew dreamy. 'And that campsite we went to. The swimming pool...'

'With the pink granite fountain.' The seam of a smile on her father's face always, with each summer's holiday, began to look as if it belonged there, though it never failed to surprise Jess. And it never failed to go away again. 'Wait.'

She darted upstairs, retrieved her precious piece of pink granite, and ran down to the kitchen again. She handed it to Louisa where it nestled in her sister's palm, pink stone shot with jet black chips, washed and polished many times since its days by the sea.

'Bloody hell.' Louisa laughed. 'You even kept this?'

Too right she had. 'It came from the Ile de Bréhat.'

Louisa nodded. 'I remember.'

Jess reached out to touch the contours of the stone. Bréhat was an island full of Mediterranean flora, narrow winding lanes, fern-decked cliffs and pink-red beaches. But it wasn't Bréhat itself that she had so desperately wanted to remember, it was her father's pleasure. His voice telling her what a lovely stone it was, suggesting she keep it, showing her the best way to polish it, saying they would remember this day. Had he remembered? Jess felt a tear on her face and the sudden warmth of Louisa's arms round her.

'You miss him too.' It was a statement, but Jess sensed Louisa's surprise.

'Not him.' She could never do that, too much had gone before. 'I miss what we were in Brittany. What we could have been the rest of our lives.'

Louisa touched the stone with a fingertip. 'Most of the time he gave you hell.' She seemed subdued; there was a note in her voice that Jess couldn't quite identify.

'Not really.' Carefully, Jess took the piece of granite from her sister's hand and placed it on the shelf of the dresser. 'He just loved you more.' She tried to disguise the hurt she still felt, always would feel, in the baldness of this simple fact. But it was a fact that she had never been able to state to her sister before.

'But you still kept the pictures.'

'You had pictures too,' Jess reminded her.

'I didn't keep any.' Briskly, Louisa flipped over the pages of the album. 'I didn't want to.'

'Why not?' Jess put her hand very gently on her sister's. It was trembling.

'Baggage.' Louisa's eyes closed. 'I wanted to be free from baggage. It only weighs you down. You can't carry baggage when you have to keep moving.'

But why did she have to keep moving? 'So you chucked

220

out everything from our past?' They might have a shared bond of childhood, but how different they were.

'Everything except for Scarlet.' Louisa's voice was low but she was trying to smile.

'You kept Scarlet?' Jess remembered that teddy bear. Louisa had always wanted it with her, even as she got older, past the age when teddy bears were supposed to be consigned to an attic in order for a child to become whole or independent or something. 'You've still got Scarlet?'

'Scarlet didn't deserve to be thrown out. He's not going to leave me, is he? He's under the duvet upstairs.'

Jess suppressed a grin. It was strangely reassuring to know that Louisa, who had thrown so much away, who was so sassy, sparky and independent, still had her childhood teddy bear. 'I can see that you didn't want to be weighed down.' Jess struggled to understand. 'But love isn't baggage.'

'Love is supposed to be about one person accepting another as they are,' Louisa said obliquely. 'Not having unreal expectations. You know what Dad was like. He didn't love who I was.'

'But—'

'He loved what he thought I was.' Louisa shook her head. 'The two were miles apart. I was never Miss Perfection. It was only a matter of time before I would slip up and let him down.'

Jess was surprised. As a child Louisa had seemed to have it all, and what was more, she had seemed to know exactly what to do with it.

Louisa flipped over another page. 'Look at her. She could never stand up to him, could she?'

Jess peered over her shoulder at the photograph. Her parents stood awkwardly between two giant boulders at Ploumanach, her mother small, hanging on to his arm; her father tall and broad, dominating the photograph just as he had dominated their mother, dominated life.

221

And Louisa was right. When Jess thought of them, of her upbringing, of her childhood, she always thought of her father, not her mother. It was odd. She had loved her mother – Amelia Parris had tried to be kind. But she had tried even harder to be everything her husband wanted, and that rather left material impulses in shadow. Jess's feelings for her father went far deeper and were far more disturbing, come to that. But they couldn't be love; not when they included such hatred.

'She wasn't strong enough.' Jess searched Louisa's narrow face, sometimes young, sometimes weary, for clues. Her high cheekbones were accentuated by the brightness of her eyes and the dramatic cut of her blue-black hair. And as always, there was that bruised sheen to her skin that made her look younger and more defenceless than she really was. Louisa was tough. Surely, *she* was strong enough?

'I always loved it here.' Louisa pointed to the Brittany landscape. 'I always felt safe.'

Safe. Jess followed her gaze. She saw two children becoming two young girls, growing summer by summer against the backdrop of the Côte de Granit Rose – the pink rocks of Trégastel, Ploumanach, the Ile de Bréhat. The two girls became two young women. Two young women who both needed to feel safe. Louisa had always seemed secure. But for the first time it struck Jess that it might be as bad to have too much love as it was to have too little. At least if it was taken unexpectedly away...

Later, watching a harassed Jess fly about the kitchen in her woollen marmalade dress fetching food for her guests, Louisa wondered about her sister and Felix.

Felix. She watched him. He was the perfect host – organising drinks, being witty and charming, bringing anyone into the conversation who might be lingering on the sidelines. And most importantly not paying *too* much attention to the sultry Marilyn Beck who was wearing a sexy satin Chinese print dress with slits practically to her waist. He had learned some lessons then – though he might not be the faithful kind. But Jess wasn't happy. Life for Jess was nowhere near as perfect as she'd imagined. Nor was it safe.

'Wow.' Peter was admiring the kitchen. Jess had fixed up a bamboo screen to separate the table alcove from the cooking area; the up-lighting in the alcove was muted and Louisa had to admit that it complemented the old pine and Jess's fennel and terracotta colour scheme beautifully. On the dresser, her sister's collection of fifties green glass glittered in the light of a beeswax candle. 'It looks great. Did you get someone in?'

'Nope.' Felix put an arm round Jess's shoulders. 'It was all this lady's own work.'

He was proud of her, Louisa could see that. And he loved her; the tell-tale signals were there, in the tender way he spoke her name, the way he had to keep touching her, the way he watched her as she moved from his side. So that was good, wasn't it?

'Jess is starting on other people's houses now,' Louisa told Peter. 'Let's hope Felix doesn't feel too neglected.'

His expression told her that if he did, she would be the last to hear about it. 'It's been sixteen years since we last saw Louisa,' he told them, changing the subject as smoothly as he did everything else. 'She's been just about everywhere, done just about everything.'

'Hardly.' But Louisa smiled. Her guess was that he *would* feel neglected, that he would much rather his wife stayed at home. Felix was a man who liked boundaries, for things to be spelled out for him, so nothing could take him by surprise. Yes ... everything about Felix was well defined, from the lines of his dark, layered hair and the depth of the dark blue eyes (how many women had got lost in those?) to the immaculate suit that clothed a firm and well-toned body.

Louisa got to her feet to help her sister bring in the starter. She found her holding a piece of blue fabric up to a spotlight. 'What on earth are you doing?'

'Just had an idea.' Humming to herself, Jess shoved the material away in a drawer and started doling out fried Camembert.

'Typical. You can't stop, can you?' And Louisa would like to bet that Jess provided him with plenty of surprises. No wonder he didn't know how to handle her. Unlike Felix she was a mass of possibilities and contradictions. She was wearing little make-up tonight, and her hair – originally brushed and shining – now looked as if she'd just walked along the cliff in a force eight gale. But it didn't matter. The wildness of it suited her, it complemented the unpredictability of her sudden smile.

'Let me do that.' Louisa took the plates through before she had the chance to go off on another tangent and get out some paint samples or something. And unlike their mother, Jess was strong. Perhaps that was what continued to fascinate a man like Felix, Jess had huge reserves of inner strength that half the time she didn't seem to know she possessed. There was a good deal of Jess that was slightly out of reach, half-hidden. And it felt right to be here with her. Louisa let out a small sigh. It wasn't easy to recapture her old resentments. What she wanted now was a new honesty between them.

'And how do you like living in Dorset?' she asked Marilyn when they were all seated once more. She might not be accustomed to dinner parties, but bar-work had made small talk a doddle.

'It'll do.' Marilyn seemed to be eyeing Felix over the rim of her glass. 'For now.'

'I love it.' Peter, a huge man to whom Louisa had taken an instant liking (when he kissed her sister on the cheek, gave her freesias and bitter chocolate mints and called her

224

Jessie) demolished half his Camembert in one mouthful. 'I got the bug when we used to visit Marilyn's mother.'

'Very occasionally,' Marilyn put in. She was one of those women who managed to look both disapproving and inviting at the same time, Louisa thought.

'And when the chance came up,' Peter glanced at Felix, 'it seemed too good to miss.'

'So you wouldn't move again?' she asked him.

'Not unless I have to.' This time Peter glanced at his wife, a glance that was not lost on Louisa. So why had he moved the first time? She decided to quiz Jess later.

'I can't imagine being able to put down those sort of roots.' Louisa denied the thought that perhaps she was already beginning to. It seemed almost too easy to sink into life at her sister's. She had even caught herself wondering if the pub in the village might be taking on staff. What was it about Dorset? Why did it seem to be pulling her to stay? This morning she and Jess had tramped along the cliff path and Jess had shown her the Spittles. It had meant something; Louisa had returned from the walk with her cheeks flushed, feeling good about herself, good about life.

And there were other attractions in the area, not least the rather enigmatic man living next door. She sneaked a glance at him. Earlier, she had watched, fascinated, as he pulled his tobacco pouch from his back pocket and rolled one of those thin cigarettes, in just a few crisp and confident movements. Now, his long brown fingers were wielding a fork with equal dexterity. Lovely hands. Jess had told her he restored antique furniture. And wouldn't she like to watch him working, to see him glance up at her with that hungry look that turned her on something rotten. Not that she wanted a man, she reminded herself firmly, tearing her eyes away. But he was her kind of guy: real, direct and extremely sexy.

'I'm not like you.' Peter was still talking about the travelling bug. 'Though I often wish I were.'

225

Privately, Louisa doubted that. Some people travelled to gain experience and see the world – fine, but they always seemed to have somewhere to come back to. Others – and she counted herself among this number – travelled because they were searching, for a sense of belonging, for an elusive sense of security. She wouldn't wish that feeling of dislocation and rootlessness on anyone.

'When I don't feel at home,' Peter said thoughtfully, 'when I'm somewhere I can't settle, I'm not at ease, I can't—'

'Can't create.' Marilyn tapped her long claret-coloured nails on the table and looked bored.

Bitch. 'I can understand that,' Louisa said quickly.

Peter didn't seem to have even noticed his wife's scorn; or perhaps he had grown accustomed to it. 'You must have seen some interesting places. Which was your favourite?'

'Brittany.' Louisa glanced at Jess. 'Trégastel beach in Brittany. The pink granite coast.'

'Nowhere more exotic?'

'Who needs the exotic?' Louisa raised her glass towards her sister. 'When there's something special so close to home?'

'And while we're doing toasts...' Marilyn winked at Felix. 'Here's another one – since it's Christmas.'

Everyone waited. Louisa noticed Felix shift uncomfortably in his seat.

'To Beck and Newman, the perfect partnership.'

A soft sigh of relief seemed to pass round the table.

'I simply won't have you two snarling away at each other's throats.' Marilyn looked from her husband to Felix and then back again. 'Especially since you have absolutely nothing to fight about.' She smiled slowly. 'Well, have you?' Her husky voice had thickened, and Louisa wondered how much wine she'd had already. She had barely finished her deep-fried Camembert in redcurrant sauce before lighting yet another cigarette.

'No more infighting.' Felix slammed his hand down on the table so hard that the wine glasses shuddered and everyone looked at him in surprise. 'How about it, Pete?'

'Sure.' Peter looked surprised, but not displeased.

After only a few drags, Marilyn ground her cigarette into the ashtray. 'I'm thrilled,' she said.

Hardly... She was a troublemaker, the sort of woman who wanted people to fight. And she was also the sort of woman whom Louisa's lifestyle to date had enabled her to avoid. She leaned back in her chair, watching Felix as he got up to clear away some of the debris on the table and pour more wine. This was all so different to the way she had become used to living. Was it too different? Was she mad to think she could adapt to it; that she could settle anywhere?

After coffee and liqueurs in the sitting room accompanied by an Italian aria on the CD player, the party began to break up. Sophie came downstairs and got talking to Peter about jewellery, Marilyn disappeared up to the bathroom, and Felix went to fetch coats.

'Time for some beauty sleep for me then.' Rupert Sumner was, Louisa realised, one of the few men she had ever had to look up to. And he didn't need beauty sleep.

'I'll see you out.' Who could tell? A little encouragement and he might invite her next door for a nightcap. She opened the front door and they both slipped outside. Louisa breathed in deeply. 'It's a lovely night.' And right now she didn't want it to end.

Together they walked down the path and on to the narrow pavement until they were almost out of sight of Cliff Cottage, half-hidden by the buddleia tree that stood in the near corner of Rupert's front garden. For a few moments they stood, savouring the softness of the night air. There was silence apart from the distant notes of another aria, and

227

then the click of Jess and Felix's front door.

Louisa stuck her head round the buddleia and saw Marilyn emerge, followed by an irate Felix.

'You're crazy,' he whispered to her, his back to the door. 'You shouldn't have come. Anyone—'

'Ssh.' To her amazement, Louisa saw Marilyn wind her arms round his neck, and as she ducked out of sight, she heard rather than saw Felix push her away. Well now...

'For Christ's sake,' she thought she heard him mutter. Then something about 'risk', then the door clicked again and Jess and Peter were there too, and everyone was laughing and talking a little too loudly, with thanks and kissing this time breaking the silence of the night.

Louisa glanced at Rupert. His face was stony and impassive. But he must have heard it too. 'For Christ's sake,' she said. 'Not her.'

He didn't comment, but the look he gave her told her his feelings far better than words. It passed between them like a secret, and in that moment she knew that he'd say nothing, that they were somehow accomplices. And then with a brief lift of his hand, he was gone.

Louisa went back up the path to say her goodbyes. Jess and Felix were folded together in the doorway, every inch the ideal homemakers. But she saw Felix's eyes narrow slightly when she came into view. He must be wondering where she had been, how much she'd heard. And she had no intention of enlightening him – at least not yet.

Louisa tucked her arm into Jess's. She felt the urge to protect her, the need to make it better. She realised that now she simply did not want to leave. But as for honesty between them – well, that was another thing again. Because what did you do when honesty went hand in hand with pain?

Chapter 17

Jess slipped her Venetian Chardonnay, took another forkful of her farfalle cooked in a delicious sauce of Parma ham, walnuts, cream and Parmesan, and savoured the sight of life on the Grand Canal of Venice.

She and Felix had arrived last night and spent the day wandering the warren of narrow streets, alleys, bridges and canal-side paths, every one of which seemed to lead back to Piazza San Marco. And that was where they all congregated – the tourists, the sightseers, the students, the well-heeled, of every nationality: in a vast and spectacular square, surrounded on three sides by graceful sixteenth-seventeenth-century arcades draped and shaded from the sun, once the lavish apartments of Venice's highest-ranking officials, but now the homes of the most upmarket shops, cafés and restaurants in the city.

'Are you enjoying yourself, Jess?' Felix's deep blue eyes were only half-serious.

And all she had to do was smile back at him, because of course she was. How could anyone not? From the moment she'd stepped out of the plane, felt the gentle warmth of the mid-March Italian sun touch her bare shoulders like a lover, she had been transported away from her worries and an English winter that never looked like coming to an end.

Transported into the careless, crazy bustle of a world where *no problem* seemed to be the order of the day.

Felix was studying his guide book, even as they ate. He had to organise their short stay, pack everything into three days that he possibly could, so that nothing would be missed, so that no one back in England could, for example, ever say to him, *Oh, but didn't you get to see the Accademia Gallery?* Jess took another forkful of pasta. Stop it, she told herself firmly. This had been his idea – a wonderful idea. If not for him she wouldn't be here, sipping her Chardonnay less than twenty feet away from the Grand Canal. Being Saturday, there was even a wedding party being taken up the Canal in style in a narrow black gondola decked with flowers arranged on a red velvet cushion. The Venetians, Felix had told her, were sensible enough to hire a gondolier only when they got married. The cost was prohibitive.

'How about a trip to San Giorgio tomorrow?' Felix suggested. He dipped into his seafood pasta in a tomato and basil sauce. And was it her imagination, or was she taking a lot more interest in food just lately?

'San Giorgio?'

'It's an island. From the Campanile there's a great view of the entire city, apparently. You can get there in a vaporetto.' He tried to hand her the book, but she waved it away. More information she did not need.

'OK. Sounds lovely.' Today, after coffee alfresco (complete with musicians in black suits and ties) at the hideously expensive Florian's, ex-haunt of many very famous literati, they had explored the mosaics, marbles and carvings of the Basilica di San Marco, the building that dominated St Mark's Square, until her head was positively reeling. Venice was glorious, but if she was honest, once she'd seen one mosaic, she'd seen them all.

After lunch, she had been relieved to hear Felix's suggestion that they boat up the Grand Canal in a water-bus. This was much more relaxing, more her thing; they could sit back and admire the parade of *palazzi*, as the old palaces were called, on the canal banks; some of them were still spectacular, some sadly dilapidated, with façades lacking their former glory, and only a plaque to remind the tourists that Byron had stayed in this one (and his mistress had once thrown herself into the Grand Canal, Felix informed her), Vivaldi had composed in this one, and so on.

And now there was dinner. For a moment Jess closed her eyes in pure pleasure. It was wonderful to have the chance to see everything, but now she wanted simply to soak up the atmosphere that was unique to the city. Because the sights – tourists and all – were almost too much to take in, at least in one mouthful.

Felix helped himself to more salad. 'And then in the evening...'

She knew what was happening in the evening – Felix's *pièce de résistance*; they were going to a performance of *La Traviata* at the best-known opera house in Venice. He had booked seats at the same time he booked the holiday. And she knew how much he was looking forward to it.

'Want a mussel?'

Jess selected one from his place. 'Mmm. That's good.' Though it reminded her, inevitably, of the food she had shared with Matthew Hill three days ago. Three days...

She tried to turn her mind away, back to Venice, the Grand Canal, back to the attractive man sitting opposite her – her husband, for heaven's sake. But when she thought of Felix she just felt sad and unsure, and when she thought of Matt it was with total confusion.

During the first two weeks of January, Jess had made plans, done sketches, brought in samples, swatches, colour boards and catalogues, and spent hours discussing Matthew Hill's hallway with the man himself. He was easy to talk to, and if the talk tended to veer away from design and decorating matters and towards the personal, it had never seemed to matter. While Felix brushed her worries over Sophie under the nearest carpet, Matthew listened, was sympathetic, and offered sensible advice. While Felix showed no interest in her designing and decorating, Matthew was enthusiastic, and seemed to understand her feeling of a new life beginning. So when she talked about college it was to Matthew. He was there, he was interested, and...

'And you fancy him,' Louisa had said, one evening when they were alone together for half an hour before she went off to do her evening shift at the Lamb and Flag down the road. Louisa seemed almost settled here in Dorset, but she was also acting strangely at times, as if something were weighing heavily on her mind. Jess didn't press her; Louisa would tell her when she was good and ready, and not before.

'I do not.' She knew she should feel a little more outrage. 'I just like the man.' But she knew then, and she knew now, that her feelings towards Matthew were not exactly the designer/client feelings she had envisaged. They were far from impersonal, in fact extremely friendly, and during the rest of January and February as she got to work on the hallway, she had to admit to feeling a sharp stab of excitement whenever she heard the sound of his key in the door. And if it were time to go and he had not yet returned from the surgery, she caught herself lingering, finding just a touch more brushwork that couldn't wait, clearing up just a little more thoroughly than she would otherwise have done. Of course, it could be simply that she needed his encouragement and enjoyed his praise. She didn't want to consider the alternatives.

And over the past ten weeks she had come to learn quite a lot about the busy GP who kept a picture of his ex-wife in the sun-room, and who loved good food. Not only did he enjoy it, but he loved cooking it too.

Jess blinked back at Felix who was describing the delights of the Doge's Palace according to the guide book. Sometimes, when she'd been busily rolling the raffia walls, picking out some detail on the cornice in cornflower blue, respraying the radiator, varnishing the new balustrade, or fixing up a light sculpture to greet this man when he returned from work each day, Matt would come home. He would rush in, admire her efforts, fix them both a drink, and in less than fifteen minutes she would be positively assaulted by the fragrances of spices or herbs wafting through to her from the kitchen (or tin can as he persisted in calling it). The first time it happened she assumed he was having a dinner party – it seemed incredible to go to so much trouble to cook for one, but Matthew had put her right on that score.

'I love preparing food, Jess,' he had said, looking more sexy than ever. 'And cooking it, looking at it. And eating it, of course. But I don't want to cook simply in order to be nourished. I want to take pleasure in it.'

She understood. And that was how she felt about Venice. She wanted to soak it up, to be a part of it, not just an observer – a tourist with a camera – who spent all day darting around the sights and missed the very heart of the place.

On the day Jess finally completed the hall, Matthew came home early (she didn't dare ask if it were intentional).

'It's perfect,' he told her.

'Rubbish. Perfect isn't a word in my vocabulary.' But she was gratified. It was her first commission, and it had taken her a ridiculous amount of time to complete, snatching an hour here and an hour there in between lectures, homework, preparation, not to mention ensuring that her husband did not feel neglected.

'You will never put so much effort into a living space again,' Matt told her.

233

'Living space?' Jess laughed. 'Now you're speaking designer jargon.' But what he said was true. And it wasn't just because he was her first client. She wanted it to be right for him because she liked the man so much.

'I had the best teacher. Wait here.' He disappeared into the kitchen and returned with a bottle of champagne and two glass flutes on a tray.

'Matt...' She had to laugh, he looked so pleased with himself. 'I'm driving, don't forget.'

'One small glass.' He shook the bottle and let the cork go with an explosion that made her fear for his new light sculpture. 'Let's drink to the day that I decided to get in an interior designer.'

'And why did you?' She accepted the glass and took a sip of the delicious, bubbly wine. Matthew Hill wasn't exactly the sort of person she had expected to answer her advertisement. She had foreseen doing battle with some iron-grey harridan with more money than taste, who would never know what she wanted and would keep changing her mind when she did. She had thought the glamorous side of designing would be far overshadowed by the need for diplomacy, flattery, charm, and psychology too. Even in Immaculate Interiors she had done her fair share of all that. But it had not been in the least like that with Matthew. It had been fun.

'You mean apart from not having time to do it myself?' His light eyes were examining hers. But Jess was becoming accustomed to the scrutiny of Matthew Hill.

'You could have got any old painter and decorator in,' she pointed out.

He smiled. 'I liked your ad. It shouted out to me. My house wanted a face-lift, I wanted a face-lift.'

'I can't do that.'

'You have done that.'

For a moment there was silence between them.

She didn't want to say it, but she had to know. 'How?' she whispered.

'After Pamela left. . .' His voice trailed off.

But he didn't need to continue. Jess understood only too well. 'You wanted to change things,' she said.

'Exactly.' He beamed at her. 'And you managed it just perfectly.'

'To the hallway, then.' Jess was pleased and gratified. Every designer surely longed to see their ideas turn into reality, with someone using the space that they had brought to life for him. But she should divert Matthew; she was always conscious that she must stop him from getting too close. 'May it always welcome you with open arms.'

'It will.' He beckoned her closer. 'And I have another surprise for you.' He took her arm – lightly, no pressure, though Jess felt branded by the proximity of him. And he led her into the kitchen where a huge pan of water that he must have put on earlier was coming to the boil.

While she watched, fascinated, he pulled on his blue and white apron, began preparing a sauce from ingredients that were already laid out on the worktop in front of him and chucked a basketload of mussels into the pan.

'Is this what's on your menu for tonight?' Jess watched, amused. There was something very sensual about the way Matthew prepared food, erotic even, if she could dare to think such a thing. 'It looks pretty tasty.'

He turned, assessing her with those unusual eyes of his. 'Tonight, I'd like you to join me, Jess.'

'Oh.' She blinked, taking a quick sip of champagne to disguise her discomfiture. 'But I'll be eating later with—' Abruptly, she stopped. It struck her that as often as not she didn't eat with Felix, since one or other of them usually got back late or went out early. Secondly, unless Felix or Louisa had cooked, there was nothing prepared, and she would be going back to face a freezer full of unprepossessing ready-mades. And thirdly, she very much wanted to share some food with him.

Matthew returned to the mussels. They had opened their shells and he drained them with one hand, shaking a colander in which the black shells rattled around, while putting the finishing touches to a garlic, cream and thyme sauce with the other. He was a dab hand, to say the least. 'Don't panic, Jess.' He sounded tetchy. 'This is just a taster.'

And that was exactly the problem, Jess thought, as she looked across at Felix and the Grand Canal. A taster had been exactly what it was. A very decadent and delicious taster. She was in Venice with her husband, eating delicious food (though not quite up to the standard of Matthew's as sampled so far) thinking of Matt rather than listening to Felix, and swallowing guilt along with her pasta. Because it had been a taste she was unable to forget.

The following day he had phoned her. 'I wondered if you were free.' And *she* wondered if he could hear her heart thumping.

'For what?' She kept her voice cool. This is a dead end, she told herself. A very dead end of a dangerous alley. Hah, hah.

'For the sitting room.' She heard the laughter in his voice. 'That was what I wanted you to do originally. Remember?'

Was he joking? Of course she remembered. 'Ye-es, but. . .' There were a thousand reasons why she shouldn't go back to work for this man. Nothing was right with Felix any more, and Matthew was part of it. She had college work, she should be at home more to cook and clean and do all the stuff wives were supposed to do. But on the other hand. . .

'Well, we could discuss it.' She had to work, she needed the money, she must stay independent if it killed her. And more to the point, she missed both Matthew and the challenge that his house had provided.

'Good.' His tone was entirely noncommittal. 'That was exactly what I wanted to do – discuss it.'

Jess looked at the calendar. ITALY was written in huge joyful letters over the following weekend. 'I won't be able to come over until next Tuesday, after college,' she said. 'I'm going to Italy for a long weekend.'

'Italy.' For a moment he was silent. And was it her imagination or was his voice when he spoke again a few degrees chillier than before? 'Well, have a lovely time.'

'I will.' Jess felt a pang of sadness. 'We will. Felix and I are going to Venice. I've always wanted to see it.' She didn't tell him that Felix had said it would be like a second honeymoon. That would be going much too far.

'D'you want these books or what?' Sophie glared at Karin.

'Aw, c'mon, Sophie, what did he say exactly?'

'He said,' Sophie took a deep breath, 'that if I'm not prepared to work, then what exactly had I come here for?'

'And what did you tell him?'

Sophie paused in the action of clearing the bookshelf in her study bedroom in one clean sweep. A clean sweep, that was what it was all about. And boy, could she do with one. 'I told him that I didn't know, that I wasn't sure what I was doing here, that it all seemed rather a waste of time.'

Karin groaned. 'That was absolutely the worst thing you could have said.'

'It was the truth.' And Sophie was getting very fed up with lies.

'Yes, but tutors don't like truth.' Karin was contemptuous. 'They want grovelling apologies. They want to be told that you see the error of your ways, and are going to make a fresh start next term and could they please give you another chance if you promise to try harder, and all that sort of stuff.'

Sophie threw the books in a heap on the bed. She wouldn't grovel for anyone. And if Karin didn't want the books she'd just give them to a charity shop. She required no reminders. 'They know what they can do with all that stuff,' she said.

Karin let out a deep sigh. 'So what did he say to that? He didn't throw you out, surely, I mean you have been working,' she glanced at Sophie, 'a bit.'

Sophie knew as well as Karin did that her personal tutor (a right sad git) couldn't throw her out for what he called underachieving, not at this stage, not until she flunked her exams or something equally dreadful. But she also knew that she was wasting her life here. 'He suggested that I take some time out to consider my future, if *that* was my attitude. He said that he understood that university didn't suit *some* people, and that I should think very carefully about my future before I made any commitments elsewhere.'

'And have you?'

'Have I what?' Sophie picked up the photo of Nick that she kept in a silver frame on her bedside table.

'Thought about the future. Made any commitments?'

'No commitments.' Commitment was a dirty word as far as Nick was concerned. Sometimes he just wouldn't listen.

'But if you'll never leave Barbara,' she had said to him the last time they met (it had become, against her will, a frequent topic of conversation – her conversation, his silence). 'Then what is the point?' Of this, she had meant. Of us.

'Fun.' He kissed her neck. 'Don't we have fun?'

Sophie had nodded, which was difficult when someone was kissing your neck. But did they? Sometimes what she felt was a blank, nothing but a blank, with fun a very long way left behind them.

'And the future?' Karin was asking, in another world, in another time.

'Oh, yes. I think about that. A lot.' She had hardly done

anything else. 'And I really want to leave here.' She felt a sudden jolt of sympathy for the girl standing by the bed. Karin had tried to be a good friend, she had covered for her where she could, offered what she thought was good advice, been there for her when Sophie needed a listening ear. But once a boff, always a boff. Karin might try, but she would never really understand. 'I'm sorry, Karin.' She touched her arm. 'But I have to go.'

'You're sure?' Karin looked as if she could hardly believe it. 'You won't change your mind?' She hesitated. 'Whatever happens?'

She knew exactly what Karin meant – she was thinking of Nick, and it was a tribute to her that she didn't say as much. 'I'm sure.' Sophie handed over the books. Better to go to someone who could really make use of them. Karin's family were not at all well off and half her books were borrowed from uni. She kissed her friend firmly on the cheek. 'And I won't be coming back.'

Chapter 18

Jess and Felix were packed and ready to leave. And maybe it was silly, but Jess felt a small thrill at the idea of getting back to Dorset, back to college, back to Cliff Cottage and her little garden on the cliff. And back to Matthew Hill?

It might not have been the second honeymoon that Felix had hoped for, but he had seemed to enjoy himself anyway. Especially the opera last night; even Jess had been enthralled at the atmosphere, the amazing costumes and the sheer emotion of the thing. And even if they had not rediscovered that elusive closeness then at least they had enjoyed one another's company. Could that be enough?

Jess waited in the foyer while he paid the bill, looking around at the abstract prints scattered, apparently at random, in groups around the walls of the wide foyer. The style was modern, the colours bold, both in total contrast to the quiet classical elegance of this Venetian hotel. Yet, somehow, it worked. And it gave her food for thought. Classical juxtaposed with modern was daring, and it was different.

'Susie and Bruno would love to see this,' she said to Felix as he joined her.

'Yes, well.' His mouth tightened. 'I don't even know all these college friends of yours, do I? And I doubt if they're the sort of people to have the wherewithal for a trip to Venice.'

Jess looked at him in surprise. She had told him all about Susie and Bruno. And so he knew (if he'd been listening) that Bruno was an architect. But Felix had never shown the slightest desire to meet them. 'Bruno's probably been to Venice lots of times,' she murmured. She wouldn't argue with him, not now.

In fact, in the informal tutorials at college, she had found several people she got on with rather well, men and women who shared her interest in colour and design. And on a few occasions they had met for lunch or for a drink, some of them bringing their partners. She had asked Felix, but he always found an excuse not to go, and Jess almost preferred it that way. But her favourite fellow student by far was Susie, ten years her junior, blonde, bubbly and only five feet tall, whose enormous brown eyes were always outlined in kohl and whose tiny hands could produce the funniest and most accurate caricatures Jess had ever seen. Her boyfriend, Bruno, was about twice the size of her, very successful and equally likeable.

'I'd love to invite them over to Cliff Cottage,' she said to Felix now. 'They could come to dinner.'

Felix made a noise halfway between a laugh and a snort, but it could have been because he'd just picked up the suitcases.

'Felix? What do you think?'

'Bloody students.' Felix heaved the cases down the steps and waved to the water-taxi he'd ordered that was approaching down the canal.

'What?' Jess stared at him. She was a bloody student too.

'And anyway, Bruno isn't a—'

'Oh, forget it, Jess.' Felix didn't seem to have any idea of what this meant to her. 'It's just that sometimes I feel that your bloody student friends are taking over our lives.'

And that was the moment when she knew for sure. Her life

– her new life, as she thought of it, which incorporated her career aims and her design and decorating – and Felix's life were no longer chugging along in parallel. Hers had veered sharply away, and though she had tried to reach out to him, tried to pull him over to join her, it wouldn't happen. He had made up his mind even as she was drifting further out of reach. And Felix wasn't a man for compromise.

Jess watched him as he climbed into the water-taxi that would take them back to the airport. The only way they could stay in touch with one another would be if she stepped back from all the things that were new in her life, all the things that were giving her this sense of direction, this wonderful sense of fulfilment that she'd never really felt before. And could she do that for Felix? Did she want to do that for Felix?

Sophie was sitting in a café drinking her third cup of coffee and gazing blankly at the house opposite. She had left her bags at Amy's. Her mother had been a little surprised but she had told her some story about leaving uni early for the Easter holidays and having to see someone to sort out a place to live. Too right she had to see someone. She had to see Nick – which was why she was sitting in the café on the corner of his street. It wasn't marvellous, a bit greasy-spoon actually. But it had the advantage of a clear viewpoint from her window seat to Nick's front door.

Moodily, Sophie stirred her tea. She had tried three times to phone him before she left Surrey, but the woman at the office number said she thought he was out with clients, and his mobile was switched off. She'd called again when she arrived in Brighton – zilch, and then, getting panicky, had gone to the flat; she could keep calling from there until she got through.

But the bloody key wasn't under the broken flowerpot. Sophie could hardly believe it – it was the first time this had happened. Granted, Nick had told her it was always possible, and granted, he usually knew when she was coming. But even so... She had wanted to sit down in the middle of the pavement, bags and all, and weep.

But Sophie was made of sterner stuff. She had sniffed, sworn loudly, and found a taxi to take her to Amy's instead. Luckily, Amy's mother (although unfortunately not Amy) was there, so she could at least unload the bags. But where the hell was Nick? Why was he making himself so unavailable?

From the phone box at the end of Amy's road, Sophie phoned again, feeling a right twit by now, leaving a message this time for Nick to call Amy's house. Which meant she could hardly phone them again. The mobile was still switched off, but by this time she guessed he might be home so she dialled his number with shaking fingers. He would go ballistic – but what choice did she have?

All she got on his home number was a bloody answerphone with Barbara's bloody voice on it announcing that *Nick and Barbara can't come to the phone at the moment.* This made her squirm. She most definitely could not leave the message that the Barabara-voice suggested she leave, so she hung around at Amy's house instead, waiting for him to call. She waited and waited until Amy's mother began looking at her very strangely and asked did she want to phone her mum? No way – Mums would be back from Venice by now, but she would flip and probably insist on driving all the way to Brighton to pick her up or something. And then it struck her that even if he got the message from his office, Nick wouldn't dare to phone her at Amy's, would he, not when he knew the family?

So Sophie made her way to his house. She had always known the address (by heart) but resisted the impulse to go – even just to look. She was not, and never would be, one of those sad, moony individuals who *just wanted to see where you live...* If she had gone before, it would have been to see his wife, to find out what she looked like, assess the competition. Nothing wrong with that, a bit of healthy competition never hurt anyone, and it was only sensible to find out the strength of the opposition. But she hadn't; until now.

And even now she had no intention of marching up to the front door; she was far too sensible for that. But at least she could vet the premises (and his wife?) maybe even hang around until she knew he was home, then try phoning again. She had to talk to him. It was a piece of pure luck that there was a café right there on the corner. And did she need some luck...

Sophie drained her cup – any more coffee and she'd need the loo. And she was sick to death of looking at his house. Considering that Nick was an estate agent, he had certainly been a little unimaginative in his choice of a home. It was brick, fairly new, semi-detached with an up and under garage. It had double glazing, frilly curtains at the windows that made Sophie's lip curl with distaste, and a mock-Victorian front door complete with stained glass window. Pretty yuck really, and just like all the others in the street. It was so boring – clearly Barbara's taste. She was probably a twin set or slacks kind of person, although Sophie had to admit that Nick had his moments. She had been unable to prevent herself yawning once or twice lately when Nick had been sounding off about politics.

Sophie sighed. No, he was lovely, he really was. And she was desperate to see him. But he wasn't terribly good at listening to other people. And what she wanted, more than anything right now, was to find someone who would listen.

Louisa walked along the damp and muddy cliff path, head down, listening to the determined *swoosh* of the water as it launched into rock and pebbles, the loud hiss as the tide gave up and departed. It was a grey day, hardly spring-like at all, and very different from early spring on the Mediterranean. But – and this thought made her want to laugh out loud – she liked it.

Jess and Felix had arrived back from Venice smiling but looking very *untogether*. Louisa knew, because she'd been watching out for it, watching and waiting and trying to decide whether or not she should tell Jess what she knew, or thought she knew. What she and Rupert had overheard the night of the dinner party ten weeks ago – God, had she really been living here for almost three months? – had not been exactly conclusive. Okay, it had *sounded* as if Felix and Marilyn had some sort of thing going, but it could have been just Marilyn coming on to him. And by now it could be over.

If she told Jess her suspicions, and they were unfounded, then couldn't that do more harm than good? It was her sister's marriage that might be at stake. Did she have any right to interfere, to make it more fragile than it already was? But then again, what about honesty?

'Oh, hell!' The boots that she'd borrowed from Jess slipped on the mud, and Louisa cursed as she struggled to regain her balance, emerging from the slip with a handful of gorse. 'Ouch.' There was honesty and then there was considering the feelings of others. Was it all a question of trying to get the balance right?

She brushed the gorse from her palms and thrust her hands into the pockets of Jess's waxed jacket which smelt of Jess and the outdoors, grass, mud and the damp of the workshop. And she stared out to sea. The waves were wild, undisciplined, noisy; the landscape was bleak, empty and seemed to offer both nothing and the entire world at the same time. It was weird, this pull on her. The landscape reminded her rather of the Brittany coast, and yet Dorset was pure Englishness, with its patchwork fields, hills and valleys, copses, rivers and green green grass. She had missed it. She walked on, down towards Brocklemouth Bay.

And then there was Rupert. Louisa had never found it difficult to attract men, but Rupert, unfortunately, was different. With Jess, he was warm and friendly, or at least they had the kind of close relationship that allowed rudeness without giving offence. But with her ... Rupert was cool, standoffish even. As if he only tolerated her because she was Jess's sister. And apart from that, he was a loner, incredibly self-sufficient, seeming not to need anyone to talk to, to be with, to... OK, say it, to have sex with.

As she reached the bottom of the cliff, Louisa paused to run her fingers along the grey rock. It was smooth and sensual to the touch, like clay; the grey was an outer layer of mud that she could easily scrape off with her fingernail to reveal the rock beneath. She did this now. But *she* needed love. Not the kind that left you vulnerable. But sex and the emotions that came with it. She was feeling a little frustrated these days, especially with such a gorgeous man in such close proximity.

Louisa sighed. On both sides of the path were the early fallers from a long-ago cliff face; great, grey boulders, piled one on top of another, not worn and smooth but a granite that had been hardened by years of abuse by water, salt, wind; now encrusted with ammonites and minerals. She moved towards the water's edge, looking among the smaller stones for evidence of a history that was speaking to her here in this battered bay; even without Jess's voice in the background of her mind, telling her of fossils and ammonites, or archaeological finds galore.

She wanted to find an ammonite of her own. She didn't care how long it took, she just wanted to, though she didn't know what the hell for. So she scoured the rocks, scrabbled among the smaller pebbles and driftwood, the weed and odd bits of human rubbish on the beach. But there was nothing.

She crossed the stream that flowed down to the sea, by its stepping stones, and sat for a moment watching two young children – a brother and sister perhaps – who were climbing on the rocks closer to the shore, kneeling by the rock pools, fishing with a little net on a stick. She and Jess had explored similar rock pools in Brittany, dresses tucked into their knickers, seaweed floating wraith-like around their ankles, stubbing their toes on barnacles, poking scuttling crabs and netting dancing shrimps. Louisa hugged her knees. She thought of Jess's daughter, of Sophie, and of the childhood she had missed.

When Jess was pregnant with Sophie, it had seemed to be merely a door to another experience for Jess, a door slammed in Louisa's face. Her sister's life had taken so many different turnings from her own; it had been easy to tell herself they were strangers, they shared nothing.

But now... Louisa watched as the girl yelped in delight, held up the net, carefully transferred its contents to their bucket with a splash of seawater over the sides. Now she could see how Jess had come to make her choice. Jess had needed Felix, needed to be safe, to be loved. After their parents' death she had needed to put down roots just as surely as Louisa had needed to get away. Roots. That was what children were – they fixed you in time, in a generation, in a place, in a home. And what about Louisa? Was her time running out? Was that what was pulling her down to earth?

Abruptly, she jumped up, almost tripped, fumbled for a hand-hold on the nearest boulder, and spotted lying at her feet a small piece of grey granite with deep ridges and indentations. She picked it up, smiled. An ammonite – not a perfect one, but an ammonite nevertheless. Beginner's luck. She clutched it in her palm, feeling the cold stone, tracing the thick ridges with her thumb. And she wondered at the pleasure she felt. Was she going barmy? Was she still Miss

Nowhere, or had she found a little of what she was looking for at last?

Sophie felt the thrust of excitement as she recognised Nick's blue Ford Mondeo. It pulled up outside his house, and she half-rose to her feet, wondering, for a mad moment if she had time to rush out there, to stop him before he went in.

But then she realised there was someone in the passenger seat. Oh, God. She shrank back from the window of the café. It was a woman – obviously Barbara – sitting there beside him. No wonder he'd had his mobile switched off, and no wonder the office coudn't contact him: he was with his wife.

Nick jumped out of the car, dangling his keys. He looked happy – Sophie registered this with a stab of anger. What right did he have to be grinning his socks off, when she felt as if the weight of the whole world was on her shoulders? And when she had been waiting for hours to see him.

Barbara, looking very un-Barbara like, for this Barbara was small and fair, and dressed not in a twin set or slacks but in rather trendy baggy trousers and a jacket with a classy cut, also got out of the car. She had her back to Sophie; she said something to Nick and he laughed. That was another surprise – that she could make him laugh.

But she didn't jump out of the car as he had. And she was moving rather slowly. Sophie stared in disbelief as Barbara turned, as Nick took her hand and they walked together up the path. She didn't jump because not only was she small and fair and rather nice-looking, she was also about six months pregnant.

Chapter 19

Sophie got to her feet, but she didn't charge over the road and confront them. What was the point? Instead, she found the nearest phone box, her stomach churning.

'Nick?'

'Yes?' His voice changed just slightly. He was nervous now and irritated. He knew it was her, but he wouldn't use her name.

'It's Sophie speaking.' If it weren't so awful, she would be relishing his discomfort.

'Hmm, yes.' She could picture him, looking towards the doorway of whatever room his wife might be in, silently cursing Sophie. 'Thanks for calling. Are there any messages for me?'

Ah, a good one. Pretending she was a girl from the office. Very neat, very practised.

'Yes, I have got a message for you, as a matter of fact,' she said sweetly.

'And what's that?'

'Get stuffed, you cretin. You're dumped.' And so what if it made him sound like a bag of garbage? In this case it was appropriate.

Nick was quiet for several seconds. 'Can we talk about

this?' he said at last. 'Do you want to fix up a meeting?'
Playing a part to the end. 'No.' She was about to put
down the phone, but she had to say something else. 'She's
pregnant, you bastard,' she managed to whisper, and then
she slammed down the phone and pushed her way out of the
red box. With difficulty, since the bloody doors were always
so stiff. After everything he had told her! After what he had
let her think!

Good bloody riddance, she told herself, as she marched
along the pavement. No more sneaking around, no more
being second best, no more wondering what he was doing
and being unable to phone him just for a chat. Sophie
sniffed. No more having to listen to him droning on about
the flaws in New Labour, no more pathetic stories about
what fun they had in the office, no more being sad because
he just wouldn't listen.

Sophie felt the tears trailing down her cheeks. Irritated,
she brushed them away. No more rushing off to the flat to
play house. Hadn't she been pathetic? Cooking for her man.
What was she, just another doormat, only in a different
colour – the kind that had *WELCOME: I WILL BE YOUR
SLAVE*, emblazoned on it? No more Häagen-Dazs, no more
heady, glorious lovemaking. But equally – come on, girl –
no more rough (and ever so slightly sordid) sex in a lay-by.

Eventually, she got back to Amy's.

'I would like to phone my mother now, please,' she said
to Amy's mum, feeling about twelve. Home was where Jess
was, and she wanted to be there with her. Suddenly the real
world was awfully scary.

'Mums? I've left Bishop Otter. For good. I'm in
Brighton. I'm going to get a train tomorrow. I'm coming to
Brocklemouth.'

'Sophie? Are you all right?' She didn't flip and she didn't
shout, thank God. She was just Mums, very calm, very
concerned. 'Phone me when you know what time you'll be

250

arriving. I'll meet you at Axminster.'

'Thanks, Mums.' If Jess had been there, she would have hugged her so hard she might have thought Sophie was never going to let her go.

Even Pavarotti laying into Marcello di Capua's '*O Sole Mio*' on the CD player failed to lift Felix's spirits as he mooched around Cliff Cottage supposedly getting ready for work. He had tried to talk to Jess again this morning – he kept trying to talk to her, but she was always so damned busy these days. This morning she went haring off to college, and no, she told him, sorry, but she would not be free for lunch as she had a business appointment. A business appointment? Felix flipped through his shirts. Half of them still in the wash or waiting to be ironed as bloody usual. What the hell did business appointment mean? Another session with that damned doctor of hers?

A cool blue, he decided, inspecting the laundering. And in the afternoon she had to pick Sophie up from the station – apparently something was very wrong and they would both have to be very careful what they said to her. Good God, treading on eggshells, that was all he needed right now.

He found (oh, miracle) a clean pair of trousers and pulled them on, although there were two creases in each leg, and he was damn sure that before she'd started this decorating lark, Jess used to take more time over the job. He should be feeling good this week after Venice but what Felix was feeling was extremely fed up.

Venice had not been a disaster, but neither had it been a success. He had practically bust a gut to make that trip work; done the research so that they would know the best places to go, what to see, what to do. But Jess hadn't been with him, not really. The strains of '*O Sole Mio*' reaching the bedroom reminded him fleetingly of their hotel (some Domingo lookalike had done a small informal concert on their last evening) and this saddened him. She had been with him in body, but not in spirit, her eyes sometimes looking right through him as if he no longer existed for her, as if her thoughts, and that spirit that he could never tie down, had left him.

Left him... Felix shuddered as he selected a tie. Venice was supposed to be a city for lovers. It was supposed to be the perfect backdrop for a weekend of sensuality and seduction, a second honeymoon, as he had told Jess. And yes, she still responded to him sexually, but he couldn't dispel the sensation that she was merely going through the motions. At times there was a tension in her that couldn't simply be stroked or soothed away.

The problem was, of course, he mused as he pulled on his jacket and surveyed himself critically in the mirror, that she was completely caught up in this work of hers. Painting and decorating had always been a man's job until some stupid prat had started rambling on about colour and mood, creating atmosphere and feng whatever-it-was to improve your quality of life. And until all these blasted home decorating programmes on the TV. Suddenly everyone thought they could do it, suddenly it became a lot more than a man up a ladder with a paint-pot. Suddenly it became women's territory – like all that other psychological claptrap. And *he* was suffering the consequences.

Not only was there college and all these new buddy-buddys that Jess wanted to bring round to the house to meet him (no thank you, he was far too old for students, mature or otherwise; they would all be scruffy, arty-farty, pretentious – *moi*, and make him feel both old and a fool) but there was also this bloody doctor. Business appointment...

Perhaps when he came home tonight he would buy her some lilies, Felix thought. Lilies were her favourite flowers, weren't they? He had always known that. But then again, perhaps he shouldn't. He recalled the strange look in her eyes the last time he'd given her lilies. He'd seen it, half-acknowledged it, not understood it. Felix stood still now, not hearing the music, not seeing himself in the mirror. Something was very wrong between them. Something had been wrong for a long, long time.

Downstairs in the kitchen, he checked the calendar. She might have business appointments now, but Jess still scrawled everything on the calendar as she always had: dentist's, doctor's, hairdressing appointments; people's birthdays and anniversaries; messages and things she must remember to do or buy. Between *milk* and *ring P. re S.* he found *M.H.* Felix groaned. Matthew bloody Hill. So he was right. She was going to see the doctor. Again.

Felix made himself another coffee and surveyed the kitchen. It was a mess as it always was these days, and Jess's lazy sister didn't put herself out to help. In the sink a pile of dirty pans seemed to signal his wife's jubilant escape from domestic duties, but it was the view out of the window that caught him as he stood there – Jess's window, as he thought of it – into the back garden and the cliff beyond.

As soon as he'd seen this cottage he'd known it would be right for her. But where was she now? Where would she be at lunchtime? With another man, that was where, in his house, doing God knows what.

Felix moved over to the phone, the anger pumping inside him. He pushed the buttons quickly, knowing the number off by heart. There was one woman, at least, who appreciated him.

'Marilyn? It's me.'

'Oh, hi, darling. And how was the trip?' She was cool at first, no doubt wanting to punish him for taking his wife away for the weekend.

'Terrible. I missed you.' In a way, that was even true.

'Are you free today? For lunch? I want to take you somewhere special.'

The change of tone was total. But when the conversation was over and Felix had put down the phone, he moved towards the window once more and thumped his fist down hard on the drainer. He knew, damn it, what he wanted, and it wasn't Marilyn Beck. He didn't want his wife at college, he didn't want her decorating another man's house. What he wanted was for Jess to be here with him. And he wanted what he had promised her six months ago. He wanted a new start.

Jess's meeting with Matthew Hill was stilted from the first moment on, both of them circling one another with wary eyes and cautious words.

'How was Venice?' he asked her, looking over her left shoulder.

'Glorious,' she replied, equally briskly. 'Now, what did you want to do with your sitting room?'

If he was surprised at how quickly she moved on to professional matters, then he didn't show it. 'As always, Jess...' His look was cold. 'I intend to leave it entirely up to you.'

'As you like.' They discussed colours and ideas for a while, but it wasn't working. It wasn't working for various reasons. For one thing her mind was on Sophie and whatever her problems might turn out to be. She felt instinctively that this Nick person was involved, more was the pity. And for another thing, she hated this distance, this awful politeness between them. Matthew had retreated into client mode, and she was finding it impossible to respond.

'So?'

'Let me think.' But when she closed her eyes and waited for inspiration, the only picture that came into her head was that of her long-legged daughter alone on a railway platform. Sophie would have to change at East Croydon and Clapham Junction; the journey wasn't easy, and would take her over three hours.

It was no use, she couldn't be constructive in her thought processes with this man being typically vague about her swatches and colour samples yet still breathing down her neck.

'Perhaps I'll go away and think about it,' she told Matthew, when they'd talked round in circles for almost an hour. It would be better if she came back here when she could be alone.

He glanced at his watch. 'That's fine by me.'

But she only felt worse than ever. He would understand if she told him about Sophie, surely he would, but he was far too frosty for her to consider doing that. And perhaps he was right. This time they should keep their relationship on a much more professional basis. They really should.

'I might look at some fabrics this afternoon,' she said, getting slowly to her feet. But she didn't want it to be like this between them. 'I have to go into Axminster anyway to pick up Sophie.' That was his chance to ask her – if he wanted to know. Damn professionalism.

But, 'Fine,' was all he said again. The word was beginning to annoy her. *He* was beginning to annoy her. 'The same arrangement as before?'

'Oh, yes.' She wondered if he realised how miserable she felt. 'Exactly the same arrangement as before.'

Jess drove straight to Axminster. Sophie's train wasn't due for another two hours, but she wanted to think, to clear her head after Venice, after Felix's attitude, after her unsatisfactory interview with Matt in Lyme Regis.

She headed for the river, parked near the bridge at Cloakham and walked along the riverside path. At last spring seemed to be in the air, the day was warmer, a little

255

hazy, and after a short while Jess stopped to rest on a wooden bench. She closed her eyes, allowing the early afternoon sun to create pictures behind her eyelids. She felt herself slightly apart from the day, and to her surprise the colours that swam in front of her vision were those of Italy: the olive greens, the sand, turmeric and ochres, the soft apricot and terracotta. She jumped to her feet – too quickly, for she felt dizzy and almost fell over. Of course! Those were the perfect colours for Matthew's sitting room. Mediterranean shades but with a dash of spice; a touch of Mexico perhaps.

She made her way back to the car and drove into town, eager to visit the specialist textile shop in Axminster that she had discovered some weeks ago. She had the urge to go for fabric first; this was in total contrast to Sandra Slattersly's insistence on furnishings as basics, colour second and textiles last in Immaculate Interiors. But Jess still enjoyed her rebellions from the Slattersly way, and she knew that just a small piece of fabric could provide inspiration for the complete look of a room.

And sure enough, half an hour later she grabbed her change and the parcel of material that she hoped would blow Matthew away when he saw it. She would use the burnt orange and sunset yellow fabric shot with olive and burgundy for scatter cushions. It was a brilliant beginning. And at least it had taken her mind off things.

She looked out of the window, surprised to see a large and familiar figure passing by. 'Peter!' And ran out of the shop. 'What are you doing in Axminster?'

'Hello, Jess.' He seemed pleased to see her. 'Errands for Marilyn's mother. Marilyn's tied up this morning apparently.' A slight frown crossed his face. 'How about you?' He glanced at the paper parcel. 'Shopping?'

'Not really. It's what you might call a by-product.' She needed to talk to someone. And they had always been close.

'As a matter of fact, I've come to meet Sophie from the station.'

'You don't look too pleased at the prospect. In the doghouse is she?'

Jess reminded herself that her daughter and Peter had also always been close. 'You could say that. She's left university.' That was enough of a bombshell, surely? She certainly wouldn't tell him about Sophie's married estate agent although that too, was on her mind. Sophie had sounded so young on the phone, all her defences down. She was vulnerable, Jess reminded herself. Only eighteen and thinking she knew it all.

It didn't seem to be much of a bombshell to Peter. 'Is that so bad?' He shrugged. 'Maybe she wasn't cut out for it, Jess.'

All very well for him to say... But she was conscious of a glimmer of perspective. 'I suppose it's silly,' she admitted to him. 'But Sophie's so bright. I always assumed she'd do all the studying I never managed.'

'Because you had Felix.'

He was a perceptive man, she mustn't forget that. 'Because I had Felix,' she agreed. 'I always wanted her to go to university. It seemed such a waste for her not to.'

'Everyone has a different talent,' Peter said obliquely. 'She may be bright academically, but that daughter of yours is also very artistic.'

'Is she?' Jess was surprised. At school, Sophie had enjoyed art, but she had never shown the flair for colour that Jess had been aware of in her own work. She remembered all those times that Sophie had sat with Peter in his studio when he was working. Perhaps Peter had seen something that she herself had missed.

'Sure.' His expression grew thoughtful. 'Why don't you get Felix to bring her in one day? I could talk to her. I'd be glad to.'

'If she'll come.' Right now Jess had no idea what Sophie was feeling, of how much damage had been done. She glanced at her watch. The train was due in ten minutes. So she squeezed his arm, said a quick thank-you and an even quicker goodbye, and headed for the station.

Sophie was quiet and looked very pale and drawn. Quiet, but: 'Leaving university had nothing to do with Nick,' she told Jess, almost before she got off the train.

As if she had known that was the first thing Jess would say to her.

'Then why?' She didn't ask until they were driving back to Brocklemouth. Jess had always found their times in the car the easiest for confidences, perhaps because Sophie could stare out of the window and Jess had to focus on the road; both could thus avoid one another's eyes.

'Because I hated it. I told you.'

Ah yes, history is bunk. Clearly, she wouldn't get much more than this out of her. But she tried. 'Hated history or hated Bishop Otter?' Sophie could always do a subject switch, couldn't she? Other students did.

'Mums...' Sophie switched off from the scenery to reward her with a quick glare. 'I hated both.'

'Oh.' On second thoughts, perhaps it was the fact that they were trapped together in the car that made confidences come more easily. Neither could simply walk away. 'I just wondered.'

'Well, I'm sorry.' She didn't look it. 'But I'm not going back to Southampton. Or any other uni. I've made up my mind.'

'I see.' Jess frowned as a sleek black XJS hurtled past them. Roads in Devon and Dorset were not tailor-made for speed-machines. If she didn't go back, then what would Sophie do? 'And Nick?' she asked carefully.

'Nick is a self-centred, pompous bastard.'

258

'Oh.' Jess was finding this extremely hard going. 'But you're OK?' She forced herself not to look at Sophie as she said this.

'I'm fine.' She didn't seem fine.

'And you've told Nick?'

'Told Nick what?' she snapped.

'About university.' Jess indicated right. She was beginning to imagine all sorts of things. Did, *Nick is a self-centred, pompous bastard*, mean a break-up? She hoped so. God knows what sort of future Sophie had with a married man. But why was she looking so pale?

'No, I haven't told him.' She was doing her clam impression.

'But you're not in some sort of trouble?'

'Trouble?'

'Sophie...' She was getting nowhere fast, and all of a sudden Jess was fed up with Sophie being incommunicado. All right, she was upset, all right she had needed to make changes in her life (but leaving university? Had that been a spur of the moment decision? What if she regretted it later and it was too late to go back?). And Jess knew all about waiting until your teenage daughter was ready to talk to you, not putting on the pressure, being calm and understanding and kind. But she was human, damn it. Didn't she have a right to know something of what was going on?

Sophie looked as if she were about to be sick.

'Sophie, you're not pregnant, are you?' It slipped out, the concern that had been there since Sophie's phone call, that had grown when she'd seen her huge eyes in a white face.

Sophie burst into tears.

'Oh, hell.' Jess pulled abruptly into a lay-by. 'I'm sorry, darling, I didn't mean...' She put her arms round her daughter, tried to comfort her.

'No, I'm bloody well not.' Sophie pushed her away. 'But *she* is.'

259

'She?' And all of a sudden it was clear to Jess what had happened. 'My poor baby.' Her heart went out to her as she took her in her arms once more. 'My poor, poor baby.'

Chapter 20

When Rupert came into the pub, Louisa knew what she must do. He'd probably forgotten she even worked at the Lamb and Flag – but he was nice enough not to take his pint over to a table. Instead, he perched on a bar stool, grinned at her (heart-meltingly gorgeous, she almost crushed a wine glass with her bare hands) and said, 'How are Jess and Felix, then? I haven't seen either of them for ages.'

Jess, he meant. Since when had Felix and Rupert ever had a civil word for each other? 'You knew Sophie was home?' She adopted her most casual expression. Thank God she was wearing her yellow shirt, it made her boobs look much bigger than they really were.

'I thought I saw her in the garden the other day. How long will she be around for?' Quickly and carelessly he rolled a cigarette.

At the sight of his skilful hands and brown expert fingers, Louisa inwardly drooled. 'Who knows?' She leaned on the bar counter, to give herself a better view and him the benefit of a closer look at the yellow shirt. There was a sharp citrussy kind of scent to him that she loved. 'She's left university.'

To her surprise, Rupert laughed. 'I suppose Jess is devastated?'

'You suppose right.' Jess didn't show it, but Louisa could see she was at a complete loss. It couldn't be easy to accept, when you'd set your heart on your daughter achieving what you yourself had not.

'I'll have to pay her a visit.' His eyes were amused. 'Remind her that yours truly chucked in university life and never regretted it for a second.'

'It might help.'

A customer approached the bar and Louisa went to serve him, moving quickly, wanting to get back to Rupert before he demolished that pint of beer and left. She wasn't surprised that he'd gone to university – probably Oxford, he looked classy enough.

'But since Sophie's come back home...' This time she tried to look vulnerable and helpless. Claude had always said she was about as helpless as a killer whale, but it was worth a try; it tended to bring out a man's protective instincts. 'That means I'll have to move out.'

He didn't reply. Perhaps Rupert didn't have any protective instincts.

'There are only the two bedrooms, you see.'

'Yeah.'

'And the cottage is pretty crowded already.'

'Um.' Not the greatest conversationalist, was he?

'So, I was wondering...' In for a penny. Louisa had never been scared to go for it. 'Er, you're not looking for a lodger, by any chance, are you?'

'Me?' He stared at her. He looked nervous at the idea although she couldn't imagine why.

'Well, I'll have to find somewhere pretty quick. Sophie doesn't want to share her room and why should she? I've been dossing down in the sitting room, but last night Felix came home drunk as a skunk and tripped right over me.' She drew breath. It had actually been quite painful. And she didn't half pity Jess having to sleep in the same bed as him,

262

with all that beery breath wafting around. Felix was behaving rather badly just now. 'Seeing as you live next door,' she went on, 'in such a big cottage – for one, that is – I wondered...' Shut up, Louisa. You're blabbing. 'If you were maybe fed up with rattling around there on your own, or even in need of a bit of help with the rent. Or something.' She sighed. A bit over the top, huh?

He was staring at her, and smoking, his mouth turning up at the corners just slightly, his eyes hooded. Talk about strong and silent ... this guy would make Clint Eastwood look like the biggest gossip in town.

'Only as a temporary measure, of course,' she said. 'Until I find somewhere.'

Still he didn't speak, so she went off to serve another customer. Why had she bothered? It had been a dumb idea and she had blown any chance she might have had with him; blown it sky high.

'Forget it,' she said when she got back, quickly, before he had the chance to speak, to make some transparent excuse. 'It was a stupid idea. You probably like living on your own. Lots of people do. It's just that I saw you, and I thought...'

'You don't always talk this much, do you?' Rupert drained his pint.

She went on the defensive. 'Sometimes.'

'Ah.' He scrutinised her carefully.

She decided to be truthful; he seemed to demand it. 'Well, when I'm nervous, I do.'

'All right,' Rupert said, after a moment.

'All right?'

He blew a perfect smoke ring. 'A week's trial to make sure we don't murder each other?'

'You're on.' Suddenly Louisa felt much more cheerful. If she couldn't seduce him when they were living in the same house, then she really was losing her touch.

Sophie didn't particularly want to go anywhere or see anyone, but if she were forced to choose, she would choose Peter Beck and his studio.

She could tell her mother wanted her out from under her feet – not that she was there very much herself, but when she was she went into clucking mode, which made Sophie feel depressed as well as guilty. Mums and Dad had laid out the money for her to go to uni and she knew she'd let them down. And she also knew (because Mums kept reminding her in the nicest possible way) that she had to *do* something with her life. But she didn't know, without Nick, what on earth that something might be.

So when her mother suggested she might go to Abbotsbury with her father one day, she virtually jumped at it. Anything was better than sitting around here.

'Hi there, stranger.'

Sophie slipped on to the low stool beside him, attempting to peer over his shoulder. 'Hi, Peter.' She was fairly confident that he would neither judge nor lecture. 'What are you working on?'

'A brooch.' He gestured towards a sheaf of papers to her left. She picked them up, leafed through them, noting the design, face on on one sheet, in profile on another, various detail on another, a further sheet of scribbled notes and pricings. But right now his attention was focused on the piece of metal he was working on with a needle file using the bench pin – a wedge-shaped wooden support fitted right on the curve of his workbench. Below it was a tray to collect the metal filings, called lemmel. Sophie knew all this, because in the past she had drunk in any information about his work that Peter had ever made available to her.

'In silver?' she asked.

'Yes, and malachite and sodalite.'

264

'Nice.' Sophie loved being with Peter Beck when he was working. He wasn't a man for unnecessary conversation, just as his jewellery design was not riddled with irrelevant detail. It was the simplicity – almost a purity – in his work that she liked. And he had always talked to her as if she were an equal. He would never preach, nor bore her to tears.

'It's very unusual.' She fingered some pieces of silver on his workbench. Examples he had been experimenting with, by the look of it. 'Like trellis.'

'Based on an industrial design,' he explained, his light eyes focusing on the intricate silverwork in front of him. 'Somebody called Depres started the whole thing off.'

'After the industrial revolution?' she asked.

'Later than that. Very Deco.'

'So what's it saying?' Knowing he wouldn't mind, Sophie picked up some paper and a pencil and began to draw idly, a silver trellis-work of her own: a bangle for the upper arm, spiralling snakelike, then abruptly changing direction and winding back again. She pushed it aside – for some reason it reminded her of Nick. But then, right now everything reminded her of Nick.

'You mean the brooch?' Peter made an adjustment to the drawing.

'Yeah.' She knew he would understand. Peter had always maintained that each piece of jewellery had an individual voice, that each design was conveying some message – to the buyer, to the wearer, to everyone who saw it.

He worked on, taking his time before responding. This habit of his drove her father bonkers, but at least whatever Peter said would be worth waiting for. Today, as usual, he was wearing old grey overalls, probably the same ones he had worn when she was a child; they had a metallic, slightly dusty smell to them, with overtones of glue and some chemical or other. It was a smell that was strangely comforting.

265

His fair hair was sticking up on end as it invariably did, and there was a pencil stuck behind each ear, although he usually forgot about these, using another one entirely. He looked eccentric, more mad scientist than jewellery designer.

'All the industrial designs tend towards the clinical,' he said. 'Clean lines, straight lines, don't mess with me.'

'A bit cold though?' she wondered out loud.

'It would be without the malachite,' he suggested. 'It's a balance of surface and depth, a mix of temperatures.'

Sophie ran her finger across the grooves of the silver. 'And interesting to touch,' she added.

'Good.' He nodded approvingly as if she were a star pupil. 'Depres started the new thinking about surface and texture, hence the way the silver is moulded.' He waved behind him. 'There's a book over there on Deco. It has a section about him if you're interested.'

She was. Sophie got up, found the book and flipped through the pages. 'Tell me more about the malachite,' she asked. 'Is it just there for warmth and depth? What about the colour?' It was one of her favourite semi-precious stones.

'It fits in with the texture theme too,' Peter explained. 'Silk-smooth but mottled green surfaces.'

Sophie understood. Texture and symmetry were almost as close to her heart as they were to Peter Beck's.

He pushed the pad away and picked up Sophie's drawing. 'What's this?'

'My bangle.' She ripped off the paper and drew a close-up with confident strokes of the pencil.

'One you've got?' He sounded interested.

'One I want.'

He smiled at her, became thoughtful. 'Maybe I'll make it up for you. It could use a copper inlay, what do you think?'

'That would be great.' She glanced across at him. 'Peter?

266

Did you always know what you wanted to do?' He was a man who seemed dedicated to his career, and it was the kind of dedication that she too would like to feel. Only for what? 'More or less.' He paused in thought. 'I was always good with my hands – but anyone who was clever with their hands was supposed to go and train to be a plumber or an electrician or something remotely useful.'

She smiled. 'Is that what your parents wanted for you?'

'Too right.' Peter pulled his fingers through his hair until it was sticking up even more than before. 'They certainly didn't take too kindly to the idea of me making *jewellery*.' He pulled a face. 'In fact Dad started to harbour grave suspicions concerning my sexuality.'

Sophie giggled. 'Real men don't care for jewellery? Let alone want to make it?'

'Something like that. But books like these...' Peter got up and pulled another one off the shelf behind them, 'just yelled at me, you know? I loved metalwork, I loved art, and I wanted to learn how to make some of this stuff, things that people would wear, jewellery that would probably live longer than I would.' He turned the pages. 'It was all here – the inspiration. It still is.' He read aloud. 'Jewellery and artefacts of the Orient, of Egypt, of Africa.'

'Yeah.' She could see how it must have been.

'It touched me.' With a small sigh he replaced the book on the shelf. 'Very much. And it led me into Art Deco, I suppose. The same influences interest me.'

Sophie was conscious of a wave of despair. She thought of Nick and adult deceit. It made her sick. He made her sick; she felt so pointless somehow. 'I said I'd meet Dad for lunch.' Although she didn't want to; she'd rather sit here and watch Peter Beck. 'Can I come again?'

'Of course.' Peter's attention returned to his work and she knew that in a moment he'd be fully involved, that he'd probably forget she'd even been here.

267

Chapter 21

Peter Beck phoned Jess several days later. 'What would you say to me offering Sophie a job?' he asked.

'At Beck and Newman?'

'Where else?'

Jess was torn. She didn't want a job, a future, to simply fall into Sophie's lap. She wanted to wake her daughter up, make her go for it herself. 'I really don't know why you should bother.'

'I'm fond of her.'

'Ye-es.' That much was true. So far Peter had shown more concern than Sophie's own father.

'And I think she could use some – what do they call it these days – work experience?' Peter laughed. 'It's got to be better than sitting around stagnating in that cottage of yours.'

'I suppose so. But if you're doing this just to be kind...'

'Oh, don't worry, Jess. Marilyn assures me I am never kind. And Beck and Newman are not in the habit of carrying anyone. You should know that.'

'Well, good.' Of course he was right – Sophie should do something. But would she want to do this?

'After all, she's got plenty of ideas in her head,' Peter said.

'You're telling me.' The problem was that most of them concerned this Nick character.

'And she wants to go her own way.'

'Ye-es.' It was hard to give the benefit of her own experience – such as it was – to Sophie. Louisa had tried too, but Sophie seemed to have built up such an armoury around her that right now, neither of them could get through.

'But then again...' She could almost see Peter Beck's easy shrug of his big shoulders. 'I like a bit of spirit. And ideas are food and drink to a designer.'

'A designer?' Jess stared at the phone. What on earth was he talking about?

'Well, you never know.' His tone suggested he was sorry that he'd said too much. 'It's early days, but if she were to work hard...'

'Yes?'

'She's always had the interest, Jess. Even a passion.'

'Passion?' Jess had never thought of Sophie's childhood enthusiasm for Peter's studio-workshop in those terms before. But she was beginning to wonder if everyone else knew her daughter rather better than she did.

'And she certainly has a talent for design. Specifically for jewellery design.'

'Really?' Jess couldn't have been more surprised if he had suggested Sophie had the makings of a deep sea diver. But what would Felix say? 'Felix,' she began.

'Oh, let me deal with Felix.' His voice grew serious. 'Is he all right, Jess? Are you all right?'

'I don't know.' Suddenly she wished that instead of talking to this man on a telephone line, she could actually be there with him, just in case she decided to crumple up in a heap and have a good old boo. His shoulders were broad enough for sure.

'I know things aren't right between you,' he said. 'The man's all over the place, anyone can see that.'

269

'I'm sorry, Peter.' It had never occurred to Jess that his work would be suffering too. Felix had always been such a perfectionist.

'Nothing to apologise for.' He sounded quite fierce. 'Are you going to leave him?'

Put like that, it seemed awfully final, and very scary. 'I'm not sure. I almost feel it's the only way. And yet...'

'It's been a long time.' She realised that he understood absolutely. 'A long road. A daughter, shared experiences. there has to be a very good reason to leave, to upset the status quo, to turn your life upside down.' He sounded as if he might have already considered all this for himself.

'Yes. Yes, there does.' The thought of Matthew Hill pushed itself into her mind and she pushed it equally firmly away. No. Matthew Hill was a client who had become a friend – nothing more.

There was no answer to her ring on the doorbell, so Jess let herself in with the key Matthew had given her. *I want you to come and go as you please*, he had told her right from the start, and nothing had changed.

She was thankful that their relationship had improved since she'd been working on the sitting room; gone was the frosty politeness he had shown her that day when she'd dashed off to Axminster to buy fabric (in colours that would warm him up?) before meeting Sophie at the station. In its place was a kind of vague friendliness which did not quite match the warmth of before, but was fairly safe, at least, something that didn't cause her sleepless nights.

Only Felix caused her those – with his drinking, and his ... surely he was seeing someone? They no longer talked, they no longer made love; she wasn't sure how long she could go on with this, and yet she was conscious of a fierce loyalty that still made her cling to him. He had been the saving of her once upon a time. And now with this new life of hers she had separated herself from him; it couldn't be easy for Felix. She kept hoping that something would change.

She headed straight for the sitting room to assess the bits of painting she had completed yesterday and which would now be dry. The colour scheme had developed into a mixture of fire and earth, rough shades painted freehand 'Mexican style' on a wall that had first been textured with plaster bonding, to avoid straight lines and smooth finishes. Sienna and burnt orange predominated; intense earth reds that complemented Matthew's walnut bookcase and chairs, and which clashed beautifully with the touches of Aztec gold and toffee-brown in the borders she'd designed. Jess smiled as she stood still to gauge the effect. It worked.

'Hot and spicy,' murmured a voice behind her.

Jess jumped. 'For heaven's sake! You scared me to death.'

Matthew grinned. 'Don't worry – if it comes to the worst, there's a doctor close at hand.'

'Hmm.' Jess moved into the room and glanced back at him. There was a warm and crumpled look about Matthew this afternoon. 'You didn't answer the door,' she said. 'Were you asleep?'

His yawn appeared to confirm this. 'I had a few hours to catch up on. It was a bad night.' He peered at the bag she was holding. 'What have you been up to today?'

'More shopping and sewing.' She opened it and showed him the saffron-yellow roller blind she had made up herself.

'Mmm.'

She unrolled it and held it against the window so that the light shone through, muted, warm, like seductive sunshine. *Mmm* told her nothing. 'But do you like it?'

'Of course I do.'

'And do you like the room now it's almost finished?'

'Of course I do.'

'*Of course, of course,*' she mimicked him. 'Would you tell me if you hated it?'

He spread his hands and grinned. 'Of course I would.'

Jess shook her head in despair. It had been the same with the hallway. Matthew Hill had given her carte blanche, whether she wanted it or not. Her fellow students at the college were madly envious when she described the kind of canvases she was working with, but Jess was left with no meter with which to measure her efforts.

'Are you pleased with it yourself?' Matthew asked.

'I love it,' she said with sudden confidence, aware that she would adore to have a room like this one. She hadn't had a chance to do any decorating in Cliff Cottage lately, but if she did ... *when* she did, she would have a room in these colours. Exactly these colours. It's as if I've done it for myself, she thought. And that was dangerous.

'I approve of all your choices,' Matthew informed her.

'I always knew you had good taste.' She pulled the fabric back up on to its roller. It was better to keep things light and jokey. Safer too.

He came over to help her. 'Oh, I have that all right.'

Caught unawares, she glanced up at him. On second thoughts, not safe at all. He was only a few feet away and he was looking into her face, as if he were searching for something. His light blue eyes were suddenly intent, his face was drawn, his dark hair had flopped over his brow but for once he hadn't immediately brushed it back again with tired fingers. He seemed very serious. Jess gazed back at him, wondering. She didn't know how long they stayed like that – perhaps it was only a few seconds, but it seemed like much longer, as the tension stretched between them.

'I can manage, thanks.' With a sharp pull of the blind, she broke the tension, becoming the brisk professional once more. But could she manage? Could she manage him?

'So you've almost finished the room?' He sounded rather sad.

'Uh huh.' But she knew how he felt. There was a sense of achievement but also anti-climax, at the completion of a room, that she was beginning to recognise. 'Though I still have the cushion covers to finish.' They had been the beginning and also would be the end. 'I'll be doing those at home.' Perhaps the word *home* would remind him that she had one; a home with a husband and a grown-up daughter living in it.

But Matthew moved from her side and the moment might almost never have happened. 'You've done a good job.' His voice was cool as he trailed his fingers along the rough surface of the wall. 'I expect I shall think of you every time I sit in this room.'

Jess forced a laugh. 'Oh, yeah, sure you will.' Swiftly, she changed the subject. 'And then there's the floor, of course. The floor covering is coming tomorrow, isn't it?' She pulled out her diary and checked the date.

'Tomorrow?' Matthew frowned.

'Do you want me to come and supervise?'

'Please.'

Jess didn't look at him. 'Are you working, then?'

'I'm not sure yet.'

Since when had he not been sure if he had a surgery or was on call? 'OK, well I may as well put the blind up now.' Jess had decided on a simple window treatment to complement the Mexican theme; in the car she also had some fine muslin which she intended to dye burnt orange and use as a window drape. She might get that done tonight too.

Jess moved the stepladder and started fixing the blind, but Matthew didn't leave the room. She dropped the fixing screw with a ping on to bare floorboards.

They both scrabbled on their hands and knees looking for it.

'You're making me nervous.' She was back on the ladder and he was still in the room. 'Do you have to stand there watching me?' She dropped the damn screw – again. 'All right, all right.' This time he let her look for it on her own. He left the room with a quizzical expression. Jess found the screw and wished he'd come back. And a cup of tea would go down well. But Matthew had disappeared.

She was just clearing up, almost ready to go home, when he came back in with the tea she'd wanted. It was hot and strong and she drank it gratefully.

'Do you fancy a walk?' He was wearing a denim jacket and had a camera slung over one shoulder. 'Just down to the woods. There are some shots I want to get.'

Jess hesitated. She was tired, and it was getting late. She had been hoping to finish the cushions and the muslin but maybe that would have to wait.

'It's only four thirty.' He smiled, teasing her, seeming to slot their relationship back into the casual friendship she was comfortable with. 'And there's something I particularly want to show you.'

She was immediately intrigued. 'All right.' It would be a relief to get some fresh air after the paint and plaster smell of this room. And wasn't it perfectly natural to go for a walk with Matthew? She wanted to see whatever it was he wanted to show her. Back to friendship perhaps, but she couldn't just leave, she found, with this moment, this feeling, this whatever it was, resting incomplete between them.

They walked down the lane, across a muddy field, over a stile and into the deciduous wood of oak and beech that she had previously only seen from the window on the landing of Matthew's house.

'Did you marry young, Jess?' Matthew asked her, as he led the way down a grassy path between the beech trees.

Was it that obvious? She smiled. 'I think you'd say eighteen was pretty young.'

He whistled through his teeth. She waited for him to ask her if she was happy, but he didn't. 'I was twenty-one. Just a boy. A penniless medical student in fact.'

'And your wife?' she asked politely. She had found little evidence in his house of his ex's continuing influence on his life. The photograph in the sun-room was the only indication that Matthew even thought about her.

'The same,' he said. 'The same age anyway. She was studying classics.'

Clever then, Jess thought. Her teachers had persuaded her to do Latin at school but beyond *amo amas amat*, she had never grasped the rudiments. She might have continued studying though – if she had not married Felix. 'You must have been happy at first,' she suggested, not knowing what he expected her to say.

Matthew laughed humourlessly as he ducked to avoid the overhanging branch of a beech tree. 'Happy in my ignorance,' he said.

'Come again?'

'I stopped liking Pamela when I got to know her,' he explained. 'That took quite a while. But it took even longer to stop loving her, to stop wanting her back.' He held the branch away from the path for her to pass.

'But you must have got to know her before you married,' she protested. He was making it sound as if he knew nothing about his own wife. 'And you had two children together,' she said, trying to remember their ages.

'Ah, but it was much later than that when I really got to know her.'

He was still holding the overhanging branch as she joined him on the other side of the tree. She was so close to him she could read the bitterness in his eyes. She stopped walking. 'When was it then?'

Matthew allowed the branch to whip back behind them. 'When she ran off with my partner who also happened to be my best friend. Only a certain sort of person can do that kind of thing.' He stomped on down the path.

His best friend. His partner. Jess thought of Felix. Felix, she realised with a slight shock, didn't have a best friend. While she had Patti and Ruth in Sussex, both of whom phoned from time to time to share gossip and a laugh. And here in Dorset she had Susie, Rupert, and of course Louisa. Probably, Louisa was her best friend of all.

She walked on, catching Matthew up by a majestic old oak tree, just before a bend in the path. 'I'm sorry,' she said, touching his arm. 'That must have been very hard for you.'

'It was.' He looked over her left shoulder, as if avoiding her sympathy. 'But it turned out not to be the end of the world I thought it was. I survived.' He glanced at her at last. 'And I shouldn't have burdened you with it.'

'Nonsense.' Jess took a firm hold of his arm. 'It helps to talk.'

'But you don't, do you?' She was conscious that he was performing another one of his close scrutinies as they walked on down the path.

'Don't I?' The late afternoon sun was glinting through the pale young leaves of the beech trees with a promise of the summer to come. She was glad to be here. But, no, she didn't talk.

'Even though you're not happy.'

It seemed silly to say that he was a client, and it seemed almost a betrayal of their friendship to pretend. 'How can you tell?' she asked.

'I never know for sure. I just see it sometimes – a sadness in your eyes, a need to keep busy, a look – as if you want to forget. When you've felt pain you recognise it in others.'

She knew what he meant. But she didn't want to brood

276

over her own marriage. She was fed up thinking about it. Resolutely, she pushed it all from her mind. 'Why do you keep her picture in the sun-room?' she asked instead. She had always wanted to know and now seemed as good a time as any to ask.

'To remind me.'

She was about to ask him what he needed to be reminded of. But at that moment they turned the corner, she felt his body tense, and then she saw in front of them exactly what he had wanted to show her. It was a glorious carpet of blue-bells woven through the trees and undergrowth, stretching in a mass of intense blue and green almost as far as she could see.

'Wow!' She clung to his arm. 'They're beautiful.'

'I knew you'd appreciate the sight of this lovely lot.' He took a few steps forward and she let go of his arm. 'They're always a picture at this time of year.'

Jess wandered further down the path. 'You're not kidding.'

He took his camera out of its case. 'This is my first visit this year. I wanted to take a few shots in the afternoon light.'

And she could see why. The late sun was slanting through the beech leaves, illuminating some of the bluebells, leaving others in deep shadow, while more bands of shade were formed by the beech trees themselves. The whole created a contrast of light and shadow that she found strangely exciting. And she had thought that this man had no eye for colour...

While he was taking the photographs Jess sat down on a fallen tree trunk, knees to her chest, watching Matthew as he wandered in the sea of bluebells. She smiled to herself. Considering there were so many, he was being almost ridiculously careful not to trample them; he would take a few cautious steps, and every now and then he would squat among them – really low, half-hidden – in his attempt to get

277

the right angle for every frame. He was soon entirely unaware of her presence, she felt, lost in absorption in his task. And he looked younger than usual. When he pushed his hair back from his face, as he did every so often, she sensed contentment. She saw that he had lost the drawn look that his face had held earlier on, when he had been talking about his wife. And she surmised that Matthew Hill knew a lot about pain, but that he knew more than his fair share about beauty too.

'Come over here,' he called.

'What for?' But she got up.

'See that patch of grass.' He pointed. 'Go and sit in the bluebells.'

'Oh, Matthew, honestly...' But the grin on his face was infectious and she found herself picking a path carefully through the flowers just as he had done, until she reached the spot he'd indicated. 'Here?' She sat down, stretched out her legs and was immediately assaulted by the exotic scent of them, the velvet softness of the blooms, the coolness of the leaves on her fingers, and most of all by the intensity of their colour. 'Wonderful. What a feast.' She sniffed deeply, stretched out her arms and lay down full length, half-lost to the flowers but still conscious of the camera clicking, of Matthew rapidly snapping away.

At last she sat up. The noise had ceased; he had stopped taking photographs, and was standing quite still, watching her.

'I brought two films with me, and they're both finished.'

She sighed. 'It's so beautiful here, Matt. Thank you for showing it to me.' The shortened version of his name came naturally to her.

He made no sign that he'd noticed as he held out a hand to help her to her feet. 'Your husband will be wondering where you've got to,' he said instead.

The comment surprised her. Mention of Felix had no

278

place here among the bluebells. 'That'll be a first.' She took hold of his hand. It was warm to the touch, as it had been on the day of their first and only handshake. She allowed him to pull her upright so that they were standing close together once more, bathed in late afternoon sunshine, surrounded by wave upon wave of bluebells.

He put his hands gently on her shoulders. 'Jess...'

'Don't, Matt.' She kept her voice gentle, but eased herself away from his hands. Why did he need the photograph of his ex-wife to remind him, she wondered again. Of what?

'"Don't, Matt," now or, "Don't Matt," never?' he asked.

She didn't honestly know. Yes, she was drawn to him; yes, they seemed to have some understanding that did not always need words. But, 'I'm not free,' she said instead. 'You know I'm not free.'

'And I also know I never intended to fall—'

'Ssh.' She reached out to put her fingers on his lips, but he caught them and did not relinquish her hand.

'We should go back,' she said, looking down at their intertwined fingers. But could they?

He nodded, released her hand; she saw the weariness return to his face, the smile leave his eyes.

In silence they returned the way they had come – down the path, out of the wood, over the stile and across the field. They walked up the lane to his cottage.

'Come in for a drink,' he said, as they reached the gate.

She sighed. 'Matt...'

'I want to tell you something.'

And Jess realised that she too had something she wanted to say to him. It was pointless running away from it.

She followed him into the house. He went to the kitchen to open a bottle of wine; Jess headed straight for the sitting room. She turned the dimmer switch that controlled the wall lights; the lamps were diffusing the light in a soft glow, illu-

279

minating the fiery tones of the room just as she had hoped. 'Lovely,' she whispered.

Matthew came to stand by her side and handed her a glass of wine. 'Thanks for creating me such a stunning room,' he said.

'You really like it?' And this time she could see that he did.

'But I'm beginning to dislike my bedroom intensely,' he went on conversationally.

'Matthew...'

'I liked it better when you called me Matt.' Lightly he touched her cheek. 'You did this room much too fast. The bedroom should take a bit longer. I'd rather like handmade fitted wardrobes.'

She turned to face him. 'Matt, this isn't right.'

'Why not?' His expression changed once more.

'Because it's like playing house, when you and I are...' She knew he was waiting for her to finish. But *what* were they?

'You being married to someone else doesn't feel right,' he said.

'But I am, and I can't go on working for you if you want something more.'

'What's holding you to him, Jess?' He said this softly, his voice so close to her his lips were almost touching her hair. 'If he makes you unhappy. And he does, doesn't he? I know it.'

It was all so simple, she thought, for those who weren't involved. Felix had once made her feel beautiful, ecstatic, glad to be alive. Felix had caused her pain, but he had also saved her from worse than pain. When she'd had no one, Felix had been there. He was still there, still wanting her. Still loving her...

'Is it other women?' Matthew asked. 'Does he treat you badly?'

280

Jess shook her head. 'No, he doesn't hit me.' He loves me, she thought. Matthew was assuming some great drama; or he thought her marriage had slunk into middle age, becoming boring, ordinary, unexciting, sexless. It simply wasn't like that.

'Why do you stay with him?' Matthew persevered.

She thought of her talk with Peter. Love, habit, the lack of a strong enough reason to leave. She looked into Matthew's face. She owed him total honesty. 'I can't imagine life without him,' she said. 'I don't want to lead you on, Matt.' That was what she had needed to say. 'I don't want you to think I'll ever be your lover.'

'A woman of loyalty.' He smiled, but his eyes were solemn once more as he traced a fingertip from the bridge of her nose to her lips.

'Hardly.'

'Well, I don't want to lose you. That was what I wanted to tell you.'

And Jess realised that she felt the same way. Matthew and his house were a big part of her new world.

'So will you redesign my bedroom? If I promise to keep your reputation intact?'

She smiled. 'Bedrooms are very personal.' It was taking a tremendous effort of will to resist him, and she wondered if he was aware of this. 'But I might.'

'And I want to be more than a client,' he murmured, bending, so that his lips were very close to her ear. She could feel his breath, warm on her bare neck. 'That was another thing I wanted to tell you.'

'Oh, you are.' Just for a second she allowed herself to close her eyes. Just for a second she would let herself feel... And then she would move away. She would...

But he released her.

Jess opened her eyes to see the bitter-sweet expression in his. Did he really understand?

'And the third thing I wanted to tell you,' he said.

'Three things,' she murmured.

'Was that I'm willing to accept it.'

'Accept it?' She was confused.

'Us being just good friends.'

'I see.' She should – she really should – be glad.

'Friends then?' He held out his hand in a way that was, she felt, unnecessarily businesslike.

'Friends.' She took it.

'And the bedroom?'

She smiled back at him. 'Of course I'll do it.' She couldn't for the life of her think of any reason why not.

'Good.'

Jess drained her glass, picked up her bag and headed for Matthew's front door and home. It was only when she stood outside, that she realised he had somehow managed to trick her. But at least she wouldn't have to stop seeing him. And she would create him a wonderful bedroom. One to die for. One that even she would be satisfied with.

She unlocked her Renault. There was absolutely nothing wrong with spending more time with Matthew Hill, nothing remotely wrong in having lunch, a drink, a walk, a talk. Because he had become a friend. And wasn't that what friends were for?

Chapter 22

Louisa read her one letter with mounting excitement, waited until she saw Felix's car snaking its way down Jupps Lane, and then ran out the back way to the cottage next door. The letter had given her a wonderful idea.

Her sister was in the back garden, apparently watering the stream.

'Jess?' Louisa stopped in her tracks. 'What are you doing? Is the water level too low or something?'

'After all that rain we've had lately? You must be joking.'

And she was right, the pond was full to bursting point.

'So.' Louisa narrowed her eyes. 'What *are* you doing?'

Jess pushed the tangle of wild hair from her face. She was wearing jeans, a vest top, and a blue fleece. 'It's the only time I get to do the gardening,' she complained with a good-natured smile. 'I'm due over at Matt's in half an hour.'

'Matt's?' Louisa raised one eyebrow suggestively. Her sister was spending so much time there; she was beginning to think she'd been right to tease her.

'Oh, don't you start.' Jess flushed. 'It's only because he wants so much work done. And I haven't exactly had prospective clients banging on the door. Maybe Felix is right. Maybe they don't want a student to do their decorating.'

283

'And maybe Felix is jealous.' Should she tell her? Rupert had let slip over dinner last night that he'd seen Marilyn Beck in Felix's car in Lyme the day before. Which seemed to indicate that Marilyn was still in his life. And that Jess was still ignorant of that fact.

'Hmm.' Jess started making a whooshing noise, as she sprayed the stream with more water. Had she gone completely loopy?

'For God's sake, Jess. What on earth are you doing?'

'It's the watercress.' She looked faintly apologetic. 'Felix thinks I'm mad, but it works. Honestly. They want a fast-running stream, so twice a day I come out here and pretend to be a waterfall.' They both laughed. Loopy, ah, yes, no doubt about it.

'So do you have time to make me a coffee?' Louisa followed Jess through the workshop and into her kitchen. She waved the letter at her. 'I have news.'

'In the pot.' Jess indicated the fresh coffee and Louisa sniffed appreciatively. She liked living next door but there were some things she missed about Cliff Cottage, and Felix's liking for fresh, strong coffee in the morning was one of them.

'What news?' Jess paused to smile at her. Louisa was looking particularly young and innocent this morning (it just showed how deceptive appearances could be) with her dark hair framing her narrow face and her green eyes gleaming. She was wearing a pair of dungarees with an embroidered smock; she looked like a flower child from the sixties. She was also flapping some airmail letter around and looking ridiculously smug.

'When does your term finish?' Louisa demanded.

'This week.' Jess checked the calendar. Two more days. It was fun, but some breathing space – at last – was a welcome prospect. And it would give her a chance to get on with Matthew's bedroom. 'Why?'

'Because,' Louisa sipped her coffee,' I'd like to drag you away for a while.'

'To do what?' Jess began to throw things into a canvas holdall. She would be going straight on after college, so she needed stuff for Matt's, stuff for tutorials. She was concentrating so hard, she barely heard what Louisa was saying.

'I've had a letter from Claude.' She waved it in the air again. 'Remember Claude?'

'Vividly.' Some of Louisa's stories had left her in stitches. He sounded quite a character.

'Well, he's been left some money...'

'Lucky Claude.' Now, Jess began throwing books into a huge shoulder bag. She added some pens and a large sketchpad, and zipped up the bag.

'And so he's bought himself a little bar.' Two bright red spots appeared on Louisa's cheeks.

'Lovely.' Jess did one of her rapid whizzes round the kitchen to make it not quite so awful to come home to. Dishes in the dishwasher, table wiped, cereal away. The rest could wait.

'With a couple of apartments. And...' She paused.

Jess grabbed both bags. She felt as if she had at least two lives as well. And now it was time to go off to one of them. 'And?'

'And he wants me to visit.' Louisa followed her down the hall.

'Sounds wonderful, darling.' Jess kissed her. 'Then you must go.' Lucky Louisa to have no adult responsibilities. Always such a child. Look at the way she dressed, for a start. She shook her head in part amusement, part despair.

'I think we should both go,' Louisa said firmly, opening the front door for her.

Jess stared at her grinning face. 'You and me?'

'Why not?' Louisa was waiting, she could see that. Louisa knew quite well that Jess had not been back to

285

Brittany, and so she certainly knew what she was suggesting. 'I came here to spend time with you,' she said softly. 'And now you're so busy I hardly see you.'

'Oh, Louisa...' Didn't she have enough of that, from Felix?

'No, it's good – what you're doing, I mean.' Louisa touched her hair. 'I admire you for it, really. But...'

Jess stood on the doorstep and waited for her to go on.

'But I want to go back to Brittany.' Louisa sounded thoughtful. 'Just for a couple of weeks. With you.'

'Can you get time off from the pub?' And did Jess want to resurrect those memories of childhood?

'Of course I can.' Louisa dismissed this with a wave of her hand. 'And it's perfect for you – it's the Easter holidays.'

But then, she didn't know about Matthew. Jess felt a sharp jolt of fear.

'You need a break,' Louisa said.

'Do I?' She could certainly do with a break from Felix. 'But what about Sophie?'

'Don't be daft.' They both knew that Sophie's independence was growing. She was eighteen. There was no way on earth she needed her mother to show the way forward. And she wouldn't even be alone in the house since Felix would be around.

'Well...'

'Where's your spirit of adventure?' Louisa whispered.

'Maybe I haven't got one,' Jess whispered back, laughing at her.

'It'll be fun.' Louisa grabbed her hands, forcing her to drop the holdall on the ground. 'Let's go the day after tomorrow if we can get a crossing.'

'The day after tomorrow?' Jess hadn't conceived of going so quickly. She would barely have time to pack.

Louisa shrugged. 'What do we have to wait for?'

And all of a sudden Jess couldn't think of anything. She had always envied Louisa her easy-come, easy-go lifestyle. And this must be what it felt like: not to plan, just to live. 'OK,' she said. It felt good. A chance to get away, to be with Louisa, even to confront some of those ghosts from the past perhaps. It might not be so terrifying after all.

It would be good timing, Louisa thought, as she waited for the bus to take her into Lyme, if she could get a little closer to Rupert before they left for France.

Consequently, when she'd finished what she had to do she walked along to his shop. Jess had told her where it was, but she hadn't got round to visiting. With Rupert, she felt she had to tread so damned carefully, in order not to send him racing in the opposite direction from her welcoming arms.

As Jess had said, the shop was situated on the street that led down to the Cobb, squashed between a baker's and a fossil store. And as Jess had also said, Louisa recalled as she opened the door, watching him stoop as he examined the casing of a huge bookcase, the shop was much too small for him.

'I just called in...' she paused, as the dust made her sneeze loudly, 'to tell you that I'm off to Brittany in a day or two. Only for a couple of weeks.' Yes, of course she could have told him tonight. But she had a good reason for wanting him to know now. Louisa draped herself decoratively across a high-backed wooden chair, and examined his expression. Was he pleased? Was he sorry? Did he care?

'Right.' It was impossible to say. Apparently his attention belonged exclusively to the bookcase.

She took a deep breath. 'And do you fancy fish and chips for lunch? By the Cobb?'

At last she had his attention. He turned to face her, his fingers raking ineffectually through his cropped hair. 'Lunch?'

'Well, you do eat, don't you?' He certainly ate at home, although the standard left much to be desired. Louisa wasn't one for home cooking and had taken to eating her main meal in the pub on the nights she was working.

'Oh, yes, I eat all right.' He grinned.

Very tasty. His nose was not so much beaky as aristocratic. And his profile wasn't pretty, but it was pretty damn interesting. Louisa kept her hands interlocked behind her neck. She wanted to grab hold of him. She wanted to grab him and kiss him long and hard, and then perhaps jump on top of him right here in this poky, dusty little shop crammed with furniture, tools and polishes.

He wiped his hands clean on his jeans, caught her eye, grinned again and moved out to the back of the shop where she supposed there was a washbasin.

'Going to France on your own, are you?' he called.

'No.' She watched him as he reappeared looking exactly the same as before. His cropped head very nearly hit the ceiling. He was long and lean and irresistibly angular; and his body was unexplored territory. Louisa had always been an explorer at heart. Would he ask who she was going with? Did he ever think about her *that way*? Who knew? As far as Louisa was concerned, he was too much in control. He clearly never let anything get to him and that was half the trouble because it meant *she* couldn't get to him either. Any emotions he had must be tightly packed inside. What would it take to make him pounce?

'I'm going with Jess,' she told him as they walked down the street to the Cobb. 'We're exploring our shared past.'

This time there was at least a flicker of emotion. 'It'll do her good,' he said. And then, romantic as Prince Charming, 'Haddock and chips, or what?'

What, she thought. What, being some lovely, tempestuous, wild, glorious sex. 'Cod, please,' she said.

Of course there was one possibility she hadn't considered. Surely not? If Claude were here she'd know for sure. But not Rupert. He couldn't – could he? – be gay?

When they were sitting on the rocks by the harbour, joined every now and then by a hopeful seagull or two, Louisa continued to work out her plan. A girl must have a plan. Faint heart never won man (or should that be lost man? It could be very confusing for a modern girl). No, she decided, thinking of Claude. Occasionally she seemed to detect the faintest glimmer of lust in Rupert's eye. So if he wasn't gay, perhaps he didn't like sex? Maybe he was impotent? She could certainly help him with *those* kinds of problems, once she got her foot in the bed, so to speak.

'Working tonight?' Rupert asked with apparent indifference. Not promising. Perhaps, Louisa thought, he simply didn't fancy her.

'I guess so.' Although if something were to prevent her (like taking part in a seduction scene) she wouldn't lose any sleep over missing a shift. Casual staff were just that – casual. It was one of the perks as far as Louisa was concerned.

'And...' She moved easily into stage two. 'I thought I'd cook dinner.'

'Really?' He seemed shocked.

'Yes, really.' She glared at him over her cod. OK, so she hadn't exactly made much use of the kitchen since she'd been living at Rupert's. But she was a liberated woman, and she'd been around. She might not like cooking, but she had developed a couple of star pulling-meals over the years – nothing fancy, but perfectly adequate if you drank enough decent wine with them. And one of those dishes (lamb korma) was already prepared and waiting to be slowly simmered as and when it was needed.

'Sounds good,' Rupert said vaguely, scrunching his fish

and chip paper into a ball and rolling a cigarette. He leaned back against the rock to smoke it and closed his eyes.

Louisa felt quite weak. The sun was warming her skin, her body was attached to his by some magnetic force that he was clearly unaware of, and it was all she could do not to throw herself into his arms. But the time wasn't quite perfect; she must get everything right, and a public beach wasn't by any means the ideal location. She needed a little privacy in which to express herself more fully.

When he'd finished the cigarette, he got lazily to his feet and pulled her up with a firm grip that got on with the job and didn't linger. 'Back to work, then,' he said.

She mustn't blow this. She took one step towards him and then stopped. 'Why don't you shut up shop and come home early for once?' That sounded about right. Not wheedling or whiny but a bright and logical suggestion with just a hint of the homey. 'It's such a lovely afternoon. We could walk back along the cliff.'

'It's a bit early.' But she could see he was tempted.

'Go on, live dangerously.' She laughed. 'It's only work.'

'Yeah, why not?' Rupert laughed too, already moving more easily, his manner more relaxed. 'You're right. Let's make it early closing day.'

Stage two completed. Louisa felt very confident. So far so good, you might say.

In the jewellery studio where Sophie now worked as Peter Beck's apprentice, Tom Ford was leaning over her shoulder, looking at her drawing. She remembered him of course, from Hilary and Bas's wedding, which seemed like years ago instead of six months.

'Bloody difficult to make,' he observed.

'Why?' She held the pad at arm's length and squinted.

'All those fiddly bits.' He pointed to the delicate daisy pattern she planned to engrave on the brooch.

Sophie sighed. 'But that's the key of the design.'

'It'll take longer, that's all I'm saying.' Tom moved away. 'And time is—'

'Money, yes, I know.'

When Sophie had started working for Beck and Newman she had been excited at the thought of designing her own jewellery, pleased at the prospect of working with Peter in an environment she had always loved, and amazed that she hadn't ever seen it as a career prospect herself. But she had very soon discovered that practical restraint was the company's motto. It might be the only way they could ever make money, as Peter kept telling her, but it was restricting and very frustrating indeed.

'The cost can reflect it,' she told Tom, who was young, but whose position as Peter's right-hand man in the factory meant that he knew an awful lot more than she did about making jewellery. 'It'll just have to have a high selling price.'

'It can reflect it, yes,' he said doubtfully. 'But only up to a point.' And she knew he was right. She wasn't exactly a name – yet.

'OK, don't say another word.' She held up her hands in submission. 'I'll change it.' To begin with she had always asked for a second opinion, confident that Peter Beck would see the artistic value in her drawing and consequently support her. But so far he had sided with Tom every time. She was beginning to realise that artistic talent didn't count for much. And that she had an awful lot to learn. She was only an apprentice at the end of the day, and most of the time she was expected to be general dogsbody and absorb the knowledge Peter, Tom and the others could provide. Peter allowed her the occasional 'bit of fun' as he called these early forays into designing. But there was no room for a prima donna at Beck and Newman.

'Sorry, Sophie.' But Tom lingered, as if he had more to say.

She ripped up the paper and started drawing again, watching him from the corner of her eye. He was a nice enough guy. Not her type, but friendly. 'What?' she asked, when he still didn't leave.

'It's just that a bunch of us are meeting up at the Swansong tomorrow night. For a drink and some food. We wondered if you'd fancy coming.'

Would she? Sophie smiled. 'Yeah, that would be cool. I'd love to. Only how would I get back to Brocklemouth?'

'Can't you crash somewhere?'

'Yeah, maybe, but...' The point was, she didn't *know* anyone in Abbotsbury. She could hardly turn up for a night out with a bunch of people she hardly knew and then ask if she could stay the night with one of them. They would think her a right nerd. And she couldn't get a taxi from Abbotsbury to Brocklemouth. It would cost a small fortune. 'Oh, hell.' It was so hard to build a social life when you lived miles from anywhere, when your father took you to and fro from work, and when the friends you'd gone to school with all lived in another county.

'What's up?' Peter Beck's burly figure swung into the studio.

And Tom slipped out, saying, 'Around eight if you can make it.'

Sophie told Peter. 'And Brocklemouth is miles away,' she complained. 'It's the back of beyond.'

'You could stay the night with us,' he said. 'Litton Cheney's only a couple of miles out of town. I'll give you a lift into Abbotsbury and then you only have to stump up for a taxi fare one way.'

'Could I?' Sophie didn't much care for Peter's wife, but it would be worth it for a good night out.

'Any time.'

'But now that I'm working here...' Sophie was thoughtful. Things should change. She was a working girl now. She

292

wasn't sure that her mother had forgiven her for dropping out of university; her father had certainly not forgiven her for choosing to work in the design field with Peter rather than in sales with him. Mums was always busy, and though they talked, Sophie wasn't sure that they were communicating as well as they might.

'You could save up for a car,' he suggested. 'I'd gladly give you some lessons.'

'That's kind of you.' Sophie drew a curve on her pad that actually *was* a daisy petal. She smiled at it. 'But I want to move out,' she said.

'Ah.'

'I don't want to have to come to work and go back home with Dad every day.' And if she heard another Italian tenor strutting his stuff at eight in the morning she would scream.

'Hmm.'

'And I want to be on my own sometimes.'

'Understandable.' Peter nodded. 'You want to stretch your wings.'

'Something like that.'

'If we paid you a bit more,' he said, 'you could afford to rent a little place. A bedsitter, a room in a house, maybe.'

Sophie's spirits leapt. 'Here in Abbotsbury?'

'Why don't you ask Tom?' Peter said. 'He knows a lot of people around here. And he shares a house with a couple of other blokes – his landlord might have somewhere that's up for grabs.'

'I'll do that.' Sophie decided to try her new idea out on him at the same time. She got to her feet.

'But don't shut the door, Sophie.'

'Huh?' She peered back at him.

'On your parents.' Peter was assembling materials at the other end of the workbench, seemingly engrossed in them. He was working on some carved jade and coral in exotic motifs à la Cartier. As usual, his fair hair was standing up

293

on end as if he'd had a shock or two this morning. 'Don't shut the door,' he said.

'What were you like as a teenager?' Louisa asked Rupert as they walked back along the cliff. 'Were you horrid?'

'Aren't all teenagers?' He stared out to sea. 'I grew upwards – so fast I couldn't keep up with myself, I became a socialist and I rebelled against the middle classes.' His tone was lightly mocking. It was one of the longest speeches she'd ever heard him make.

'And your parents were the middle classes?' she guessed.

'Oh, of course.' He treated her to one of his lovely smiles. 'Don't we all want to rebel against the people that brought us into the world? Are we blaming them, do you think?'

'Probably.' Although she hadn't had the chance to rebel. And she might even have been too scared to. 'What were they like?'

'Materialists.' This time Rupert stopped walking. 'The only working-class person I knew was our cleaner.'

'Why materialists?'

'They had a big house and a flashy car with another run-around for town.' His voice was bitter. 'My father was a solicitor who was excellent at golf and at getting rich on other people's problems. My mother didn't *have* to work.' He laughed. 'So naturally, she didn't.'

'You sound as if you hate them.' This was some pile of emotion she'd uncovered.

'I thought I did, once.' He paused. 'They seemed to sum up everything I couldn't stand about the world.'

'And now?' she asked. 'You don't hate them now?'

'I hardly know them now.'

Louisa thought she could fill in some of the gaps. He had made himself a loner, separated himself from his background, his roots. And in a way she had done the same thing – at least

294

for a while. But the difference was that she was in no position to go back and resolve whatever differences they had known; to meet her parents as an adult, as an equal, to sort out her childhood in her head. And if she could have, would she? She cast a sideways glance at the tall man striding along beside her. She thought that she would be interested to meet his parents. If only to find out a little about where the guy was coming from...

Back at the cottage she made tea and they lounged in the garden enjoying the sun. It was easy and relaxed; Louisa was feeling good. Maybe she would be missing work tonight after all. Soon, it would be time to put the lamb korma on to simmer.

'I'm glad you came into the shop today.' Rupert spoke so abruptly that she jumped.

'Oh?' Her heart went for it. Thumpety-thump, crash bang wallop. 'Why's that?' She was amazed she managed to get the words out at all.

He sat up straighter. 'Well you can see I need a bigger place.'

'Ye-es.' This wasn't exactly what she'd had in mind, but she supposed it was a start.

'And you know Jess is having problems starting out, getting clients?'

'Yes of course I do.' She became brisk. 'But that's because she's still a student. She told me as much today. Once she's qualified—'

'She'll only be qualified for certain design techniques. She may want to take it further. In another year she could do the professional interior design course. Get her advanced certificate.'

'So what are you getting at?' Louisa felt slightly irritated. He seemed to know an awful lot about Jess and her future plans.

295

'I was thinking of asking her if she wanted to join forces with me.'

'Oh?' She was cool. What exactly did he mean by that?

'In the business. If I expand. Restoration and redesign, one fell swoop, you know? Antiques and soft furnishings all in one venue.' All the emotion and enthusiasm she had been looking for was in evidence now. Rupert's eyes were shining with it, he was grinning, his hands were waving around like a traffic policeman's. 'Her course will only be part-time. She could use it as a base for now. What do you think, Louisa? D'you think it would work?'

'It would cost you.' She tried to analyse why she minded. Was it just that Jess had seemed to have it all, and now, without trying, she had the emotion and enthusiasm of this gorgeous man as well?

But he only laughed. 'Money isn't an issue, Louisa.'

Not from where she was standing. In her experience, the only people who didn't think money was an issue were those who had oodles of it to spare.

After a decent period, she went to get them a drink – alcoholic, this time, she was in need of restoration herself, and luckily there was a bottle of Rupert's extremely potent dandelion in the fridge, only just opened. She came back with the drinks, seated herself much closer to him than before, and practised her enigmatic smile.

When they got to drink number two, she shivered slightly and suggested they go inside. Rupert didn't object – she hoped he would be putty in her hands. And as for the drinks, two was a good number – enough to loosen up the inhibitions but not enough to mar performance. Inwardly, she grinned. Wishing...

Once inside, with Rupert on the sofa and Louisa stretched out like a cat on a floor cushion, she moved seamlessly into the next stage of the plan. 'I like you, Rupert,' she said.

'I like you, too.' He didn't move, not towards her, not away. Was that amber, or could it possibly be green?

'Ah, but I like you a lot. And I'm sorry, but I just have to do this.' In one movement, Louisa eased herself on to the sofa beside him, leaned over so that their eyes were only inches apart, took his face between her hands and kissed him long and hard, exactly as she had wanted to kiss him from practically the first time they had met.

And that was when the doorbell rang.

Chapter 23

'And I was feeling in need of some exercise.' Hilary Nicholson spun slowly round on her chair. 'So I booked a badminton court,' she said into the telephone. 'Do you fancy a game?'

'I'd love to. But isn't there someone else you usually play with?' the female voice on the other end of the line enquired.

Not half. Hilary looked across the office at Felix's closed door. Although even that wasn't true any more. Felix had given her some claptrap about his wife and a new start, which was a terrible pity, given that Bas had become boring as hell. But she had known there was someone else, and by now (after monitoring his phone calls and rifling his private diary) she had a good idea who it was. MB didn't leave a lot to the imagination, given the signs. 'The girl I usually play with is tied up,' she said.

'Oh, well, I suppose...'

Felix had left already, mumbling something about needing to get home. But was he going home? 'You're not too busy?' she asked Marilyn Beck. 'Only there was something I rather wanted to have a little chat with you about.' That was bait and a half. 'It is important.'

'Really?' Hilary could almost hear her mind beavering away. 'Well, I'll have to make a couple of calls.'

'That's OK,' Hilary told her. 'Phone me back in ten minutes? I'm counting on you, Marilyn.'

She smiled as she replaced the receiver, smiled even more as she imagined Marilyn calling Felix on his mobile. But she would teach them both. She would not be taken for a fool by anyone.

'Shall I get it?' Rupert enquired in dry tones. 'Or will you?' Louisa couldn't read the expression in his eyes. Neither had she been able to read the kiss – though since it had been rudely interrupted, that was hardly surprising. 'We could always ignore it,' she suggested hopefully.

'Not really.' He looked past her. 'It's Sophie, and she's peering in through the window.'

Louisa silently cursed her niece. 'I'll go.' She heaved herself upright. In the corner by the door she noticed his violin in its battered leather case. She hadn't heard him play for a while.

'Hi, Auntie mine. Have you seen Mums?' Sophie was leaning against the porch. She was also grinning, which would have been a nice change (had Louisa been in the mood for it) since she'd been a bit on the hangdog side lately. That, she reminded herself, was what married men did for you. And she was beginning to wonder if the Rupert Sumner kind were any better.

'No. I—'

'Ugh. Yuck!' Sophie wrinkled her nose in distaste. 'What on earth is that smell? Have you been burning coconuts on a bonfire or something?'

'Bloody hell!' Louisa spun round and made for the kitchen. Her lamb korma was no longer simmering; it was burning. Its potential as a pulling meal was clearly lost; going by the state it was in it would be hard pushed to even manage nutrition.

'Whatever was that in its other life?' Sophie had followed her in.

299

Louisa told her. 'It was for me and Rupert,' she said pointedly, hoping Sophie would catch her drift.

'Looks like he's lost interest in dinner.' They both watched as Rupert emerged from the sitting room and grabbed his jacket.

'I've got a few things to sort out,' he told Louisa, not quite meeting her eye. 'Hi, Sophie.'

'Hi.' She was watching him appreciatively.

Coward, Louisa thought. She felt like a cross between Medusa and the Wicked Witch of the West. 'And I have to get to work.' If Sophie would go, she might be able to get all this sorted out in her head. What was Rupert so afraid of?

But her niece took her time in getting to the front door. 'He's very sort of dark and hungry-looking, isn't he?' She watched him disappear out of sight.

Her eyes were so like her father's. And yet bits of her were pure Jess – like seeing her sister as a teenager all over again. She had the same dreamy quality; it made you wonder what she was thinking, what she was hiding, who she really was. 'I suppose he is.' Although she wasn't sure she wanted to discuss it right now.

'Yeah, like a real romantic hero – Heathcliff or Darcy; very English but wild underneath.'

A *real* hero? 'Was Darcy wild underneath?' Louisa frowned. She obviously hadn't paid enough attention to her Austen.

'Oh, I expect so.' Sophie made it to the doorstep. 'And of course he had a hidden passion too.'

'He did?' Louisa had got lost in this conversation somehow, a sensation she was pretty used to from talking to Jess.

'Mmm, he had Elizabeth. And Pemberley. Only he thought Elizabeth was busily engaged elsewhere, with Wickham. And of course he was a terrible snob.'

'Rupert isn't a terrible snob,' Louisa objected.

'No.' Sophie backed off down the path. 'But he does have a secret passion.'

'Oh?'

'You know.' She winked and grinned.

Louisa was trying to be patient. 'I'm not actually living with him, Sophie, as such. Rupert and I aren't an item.'

'Oh, I know that.' She laughed. 'He's mad about Mums, isn't he? Besotted, actually. It's quite sweet.'

'Jess?' Louisa hung on to the door.

'Of course it's absolutely useless, since Mums is batty about Dad and always will be. But it's rather romantic, isn't it, to see old Rupe pining away for love of her.'

'Pining away?' Old Rupe? Louisa was stunned. Of course it was ridiculous. Rupert wasn't pining for anyone, and as for being in love with Jess – well, that was just a teenage girl's over-vivid imagination. It couldn't possibly be true.

Sophie had reached the pavement. 'Perhaps you should save him, Auntie Louisa,' she called cheerfully. 'You know—'

''Bye Sophie.' Thankfully, she closed the door. It *was* ridiculous, wasn't it? He and Jess were friends, they even confided in one another – but friends did that. He had been angry about Felix, but who wouldn't be? Then again, he always seemed more interested in conversations that included the subject of Jess. Come to think of it, he even wanted to go into partnership with her now.

Business partnership. That was all. He had money; he must have (like Darcy...) He wanted to help her sister.

She ran up the stairs and brushed her hair until her scalp ached. She had made a complete and utter fool of herself, of that she was sure. But the rest couldn't be true. It just couldn't.

Hilary was beginning to enjoy herself immensely. She ensured that her first shots were woolly and weak – the shuttlecock tossed high in the air to the small figure in black on the other side of the net – but this was merely in order to ascertain her opponent's standard of play. Hilary meant business. She didn't merely want to win. She was after total annihilation.

'Well done!' she called to her opponent in a condescending tone, every time Marilyn managed an easy smash. Not only was Marilyn's game weaker than her own, but the other woman also had a distinct lack of puff. It was fun to let her almost catch up in the first game, even funnier to get her dashing madly round the court to no avail in the second game. And Hilary had another great advantage over her opponent: she knew this wasn't just about badminton. The final game she won to love.

'I haven't played for ages.' By now Marilyn was rather sweaty and very cross.

'Me neither.' She smirked. She wasn't even out of breath.

Marilyn grabbed a towel. 'And you never told me you were good.'

Hilary added insult. 'I'm not especially.'

'Thanks a lot.' Marilyn glared at her. Keeping a safe distance between them, they headed for the showers.

Hilary could tell that she was finding it hard to maintain the surface politeness that was part of the game. All to the good. Marilyn had been defeated; she now had to be made angrier still. 'You weren't that bad,' she said magnanimously.

'Too many ciggies,' Marilyn grumbled.

'Or not enough exercise.' Hilary nipped into the first cubicle and stripped off. 'Is Peter letting you down in that department these days?' Her laughter was bright and ever so slightly sympathetic. Was Marilyn feeling enough of a failure yet?

'Peter is fine,' came the reply from the other side of the partition. 'And Bas?'

She was putting up a fight. Hilary smiled to herself. She

302

liked that. 'Bas is nice,' she said. The hot water shot on to her shoulders and she shivered with delight as it rippled down her spine. 'But he's not up to Felix Newman's standard. I can assure you of that.'

There was silence from the other cubicle.

Hilary stuck her head through the curtain. 'You did know about me and Felix?'

'Didn't everyone?'

Hilary smiled to herself. 'Once you've had Felix...' She turned and the water rained on to her breasts. 'You're spoiled for anyone else.'

'Really?'

'Oh, yes.' Hilary began to lather her body, soaping her legs and arms, lingering on her belly and her breasts. A shower was such a sensual experience, she found. She and Felix had showered quite often together in the good days in Sussex when she had rented her own flat. (Although the office had always been fun too.) And just thinking of it now, remembering his hands on her wet skin, water in her hair, her eyes, her mouth ... she felt her fingers creeping towards the top of her legs. But, no. Not now. Now, there were other more pressing things to deal with, like getting confirmation that Marilyn Beck was *the one*, for example.

She would never have guessed that Felix would be so stupid, although of course men were – especially when it came to matters sexual. But his secrecy alone had as good as told Hilary it must be someone risky. And then there were the phone calls and MB in the diary. It was still a hunch; but Felix's habitual expression these days told her that he certainly had *something* to look guilty about.

'How on earth do you manage now that you're married, then?' she heard Marilyn enquire with admirable sarcasm. 'Being restricted to just one man, I mean?'

The plan was working. She was giving her the slut

treatment. Hilary rinsed off. Marilyn was making her feelings too obvious. And that must be because she was beginning to dislike Hilary intensely.

Hilary wrapped herself in her towel and swept through the curtain, to find Marilyn on the other side.

'What makes you think I have only got one?' she asked as they headed towards the changing room. 'One man, I mean? What makes you think Felix and I are no longer an item?'

'Are you?' Marilyn stared.

Hilary laughed for longer than perhaps she should have, as she held the door open for her rival. 'You're right,' she conceded at last. 'It is over with Felix, more's the pity. And that's what I wanted to talk to you about.'

'I don't see what it has to do with me.' Once in the changing room Marilyn began to rub herself dry.

Deliberately Hilary turned her back. 'I told Felix that once I was married, he'd have to find someone else. Silly of me, don't you think?' She allowed this to sink in. 'But I've changed my mind. I miss him. So how d'you think I should play it? Men like Felix have such big egos, don't they?' She giggled. 'And not just egos.'

Marilyn stared at her. 'Why are you asking me?'

'You know what he's like. He won't admit that he still wants me, not outright anyway, just because I turned him down.' Would she swallow it? In Hilary's experience, women believed almost anything about men – if it were said convincingly enough.

There was a long pause. She guessed that Marilyn was struggling with conflicting emotions, not to mention her sense of caution. 'What if Felix simply isn't interested?' Marilyn asked at last. 'Have you considered that?'

Catty. That was good. Hilary began to dress. 'Felix is so sexy,' she said, smoothing the silk of her knickers with the palm of her hand. 'And I was good for him. We were *great* together.' She bent forwards to put on her bra. 'I'm positive he still fancies me.' And at last she turned back to face Marilyn. 'He as good as admitted it.'

'Perhaps he was trying to make you feel better,' Marilyn snarled.

'Oh, no, it wasn't that. I know it's true. I can tell from the way he looks me up and down when I come into the room. You know...' She giggled girlishly. 'Do you think he's waiting for me to take the initiative and have him on his desk like I used to?'

Marilyn was almost fully dressed already. She looked as if she couldn't get out of the changing room quick enough. 'I don't give a shit what you do, Hilary,' she said.

'But what would you advise?' Hilary asked, pretending to ignore the tone of her reply. Still in her bra and knickers she pulled a hairbrush out of her bag and went to stand in front of the mirror. Come on, damn you. 'I know you're older than me,' she said in desperation, seeking Marilyn's reflection in the glass. 'I know you're a woman of the world, and that's why—'

'I think you're wrong. I think that Felix Newman doesn't miss you in the least,' Marilyn said. Her face had darkened into anger. She was pulling a comb through her hair, but her mind didn't seem to be on the job.

Geronimo... 'And how would *you* know?' Hilary let herself sound hurt. After her own behaviour a woman like this would not feel a shred of sympathy. Come on, Marilyn, she thought. How much do you hate me?

'I know because he told me.' It was Marilyn's moment. But Hilary had given it to her.

'And when did he tell you that, may I ask?' Hilary put her hands on her hips.

Marilyn was nervous – Hilary could see it in the way she licked her lips, before she bent to put on her shoes. She was probably dying for a cigarette, poor cow, but it was no smoking in the leisure centre, and Hilary was glad.

305

'He told me last week.' It was an exit line, and Hilary had timed it beautifully for her. She watched as Marilyn picked up her sports bag and made for the door. 'He told me when we were in bed together,' she said as she walked out of the door. 'He told me when we were making love.'

Perfect. And yet Hilary felt a twinge of envy behind the sense of mission accomplished. 'I suppose we have to assume then,' she said sadly to herself as she slipped on her sweater, 'that it's true.'

Chapter 24

By the time he heard Jess's key in the lock, Felix was on his fourth whisky. He was sitting morosely in his favourite armchair, feeling more than a little sorry for himself. Even Sophie had disappeared next door saying that Rupert had promised to play some Beastie Boys number on the violin for her (Beastie Boys? What was the world coming to?) And, *Wasn't Rupert gorgeous?* she added. Felix would have liked to punch him in the throat – that was the kind of mood he was in.

'Hi! Anyone home?'

She sounded cheerful. That annoyed him for starters. What did she have to be so cheerful about? He decided not to answer.

He could hear the sound of her humming as she dumped her bag in the hallway and made her way into the kitchen. Some crappy pop song; he'd heard Sophie humming it too. What was wrong with everyone? Didn't anyone appreciate decent music any more? And what would Jess do now? Make his dinner, perhaps? He hoped so, because despite all this emotional trauma, he was bloody starving.

He strained to listen, heard a drawer being opened, registered the sound of her scrabbling through the contents. That sounded hopeful. There was a moment's silence and then the noise of a cork being pulled and the splash of wine into a glass. Typical.

The phone rang, to be silenced almost immediately.

'Oh, hi, Matt,' she said. 'Yes, I've just got back.'

Matt? Felix detected a caressing note in her soft voice and he squeezed his glass of whisky so hard he thought it would break.

'No, I didn't...' A pause. 'Yes, of course I will.' Another pause. 'Mmm...' What the hell had he asked her? 'All right. Tomorrow. Oh yes, and – oh, I'll tell you that tomorrow.' He heard Jess put down the phone.

Felix took another slug of his drink. A meaningless conversation perhaps. Nothing he could pick up on, nothing he could use as ammunition. But it was the way she'd spoken. As if this man weren't simply a client. As if he *mattered*.

He heard footsteps in the hall, didn't move and watched her as she entered the sitting room.

She gave a little jump when she saw him. Guilt perhaps?

'Felix.' He watched as she adjusted her expression. Her eyes had been dreamy, glazed, her thoughts quite obviously elsewhere. Happy? Had her eyes been happy? 'I didn't know you were home.'

'Obviously.'

Now her eyes grew wary. He watched in fascination. Perhaps she was trying to remember what she'd said to that doctor on the telephone. 'Why didn't you answer when I called out?'

'I'm not in a talkative mood.' He looked away. That would tell her.

'And where's Sophie?'

'With lover boy next door.'

He heard her sigh; she was wondering how to deal with him. 'What is it, Felix?' She waited, hand on hip, looking as if she didn't really want to know. 'What's wrong?'

He shrugged. Would she think him childish? Perversely, whisky seemed to have that effect on him.

'There must be something.' She was losing patience, he could tell.

Felix came to a decision. 'I've been thinking...'

'Yes?'

Well, why not test her? With the drink inside him he couldn't think of any good reason why he shouldn't. It might make you behave childishly, but it also helped a man see a situation more clearly. And he could date the time when their problems had begun. 'I don't like the idea of you doing this decorating lark,' he said.

He saw her stiffen, saw the eyes he loved become cold against him. But sometimes, he told himself, you had to be cruel to achieve a greater good, a greater kindness.

'Why not?' Her voice was so brittle he imagined it bouncing off the very walls and snapping in two right there in front of him.

He was ready for this. 'Because it's dangerous. Going to the houses of strangers you don't know from Adam.' Not to mention doctors.

'I take precautions.' She glared at him.

'What kind of precautions?' he pressed.

But she wasn't playing this game. 'That's my business.'

Felix realised he wasn't getting very far. 'You don't need a job,' he said. 'I—'

'That's exactly where you're wrong,' she cut in, her voice becoming strident now. She sounded very unlike the Jess he knew and loved. This one was confident and sure of her own mind. 'A job is precisely what I need.'

'You don't. I earn enough for both of us.'

'Who's talking about money?'

'Well...' He wasn't sure where to go from here. 'All right. Why do you need to work anyway? Tell me that.'

Even as he spoke, he realised this was probably a mistake.

Sure enough... 'I need a job for myself, for my own...' Yes, he thought, she was really going to say it. 'For my own personal fulfilment.'

'Loadacrap.' He hadn't exactly meant to say this. 'Loada feminist crap.'

'It is not.' She seemed taller than usual as she stood there looking down on him. Her hair was as wild as ever, forming a tangled halo around her face. But Jess was in control. 'Would you prefer me to stagnate at home?' she asked conversationally, as if they were discussing the dinner.

He wasn't fooled. 'No.' But, he would prefer her to *be* at home, obviously.

'Then why is it,' she began, 'that when I'm doing some-thing that's important to me, you simply can't take it?'

'I can.'

'It doesn't look like it.' Jess sighed. 'You want to stop me working, don't you? You've just said so.'

'I'm only thinking of you.' But he realised immediately from her expression that this was not the right thing to say. 'Of your safety,' he blustered.

'You are thinking of Felix,' she corrected smoothly. 'You are always thinking of Felix. That is what you do.'

'But—'

'Are we in such trouble, you and I?' He realised she was close to tears. 'That you have to try and stop me from living my own life? From doing what I want to do, what I need to do?'

'But that's just it.' It dawned on Felix that honesty was the only way forward now. This conversation was worrying him. *She* was worrying him. 'You're living your life and I'm living mine. We're not living together like we used to.'

'I know.'

For a moment they both remained silent, as if absorbing this truth.

310

'And I want it to be like it was,' Felix said. Couldn't she see?

'One thing I do not want,' Jess said, turning away from him, 'is for it to be like it was.'

'Shit.' This bloody psycho-analysing was too much for him. Especially after a few drinks. Felix banged his fist on the arm of the chair. She was talking in circles and he was getting lost on the way. She had twisted everything he had tried to say, and now it was even more wrong than it had been before. He got to his feet. 'I'm going out.'

'Fine.' She left the room without even looking at him.

Not a sad look, not a tear. He must have imagined that she was close to it before. Now, she just looked cold. Cold as bloody ice.

Somehow, Louisa was not surprised when she looked up to see Felix entering the pub. He came in the Lamb and Flag from time to time, usually for one drink before going home, but it wasn't because of that. It was because of what she had been thinking. She couldn't get the thought out of her head – Rupert and Jess ... Jess and Rupert ... like some damned chorus line, some song with a happy ending.

'Hi.'

'Hi.' He drifted across to the bar, parked himself on one of the high stools.

'What can I get you? A smile?' Tonight, Felix was looking especially miserable. He was an attractive man, and a few worry creases around the eyes and mouth did nothing to detract from his appeal. But it was the expression in those eyes that had it. There was a blankness about them where before there had been laughter. Life, she supposed. She was becoming maudlin herself; she must stop.

'Very amusing. I'll have a half of best and a Bell's.'

He drank quickly, making no move to go or to talk, apart from to order more drinks and a toasted sandwich.

'What's up?' she asked at last, when they were quiet and the pub relatively empty. Not that she expected him to tell her. They had never done much more than tolerate one another.

'I feel like she's moving away from me,' he said.

'Jess?' Though of course, she knew.

'This college thing, this bloody decorating...'

Louisa took a step backwards. This was awkward. She wasn't sure she felt comfortable discussing her sister's behaviour with Felix. But clearly he needed to talk.

'And I can't stop it happening.' Felix swirled the whisky around in his glass before downing it in one.

And why shouldn't he get pissed? Louisa began to feel vaguely sorry for him. OK, so he had indulged in an affair or two – but that wasn't exactly criminal. Lots of people did it; who was she to judge them?

'Pint of bitter, please, love,' someone called.

'I'm on my way.'

Louisa glanced across at Felix as she pulled the pint. It didn't seem right, a man like Felix looking so pathetic. He had never looked remotely pathetic before.

Having served the new customer, she returned to where Felix was sitting. She leaned on the counter. 'Maybe this is just something Jess feels she needs to do,' she said, trying to smooth the waters. 'It doesn't have to threaten your marriage.'

'It's a threat all right.'

'But if she needs—'

'Yeah, but it's all *her* needs, isn't it?' Felix shook his head. 'Right now, I'm more bloody concerned with mine.'

Louisa repressed a smile at this. Hadn't he always been?

'I'm not in charge any more,' he muttered, in what she guessed to be a moment of rare honesty. 'And I don't bloody well like it.'

Funny, she thought, as she moved away to serve another

312

customer, how control was so important to men like Felix. Women struggled to take control of their own lives; they probably never meant to take it away from the men who seemed to think they had some sort of monopoly on it. And she could understand wanting control of your own life. But why want control of someone else's too?

Time was called, and she began to clear up, noticing that Felix was still hanging around, one of the last stragglers to leave.

'Got anyone to walk you back?' he asked as he got unsteadily to his feet.

'Not tonight.' Sometimes Rupert came over; the first time she had hoped this was significant, but she had soon learned it was nothing of the kind.

'I'll walk you.'

Louisa took hold of a tray of glasses and began to unload and stack them for cleaning. 'I'm quite capable of walking on my own,' she said. She wasn't some hometown girl who knew nothing of the world and all its dangers.

Felix shrugged. 'Suit yourself.'

After he'd gone, Louisa wished she'd been nicer. He wasn't to know what had happened tonight with Rupert – or more to the point, what hadn't happened. The guy had problems of his own; she shouldn't have cut him dead like that.

But when she got outside half an hour later, he was waiting for her.

'I didn't like the idea of you walking back on your own,' he said in reply to her unspoken question. 'There's a lot of weirdos about. That's what I tried to tell Jess.'

'I never had you down for a gentleman.' But Louisa smiled. She wasn't the nervous kind, but she could do with his company.

'No, you had me down for a bastard.' He chuckled.

She sneaked a look at him. 'Well, you are rather, aren't you?'

'Sure.' He took her arm but she wasn't conscious of any threat. Felix was as harmless as they came tonight. For a start he was half-cut, or he ought to be after the amount he'd put away this evening. 'You know, don't you?'

'About Marilyn Beck?' The moon was big and strong tonight, almost a full one, and this subject of conversation had been on the cards for sure.

He nodded. 'You heard us on Boxing Day, right? But you never told Jess.' He stopped walking and stared at her as if he'd never seen her before.

'I didn't want to interfere,' she said primly, half pulling him forwards. 'It's your marriage. I suppose you love each other, still.'

'Love!' He stumbled. 'Yeah, I guess I do.' He glanced at her. 'Don't suppose you've ever been troubled in that department?'

Little did he know. 'Once or twice,' she compromised. 'It happens to us all.'

He stumbled once more, this time on an uneven paving stone. 'Well, I do love Jess,' he said. 'Even though ... even though I—'

'Sleep around?' She was beginning to see how vulnerable he was. He was the sort of guy who needed sexual conquests to convince him he still had what it took. But that was no compensation for Jess.

'You sure do say what you think.' His words were slurring, and his voice was betraying those years spent in Australia more than it usually did. He gave her arm a small squeeze. 'But I wanted Jess. I always wanted her.'

It seemed that everyone did. Their father had once made her think that she, Louisa, was the one everyone wanted, the one who was special. But the reality was very different. 'Self-pity doesn't suit you, Felix,' she informed him tartly.

''S'easy when you're drunk.' He swayed dangerously to

314

one side and she eased him back to the strictly vertical. Just who was walking whom?

They took the next turning on their left, and all at once the smell of the sea grew stronger and sweeter, as it always did at this point. Nearly home – if she could call it that after the fiasco with Rupert tonight. It was a good thing she and Jess were going to Brittany. But what would happen after that? Would she be flat-hunting in earnest?

At last they reached Rupert's cottage. 'Will you be OK?' she asked. He didn't look it.

'Hell.' He slumped heavily against the buddleia tree. 'I've messed up.'

She could see his face quite clearly in the moonlight and she could see the pain – as clear as it ever got. Despite her better judgement, her heart went out to him. 'It may not be too late,' she said, lightly touching his cheek.

'If I thought that...' His voice trailed off and he grabbed her hand. 'Why are you being so nice to me?'

'Why shouldn't I be?'

'You never have been before.' He looked at her, peering into her face, seeming suddenly sober. 'You're beautiful.'

There was a moment when she could have drawn back; there always was. But she was still smarting from her humiliation with Rupert. And then there was Jess. Everyone wanted Jess...

So when he kissed her, she kissed him back, to make the pain go away. His lips were hot with the taste of whisky; his breath seemed to burn her throat. She kissed him back and she wouldn't have even cared if Jess and Rupert had been at their windows watching them. Probably.

Jess hurried to Matthew's to find only an empty house.

What now? After a moment's hesitation she wandered upstairs, lingered on the landing, took a deep breath and strode into his bedroom. She stopped. The duvet was crumpled, his clothes were thrown all over the floor; and the room was pure Matthew, it even smelled of Matthew. How could she deal with this room?

She smoothed the duvet (help! She was becoming homey), unloaded a pile of magazines and catalogues from her bag on to the bed, and sat down to flick through them. Handmade wardrobe space, he had said. What did he think she was, a carpenter?

She began to make notes on storage space and general structure, drew a few rough sketches on her pad. The room as it stood was plain and entirely rectangular. She wanted a series of curves that would draw the eye along and give the illusion of a bigger, more rounded space. In bedrooms lighting was paramount: some reading light, some muted light, a soft pool for a welcome (to whom?) a light for make-up... Make-up? She stopped abruptly. Just who was she envisaging here? Herself? Some other woman?

Oh God. She got to her feet. Would this be easier with Matthew in the room with her? Probably not; they might end up on the bed in a much more literal sense.

When she heard him opening the front door, she jumped guiltily and retreated to the landing. 'Hi! I'm up here.' In your bedroom, she almost said. Well, at least she had stopped short of sniffing the duvet, she wasn't quite that desperate.

'Hello.' There was a tender note in his voice and he almost ran up the stairs. 'Sorry I'm so late.' He flipped the hair from his brow and it flopped straight back again. 'Morning surgery went on for ever, and then there were some inoculations to do.'

'It's OK.' She advanced tentatively into the bedroom again and indicated the mass of paperwork on the bed. 'I've brought some ideas.' But what about colour? It would have to be something brightish to maximise the light, because the window wasn't huge although there was a magnificent view.

316

She wandered over.

Matthew came up behind her. She thought – for a moment – that he might kiss her, she felt – for an even shorter moment – like a character in some TV movie.

Then she turned to see him pick up *House Beautiful* instead.

'So this is where you get your inspiration.'

'It comes from the most unexpected places actually.' She was sorry he hadn't kissed her. Kind of. 'But in the next week or so you might like to look them over,' she said. 'See what appeals to you.'

He raised one eyebrow as he surveyed her. 'What appeals to *you*?'

'It's your bedroom, Matt,' she said softly.

'But I want you to design it.'

They stared at one another. I can't do this, Jess thought. She could not pretend that he was just a client, and he could never be just a friend. If her marriage was ever to get back on track, she would have to cut Matthew Hill out of her life.

'I'm going away for a while,' she told him.

'Again?' One eyebrow twitched up. 'You've barely come back from Venice.'

'That was only a weekend.' She felt a slight nudge of betrayal. 'This time I'm going away for a couple of weeks. With my sister.' Would Louisa want to move back in now that Sophie looked set to find a place of her own in Abbotsbury? It would be good for Sophie; she didn't want her cooped up in Brocklemouth; she needed to find friends of her own age, be able to go out and have a good time. But as for Louisa ... perhaps it was best if Cliff Cottage continued to belong to just Jess and Felix for a while.

'I see.'

'I didn't want to tell you on the phone.' Heaven knows why. 'But I need a break. And I want to spend some time with Louisa.'

'Of course.' Matthew's expression had changed, as if he knew she was about to leave whatever they had behind.

'So if you have a think about what you might like.' There was yet another awkward silence. 'When I come back, maybe we'll get started.' Or maybe not. Maybe she wouldn't do it at all. Couldn't do it.

She walked to the door. It was no good. The colours weren't coming to her. All she could think of was what she would like (midnight blue ... very romantic, very impractical; a huge brass bed with flowing drapes – hardly suitable for Matthew's lifestyle; a giant Deco mirror in a frame of beaten silver). There was nothing more she could do at this stage, and suddenly she felt unable to stay here any longer. Her idea to spend some time with him before she left seemed a stupid one. She wasn't free to do anything of the kind. 'Goodbye, Matt.'

'I'll see you out.'

She went down the stairs first, in front of him, turning at the bottom to watch his descent. She could not, for the life of her, interpret his expression.

'Why do you keep that photo of Pamela?' she asked him, as he opened the front door. 'What is it you want to be reminded of?'

'That's easy.' His smile was lopsided and she wasn't sure how much of it to believe. 'I want her picture there to remind me of what happens when you fall in love.'

Jess frowned in confusion.

'It opens you up,' he said. His eyes still told her nothing. 'And do you know what's the worst thing, Jess?'

She shook her head.

'Nobody even offers you a general anaesthetic.' Very softly he shut the door behind her.

Chapter 25

Jess and Louisa crossed the Channel on the ferry from Poole to Cherbourg the following day, and drove on to St Malo. Jess's Renault might be slightly battered, but it proved equal to the task.

St Malo with its walled city and castle was picturesque, but this wasn't the Brittany of their childhood, and Jess was eager to go on. So they stayed only one night, before driving through the Rance valley and along the Côte d'Emeraude towards the Côte de Granit Rose. And as they passed St Brieuc, heading towards Paimpol, where they planned to stay the night, Jess could feel excitement and trepidation growing in about equal doses.

She had a reason for wanting to stay in Paimpol rather than pushing on to Trégastel and Claude's new bar and apartments, although she knew Louisa was keen to see both. 'Tomorrow I want to go down to Pointe de L'Arcouest,' she told Louisa over dinner.

'Oh yeah?'

There was no need for Jess to tell her why. The Point was well known for only one thing – the ferries that took people over to the Ile de Bréhat.

'It's not like it used to be.' Louisa poured more red wine from the jug on the table.

'I suppose it's become very commercialised?' Jess ate another mussel and thought of Matthew. Never again would she be able to eat mussels without him encroaching on the experience, she thought crossly. In Matthew's hands culinary skill was erotic; she had never dreamed she could be so turned on by watching a man move expertly between skillets and pans, ovens and woks.

'No, that's the problem. They still don't allow any cars on the island and it's stayed fairly unspoiled.'

'That's a problem?' It sounded perfect to Jess. She wanted the place to be exactly as it had been before.

Louisa pulled a face. 'It's a problem because since the whole world and his wife base their Brittany holiday on the Michelin guide, and since the guide says it's beautiful and unspoiled...'

'They all flock there?'

She looked gloomy. 'In droves.'

Jess shrugged. 'I don't care. I still want to go. The pink granite's still there, isn't it?'

'Course it is. It would take a bloody big bulldozer to crash the entire lot into the sea.'

'I don't care about the people.' Jess wiped fingers coated in garlic butter and parsley on her napkin. 'The pink granite's what I want to see.' The Côte de Granit Rose stretched way beyond Perros Guirec, even farther than Trégastel, but this was a special part of the coastline. It was a dangerous memory, this lone example of paternal approval that she held in her head. But she had the piece of granite at home in Dorset to remind her. Pathetic huh? Only a stone, hardly of earth-shattering importance. But to Jess at the time it had held all the hope of a new beginning.

Louisa was looking slightly smug, as if she knew what Jess was thinking. But, 'Then that's what we'll do,' was all that she said.

*

Although she had worn a warm jacket, Jess felt the wind's cold fingers trying to inch their way through the fabric, scenting out the gaps to squeeze into, as the boat took them over to the island. The sun was weak, but managed to give the maze of islets and granite reefs poking their heads out of the sea a pink and surrealist glow.

Jess recalled trying to count them all. She had got up to twenty, when her father consulted the guide book and informed her that there were eighty-something. She couldn't remember exactly how many, only the feeling that there wasn't much point in counting any more.

The boat skirted the indented coastline, drew closer to the craggy face of the pink rock, and drifted into Port Clos. The engine was shut off and disembarking commenced. Jess shivered, although without the sea breeze chilling her, she was now quite warm.

'Here we go.' Side by side they walked up the landing stage and over the beach, tramping up the lane with all the other tourists.

Tourists ... Jess pulled a face of horror, but Louisa leaned closer towards her and whispered, 'And it isn't even high season yet.'

Jess was beginning to see her point.

Following the signs, they went on towards Le Bourg. Everyone was either walking or cycling. What on earth must the residents think of them – these odd sheep-like people who so regularly invaded their little island with its temperate climate and Mediterranean flora. 'They must hate us,' she whispered, feeling ashamed.

'They don't hate the money we bring with us,' Louisa remarked, more philosophically.

'I suppose not.' On they went. It was beginning to feel like a pilgrimage.

'Did you never want to come back to Brittany before?' Louisa asked as they reached the small central square of Le

321

Bourg. It was predictably stuffed with people but also lined with attractive plane trees. They sat down on a bench to rest for a moment.

'Often,' she said.

'Then why didn't you?'

Jess gazed round the square. The island was peculiar – a kind of superficial time warp; it seemed to exist merely for people like herself and Louisa and all the other boatloads of tourists, who wished to remind themselves of what life might once have been like. Simple, like this square; a community based round the church, whose tower she could just see from here if she craned her neck; a community living off the land with only tractors for transport. And yet the irony was that while nothing had apparently changed, *everything* had changed. The islanders lived off the tourists who ruined their island; they were unchanged for the tourists who ruined their island. The place was a living paradox.

She sighed as she considered Louisa's question. 'I suppose I wasn't brave enough,' she admitted at last.

'And I was scared to come back to England,' Louisa said.

Their eyes met. 'But I'm here now.' Jess felt drawn to her sister once more. Admitting a shared weakness was a great leveller.

'And what does it feel like?' They got to their feet, took another turning down another lane that seemed exactly the same as the first one to Jess, once again lined by dry-stone walls and fields. Eucalyptus, fig trees, honeysuckle. When the summer flowers joined the spring ones it would be a feast for the eyes indeed.

'Very different from before.' Jess struggled to explain. She had seen these lanes in her mind's eye many times but the reality had made her doubt her own accuracy. 'It feels as if my memory has been out of kilter for years. As if it started with a wrong image.'

'As the child saw it,' Louisa said.

She nodded. 'As the child saw it. And the distortion has kind of increased with time.' It was most odd.

'I know exactly what you mean.'

In step, in tune, they turned off the lane on to a narrower path leading in a south-easterly direction. They were walking downhill and Jess guessed that sooner or later they would reach the sea – the island was only about a mile wide.

'I'm not sure I can even find the real memory,' Jess said after a while. She thought they were coming to a beach – a cove maybe. But would it be *the* cove?

Louisa stopped dead in her tracks. 'But why does it have to matter for us?' she demanded. 'Every adult in the world has weird memories about their childhood. Everyone knows that memory isn't reliable, that it's subjective, suspect, all that stuff. Everyone gets things wrong.'

Gently, Jess took her arm and they walked on. 'I think it matters more to us, because we lost them so early,' she said. 'We lost the people who could have said, *Remember that time you caught a crab in a rock pool on Trégastel beach?* Or whatever it might be.'

Thoughtfully, Louisa nodded. 'We lost our reinforcers,' she said.

'So we only have a child's memory left.'

Louisa laughed. 'And it tells too many fibs.' She was silent for a few moments. 'But perhaps it's better that way.'

Jess knew what she was saying. Their childhood had not been exactly idyllic – even Louisa's, that had once seemed so perfect. 'It's a bit like painting by numbers.' The more she thought about it, the more it all fitted. 'Remember doing that?'

'Oh, yes.'

Jess had loved her painting by numbers set. Five=lime green, seven=crimson. Things had been so straightforward. 'And you know there's a true picture in there somewhere. It's printed on the box.'

Louisa nodded. 'But if you get a bit wrong—'

'You can never make sense of the blasted thing.' If one section was the wrong colour, the whole lot got twisted. 'So what do you do to put it right? To... Louisa seemed to be struggling to find the words she was looking for. 'To *deal* with it, you know?'

They came to the bottom of the path. As Jess had expected, it opened up on to a pink shingle beach. There were plenty of rocks, millions of stones. She had come this way guided by instinct. But was it *the* cove? 'Maybe you have to go back to the beginning. To see where you went wrong.' Which was, in a way, precisely what she was doing now.

She clambered on to a boulder, standing high to get the lie of the land. She didn't think this was the cove but to the west, beyond the great jutting orange-pink face of the weathered old cliff...

Louisa was watching her. 'What did you miss most?' she asked. 'When they died?'

Jess took Louisa's arm as her sister helped her down from the boulder. 'Being looked after,' she replied without hesitation. 'By someone strong and sure of himself.' That was easy. That was why Felix had been the answer to her prayers. 'What about you?'

'Love.'

Jess nodded. So much love, to be taken away. It was hard to lose love. She thought of Matthew. No wonder they were both so wary of being hurt like that again, Louisa and Matt. Maybe Rupert too. Loving and losing... Though if you didn't open yourself up to love, it wasn't really living, was it?

Louisa gazed out into the distance towards the sea and the maze of pink reefs. 'Oh, yes. I missed love,' she said.

They stayed on the beach for half an hour, Louisa sitting on the shingle, getting the most from the watery spring sunshine, and Jess poking about in rock pools. She was rest-

324

less; she wanted to move on.

'I want to walk round the headland,' she told Louisa.

'All right. I'll come with you.' Lazily, Louisa got to her feet to follow.

The tide was fairly high, and there were enough boulders to make rock-hopping easy. It took them twenty minutes, and then the cove was in sight.

Jess stopped. 'Isn't this it?' she said in excitement, forgetting that she hadn't told Louisa what she was looking for. 'The cove where we had that picnic. When—'

'You found that red rock.' Louisa was standing hand on hip surveying her. She was wearing that same enigmatic smile that Jess had caught on her face a couple of times already today.

'Pink.' Jess remembered that she'd shown her the stone on Boxing Day when they had been looking at all those old photos.

'No, red.' Louisa continued to rock-hop.

Jess went a slightly different way, wanting, childishly perhaps, to get there first.

'The whole beach was pink,' Louisa went on. 'The whole island is pink. You found a rock that was red.'

If they were painting by numbers then the colour would rather depend on who was looking at it.

They reached the shingle at the same moment, looked across at each other and laughed. 'Do you wish you'd found it?' Jess asked her.

'Of course I do.' They laughed even harder. 'I was jealous as hell,' Louisa went on. 'Can you believe it? And all over a bloody rock?'

Considering the rivalry that had always existed between them, Jess supposed she shouldn't really be surprised. 'Only a rock, but a beautiful rock,' she said.

Once again Louisa sat down while Jess explored. That was why, Jess thought, she had been the one to find it. Of

325

the two of them, Louisa had always been the hedonist. And yet holidays had brought them together into a kind of friendship that had been impossible for the rest of the year. Yes, there had been rivalry, but they had liked having one another around, she was sure of that much.

'You'll never find another one like it,' Louisa called out to her.

How did she know Jess was looking? But she was probably right. And at least she had found the right cove, that was something. The cliff behind was an impenetrable mass of orange-pink. There was no path that she could see; it looked as if the only access was the way they had come. And that was probably why it was deserted. Peace at last. That proved, didn't it, that even in Bréhat there were hidden and unchanged places if you were prepared to look hard enough.

'It was a freak,' Louisa said.

'I suppose it was.' In more ways than one. A freak occurrence, but at least she had kept it, at least it had shown her how things might have been.

'My God!' Louisa shrieked.

'What?' Jess followed the direction of her gaze. The tide had come in more swiftly than she would have believed possible. It had come in and virtually cut them off from the big shingle beach.

Already Louisa was tearing off her trainers. 'Come on, Jessie, hurry up, we'll have to wade back.'

'Or swim.' But Jess followed suit.

They rolled up their jeans and plunged their feet into the icy water. It almost reached their knees. They shrieked – in unison this time, clutching one another by the arm.

'Come on.' Jess, the older, took charge as Louisa hesitated. 'It's the only way.'

So they plunged on, their bare feet poked and battered by sharp stones and hard rock, their ankles numbed by the ice-cold bracelet of the water as it gripped them. They went on, hand in hand, alternately stumbling over rocks they couldn't see, alternately helping the other remain upright; needing one another more than ever before. They went on, knowing they had to keep going and fast, to get to the other side of the headland before so much beach was swallowed by the invading sea that they would have to swim for it. And both of them knew that Jess was not a strong swimmer.

'Remember that time Dad slipped off a rock at Trégastel beach and got a ducking?' Louisa half-panted, half-yelled. Jess wanted to tell her to save her breath but she knew this was Louisa's way of keeping them going. 'Yeah.' She ploughed into another wave. She was scared, but not as scared as she had been of coming here in the first place. They would make it, she was sure.

'He came up spluttering and shouting. We waited to see who he was going to blame for it.'

'Probably me,' Jess muttered. 'Or Mother.' The water was up to her thighs.

'He was a tyrant,' Louisa shouted.

'Yep.' The roll of denim above her knees was wet and heavy, pressing into her flesh.

'But we survived.'

'We did.' There was a moment when their glances held once more, they almost stopped walking, and then they realised that the water was getting shallower, that they were rounding the headland, that there were people on the shingle beach staring at them and shouting. It was a moment of closeness, Jess realised, a moment she would always remember.

Peter and Sophie were just discussing the merits of amber, and its recent rise to popularity in the world of modern jewellery, when the sound of spiked footsteps outside indicated a visitor to the studio. The delicate clearing of a throat announced it was female, and a blonde head stuck apologetically round the door meant it was Hilary Nicholson. Sophie tensed.

'Hilary?' Peter sounded polite, but Sophie, who was beginning to know him well, recognised immediately that he disliked her. She was ridiculously pleased.

'Hello, Peter.' Hilary entered the studio, bringing with her the kind of brittle frailty that Sophie associated with tiny gold lockets or crucifixes on very fine chains.

She fingered her own dangling copper earrings and recrossed her legs.

'And Sophie.' She could see Hilary's glance lingering on her silver nose stud. 'How nice.'

Patronising cow. Hilary was wearing a black and gold outfit that, in Sophie's opinion, did nothing for her complexion. It did a lot for her figure however, clinging suggestively to her slender body, so no doubt it did the job intended. Her nose twitched as she caught a waft of Hilary's perfume.

'So...' Peter ran his fingers through his fair hair. It spiked up obediently. 'Was there something you wanted, Hilary? Problems upstairs?' His voice was mild, but it was saying that she was in their way, that she didn't belong with them, that she should say what she had come to say and then go.

And Sophie was glad. She had never known for sure about her father and Hilary. Well, Mums had denied it (she would). But she still didn't trust Hilary; she could see the spite in her eyes.

Hilary looked first at Peter and then at Sophie. 'Could I have a word, Peter?' Her voice was surprisingly girlish.

Sophie was immediately suspicious. In her limited experience women who pretended to be babies in order to get their own way were not to be trusted one bit.

He spread his hands. 'Of course.' Although they all knew that Felix dealt with personnel, and that Peter was supposed

328

to be left alone as far as possible, to get on with the creating and the manufacturing side of things.

Nobody moved. All three were waiting.

Hilary hesitated. 'In private.'

Sophie unwound her legs and got to her feet, towering briefly and maliciously over the other woman. 'I'll take a hike, then.'

'Only it's not for young ears.'

Sophie winced. Who said she wanted to stick around? 'It's all right. I need to see Tom anyway.' She stumped out of the studio, shut the door decisively and walked away very loudly, before tiptoeing back. She wasn't an eavesdropper – well, not usually. She bent and put her ear to the door. But for some reason she had a bad feeling about this one.

'Are you glad we came back?' Louisa asked. They were on the boat speeding back to Pointe de L'Arcouest.

A shot of brandy at the insistence of one of the café proprietors, and the chance to dry their legs and jeans in the sun, had restored their equilibrium, even though as Louisa pointed out they still didn't have one piece of that bloody red rock to show for their adventure. It had been a sobering experience, and one that Jess had no intention of repeating – red rock or no.

'Of course I am.' Sometimes you had to go back to go forward. There were no answers, but to return was to find perspective; a balance of good and bad, bitter and sweet. To return was to find some sort of truth, if only to find out what had gone wrong with the picture.

'I don't think I'll ever have a child,' Louisa announced.

'Why ever not?' Jess wondered when she would stop shivering.

'Because there's too much to get wrong.'

'Oh, it's not so bad.' Jess put her arm round her. 'And

329

how come you knew I was looking for another piece of red rock anyway?'

Louisa smiled. 'You were looking for the past.'

'Mmm?'

'Well, I'd already done it.'

'You mean you'd already been back?' Jess was astounded.

'It took me two visits. But I found that cove.' She giggled. 'I didn't get cut off by the tide. But I never found a piece of bloody red rock either.'

Chapter 26

'So...' Louisa leaned over the chrome and blue glass table in Claude's bar towards Jess. 'Do you like him?' It mattered to her.

Claude was behind the bar dressed in his regulation tight black trousers, white shirt and red cravat, mixing cocktails in a shaker, flirting outrageously with the young barman in what he had already referred to when they were chatting earlier as their *double act to draw in the crowd,* chérie. And it probably would.

Jess glanced over, turned back and shot Louisa one of her generous smiles. She was looking good. She had scrunch-dried her hair tonight, standing with her head upside down so that Louisa had been compelled to kneel on the floor to talk to her properly, and when she'd complained, Jess had merely muttered something about volume at the roots. Then she'd slicked the ends with hair wax so that it looked wilder than ever tonight – for the after-hours party that Claude was planning. Louisa grinned. Jess seemed very liberated here in Brittany. And it felt good, just being here with her.

'Of course I do,' Jess told her. 'How could I not like him? He's young, French, good-looking, fun to be with...'

She broke off to sip her wine. 'And he runs his own bar. I adore him.'

'And he's gay,' Louisa added, just in case she'd forgotten.

'Exactly. What you might call a perfect combination.'

Louisa looked a question at her sister.

'No worries about the sex thing,' she explained.

'Ah.' Louisa knew exactly what she meant.

The object of their discussion sauntered over to their table, looking very much the man in charge and loving every minute of it.

'Everything is good, no?' he asked them.

'Everything is wonderful.' Jess looked enthusiastically around her.

'And I think...' He addressed himself to her. 'It is your turn to dance with me.'

They took to the floor.

'I am glad – so glad – to meet you at last,' he murmured, as they danced practically cheek to cheek. Typical Frenchman. His liquid brown eyes were admiring, his voice as soft as a lover's might be. She thought of Matt and sighed.

'The feeling's mutual. Louisa's told me so much—'

'*Non!*' He released her abruptly in a gesture of mock horror. 'Not too much, I hope?'

'Oh, but yes.' Jess reclaimed him. 'It sounds a lot of fun. And this place you have here *is* wonderful. I mean it.' She glanced up at the canopy above them. Shades of blue dominated the bar and attached to the ceiling was a fabric canopy in deep navy, billowing in the air flowing from the ceiling fan, and decorated with hundreds of tiny silver stars. It created a rippling night sky that reminded Jess of her plans for Matt's bedroom. Very effective, very different. Could she adapt such an idea for use in her own portfolio? Would it work in a bar in England?

'And what do you think of our beautiful Brittany?' Claude enquired.

'I love it.' Jess felt confident that she had gone some way to putting the past in order. And she'd learned more about herself, about Louisa, about the truths to be found behind every façade – though perhaps that was a little too glib and easy. At any rate, she had come closer to discovering what things had really been like for herself and for Louisa, now and before.

'I've always loved it,' she added. She felt at home on the wild and jagged coastline, the long smooth beaches, the jumble of rocks and reefs in every shade of grey, brown and pink, and the streams and grottos of the woods inland. She admired the historic cities with their castles and timber-framed houses, the châteaux, the open-air cafés selling mussels and oysters that slipped down the throat as easily as the wine. Ah, Matthew...

'Since the childhood *vacances*?' His voice was soft.

'That's right.' Perhaps her most important discovery had been how mistaken her old memories could be.

'You will always be welcome here,' Claude said rather solemnly. 'For a holiday. To work. Whatever. Any time.'

'To work?' Jess was thoughtful.

'We all need ... what do you say?'

The song ended, and before Jess could protest Claude swept her off into another dance. 'We all need the break.'

'Oh, yes. A break.' She glanced across the room towards Louisa. She too looked at home here; tall, but never awkward, possessing the careless chic of the French, shaken but not stirred with more than a dash of English eccentricity.

Claude followed the direction of her gaze. 'You are good for Louisa. Maybe good for each other, *non*?'

She considered. 'I think perhaps we are.' It had certainly

333

seemed so this afternoon when they'd plunged through the rising tide at the Ile de Bréhat. 'We're very different,' she said, speaking her thoughts aloud.

'With different kinds of strengths,' Claude said.

Jess drew back and scrutinised him. She would never have guessed him to be such an amateur psychologist.

He pulled her back into the dance. 'We all need someone.'

'Oh, yes.'

'For the support, you know? The deep-down stuff?'

Jess had the feeling that he was trying to tell her something. 'I know,' she said.

'So, I am glad.' He nodded. 'You have found her. She has found you.'

'We certainly took our time.'

The song ended, and at last he took her arm to guide her back to their table. 'Good relationships don't jump up overnight,' he said.

'Spring up. And neither do bad ones.'

He nodded. 'Times passes. Things – they change. We see nothing. We let ourselves see nothing. And then, all at once our world is a different one.'

'Goodness.' Jess stopped and stared at him. 'How the heck did you get to be so clever?' she demanded. Amateur psychologist no way, she was talking to a professional.

'Me?' He winked at her as they approached the table. 'I never passed an exam in my life.'

Somehow, that didn't surprise her in the least. Jess laughed. 'Exams? What have exams got to do with it?'

*

'You don't have much stuff, do you, Sophie?' Tom was leaning in the open doorway watching her.

She would have to get used to this in a mixed house, remember not to wander around half-dressed as she often did at home. 'I prefer it that way.' She thought of her Aunt

Louisa. 'If you travel light, it's easier to move on.'

'What, already? You've only been here a day.' He laughed, and Sophie heard herself laughing with him. She felt the tension unwinding in her body for perhaps the first time since that awful conversation she had overheard this afternoon. Not even a conversation really, just Hilary Nicholson and cruel words.

Sophie had listened, and it had been as if Hilary were standing over her with a knife, digging deep. *Felix and Marilyn.* She heard the words, felt Peter's sharp intake of breath as if she were in the room with them, sensed his disbelief mingling with her own. *Your partner and your wife.* A disbelief which was to be replaced very soon by certainty. His would match hers. He would know it to be true just as she knew.

'Sorry.' With an effort, Sophie pulled herself back to the present, to the unfamiliar bedroom in her new house, to the tall young man with the long fair hair who was one of her new housemates. The others were Jane, who worked – and virtually lived, according to Tom – at the riding stables, and Martin, who was also young and who worked at the swannery.

'We need a female in the house,' Tom had rolled his eyes when he discovered she was looking for a place. 'We were about to advertise. So look no further.'

'Why do you need a female?' It was still strange to Sophie to be so easy and relaxed among the opposite sex. Perhaps it was because she had no brothers; perhaps it was the influence of the all-girls school she had attended. And she hadn't exactly given university much of a chance. As for Nick... But she wouldn't think about him. In some ways she had been sheltered, and now she was out in the big wide world and she was determined to make a success of it.

'To clean the house and do the cooking, of course.' He laughed at Sophie's horrified expression. 'For balance, actually. We're two men and one woman.'

335

'Yes?'

'And despite the divorce rate, it's a well-known fact that men and women – when they're not involved with one another – live best together.'

'They do?' Sophie was beginning to get the hang of his banter. Tom was apparently rarely serious.

'They certainly do.'

Intrigued, she went to see the house, a three-bedroomed terrace in the centre of the village, which had a dining room converted to make a fourth. She met Martin and Jane and liked the entire package. The house was messy and no one cared; the house needed decorating and no one was lurking with a paint brush. It was heaven. She couldn't wait to become a part of it.

'I'm on edge. I had such a bad day today,' she told Tom now. He was kind, but she couldn't tell him more than that.

But this seemed to satisfy him. 'Even Peter was a bit shirty this afternoon,' he remarked. 'Don't let it get to you. It's only a job. And you are the boss's daughter.' He strode off towards the kitchen.

'Unfortunately for me,' she muttered to herself. She wished it was just about the job. That would be easy.

After Hilary had left she had given Peter half an hour before going back to his studio. His kind eyes were glazed. He might even have been crying, though she couldn't tell, and his head was bowed, but he was functioning almost as he always did.

What would he do? Sophie looked at the defeat written on his face and she felt a deep hatred for Hilary Nicholson.

Now, she closed the door and flung herself down on her new bed. She was glad to be here, but she could do with talking to her mother. No chance of that. Mums was away, and in any case, how could she talk to her about this?

She punched the pillow experimentally, like a child, pretending it was Hilary. As for her father, he had betrayed someone she cared for – Peter, a man who had rescued her, given her life some meaning.

She punched the pillow again, still wanting it to be Hilary Nicholson. But it wasn't, it was her father. How could he have put her in such an embarrassing position? And how could he have done this to Mums?

Three hours later Louisa watched Jess as she flopped on to the bed. 'God, I'm exhausted.'

The dancing had been followed by eating, and then more drinking and dancing into the small hours, punctuated by coffee and seemingly endless talking in a super-fast French that left Jess, and sometimes even Louisa, way behind.

'I don't know how he can keep up the pace,' Jess said.

'Claude?' Louisa went over to the washbasin and splashed cold water on her face. She didn't want to be drunk or tired; she didn't want to sleep. She filled up the bowl and stuck her face in.

'Mmm.' She could just hear Jess's voice over the steady hum of the water. 'Do you think he's in love with that barman of his?'

'According to Claude...' Louisa surfaced and grabbed a towel. 'That boy is as straight as a *couleur*.' She put on an atrocious French accent.

Jess's eyes were closed. 'A dye? Poor old Claude.'

'Claude will survive.' Louisa threw the towel down on a chair, kicked off her shoes and sat next to her sister on the bed. 'Can we talk?'

Jess opened her eyes and Louisa almost lost her resolve.

'You look,' Jess murmured, 'as if you're going to tell me something I shan't want to hear.'

Louisa reached out and touched her hair. It still looked wild and waxy. 'It's about Felix.'

They stared at one another.

'Maybe I should have said something before.' Haltingly,

337

she told Jess of what she and Rupert had seen and heard; how Rupert had seen Felix with Marilyn in Lyme; the whole bit. And as she spoke, she watched her carefully. The little make-up Jess had worn tonight had faded, and her face was pale in the rather eerie glow of the light bulb right above their heads. Her wide mouth was pinched; the lines of laughter round her eyes matched those of worry on her brow.

'Why tell me now?' Jess didn't seem surprised. There was a soft kind of disappointment in her eyes, but then she closed them once again.

Pulling down the shutters, Louisa thought. Like she always had before. 'Because now I know it's true. Because you should know. Because you always said we should be honest with each other.'

'I see.'

Jess seemed to be taking this in a rather unexpected way. Was she too drunk to appreciate what Louisa was telling her? She didn't seem drunk. 'And I let Felix kiss me the night before we left,' she blurted.

'What?' Rather disconcertingly, Jess burst out laughing. 'Why on earth?'

'I felt sorry for him.' She decided not to say any more about Rupert – not yet. 'It didn't mean anything.'

'Of course it didn't.' But Jess got to her feet.

'Where are you going?'

'I just want to be on my own for a bit.' Slowly, she walked out of the door.

Louisa picked Scarlet up from the bed and hugged him tight. 'Now she knows it all,' she whispered to the bear. And she wasn't sure whether to be glad or sorry.

Chapter 27

It was the middle of the night when Felix was woken from an uneasy sleep by the strident ring of the doorbell.

Sophie? He struggled to wake, fumbled for the light switch, blinked in protest as the glare obediently smashed into the room. He heaved himself out of the bed and into his slippers and grabbed his dressing gown from the hook. The bell continued to ring. 'All right, all right, I'm coming,' he yelled.

It had been a bloody stupid idea for Sophie to move out and into that house in Abbotsbury. Probably Peter had encouraged her, just as he'd encouraged her to work with him at Beck and Newman instead of with her father in sales. Designer indeed. But what was wrong with her now? The bell continued to ring.

Felix took the stairs two at a time. He only hoped she wasn't in some sort of trouble – especially with Jess away.

He pulled open the door. 'What the hell. . . ?'

It was pouring with rain and Peter Beck was standing dripping on the doorstep. He looked like a man possessed.

'I want a word with you,' he growled.

Felix gaped. Was he dreaming? 'What sort of time do you call—'

But Peter did not let him finish. He took a step closer, grabbed the lapels of Felix's dressing gown, half-lifted him from the ground and pushed him inside.

'What on earth...?' But it didn't take a genius to work it out. Peter knew. And it was pretty pointless to deny it now. Still, Peter hesitated.

'Hit me, then. Go on – hit me.' Felix had always found that an angry man will do the opposite of what you tell him to do. And this man was angry. Bloody angry.

Peter hit him – hard, and right on the jaw.

'Jesus.' Felix staggered back. A series of flashing lights accompanied a slow thud of blood to the head. He'd never been thumped like that before. Was this what he'd heard referred to as seeing stars? A double version of Peter was standing looking down at him. He was unable to read his expression.

'Does that make you feel better?' His jaw hurt when he spoke. He fingered it cautiously. Was there any blood? Was anything broken?

Peter was still standing there, shaking. Felix felt a flood of injustice. They always blamed the other man, didn't they, these jealous husbands? Never took it out on the people who had actually betrayed them: their own wives. Perhaps they didn't like the idea that they weren't enough for their women – that some other man could give them what they wanted. And this was *Peter*, for God's sake. 'Does that make you feel more of a man?' he asked unwisely.

'Not yet.' And Peter hit him again with a glancing blow to the shoulder.

Felix folded once more. 'Bloody hell.' He couldn't believe this was happening to him. This time he was sure he'd ruptured something.

'Get up,' Peter said.

'I'm not going to fight you.' Felix's brain was working overtime. This was no joke. This was assault. Felix was fit

340

but Peter was a big man with heavy fists and a lot of fury on his side. He was probably capable of killing him, and Felix did not want to die.

But to his surprise, Peter only said, 'Get me some coffee, for Christ's sake.'

What was he going to do? Pour it all over him? Best make sure it wasn't scalding then.

But Peter appeared to be calming down. He followed Felix into the kitchen and sat at the table. 'I knew you were a bastard, but I never dreamed you'd try it on with Marilyn,' he said. 'You're obviously a much bigger bastard than I gave you credit for.'

Felix considered this as he filled the kettle. It was hardly his fault. A woman was fair game if she sent out the right signals, and Marilyn had certainly sent out enough of those. But it didn't seem the time to remind Peter that it took two to fornicate. With him in this mood it was all about damage limitation. 'It's over between us,' he said instead.

'Too right it bloody is.'

'Peter, I—'

'I don't want to hear it.'

Felix took the coffee jar out of the cupboard and spooned granules into two mugs. That was the trouble with men like Peter. Artists... He didn't live in the real world – and he wasn't willing to hear about it either.

Peter was still talking. 'I don't want excuses, reasons, justifications. Like I said, I know what a bastard you are, what a bastard you've been to—' He broke off abruptly. 'Does Jess know?'

'Of course she doesn't.' Felix didn't want to bring Jess into this discussion. Neither did he want to consider that *he* might now be the cuckolded one. But one thing he was sure of – Peter Beck was too damn soft on her to tell her. Thank God.

Absently, Peter stirred his coffee. 'Have you any idea what you've done to your family?'

341

'I know, I know.' And that was what came, Felix thought, from being able to read the signals women gave off. It was like animals on heat. He always sensed it, and was it really his fault if he responded like a normal red-blooded male? 'I tried to stop things getting out of hand.'

'But you're weak,' Peter said. 'And greedy.'

Felix thought this was going a bit far. But perhaps it was safest to agree. 'You've talked to ... er, Marilyn?' He felt awkward saying her name, and he could see that Peter didn't like it either.

'Oh, yes.' Peter's pale eyes scanned him as if he were a piece of dirt. 'She told me how you pestered her.'

'What?' He couldn't accept *that*. 'I wouldn't say—'

'I wouldn't say anything if I were you, old chap.'

He couldn't detect a threat in Peter's tone, but his jaw was still aching, and that was deterrent enough.

'I have to take some of the blame,' Peter went on, as if talking to himself. 'I've been working long hours, I suggested we move to Dorset in the first place.'

What about Marilyn's mother? But then, the way Marilyn had told it, her mother had never had much to do with the decision. As far as he remembered, Marilyn had been more than willing in rather a lot of ways. He kept quiet.

'I've neglected her.' Peter took a gulp of coffee. 'And I should have known better. But you...' He glanced at Felix. 'You're the lowest of the low, you are.'

Felix sighed. Time for a bit of humble pie. 'I don't know how I can make it up to you, Peter.'

'I do.'

'Oh?' He seemed different. And it wasn't just the anger in him. He seemed hard and determined, and this worried Felix even more than the physical threat he had posed. 'How?'

'You can make it easy for me to take over your shares in the company. I'll even buy them at a fair price.'

342

Felix stared at him. Was he mad? Didn't he know how much blood and sweat Felix had put into this company of theirs? Did he really think that Felix's role was so minor? 'But you can't do that,' he muttered.

'Why not?' Peter slammed his mug down on the counter. 'There's no way I'm going to be the one to leave, this time.'

'Because of what I bring to the company, that's why.'

Peter laughed.

But he was a fool if he thought Beck and Newman could survive five minutes without Felix. He was the businessman, not Peter. He should never underestimate business. A company could not survive on pretty designs.

'I think I could replace you with another salesman,' Peter said with a slight sneer. 'Someone with a few brains who could gen up on the insurance details, someone who's interested in jewellery and antiques, someone who can chat up the customers without taking them to bed.'

'Oh, come on, Peter.' He couldn't be serious. 'You'd really do this, because of me and—'

'Too bloody right, I would.' Peter's lips closed into a line of distaste.

'I'm not the first though, am I?' This might be risky, but Peter could hardly deny it.

He didn't; he ignored it. 'I'm waiting, Felix.'

'And if I say no?' Why should he give in to what amounted to blackmail?

'Then I withdraw my share.'

'Your share?' That meant money. More money than Beck and Newman could stand to lose. Without Peter's money, Felix would need a substantial loan. Without Peter there was no designer, no kudos; they might as well be some high street jeweller selling nothing but tat or overpriced antiques.

'You'd do better with the first option,' Peter said, as if he were offering impartial banking advice. 'That way you'd at least have some cash to put into something else. Whereas if

343

I pulled out, you know the company wouldn't survive.'

'But you wouldn't do that.' Because Felix also knew that the company meant more to Peter than he was making out. It was his baby as much as it was Felix's. He couldn't be such a fool – and over a woman... 'And if I sell you my shares – I'd have to tell Jess.' No, not that. 'You wouldn't do it to me, to us?'

But Peter didn't look much like Peter tonight. He got to his feet. 'Just watch me,' he said.

Jess walked around Claude's garden, deserted now that the last stragglers had left the party. She needed this quiet, this darkness that cooled her cheeks and soothed her senses.

She sat for a moment on the steps of the terrace. The garden enclosed three sides of the bar; it was bordered with fence and trellis and both levels were crammed with café tables and with pots already stuffed with plants. In the summer, the garden would be a mass of colour. She could picture the vibrancy of it: the red and white of geraniums and gladioli, the pinks and mauves of cornflowers and stocks; she could almost hear the babble of French voices, the chink of glasses; she could smell the enticing fragrance of fresh coffee in the air.

Yes, it was peaceful, and although she was in Trégastel village, a short distance from the beach, she thought she could still hear the distant wash of the sea on sand and rock, that reminded her of home.

As for what Louisa had told her, she had guessed as much. But it was different being told. She had listened and she had waited – for something. For the pain of betrayal perhaps? Or was that too fanciful by half? But she had felt less than nothing; not even surprise.

'It can't go on,' she murmured now, to the night air, to the breeze that chilled her bare legs. Because it hadn't hurt her at all.

She reached out to touch the early-flowering jasmine growing along the trellis of the upper terrace. The delicate scent was at its best at night-time. Delicate, but heady if you sniffed deep. Jess contemplated the tiny flowers. And since it hadn't hurt her at all...

But she was growing cold, and at last she reluctantly left the night-time garden, made her way back inside, let herself into the apartment.

Only the bedside lamp was on. Louisa was lying on the bed clutching that silly teddy bear of hers, staring into space.

'Jess?' She sat up.

'It's all right.' Slowly, she began to take off her clothes.

When she was naked Jess stood still, stared at herself in the long mirror. She was thirty-seven years old. At the moment her body was still firm, even though she had faint stretch marks, some definite cellulite around the thighs and a few other miscellaneous lumpy bits. But in this light she still looked pretty good.

Louisa was watching her. 'I didn't want to hurt you.'

'You haven't.' She began to brush her hair. 'I'm leaving Felix.' Now that she'd made the decision at last it seemed very straightforward. Patti had been right. A good deal was not enough; she wanted more. Trust, for starters. And it was no use changing just the look of the thing. It had to be changed at root.

'Because of Marilyn?' Louisa's voice was small.

'Not really.' Knowing about Marilyn had made little difference (what did it mean, really?) and at the same time the vital difference. Because she could forgive one mistake. But two women couldn't be a mistake. Two women formed a pattern. And she and Felix could not go on.

'Does that mean...?' Louisa looked rather weird. What on earth was wrong with her? 'Does that mean that you and Rupert...?'

'Rupert!' Jess laughed out loud. What was she on about? 'Are you going a bit doolally tonight, or what? I rather thought Rupert was your department.' She stopped brushing. Louisa was looking very sad. 'You don't mean to tell me that you haven't had your wicked way with him yet?' Truly amazing. If he hadn't responded to her sister living in the same house as him, then surely it must be true? Rupert had a disastrous love affair closeted in his past.

'But I thought, you and he...?' Louisa avoided her eye.

'Good God, no. Oh, no offence.' She sat on the bed beside her. 'I love him – but not in that way. It's a bit like you and Claude only without the gay bit.' Who could have put that idea into her head? 'And anyhow.' She hugged her knees and thought of Matt. 'The last thing I want is to run into someone else's arms. Well,' she amended, 'maybe their arms, but not their lives.'

Louisa seemed confused, poor lamb. 'So what will you do?'

'That's easy.' Now, Jess felt truly liberated. 'Whatever I feel like doing – that's what I'll do.'

'Why?' Felix glared at Hilary.

'Why what?'

She was cool, he'd give her that; it was hard to recognise the woman who had crumpled underneath him the last – and final – time they'd had sex. Now, there was not an ounce of need in evidence. She seemed remade into the Hilary of old, but now, no shred of sexual desire remained in him.

'I've already talked to Marilyn,' he told her. Not that she'd wanted to see him. Typically, Marilyn was now busily playing the penitent wife, clinging to Peter as if he were her saviour and Felix the devil incarnate. But who could blame her for simply knowing which side her bread was buttered on? One look at Marilyn and it had become patently obvious that *she* had not been in the confessional box. No, Hilary

346

was responsible, he knew it in his bones. She had virtually threatened him with it not so long ago.

Hilary merely wrinkled her nose at him. 'What about?'

'You know bloody well what about.'

She put on a silly and mock-shocked expression.

Felix lost patience. 'Don't pretend with me. I know you too well. I always knew you too well.'

'Then you should have *known*,' Hiliary responded as she whirled round to stare out of the window, 'that I would never accept second best.'

'Second best?' Felix was baffled. He scrutinished her slim back but it provided no clues. Even before, there had always been Jess.

She whipped round again. 'Before, I knew exactly what was going on. I understood what you needed. I didn't *care*.'

She turned to gaze out of the window once more. Her arms were tightly folded in front of her.

'I never realised—' he began.

'Don't flatter yourself,' she snapped, treating him to a rapid once-over clearly designed to reinforce her words. 'A woman gets older while a man stays the same.' Her eyes narrowed as she surveyed his waistline. 'Or at least, he only gains a few inches and the odd distinguished grey hair,' she conceded. 'You became an unhealthy addiction, that's all.'

'Thanks a lot.' His stomach was as flat as it had always been – well, almost.'

'But when I met Bas...' After her initial reluctance, Hilary now seemed positively determined to unburden herself. 'And he wanted to marry me...' She glanced at Felix. 'I liked the thought.'

'Of marriage? Absolutely.' Felix nodded approval.

But Hilary flashed him another of the contemptuous looks she was so good at. 'The thought of having someone to care for me. It was a chance I couldn't turn down. Like I said, we're all getting older.'

347

'So what went wrong?' There must be more to it than that.

'I found I was already too tied down to you,' she said simply. 'It wasn't easy to respond to Bas, with you still around, especially when I knew you'd found someone else. Someone who wasn't just a casual fling to you. Someone who you wanted to keep secret.'

'*Needed* to keep secret,' he corrected. 'For obvious reasons, I would have thought.'

'The *obvious* thing,' she said, 'would have been never to get involved with Marilyn Beck in the first place. I mean, for God's sake – Peter's wife, what were you thinking of?' For a moment, her guard was down.

'It was an accident.' What sort of a man did she imagine he was? 'I didn't go out one day with the express intention of starting an affair.'

'But she was just so appealing, so incredibly sexy...' There was a sneer in Hilary's voice that was remarkably unattractive. 'That you just couldn't resist her.'

Felix shrugged. It was pretty pointless arguing with her in this mood. In her opinion Marilyn had usurped her place, and nothing he said would make her think otherwise. 'I didn't know you felt that way,' he said. It was a shame really that women were so different from men.

'I'm not talking about love.' Hilary took a pace towards him. 'Don't think that. But I wanted you back. I wanted to have you *and* Bas. Why shouldn't I?' She seemed peeved. '*You* had it all.'

Yes. 'And it was good,' he murmured, remembering. 'You know we were good together.'

'Yes, it was good.' For a moment their gazes locked, before she looked towards the window once more. 'And then you walked away.'

'To Marilyn.' Felix was aware that he had messed up. And not just because of Marilyn. He should never have allowed himself to get so involved with Hilary. It had been nothing short of ridiculous to imagine she had no emotions – she was a woman, wasn't she? She was just good at keeping them in check. Or she had been.

'Yes, to Marilyn,' she said. 'But not any more.'

He read the satisfaction in her small smile. 'Darling girl,' he said. 'After what you've done, it's likely there'll be no company any more.'

'And Jess?' Her expression was inscrutable.

'Jess has nothing to do with it.' He spoke automatically.

Hilary laughed. 'No, she never did have, did she?'

Felix absorbed the bitterness. What did she expect of him now? His thanks perhaps? Or did she want to be screwed on the office desk in the way he'd done so often? Whatever she wanted, she would be disappointed this time. 'And incidentally – you don't have a job any more,' he told her.

'Darling man...' Hilary moved towards the door with almost her old aplomb. 'I'm married to Bas Nicholson,' she said as she left the room. 'Do you honestly think I need one?'

Chapter 28

Louisa was about to put her key in the lock when she heard it. She didn't know the music. But any fool could recognise what it was saying. It was low and plaintive, a sad melody; the violin was crying, almost gasping for breath, and then gathering momentum; building to an emotional climax—

Abruptly, the music ended with the jarring grate of bow on strings. She could almost see him flinging the instrument to one side.

Warily, she made her way into the cottage. What was she in for? How would he react when he found out about Jess and Felix? Would he still want her hanging round the place like some grisly reminder of a seduction scene gone horribly wrong?

'Oh, hello.' She glanced up as Rupert loped into the hallway and grabbed her bag. And the rather pleasant tingle that spun its way through her whenever he was nearby hadn't gone away. Unfortunately for her.

'Hi. Good trip?' He seemed friendly enough. But she needed to know.

She leapt in. 'So, do you want me to move out?' Now that I've kissed you, she added mentally.

He shook his head and gave her an odd look. 'Nope. Do you want me to take this upstairs?'

Louisa shrugged. 'All right. Thanks.' She couldn't make him out. 'Well, anyway, when something turns up...' He was halfway up the stairs by now, so she couldn't see his face. 'I'll take it.' It shouldn't be too difficult; though she might have to move closer to civilisation, which in turn might mean losing her job at the pub.

'Actually...' He leaned over the banisters to look down at her. 'I kind of missed having you around,' he said.

'I missed you,' Felix told Jess. He was pacing up and down the sitting room, Pavarotti was singing 'Rondine al nido' through the speakers of the hi-fi, and Jess was sitting cross-legged on the sofa.

How could she tell him? Why wouldn't he stay still for five minutes? It was making her exhausted just watching him. 'Has something happened while I've been away? Is Sophie all right?'

'It's Peter.' He didn't look at her. 'He's got the hump over ... over some decision I made that he didn't agree with. And now the idiot wants to wind up the company – or at least he wants to buy me out.' He barely paused for breath. 'Can you believe it, Jess? After all we've achieved?'

So that was it. 'He's found out,' she said blankly. Poor Peter.

'What?'

'About you and Marilyn.' Please God, don't let him bother to pretend.

He stared at her. 'You knew?' And then his expression changed. 'How? Did Louisa tell you?'

Angrily, she shook her head. 'It doesn't matter *how* I know, I just do.'

'Oh, Jess, I feel so bloody dreadful.'

Here we go, she thought. *I never meant to hurt you. I*

don't know how it happened. Will you ever forgive me? No.
'I honestly never intended to hurt you, as God's my
witness. I don't even know how the hell it happened. She
was there and—'

'Stop!' She drew breath. 'I don't want to hear it.'

'But—'

She stopped him again, this time with a fierce glare. 'And
you certainly can't blame Peter for reacting that way. Why
should he want to go on working with you after this?' Her
voice held scorn, and she didn't mind him knowing it. That
was how she felt.

'You don't understand.' He resumed his pacing. 'We
could be losing the company. That's what matters.'

Jess almost laughed. He was so unaware. 'You have no
idea what matters,' she told him.

'Of course I do.' He moved into the light. 'How the hell
do you think I'll find another job at my age?'

At his age... 'Felix.' She gazed at him. There were fine
lines around his eyes and mouth, and once she had thought
she would like the time when he began to look older. She
had imagined that as he got well into his forties... What?
That he might grow up? That he would look at his thirty-
something wife and realise that she was enough for him.

'Yes?' he was close to her now. 'Listen to me, Jess, you
have to. I never meant—'

'Don't. I know what you never meant to do.' But he was
still very close and she spotted the faded bruising. 'You've
hurt yourself.'

'It's nothing.' He turned away again.

She realised what must have happened. 'Peter hit you.'
Involuntarily, her hand flew to her mouth. 'Didn't he?'

'He bloody well came round in the middle of the night to
hit me,' Felix said, as if the timing of it had been the main
insult. He fingered his jaw carefully.

'My God.' Peter was the mildest of men.

And then he dropped to the floor at her feet, taking her completely by surprise. 'Jessie. . .'

Yes, she knew what he wanted. Forgiveness, comfort, all that stuff. And despite herself, she lifted her hand from where it rested on her knee, stretched her fingers towards his dark head, reaching for him. It was an old habit. He wanted to rest his sore head on her lap and have her stroke his hair, make him better, tell him it would go away. But how could it?

'Why won't you listen to me?'

'Maybe I don't feel like coming home to your problems.' There, she'd said it. Or at least part of it.

'I see.' Wearily, he got to his feet. 'My problems? You've got problems of your own, I suppose. Is that it? You don't want to be bothered with mine.' He shot her an accusing look.

Jess eyed him carefully. 'Not exactly.'

'But your problems are mine. Mine are yours. We're married. Joined.' The dark blue of his eyes seemed to be burning into her, daring her to deny it. 'I know I shouldn't have gone near Marilyn. But we're still married. You and I. Aren't we?'

Jess wondered if she should make him sit down again. 'Felix,' she said once more.

He stared at her.

She took a deep breath. 'While I was in Brittany. . .' Pavarotti was reaching the end of the aria and Jess had to raise her voice to beat the competition. 'I did a lot of thinking.'

'And?' He was right to sound wary.

'And I came to a decision.' The music ended. She dropped the volume of her voice accordingly, but now he would hear it shaking. This wasn't easy.

'What sort of a decision?'

'That I didn't want to be married to you any longer.' She heard the words drop into the new silence between them.

'Because of Marilyn?' That look of confusion on his face had once touched her heart. Once, she would have been unable to see this through. 'You don't mean it? She was nothing to me.'

'I'm sorry, Felix, but I do mean it. And it's not just because of Marilyn.' Hadn't he said as much himself? 'We've become too separate, you and I.'

He walked over to the hi-fi. For a moment she thought he was about to restart the CD as if nothing had happened, but he only leaned heavily on the shelf. There was a beaten look about him now. And that did move her.

'Is there anything I can say to make you change your mind? Anything at all?'

'No.' She was tired of thinking it was her fault – that she wasn't pretty enough, clever enough, funny enough, that she couldn't cook well enough. She was tired of losing just a small part of herself, piece by piece. If she didn't stop, she'd be all gone. She considered trying to tell him this. But what was the use? It would be totally beyond his comprehension. Louisa had understood. She had made Jess see that *she* wasn't at fault, that it was just Felix and the way he was. And maybe that was it. Maybe only another woman would understand.

'It looks like there's nothing more to say then.' Felix grabbed his coat.

'What will you do?' she asked him.

'Go out and get drunk.' He laughed without humour.

'I meant about the company.' She would hate to see him lose it. 'Maybe if I talked to Peter...'

'Don't bother.'

She was right – they were separate now.

Felix left Cliff Cottage, not even sure himself of where he was going this time. But he knew he had to leave. He couldn't stand the sympathy in her eyes. And he couldn't talk to her; not now.

Losing the company was a blow. A pretty massive blow. But he thought maybe he could recover from that if it came to it, if Peter really had the balls.

But losing Jess was different. In losing Jess he knew he had lost a part of himself.

After he'd gone, Jess sat for a few minutes lost in thought. Then she stretched, got to her feet and went to the phone in the kitchen. She knew his number by heart. She dialled, heard it ring, heard the click of his answerphone.

The soft, confident voice of the recorded message almost made her lose her resolve – but hadn't she irrevocably made up her mind about this too?

'This is Jess,' she said, after the tone. 'I wanted to let you know that I can't decorate your bedroom. In fact I can't do any more work for you. I'm sorry. But it's not real, you see. I need to do real work for people who aren't involved...' She was making a hash of this. She should have met him face to face or at least written him a letter. But she had been afraid she wouldn't be able to go through with it if she were to see him there in front of her.

'It's better that we don't see one another for a while,' she said quickly. She put down the phone. She was out of breath, as if she'd run a marathon instead of simply broken free from the two men in her life. Simply...

Chapter 29

'Winding up the company?' Sophie looked from one to the other of them. 'Are you serious?'

'Perfectly serious.' Her father's face revealed not a trace of emotion.

'It may have to come to that,' Peter agreed. And he was as bad. Both of them were talking as if it meant nothing.

Sophie clenched her fists. 'I don't understand. Why?' She wanted to lash out at them and right at this moment either one of these men would do. Didn't they understand how much this job meant to her? And it was so much more than a job. This and the house in Abbotsbury represented a new way of life. A move forward. It was as if someone had unveiled a signpost that had remained hidden for years and shown her the way to go.

Peter was the first to rouse himself and show some compassion. 'We don't necessarily have to wind up Beck and Newman,' he said, glancing at Felix as if for confirmation. 'Your father and I have come to a parting of the ways, that's all. We wanted to tell you before we told the rest of the staff. Before we decided...'

A parting of the ways, of course, she should have realised. Now, she didn't need telling the reason why. Like so many things, it was her father's fault.

'You and I could carry on, Sophie.' He jumped to his feet. 'Newmans Jewellers – how does that sound?'

'Pretty stupid, actually.'

'Sophie!'

'No.' She stood tall. She was not her mother. She was not going to let her father use his old charmer tactics on *her*. 'Without Peter we're without a jewellery designer,' she reminded him. 'What's the point of that?'

Felix narrowed his eyes. It seemed like a conspiracy. 'You could be the designer,' he told his daughter. 'It could be a family firm.' He injected into his voice all the enthusiasm he could muster. They wouldn't have Peter's money, granted, but they could start at the bottom and build. Other companies did the same. And he was willing to try if Sophie would only take a chance, show some faith.

Peter rose slowly to his feet. He was wearing an old T-shirt and jeans, and looked pretty awful. Felix had to admit that he found it difficult to face him these days, found it hard to be in the same room as him and his silent accusations. Even if Peter hadn't made the decision that had so shocked Felix a couple of weeks ago, he knew that their partnership would never have survived this.

'If that's what you both want,' Peter said. 'I won't stand in your way.' He made for the door.

Felix saw the sympathy in Sophie's eyes. Bloody hell, she knew.

'What do *you* want, Peter?' she asked softly.

He shrugged. 'To go on designing if I can. But I don't need an entire company. I don't need all this.' He made a gesture that seemed to encompass and belittle Felix and all Felix had achieved for Beck and Newman. 'I can do it alone and at home if I want to – on a much smaller scale, of course.'

'And that would suit you, wouldn't it?' Felix couldn't

hide his contempt. The truth was that Peter had never wanted the company to be big. He had never shared Felix's ambition. If not for Felix, Beck and Newman would have remained a two-man band making peanuts, instead of the prestigious firm it was today.

Sophie was looking at him, although her words were directed at Peter. 'And in this new company, would you still want me?' she asked.

Felix stared back at her. It was a body blow harder than the one Peter had dealt him two weeks ago.

But Peter seemed to stand up rather straighter at this. He looked from one to the other of them, his gaze questioning. 'Of course I would,' he said.

'I'm not trained,' Sophie told Felix quickly. 'I've still got so much to learn. Peter can teach me.'

'I see.' Felix could see all right. His daughter had made a choice between them. Beck and Newman would continue, but he wouldn't be the Newman involved. He turned to Peter. 'Then you owe me.'

'You'll be paid.' Peter moved over to the desk and withdrew a manila folder. His bulky body seemed to have gained a sense of purpose. 'All the details are in here. Shares, the lot. I had the accountant draw it up. It's more than fair, and you can leave just as soon as you like. Your notice is not required.'

'I'm sorry, Dad.' His daughter, his beanpole Sophie, was standing in front of him with her huge serious eyes locked on to his face. 'But I couldn't let you punish Peter any more. He's been hurt enough.' She paused. 'And I have to think of my future. He's been good to me.'

Hadn't *he* been good to her? Hadn't *he* put his hand in his pocket for her more times than he cared to remember? 'I don't know what your mother will say,' he muttered, for a moment almost forgetting. And blood was supposed to be thicker than water. What a joke that was.

But Sophie just stared sadly at him. 'I think she'll understand,' she said.

Jess received two phone calls that afternoon. One was from a surprisingly self-contained Sophie, who told her the outcome of the meeting at Beck and Newman.

'I don't even feel especially guilty, Mums,' she said. 'Do you think that's awful?'

'It's your life to live, darling,' Jess told her. 'And we're only responsible for our own happiness – not other people's.'

'I suppose.' At last Sophie's voice betrayed some emotion. 'But even after everything he's done, I hate to see everyone turning against him.'

'Then you should tell him that.'

Jess was thoughtful as she put down the phone. Sophie was strong, much stronger than she herself had been at her age. Sophie was a survivor and that was good. Because the upheaval in her life was only just beginning, and she would need all the strength she possessed.

The second phone call was more difficult. Jess had been expecting it; she knew Matthew Hill well enough for that. Matt would not come to the house and confront her because he would never risk embarrassing her in that way, but neither would he accept the lame explanation she'd given him on an answerphone tape.

'So what's happening?' he asked in his usual direct manner.

Jess hedged around the subject, unwilling to say too much. 'It's been lovely working for you,' she said. 'But I need experience with someone more—'

'More critical?' He laughed.

'Exactly.' She hadn't so much advised Matthew as taken over. And whatever she did was always fine by him. The

359

people she designed for in the future were hardly likely to be as uncomplaining as Matt.

'And what about us?' he asked.

This was the hard bit. 'Can we slow things down, ease off a little?' she pleaded. She had already planned what to say. But did she sound convincing? 'We both know the pitfalls ... we've both had our fingers burned.'

'This is you and me, Jess.'

'What?'

'We're talking about you and me. You sound like an article in some women's magazine. Do you have any more clichés, or are you done?'

'Matt...'

His voice changed. 'I want to see you.'

Jess gripped the receiver more tightly. She had made up her mind that she wouldn't see him, couldn't see him. Not because she couldn't trust herself; although that was a factor, since his presence did have an alarming way of turning mental resolve into physical lust. But she couldn't risk telling him in person, because she knew he'd be able to see through her flimsy armour in no time. She needed' distance from him, and yet even the sound of his voice was tempting her to give in. Any minute now she'd melt into a puddle on the floor. 'I don't think that's a very good idea,' she said primly.

'So you can't work for me, you won't be my lover, and you absolutely refuse to be a friend?'

'Well...'

'That seems rather a waste.'

Oh yes, it seemed like a waste, all right. 'There are other things I need to be involved in right now.' Jess put a briskness into her tone that she was far from feeling.

'Fine.' His voice changed. 'I presume you'll be calling by to collect your stuff?'

'Yes.' *Fine*, had he said? She thought of the brushes,

360

dustsheets, rollers and stencils. Like a woman moving in with her lover she had brought more and more things to Matt's house, and it seemed that she had taken nothing away.

'You know the surgery hours, so it should be easy for you to choose a time when I'm not here.'

His voice cut into her. Didn't he care?

'And we both want to make it easy for you, don't we, Jess?'

This time she heard his hurt. 'Matt, you told me why you keep the photo of your ex-wife in your sun-room. Remember?'

'Of course.' His voice was clipped. 'And?'

'And isn't the lesson to not get involved? Or have I missed something?' Wearily she pushed her hair from her brow. Why wouldn't he see?

'Quite. Oh, quite.'

Jess moved the receiver to her other ear. This was not the Matthew she knew. This man was cold, professional and rather scary.

'And I would say that I've been proved right,' he went on. 'Wouldn't you?'

'Oh, Matt.' Jess sighed.

'I mustn't keep you.'

God, he was really rubbing her nose in it now.

'And there's one more thing.'

'Yes?' Ridiculously, her hopes leapt.

'Don't forget to post the key I gave you back through the letter box when you leave with your things. Clearly, you won't be needing it any longer.'

'All right.' Deep inside she felt regret for what she was doing, for what might have been. And then she heard him replace the receiver. The phone went dead; their communication was at an end.

'Shit,' she said. But how had she expected him to react? It

was all very well making a resolution. But fancying a man like crazy had a way of complicating the issue – until you didn't seem to be sure of anything any more.

Louisa was astounded at the amount of stuff she had managed to accumulate since moving into Rupert's cottage. She threw the entire contents of the wardrobe into a heap on the bed. And to think she had arrived at Jess's last year with just a rucksack...

On her travels once, she had met a man (seventy if he was a day) who had decided on the day he retired to sell his house and all his possessions and just go. What was left had filled a huge rucksack, but he had made a resolution to leave one thing behind every time he stopped somewhere.

'Do you have anything left?' she had asked him, laughing. His hair was steel-grey, his face brown and lined as one of Rupert's old oak tables.

'Enough,' he had said.

And now here she was, doing the opposite. The human instinct; men had always settled when they found what they needed to survive.

'What are you doing?'

She hadn't heard him come in from the back garden where he had been out digging five minutes ago, but now Rupert was on the landing staring at the clothes strewn over the bed.

What did it look like? 'Packing.'

He stood there, hands thrust deep into the pockets of his jeans, eyes hooded, expression guarded. Louisa continued emptying drawers. If she couldn't have him she couldn't continue to live here. 'Jess and Felix are getting a divorce,' she said conversationally.

'I know.'

Well, he would, wouldn't he? She stopped what she was doing. 'You've talked to her then?' To profess undying love perhaps? Had Jess sent him away with a flea in his ear, or had she changed her mind? Since their return, Louisa herself had managed to avoid him quite successfully. Even today she had crept into the cottage and checked on his whereabouts before starting to pack. It obviously hadn't been a very big trench.

'Yeah, we had a coffee the other morning.'

'Ah.' Coffee. 'And?'

'And what?' He seemed confused. Men could be very dense.

'And did you put your idea of a business partnership to her?' She didn't dare ask about any other kind of partnership.

'Yeah.' Rupert seemed mesmerised by the clothes on the bed. Perhaps he too was amazed by the sheer volume of the pile. 'She said she'd give it some thought.' He shrugged, as though it wasn't particularly important anyway.

'Hmm.' Louisa eyed her rucksack dubiously. No way would this lot fit in here. 'Do you have any carrier bags, Rupert?'

'No.' He advanced purposefully into the room. Once, she would have done anything to get him in here. But now...

'Where exactly are you going?' he demanded.

Very forceful. 'There's a spare room at the pub.' The landlord had offered it to her at a good rate.

'So you're not going further afield, then?'

She narrowed her eyes. Was he that desperate to get rid of her? 'Not yet.' Actually, she wanted to stay in Dorset. Despite her lack of success on the romantic front, she was beginning to feel almost rooted here.

'Good.'

'Good?' Had she missed something? It really sounded as if she might have done. But she hardly dared think such a thing.

'I was hoping that you and I might be,' she knew he was

embarrassed now, and it gave her strength, 'friends.'

'Friends?' She wasn't going to let him off too easily.

He grinned. 'OK, more than friends.' He was very close now. She could smell the scent of the last cigarette he'd smoked still clinging to his old gardening sweater, mingling with the earthy smell of outside.

'When did you work all this out?' She tried to sound arch, but it wasn't easy when he was looking at her like that.

'Now let's see. It might have occurred to me when we first met. Or maybe when you dragooned your way into moving in.'

Dragooned? Cheek.

'But when did I work it out for sure?' He grabbed her round the waist. 'I reckon it was when you kissed me.'

Chapter 30

Jess held her breath as she drove up to the yellow-brick house. But his car was not in the driveway. She was safe.

She parked the Renault on the road outside, went to the front door and rang the bell, just in case. No answer. She put the key in the lock. For the last time, she thought.

The house was very quiet. She stood in the doorway of the sitting room looking at the Mexican-style room she had created. It showed signs of being lived in now; Matthew's papers were littered across the coffee table; he had put a couple of plants in the window bay. Was she throwing away something precious? She still wasn't sure.

The sound of another key in the lock made her jump, but it was too late now to run away. He would have seen her car. She moved further into the room, and tensed as she heard him come in, heard him stamp his feet on the mat, slam the front door.

'Where are you?'

'In here.' She waited for him to join her.

And when he did, he looked the same as ever with lines of tiredness around his light blue eyes, and his fair flopping over his brow. As always he gave the impression that he simply hadn't had time to get it cut.

'You have a surgery this afternoon,' she said accusingly.

'I swapped with one of the other partners.'

They stared at each other. She wanted to ask him why. Was it a coincidence, or had he guessed she would come today, knowing that she finished college early on Fridays?

'I asked you what was happening,' he said, throwing himself into a chair. 'You never told me.'

Jess sat down in the chair opposite and eyed him warily.

'Will you tell me now?'

'It's over between Felix and me,' she said. She owed him that much at least.

He nodded – apparently just another person who wasn't surprised. 'And you're upset?'

'Not really.' She knew she should elaborate. 'It was my decision. I'd had enough.'

'And how did he take it?' Matthew leaned forwards. He had such a penetrating gaze that she had the sensation of being put under a microscope yet again.

'I don't know what he minded most – losing me or losing the company.'

'The company?'

Jess explained. 'At first he said he was going to go back to Australia.' She laughed. That was fairly typical of Felix too. He had hated the country until a week ago, but now it apparently offered everything. 'Then Sophie talked to him, and he decided to stick around. He's already found a place to stay in Exeter. Peter was very generous. I can keep the cottage until the summer and Felix will have enough to set himself up in something.' Exactly what, she didn't know, but Felix was never short of ideas. 'He'll be all right.' She realised she was talking too much, but it was hard to stop, with Matthew so close and yet so very far away. 'He's decided to take a couple of weeks' holiday.'

'He'll miss you,' Matthew said.

'You don't know Felix.' She laughed once more. 'He'll

soon bounce back. He's going to Italy again. The Italian women won't know what's hit them. He loves Italian food and music and—'

'Jess.' He rose to his feet, came nearer and took her hands, pulling her up so that they were just an arm's distance apart. 'You said you would be keeping the cottage until the summer.'

She looked down at the hands holding hers. A doctor's hands, capable hands; the nails were short, square and very clean. 'When I was in Brittany,' she said. 'I tried hard to come to terms with the past. With the way it had been with my parents and Louisa. The way I'd envied her simply for leading her own life.'

'And you weren't doing the same?' Matthew asked gently.

'I never have done.' She looked away from his understanding. 'I've always lived through someone else.'

'Very unselfish of you.' Matthew lifted her hand to his lips, but he didn't kiss it as she thought he might; instead he began playing with her fingers, as if he needed to maintain the contact between them, skin to skin.

She had to put him right on that. 'It wasn't unselfish at all. It was reflecting on me. It meant I felt loved, I felt secure. Pathetic really. It meant I could live my life without taking the responsibility for any of it.'

He was looking very serious. 'But not any more?'

'Not any more.' She had got something wrong, back then, and now it was time to put it right. Just like in those painting sets of her childhood, the first time she had realised how colour could change things.

'That's good.'

She was surprised. 'You think so?'

'Oh, yes.' He let go of her fingers but put his hands on her shoulders instead. 'Your work has given you a new direction,' he said. 'That's something you can achieve for yourself.'

'Yes.' And it was a direction she didn't regret for a moment. 'But it's not enough.'

Almost absent-mindedly, his hands drifted to her neck and then moving back to caress her shoulders. 'So what do you plan to do?'

She shivered. 'I want to finish the course; I want to do the advanced City and Guilds 7839. I want to build up my work experience. Then I want to become an associate member of the IDDA.'

'The what?'

'The Interior Decorators and Designers Association. And in the summer I want to take some time for myself.' She looked up at him. What was he thinking? 'I want to go away for the summer,' she said. 'When I've finished studying I might go away for longer.'

He didn't even ask where to. Perhaps it didn't matter to him; perhaps he already knew.

'You see, I want to explore life a bit.' She felt her enthusiasm growing as she tried to communicate this to him. 'I want to explore *me*. I want to get to know myself, and—'

'You don't want to get rid of your husband and immediately be shackled to another man.' He moved towards the door. 'I need some coffee.'

She followed him into the kitchen. 'I wouldn't have put it quite like that.'

He turned to face her. He didn't seem angry; she wasn't exactly sure how he did seem. 'But that's why you don't want to see me. Isn't it?' His eyes were searching her face.

'When you told me about your wife, and the photo and everything...'

'Yes?'

'I realised that it wasn't fair to let you think I was free for a relationship.'

'Apparently you never were free.' He laughed; moved over to the coffee machine, filled it, switched it on. 'Just my luck – first a husband and then a need for self-discovery.'

Jess took a deep breath. She knew this was just his hurt speaking. 'You can laugh at me if you like. But you wouldn't really want me as I am.'

'Do you want to take a bet on that?' His voice was very soft, very compelling. He took a step towards her, then another.

'Matt...'

'What you're saying is you've got some unfinished business,' he said.

'Well, yes.'

He tilted her chin so that she had no choice but to stare into his eyes. 'And I've got some unfinished business of my own.'

'You have?' He was so close, so warm, he raked her hair lightly with his fingers; the lemon-pine scent of him seemed to be coming not from him but from somewhere inside her head.

'*We* have.'

And of course, he was right.

'I hear what you're saying,' Matt whispered into her hair. 'I accept it. But I'm not trying to tie you down to me. We're two adults, both free, both uncommitted. Can't we just stay with that?'

'What do you want, Matt?' Although she had a pretty good idea.

'Same thing I've always wanted.' He was smiling. 'I want you to continue to cast your expert eye over the bedroom. And not just your eye – I'd also like the rest of you if possible.'

'That kiss.' The clothes that Louisa had slung on the bed were a lot more messed up than they had been an hour ago. 'It must have been even better than I realised.'

'I was a bloody fool.' Rupert was no longer wearing his

gardening clothes, and his light eyes were scanning her face with genuine affection. A lot of genuine affection. 'After Estelle...' He hesitated. 'I kind of promised myself to be celibate.'

'Estelle?' Louisa wondered where Jess had come into the equation – if she ever had.

'Estelle was the big passion of my life.' His fingers exploring the niceties of Louisa's collar bone told her that the past tense was the most important bit of this statement. 'We were together for ten years. If you can call it that.'

'You loved her?' Louisa watched him and waited.

He nodded. 'She was a musician too. That's how we met. But she was also married.'

'Ah.' She would be.

'Not happily.' He frowned. 'Neil tried to make her into something she wasn't. Estelle minded that. But—'

'But she wouldn't leave?'

'She said she couldn't do that to him. And you never know, do you?'

'No.' You never knew the strength of their love if they weren't willing to prove it to you. 'So what happened?'

'We just went on.' He seemed so sad; she ached to comfort him. 'I couldn't leave her. She couldn't leave him.' He laughed, without humour. 'It was very hard for me after...'

'After?' Her voice was gentle. This was something she knew instinctively he had not even told Jess. And Jess, she realised, had never been any part of this. It had simply been Sophie's teenage imagination, fertile and desperate for romance.

'She died.' Rupert pushed her fringe from her brow with his fingertips. 'Of leukaemia. I wasn't very good at accepting it, I'm afraid. I blamed everything and everybody.'

Louisa held him tight. 'I'm sorry.' At last, she was beginning to see.

370

'It was five years ago.' He kissed her shoulder. 'I reckon Estelle would say it was about time for me to wake up. She'd be happy for me.'

'For us.' This is bloody well *it*, Louisa thought. 'I feel good,' she whispered. She didn't think it could feel more right. And for some reason she wasn't worried that it would all be snatched away from her. She had found someone even more emotionally fragile than she was herself. She could almost see herself in this man. And she could see that he could be trusted.

'Move in with me then,' he said.

She blinked at him. 'I'm already in.'

'Properly. No temporary measures.' He held her face between his hands and kissed her again. 'I'm tired of playing safe. I want to live a little. With you.'

'You still don't know me very well. I'm bossy,' she told him, as she felt his fingertips trace a pattern across her face.

'I know.'

'I'm greedy, and incredibly demanding.' Now, for example, if he bent lower and kissed her neck, everything would be perfect.

'I know that too.' His lips moved in absolute obedience.

'And I want to get to know all of you – even the parts you keep quiet about. I even want to meet your parents.' She watched him carefully. She understood about parents who wanted a brighter star. But it wasn't too late for Rupert. He had the chance for a resolution.

His eyes clouded. 'You must be psychic. You and Jess have made me think about a lot of things.'

'And?' Louisa moved her fingers through the short, cropped hair.

'I phoned them while you were in Brittany. They're coming up at the weekend. It'll be the first time I've had them here at the cottage. It'll be strange.'

'Oh, Rupert.' She squeezed his arm.

'So do I take it that this lot's going back into the wardrobe?' He picked up a leaf-green jacket with navy lining, crushed underneath them.

'I think it is. Though I might have to iron it all first.' Wistfully, she located and examined her crimson sarong.

'Bugger the ironing.' He removed the sarong from her hands while *his* hands explored a bit further.

'You're right.' Louisa flung her arms round his neck. 'Bugger the ironing. We have far more important things to do.' She had come home.

There was a moment when Jess made a conscious decision. She was not a young girl, too naïve to decide for herself, or a female so flimsy that she could be swept along – against her better judgement – by romance, let alone a man's touch or a whiff of sexy aftershave. She made the decision. And she said, 'OK.'

Hand in hand they went up the stairs to the bedroom.

'I always thought this room had potential,' she teased.

'I'm sure you're right.' He loosened his tie, undid the first few buttons of his shirt and came to stand close to her once more.

She was so used to Felix; she knew the moves so well, that she stood still, unsure with this man, of how to go on.

But he reached out, touched her face, kissed her lightly, almsot tentatively on the lips, and then gently began to undo the buttons of her blouse. She helped him, they helped each other, they were practically tripping over one another's fingers, but eventually they stood naked, almost face to face, chest to breast.

'I knew what you would look like,' he said. 'Exactly.'

She understood what he meant. She too had expected the paleness of his skin, the roundness of his hips, the soft brown of the hair on his chest. But there was more. Naked, Matthew had a strange vulnerability, a boyishness that surprised her.

372

He kissed her again, slowly, as if they had all the time in the world, a long kiss of exploration that went on and on. And as they kissed, their two bodies moved together, first with a gentle pressure and then harder, more insistent, one against the other. Need... His body was unfamiliar – his skin paler than Felix's skin, his hair lighter and not spiky to the touch, his hands not knowing exactly where to go.

And why should they? She smiled to herself. His kiss, his touch, the smell and feel of him, everything was a comparison to her husband. Louisa would say she had been with the same man too long.

After a while he scooped her into his arms and they half-fell laughing on to the bed. No longer self-conscious, Jess knelt over him, bending to kiss his neck, his shoulders, the breast-bone that protruded very slightly from the soft brown chest hair, while he held the weight of her breasts in the broad and capable palms of his hands. It was slow, easy and relaxed; she felt the tension ebb from her body; replaced by wave upon wave of sensuality – wonderful and guiltless; by desire and slow, slow satisfaction.

They were not making any earth-shattering commitment to one another, she realised. They were two adults simply taking a time of pleasure.

And quite a long time. It was two hours later before he got round to drinking the coffee he'd made earlier, and made a small pot of Earl Grey for Jess.

'I should be going,' she said, when she'd drunk it.

He made no protest, and she had known he wouldn't. Now, they understood one another. They didn't need to say that nothing had really changed.

Jess got dressed, gave her sleepy lover one last kiss, and went downstairs. She began loading her things into the Renault.

When she was sure there was nothing left behind, she let herself out of the front door and closed it firmly behind her.

Love them and leave them, with no regrets – that had always been Louisa's motto.

If she took up Rupert's business offer, her future would be safe and secure. He wanted to help her. Rupert, apparently, had come into a good deal of insurance money when he reached the age of twenty-one. But what with his socialist leanings and the fact that it was family money, it had mostly just sat in some building society gathering interest. Similarly, if she and Matthew formed a steady relationship – although when were relationships ever steady? – then she would be content. But, did she want that?

No, she owed it to herself to spread her wings a little. And she wanted to make it alone. So she would say no to Rupert for now. She would go to Brittany for the summer, make Trégastel her base, travel a little, work a little. And then she would spend some time in Sussex with Patti and Ruth. She had spoken to both of them last night; told them of her plans. Patti had said she was crazy but Ruth had seemed to understand.

And she would come back. Oh, she would come back for college, for her sister and Sophie, to Dorset (and unlike Louisa, she wouldn't wait sixteen years to do it).

But for now...

The late afternoon sun was bright on her head. She pulled her sunglasses from her bag, rescued her sketchbook as it was about to land on the path, and scrabbled for Matthew's house key. She found it, pressed the cold metal into her palm for a few seconds and pushed open the letter box. As for Matthew, she didn't want to tie herself to him, she didn't want to make any promises. But then again...

She smiled, dangled the key lightly between her fingers and dropped it with perfect nonchalance back into her open, bulging bag.